NORA ROBERTS

Dear Reader,

If you enjoyed reading about Natasha and Mikhail in the first Stanislaski volume, *Yes to Love*, you're sure to love these two fan-favorite stories featuring the two younger Stanislaski siblings.

As a child, Rachel Stanislaski envied the beauty and grace of her older sister Natasha. Now a high-powered lawyer in New York, Rachel's the one turning heads. But Zack Muldoon isn't looking for romance when he hires Rachel to defend his delinquent kid brother—he just needs a street-smart attorney to defend Nick. So no one is more surprised than Zack when he finds himself falling for the savvy lawyer.

Alex Stanislaski has always been a ladies' man—the suave charmer to Mikhail's hot-tempered craftsman. But it's Alex's turn to be charmed—and seduced—when he becomes the object of bold and beautiful soap-opera writer Bess McNee's affections.

Watch for the story of Zack's brother, Nick, as well as the story of Natasha and Spence's daughter, Kate, in the third Stanislaski volume, *Lost Love Found*.

Happy reading!
The Editors
Silhouette Books

NORA ROBERTS

WILD HEART

Includes *Falling for Rachel* & *Convincing Alex*

Silhouette Books

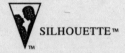

SILHOUETTE™

Recycling programs for this product may not exist in your area.

Wild Heart

ISBN-13: 978-1-335-45286-3

Copyright © 2023 by Harlequin Enterprises ULC

Falling for Rachel
First published in 1993. This edition published in 2023.
Copyright © 1993 by Nora Roberts

Convincing Alex
First published in 1994. This edition published in 2023.
Copyright © 1994 by Nora Roberts

For questions and comments about the quality of this book, please contact us at CustomerService@Harlequin.com.

Silhouette
22 Adelaide St. West, 41st Floor
Toronto, Ontario M5H 4E3, Canada
www.Harlequin.com

Printed in U.S.A.

CONTENTS

FALLING FOR RACHEL 7

CONVINCING ALEX 245

FALLING FOR RACHEL

Mary Kay, here's one just for you

Prologue

Nick couldn't figure out how he'd been so damn stupid. Maybe it was more important to be part of the gang than he liked to admit. Maybe he was mad at the world in general and figured it was only right to get his licks in when he had the chance. And certainly he'd have lost face if he'd backed out when Reece and T.J. and Cash were so fired up.

But he'd never actually broken the law before.

Not quite true, he reminded himself as he pulled himself through the broken window and into the back of the electronics store. But they'd only been little laws. Setting up a three-card monte scam over on Madison for suckers and tourists, hawking hot watches or Gucci knockoffs up on Fifth, forging a couple of IDs so that he could buy a beer. He'd worked in a chop shop for a while, but it wasn't as if *he'd* stolen the cars. He'd just broken them down for parts. He'd gotten stung a few times for fighting with the Hombres, but that was a matter of honor and loyalty.

Breaking into a store and stealing calculators and portable stereos was a big leap. While it had seemed like a lark over a couple of beers, the reality of it was setting those brews to churning in his stomach.

The way Nick saw it, he was trapped, as he'd always been. There was no easy way out.

"Hey, man, this is better than swiping candy bars, right?" Reece's eyes, dark and surly, scanned the storeroom shelves. He was a short man with a rough complexion who'd spent several of his twenty years in Juvenile Hall. "We're gonna be rich."

T.J. giggled. It was his way of agreeing with anything Reece said. Cash, who habitually kept his own counsel, was already shoving boxes of video games in the black duffel he carried.

"Come on, Nick." Reece tossed him an army-surplus bag. "Load it up."

Sweat began to roll down Nick's back as he shoved radios and minirecorders into the sack. What the hell was he doing here? he asked himself. Ripping off some poor slob who was just trying to make a living? It wasn't like fleecing tourists or selling someone else's heat. This was stealing, for God's sake.

"Listen, Reece, I—" He broke off when Reece turned and shined the flashlight in Nick's eyes.

"Got a problem, bro?"

Trapped, Nick thought again. Copping out now wouldn't stop the others from taking what they'd come for. And it would only bring him humiliation.

"No. No, man, no problem." Anxious to get it all

over with, he shoved more boxes in without bothering to look at them. "Let's not get too greedy, okay? I mean, we got to get the stuff out, then we got to fence it. We don't want to take more than we can handle."

His lips pulled back in a sneer, Reece slapped Nick on the back. "That's why I keep you around. Your practical mind. Don't worry about turning the stuff. I told you, I got a connection."

"Right." Nick licked his dry lips and reminded himself he was a Cobra. It was all he'd ever been, all he ever would be.

"Cash, T.J., take that first load out to the car." Reece flipped the keys. "Make sure you lock it. Wouldn't want any bad guys stealing anything, would we?"

T.J.'s giggles echoed off the ceiling as he wiggled out the window. "No, sir." He pushed his wraparound sunglasses back on his nose. "Thieves everywhere these days. Right, Cash?"

Cash merely grunted and wrestled his way out the window.

"That T.J.'s a real idiot." Reece hefted a boxed VCR. "Give me a hand with this, Nick."

"I thought you said we were just going for the small stuff."

"Changed my mind." Reece pushed the box into Nick's arms. "My old lady's been whining for one of these." Reece tossed back his hair before climbing through the window. "You know your problem, Nick? Too much conscience. What's it ever gotten you? Now, the Cobras, we're family. Only time you got to have a conscience is with your family." He held out his arms. When Nick put the VCR into them, Reece slipped off into the dark.

Family, Nick thought. Reece was right. The Cobras were his family. You could count on them. He'd had to count on them. Pushing all his doubts aside, Nick shouldered his bag. He had to think of himself, didn't he? His share of tonight's work would keep a roof over his head for another month or two. He could have paid for his room the straight way if he hadn't gotten laid off from the delivery-truck job.

Lousy economy, he decided. If he had to steal to make ends meet, he could blame the government. The idea made him snicker as he swung one leg out of the window. Reece was right, he thought. You had to look out for number one.

"Need a hand with that?"

The unfamiliar voice had Nick freezing halfway out the window. In the shadowy light he saw the glint of a gun, the flash of a badge. He gave one fleeting, panicky thought to shoving the bag at the silhouette and making a run for it. Shaking his head, the cop stepped closer. He was young, dark, with a weary kind of resignation in the eyes that warned Nick that he'd been this route before.

"Do yourself a favor," the cop suggested. "Just chalk it up to bad luck."

Resigned, Nick slipped out of the window, set the bag down, faced the wall and assumed the position. "Is there any other kind?" he muttered, and let his mind wander as he was read his rights.

Chapter 1

With a briefcase in one hand and a half-eaten bagel in the other, Rachel raced up the courthouse steps. She hated to be late. Detested it. Knowing she'd drawn Judge Hatchet-Face Snyder for the morning hearing only made her more determined to be inside and at the defense table by 8:59. She had three minutes to spare, and would have had twice that if she hadn't stopped by the office first.

How could she have known that her boss would be lying in wait with another case file?

Two years of working as a public defender, she reminded herself as she hit the doors at a run. That was how she should have known.

She scanned the elevators, gauged the waiting crowd and opted for the stairs. Cursing her heels, she took them two at a time and swallowed the rest of the bagel.

There was no use fantasizing about the coffee she craved to wash it down with.

She screeched to a halt at the courtroom doors and took a precious ten seconds to straighten her blue serge jacket and smooth down her tousled, chin-length black hair. A quick check showed her that her earrings were still in place. She looked at her watch and let out a deep breath.

Right on time, Stanislaski, she told herself as she moved sedately through the doors and into the courtroom. Her client, a twenty-three-year-old hooker with a heart of flint, was being escorted in as Rachel took her place. The solicitation charges would probably have earned her no more than a light fine and time served, but stealing the john's wallet had upped the ante.

As Rachel had explained to her bitter client, not all customers were too embarrassed to squawk when they lost two hundred in cash and a gold card.

"All rise!"

Hatchet-Face strode in, black robes flapping around all six-foot-three and two hundred and eighty pounds of him. He had skin the color of a good cappuccino and a face as round and unfriendly as the pumpkins Rachel remembered carving with her siblings every Halloween.

Judge Snyder tolerated no tardiness, no sass and no excuses in his courtroom. Rachel glanced over at the assistant district attorney who would be the opposing counsel. They exchanged looks of sympathy and got to work.

Rachel got the hooker off with ninety days. Her client was hardly brimming with gratitude as the bailiff led her away. She had better luck with an assault case.... After all, Your Honor, my client paid for a hot meal in good faith. When the pizza arrived cold, he pointed out the problem by offering some to the delivery boy. Unfortunately, his enthusiasm had him offering it a bit too heartily, and during the ensuing scuffle said pizza was inadvertently dumped on the delivery boy's head....

"Very amusing, Counselor. Fifty dollars, time served."

Rachel wrangled her way through the morning session. A pickpocket, a drunk-and-disorderly, two more assaults and a petty larceny. They rounded things off at noon with a shoplifter, a two-time loser. It took all of Rachel's skill and determination to convince the judge to agree to a psychiatric evaluation and counseling.

"Not too shabby." The ADA was only a couple of years older than Rachel's twenty-six, but he considered himself an old hand. "I figure we broke even."

She smiled and shut her briefcase. "No way, Spelding. I edged you out with the shoplifter."

"Maybe." Spelding, who had been trying to wheedle his way into a date for weeks, walked out beside her. "Could be his psych will come back clean."

"Sure. The guy's seventy-two years old and steals disposable razors and greeting cards with flowers on them. Obviously he's perfectly rational."

"You PDs are such bleeding hearts." But he said it lightly, because he greatly admired Rachel's courtroom style. As well as her legs. "Tell you what, I'll buy you lunch, and you can try to convince me why society should turn the other cheek."

"Sorry." She shot him a quick smile and opted for the stairs again. "I've got a client waiting for me."

"In jail?"

She shrugged. "That's where I find them. Better luck next time, Spelding."

* * *

The precinct house was noisy and smelled strongly of stale coffee. Rachel entered with a little shiver. The weatherman had been a little off that day with his promise of Indian summer. A thick, nasty-looking cloud cover was moving in over Manhattan. Rachel was already regretting the fact that she'd grabbed neither coat nor umbrella on her dash out of her apartment that morning.

With any luck, she figured, she'd be back in her office within the hour, and out of the coming rain. She exchanged a few greetings with some of the cops she knew and picked up her visitor's badge at the desk.

"Nicholas LeBeck," she told the desk sergeant. "Attempted burglary."

"Yeah, yeah…" The sergeant flipped through his papers. "Your brother brought him in."

Rachel sighed. Having a brother who was a cop didn't always make life easier. "So I hear. Did he make his phone call?"

"Nope."

"Anyone come looking for him?"

"Nope."

"Great." Rachel shifted her briefcase. "I'd like him brought up."

"You got it. Looks like they've given you another loser, Ray. Take conference room A."

"Thanks." She turned, dodging a swarthy-looking man in handcuffs and the uniformed cop behind him. She managed to snag a cup of coffee, and took it with her into a small room that boasted one barred window, a single long table and four scarred chairs. Taking a seat, she flipped open her briefcase and dug out the paperwork on Nicholas LeBeck.

It seemed her client was nineteen and unemployed and rented a room on the Lower East Side. She let out a little sigh at his list of priors. Nothing cataclysmic, she mused, but certainly enough to show a bent for trouble. The attempted burglary had taken him up a step, and it left her little hope of having him treated as a minor. There had been several thousand dollars' worth of electronic goodies in his sack when Detective Alexi Stanislaski collared him.

She'd be hearing from Alex, no doubt, Rachel thought. There was nothing her brother liked better than to rub her nose in it.

When the door of the conference room opened, she continued to sip her coffee as she took stock of the man being led in by a bored-looking policeman.

Five-ten, she estimated. A hundred and forty. Needed some weight. Dark blond hair, shaggy and nearly shoulder-length. His lips were quirked in what looked like a permanent smirk. It might have been an attractive mouth otherwise. A tiny peridot stud that nearly matched his eyes gleamed in his earlobe. The eyes, too, would have been attractive if not for the bitter anger she read there.

"Thank you, Officer." At her slight nod, the cop uncuffed her client and left them alone. "Mr. LeBeck, I'm Rachel Stanislaski, your lawyer."

"Yeah?" He dropped into a chair, then tipped it back. "Last PD I had was short and skinny and had a bald spot. Looks like I got lucky this time."

"On the contrary. You were apprehended crawling out of a broken window of a storeroom of a locked store, with an estimated six thousand dollars' worth of merchandise in your possession."

"The markup on that crap is incredible." It wasn't easy to keep the sneer in place after a miserable night in jail, but Nick had his pride. "Hey, you got a cigarette on you?"

"No. Mr. LeBeck, I'd like to get your hearing set as soon as possible so that we can arrange for bail. Unless, of course, you prefer to spend your nights in jail."

He shrugged his thin shoulders and tried to look unconcerned. "I'd just as soon not, sweetcakes. I'll leave that to you."

"Fine. And it's Stanislaski," she said mildly. "*Ms*. Stanislaski. I'm afraid I was only given your file this morning on my way to court, and had time for no more than a brief conversation with the DA assigned to your case. Because of your previous record, and the type of crime involved here, the state had decided to try you as an adult. The arrest was clean, so you won't get a break there."

"Hey, I don't expect breaks."

"People rarely get them." She folded her hands over his file. "Let's cut to the chase, Mr. LeBeck. You were caught, and unless you want to weave some fairy tale about seeing the broken window and going in to make a citizen's arrest…"

He had to grin. "Not bad."

"It stinks. You're guilty, and since the arresting officer didn't make any mistakes, and you have an unfortunate list of priors, you're going to pay. How much you pay is going to depend on you."

He continued to rock in his chair, but a fresh line of sweat was sneaking down his spine. A cell. This time they were going to lock him in a cell—not just for a few hours, but for months, maybe years.

"I hear the jails are overcrowded—costs the tax-payers a lot of money. I figure the DA would spring for a deal."

"It was mentioned." Not just bitterness, Rachel realized. Not just anger. She saw fear in his eyes now, as well. He was young and afraid, and she didn't know how much she would be able to help him. "About fifteen thousand in merchandise was taken out of the store, over and above what was in your possession. You weren't alone in that store, LeBeck. You know it, I know it, the cops know it. And so does the DA. You give them some names, a lead on where that merchandise might be sitting right now, and I can cut you a deal."

His chair banged against the floor. "The hell with that. I never said anybody was with me. Nobody can prove it, just like nobody can prove I took more than what I had in my hands when the cop took me."

Rachel leaned forward. It was a subtle move, but one that had Nick's eyes locking on hers. "I'm your lawyer, LeBeck, and the one thing you're not going to do is lie to me. You do, and I'll leave you twisting in the wind, just like your buddies did last night." Her voice was flat, passionless, but he heard the anger simmering beneath. He had to fight to keep from squirming in his chair. "You don't want to cut a deal," she continued, "that's your choice. So you'll serve three to five instead of the six months in and two years probation I can get you. Either way, I'll do my job. But don't sit there and insult me by saying you pulled this alone. You're penny-ante, LeBeck." It pleased her to see the anger back in his face. The fear had begun to soften her. "Con games and sticky fingers. This is the big leagues. What you tell me stays with me unless you want it different. But you play it straight with me, or I walk."

"You can't walk. You were assigned."

"And I can get reassigned. Then you'll go through this with somebody else." She began to pile papers back in her briefcase. "That would be your loss. Because I'm good. I'm real good."

"If you're so good, how come you're working for the PD's office?"

"Let's just say I'm paying off a debt." She snapped her briefcase closed. "So what's it going to be?"

Indecision flickered over his face for just a moment, making him look young and vulnerable, before he shook his head. "I'm not going to turn in my friends. No deal."

She let out a short, impatient breath. "You were wearing a Cobra jacket when you were collared."

They'd taken that when they booked him—just as they'd taken his wallet, his belt, and the handful of change in his pocket. "So what?"

"They're going to go looking for your *friends,* those same friends who are standing back and letting you take the heat all alone. The DA can push this to burglary and hang a twenty-thousand-dollar theft over your head."

"No names," he said again. "No deal."

"Your loyalty's admirable, and misplaced. I'll do what I can to have the charges reduced and have bail set. I don't think it'll be less than fifty thousand. Can you scrape ten percent together?"

Not a chance in hell, he thought, but he shrugged. "I can call in some debts."

"All right, then, I'll get back to you." She rose, then slipped a card out of her pocket. "If you need me before the hearing, or if you change your mind about the deal, give me a call."

She rapped on the door, then swung through when it opened. An arm curled around her waist. She braced instinctively, then let out a little hiss of breath when she looked up and saw her brother grinning at her.

"Rachel, long time no see."

"Yeah, it must be a day and a half."

"Grumpy." His grin widened as he pulled her out of the corridor and into the squad room. "Good sign." His gaze skimmed over her shoulder and locked briefly on LeBeck. "So, they tied you up with that one. Tough break, sweetheart."

She gave him a sisterly elbow in the ribs. "Stop gloating and get me a decent cup of coffee." Resting a hip against the corner of his desk, she rapped her fingertips against her briefcase. Nearby a short, round man was holding a bandanna to his temple and moaning slightly as he gave a statement to another cop. Someone was talking in loud and rapid Spanish. A woman with a bruise on her cheek was weeping and rocking a fat toddler.

The squad room smelled of all of it—the despair, the anger, the boredom. Rachel had always thought that if your senses were very keen you could just barely scent the justice beneath it all. It was very much the same in her offices, a few blocks away.

For a moment, Rachel pictured her sister, Natasha, having breakfast with her family in her pretty kitchen in the big, lovely house in West Virginia. Or opening her colorful toy shop for the day. The image made her smile a bit, just as it did to imagine her brother Mikhail carving something passionate or fanciful out of wood in his sun-washed new studio, perhaps having a hasty cup of coffee with his gorgeous wife before she hurried off to her midtown office.

And here she was, waiting for a cup of what would certainly be very bad coffee in a downtown precinct house filled with the sight and smells and sounds of misery.

Alex handed her the coffee, then eased down on the desk beside her.

"Thanks." She sipped, winced, and watched a couple of hookers strut out of the holding cells. A tall, bleary-eyed man with a night's worth of stubble shifted around them and followed a uniform through the door that led down to the cells. Rachel gave a little sigh.

"What's wrong with us, Alexi?"

He grinned again and slipped an arm around her. "What? Just because we like slogging through the dregs for a living, for little pay and less gratitude? Nothing. Not a thing."

She chuckled and fueled her system with the motor oil disguised as coffee. "At least you just got a promotion. Detective Stanislaski."

"Can't help it if I'm good. You, on the other hand, are spinning your wheels putting criminals back on the streets I'm risking life and limb to keep clean."

She snorted, scowling at him over the brim of the paper cup. "Most of the people I represent aren't doing anything more than trying to survive."

"Sure—by stealing, cheating, and assaulting."

Her temper began to heat. "I went to court this morning to represent an old man who'd copped some disposable razors. A real desperate case, that one. I guess they should have locked him up and thrown away the key."

"So it's okay to steal as long as what you take isn't particularly valuable?"

"He needed help, not a jail sentence."

"Like that creep you got off last month who terrorized two old shopkeepers, wrecked their store and stole the pitiful six hundred in the till?"

She'd hated that one, truly hated it. But the law was clear, and had been made for a reason. "Look, you guys blew that one. The arresting officer didn't read him his rights in his native language or arrange for a translator. My client barely understood a dozen words of English." She shook her head before Alex could jump into one of his more passionate arguments. "I don't have time to debate the law with you. I need to ask you about Nicholas LeBeck."

"What about him? You got the report."

"You were the arresting officer."

"Yeah—so? I was on my way home, and I happened to see the broken window and the light inside. When I went to investigate, I saw the perpetrator coming through the window carrying a sackful of electronics. I read him his rights and brought him in."

"What about the others?"

Alex shrugged and finished off the last couple of swallows of Rachel's coffee. "Nobody around but Le-Beck."

"Come on, Alex, twice as much was taken from the store as what my client allegedly had in his bag."

"I figure he had help, but I didn't see anyone else. And your client exercised his right to remain silent. He has a healthy list of priors."

"Kid stuff."

Alex sneered. "You could say he didn't spend his childhood in the Boy Scouts."

"He's a Cobra."

"He had the jacket," Alex agreed. "And the attitude."

"He's a scared kid."

With a sound of disgust, Alex chucked the empty cup into a wastebasket. "He's no kid, Rach."

"I don't care how old he is, Alex. Right now he's a scared kid sitting in a cell and trying to pretend he's tough. It could have been you, or Mikhail—even Tash or me—if it hadn't been for Mama and Papa."

"Hell, Rachel."

"It could have been," she insisted. "Without the family, without all the hard work and sacrifices, any one of us could have gotten sucked into the streets. You know it."

He did. Why did she think he'd become a cop? "The point is, we didn't. It's a basic matter of what's right and what's wrong."

"Sometimes people make bad choices because there's no one around to help them make good ones."

They could have spent hours debating the many shades of justice, but he had to get to work. "You're too softhearted, Rachel. Just make sure it doesn't lead to being softheaded. The Cobras are one of the roughest gangs going. Don't start thinking your client's a candidate for Boys' Town."

Rachel straightened, pleased that her brother remained slouched against the desk. It meant they were eye to eye. "Was he carrying a weapon?"

Alex sighed. "No."

"Did he resist arrest?"

"No. But that doesn't change what he was doing, or what he is."

"It might not change what he was doing—allegedly—but it might very well say something about what he is. Preliminary hearing's at two."

"I know."

She smiled again and kissed him. "See you there."

"Hey, Rachel." She turned at the doorway and looked back. "Want to catch a movie tonight?"

"Sure." She'd made it to the outside in two steps when her name was called again, more formally this time.

"Ms. Stanislaski!"

She paused, flipping her hair back with one hand as she looked over her shoulder. It was the tired-eyed, stubble-faced man she'd noticed before. Hard to miss, she reflected as he hurried toward her. He was over six feet by an inch or so, and his baggy sweatshirt was held up by a pair of broad shoulders. Faded jeans, frayed at the cuffs, white at the stress points, fit well over long legs and narrow hips.

It would have been hard not to miss the anger, too. It radiated from him, and it was reflected in steel-blue eyes set deep in a rough, hollow-cheeked face.

"Rachel Stanislaski?"

"Yes."

He caught her hand and, in the process of shaking it, dragged her down a couple of steps. He might look lean and mean, Rachel thought, but he had the grip of a bear trap.

"I'm Zackary Muldoon," he said, as if that explained everything.

Rachel only lifted a brow. He certainly looked fit to

spit nails, and after that brief taste of his strength she wouldn't have put the feat past him. But she wasn't easily intimidated, particularly when she was standing in an area swarming with cops.

"Can I help you, Mr. Muldoon?"

"I'm counting on it." He dragged a big hand through a tousled mop of hair as dark as her own. He swore and took her elbow to pull her down the rest of the steps. "What's it going to take to get him out? And why the hell did he call you and not me? And why in God's name did you let him sit in a cell all night? What kind of lawyer are you?"

Rachel shook her arm free—no easy task—and prepared to use her briefcase as a weapon if it became necessary. She'd heard about the black Irish and their tempers. But Ukrainians were no slouches, either.

"Mr. Muldoon, I don't know who you are or what you're talking about. And I happen to be very busy." She'd managed two steps when he whirled her around. Rachel's tawny eyes narrowed dangerously. "Look, Buster—"

"I don't care how busy you are, I want some answers. If you don't have time to help Nick, then we'll get another lawyer. God knows why he chose some fancy broad in a designer suit in the first place." His blue eyes shot fire, the Irish poet's mouth hardening into a sneer.

She sputtered, angry color flagging both cheeks. She jabbed one stiffened, clear-tipped finger in his chest. "*Broad?* You just watch who you call *broad,* pal, or—"

"Or you'll get your boyfriend to lock me in a cell?" Zack suggested. Yeah, that was definitely a fancy face, he thought in disgust. Butter-soft skin in pale gold, and eyes like good Irish whiskey. What he needed was a street fighter, and he'd gotten society. "I don't know what kind of defense Nick expects from some woman who spends her time kissing cops and making dates when she's supposed to be working."

"It's none of your business what I—" She took a deep breath. Nick. "Are you talking about Nicholas LeBeck?"

"Of course I'm talking about Nicholas LeBeck. Who the hell do you think I'm talking about?" His black brows drew together over his furious eyes. "And you'd better come up with some answers, lady, or you're going to be off his case and out on your pretty butt."

"Hey, Rachel!" An undercover cop dressed like a wino sidled up behind her. He eyed Zack. "Any problem here?"

"No." Though her eyes were blazing, she offered him a half smile. "No, I'm fine, Matt. Thanks." She edged over to one side and lowered her voice. "I don't owe you any answers, Muldoon. And insulting me is a poor way to gain my cooperation."

"You're paid to cooperate," he told her. "Just how much are you hosing the boy for?"

"Excuse me?"

"What's your fee, sugar?"

Her teeth set. The way she saw it, *sugar* was only a marginal step up from *broad.* "I'm a public defender, Muldoon, assigned to LeBeck's case. That means he doesn't owe me a damn thing. Just like I don't owe you."

"A PD?" He all but backed her off the sidewalk and into the building. "What the devil does Nick need a PD for?"

"Because he's broke and unemployed. Now, if you'll excuse me…" She set a hand on his chest and shoved.

She'd have been better off trying to shove away the brick building at her back.

"He lost his job? But…" The words trailed off. This time Rachel read something other than anger in his eyes. Weariness, she thought. A trace of despair. Resignation. "He could have come to me."

"And who the hell are you?"

Zack rubbed a hand over his face. "I'm his brother."

Rachel pursed her lips, lifted a brow. She knew how the gangs worked, and though Zack looked rough-and-ready enough to fit in with the Cobras, he also looked too old to be a card-carrying member.

"Don't the Cobras have an age limit?"

"What?" He let his hand drop and focused on her again with a fresh oath. "Do I look like I belong to a street gang?"

With her head tilted, Rachel ran her gaze from his battered high-tops to his shaggy dark head. He had the look of a street tough, certainly of a man who could bulldoze his way down alleys, pounding rivals with those big-fisted hands. The hard, hollowed face and hot eyes made her think he'd enjoy cracking skulls, particularly hers. "Actually, you could pass. And your manners certainly reflect the code. Rude, abrasive and rough."

He didn't give a damn what she thought of his appearance, or his manners, but it was time they set the record straight. "I'm Nick's brother—stepbrother, if you want to be technical. His mother married my father. Get it?"

Her eyes remained wary, but there was some interest there now. "He said he didn't have any relatives."

For an instant, she thought she saw hurt in those steel-blue depths. Then it was gone, hardened away.

"He's got me, whether he likes it or not. And I can afford a real lawyer, so why don't you fill me in, and I'll take it from there."

This time she didn't merely set her teeth, she practically snarled. "I happen to be a *real* lawyer, Muldoon. And if LeBeck wants other counsel, he can damn well ask for it himself."

He struggled to find the patience that always seemed to elude him. "We'll get into that later. For now, I want to know what the hell's going on."

"Fine." She snapped the word out as she looked at her watch. "You can have fifteen minutes of my time, providing you take it while I eat. I have to be back in court in an hour."

Chapter 2

From the way she looked—elegant sex in a three-piece suit—Zack figured her for one of the trendy little restaurants that served complicated pasta dishes and white wine. Instead, she stalked down the street, her long legs eating up the sidewalk so that he didn't have to shorten his pace to keep abreast.

She stopped at a vendor and ordered a hot dog—loaded—with a soft drink, then stepped aside to give Zack room to make his selection. The idea of eating anything that looked like a hot dog at what he considered the crack of dawn had his stomach shriveling. Zack settled for a soft drink—the kind loaded with sugar and caffeine—and a cigarette.

Rachel took the first bite, licked mustard off her thumb. Over the scent of onions and relish, Zack caught a trace of her perfume. It was like walking through the jungle, he thought with a frown. All those ripe, sweaty smells, and then suddenly, unexpectedly, you could come across some exotic, seductive vine tangled with vivid flowers.

"He's charged with burglary," Rachel said with her mouth full. "Not much chance of shaking it. He was apprehended climbing out of the window with several thousand dollars' worth of stolen merchandise in his possession."

"Stupid." Zack downed half the soft drink in a swallow. "He doesn't have to steal."

"That's neither here nor there. He was caught, he was charged, and he doesn't deny the act. The DA's willing to deal, offer probation and community service, if Nick cooperates."

Zack chuffed out smoke. "Then he'll cooperate."

Rachel's left brow lifted, then settled. She had no doubt Zackary Muldoon thought he could prod, push or punch anybody into anything. "I sincerely doubt it. He's scared, but he's stubborn. And he's loyal to the Cobras."

Zack said something foul about the Cobras. Rachel was forced to agree. "Well, that may be, but it doesn't change the bottom line. His record is fairly lengthy, and it won't be easy to get around it. It's also mostly hustle and jive. The fact that this is his first step into the big leagues might help reduce his sentence. I think I can get him off with three years. If he behaves, he'll only serve one."

Zack's fingers dug into the aluminum can, crushing it. Fear settled sickly in his stomach. "I don't want him to go to prison."

"Muldoon, I'm a lawyer, not a magician."

"They got back the stuff he took, didn't they?"

"That doesn't negate the crime, but yes. Of course, there's several thousand more outstanding."

"I'll make it good." Somehow. Zack heaved the can toward a waste can. It tipped the edge, joggled, then fell inside. "Listen, I'll make restitution on what was stolen. Nick's only nineteen. If you can get the DA to try him as a minor, it would go easier."

"The state's tough on gang members, and with his record I don't think it would happen."

"If you can't do it, I'll find someone who can." Zack threw up a hand before she could tear into him. "I know I came down on you before. Sorry. I work nights, and I'm not my best in the morning." Even that much of an apology grated on him, but he needed her. "I get a call an hour ago from one of Nick's friends telling me he's been in jail all night. When I get down here and see him, it's the same old story. I don't need you. I don't need anybody. I'm handling it." He tossed down his cigarette, crushed it out, lit another. "And I know he's scared down to the bone." With something close to a sigh, he jammed his hands in his pockets. "I'm all he's got, Ms. Stanislaski. Whatever it takes, I'm not going to see him go to prison."

It was never easy for her to harden her heart, but she tried. She wiped her hands carefully on a paper napkin. "Have you got enough money to cover the losses? Fifteen thousand?"

He winced, but nodded. "I can get it."

"It'll help. How much influence do you have over Nick?"

"Next to none." He smiled, and Rachel was surprised to note that the smile held considerable charm. "But that can change. I've got an established business, and a two-bedroom apartment. I can get you professional and character references, whatever you need. My record's clean— Well, I did spend thirty days in the brig when I was in the navy. Bar fight." He shrugged it off. "I don't guess they'd hold it against me, since it was twelve years ago."

Rachel turned the possibilities over in her mind. "If I'm reading you right, you want me to try to get the court to turn Nick over to your care."

"The probation and community service. A responsible adult to look out for him. All the damages paid."

"You might not be doing him any favor, Muldoon."

"He's my brother."

That she understood perfectly. Rachel cast her eyes skyward as the first drop of rain fell. "I've got to get back to the office. If you've got the time, you can walk with me. I'll make some calls, see what I can do."

A bar, Rachel thought with a sigh as she tried to put together a rational proposition for the hearing that afternoon. Why did the man have to own a bar? She supposed it suited him—the big shoulders, the big hands, the crooked nose that she assumed had been broken. And, of course, the rough, dark Irish looks that matched his temper.

But it would have been so much nicer if she could tell the judge that Zackary Muldoon owned a nice men's shop in midtown. Instead, she was going to ask a judge to hand over the responsibility and the guardianship of a nineteen-year-old boy—with a record and an attitude—to his thirty-two-year-old stepbrother, who ran an East Side bar called Lower the Boom.

There was a chance, a slim one. The DA was still

pushing for names, but the shop owner had been greatly mollified with the promise of settlement. No doubt he'd inflated the price of his merchandise, but that was Muldoon's problem, not hers.

She didn't have much time to persuade the DA that he didn't want to try Nick as an adult. Taking what information she'd managed to pry out of Zack, she snagged opposing counsel and settled into one of the tiny conference rooms in the courthouse.

"Come on, Haridan, let's clean this mess up and save the court's time and the taxpayers' money. Putting this kid in jail isn't the answer."

Haridan, balding on top and thick through the middle, eased his bulk into a chair. "It's my answer, Stanislaski. He's a punk. A gang member with a history of antisocial behavior."

"Some tourist scams and some pushy-shovey."

"Assault."

"Charges were dropped. Come on, we both know it's minor-league. *He's* minor-league. We've got a scared, troubled kid looking for his place with a gang. We want him out of the gang, no question. But jail isn't the way." She held up a hand before Haridan could interrupt. "Look, his stepbrother is willing to help—not only by paying for property you have absolutely no proof my client stole, but by taking responsibility. Giving LeBeck a job, a home, supervision. All you have to do is agree to handling LeBeck as a minor."

"I want names."

"He won't give them." Hadn't she gone back down and harassed Nick for nearly an hour to try to pry one loose? "You can put him away for ten years, and you still won't get one. So what's the point? You haven't got a hardened criminal here—yet. Let's not make him one."

They knocked that back and forth, and Haridan softened. Not out of the goodness of his heart, but because his plate was every bit as full as Rachel's. He had neither the time nor the energy to pursue one punk kid through the system.

"I'm not dropping it down from burglary to nighttime breaking and entering." On that he was going to stand firm, but he would throw her a crumb. "Even if we agree to handle him as a juvie, the judge isn't going to let him walk with probation."

Rachel gathered up her briefcase. "Just leave the judge to me. Who'd we pull?"

Haridan grinned. "Beckett."

Marlene C. Beckett was an eccentric. Like a magician, she pulled unusual sentences out of her judge's robes as if they were little white rabbits. She was in her midforties, dashingly attractive, with a single streak of white hair that swept through a wavy cap of fire-engine red.

Personally, Rachel liked her a great deal. Judge Beckett was a staunch feminist and former flower child who had proven that a woman—an unmarried, career-oriented woman—could be successful and intelligent without being abrasive or whiny. She might have been in a man's world, but Judge Beckett was all woman. Rachel respected her, admired her, even hoped to follow in her footsteps one day.

She just wished she'd been assigned to another judge.

As Beckett listened to her unusual plea, Rachel felt her stomach sinking down to her knees. Beckett's lips were pursed. A bad sign. One perfectly manicured nail was tapping beside the gavel. Rachel caught the judge studying the defendant, and Zack, who sat in the front row behind him.

"Counselor, you're saying the defendant will make restitution for all properties lost, and that though the state is agreeable that he be tried as a minor, you don't want him bound over for trial."

"I'm proposing that trial may be waived, Your Honor, given the circumstances. Both the defendant's mother and stepfather are deceased. His mother died five years ago, when the defendant was fourteen, and his stepfather died last year. Mr. Muldoon is willing and able to take responsibility for his stepbrother. If it please the court, the defense suggests that once restitution is made, and a stable home arranged, a trial would be merely an unproductive way of punishing my client for a mistake he already deeply regrets."

With what might have been a snort, Beckett cast a look at Nick. "Do you deeply regret bungling your attempt at burglary, young man?"

Nick lifted one shoulder and looked surly. A sharp rap on the back of the head from his stepbrother had him snarling. "Sure, I—" He glanced at Rachel. The warning in her eyes did more to make him subside than the smack. "It was stupid."

"Undoubtedly," Judge Beckett agreed. "Mr. Haridan, what is your stand on this?"

"The district attorney's office is not willing to drop charges, Your Honor, though we will agree to regard the defendant as a juvenile. An offer to lessen or drop charges was made—if the defendant would provide the names of his accomplices."

"You want him to squeal on those he—mistakenly, I'm sure—considers friends?" Beckett lifted a brow at Nick. "No dice?"

"No, ma'am."

She made some sound that Rachel couldn't interpret, then pointed at Zack. "Stand up... Mr. Muldoon, is it?"

Ill at ease, Zack did so. "Ma'am? Your Honor?"

"Where were you when your young brother was getting himself mixed up with the Cobras?"

"At sea. I was in the navy until two years ago, when I came back to take over my father's business."

"What rank?"

"Chief petty officer, ma'am."

"Mmm-hmm..." She took his measure, as a judge and as a woman. "I've been in your bar—a few years back. You used to serve an excellent manhattan."

Zack grinned. "We still do."

"Are you of the opinion, Mr. Muldoon, that you can keep your brother out of trouble and make a responsible citizen of him?"

"I... I don't know, but I want a chance to try."

Beckett tapped her fingers and sat back. "Have a seat. Ms. Stanislaski, the court is not of the opinion that a trial would be out of place in this matter—"

"Your Honor—"

Beckett cut Rachel off with a single gesture. "I haven't finished. I'm going to set bail at five thousand dollars."

This brought on an objection from the DA that was dealt with in exactly the same manner.

"I'm also going to grant the defendant what we'll call a provisional probation. Two months," Beckett said, folding her hands. "I will set the trial date for two months from today. If during that two-month period the defendant is found to be walking the straight and narrow, is gainfully employed, refrains from associating with known members of the Cobras and has not committed any crime, this court will be amenable to extending that probation, with the likelihood of a suspended sentence."

"Your Honor," Haridan puffed out, "how can we be certain the defendant won't waltz in here in two months and claim to have upheld the provisions?"

"Because he will be supervised by an officer of the court, who will serve as co-guardian with Mr. Muldoon for the two-month period. And I will receive a written report on Mr. LeBeck from that officer." Beckett's lips curved. "I think I'm going to enjoy this. Rehabilitation, Mr. Haridan, does not have to be accomplished in prison."

Rachel restrained herself from giving Haridan a smug grin. "Thank you, Your Honor."

"You're quite welcome, Counselor. Have your report to me every Friday afternoon, by three."

"My…" Rachel blinked, paled, then gaped. "My report? But, Your Honor, you can't mean for me to supervise Mr. LeBeck."

"That is precisely what I mean, Ms. Stanislaski. I believe having a male and a female authority figure will do our Mr. LeBeck a world of good."

"Yes, Your Honor, I agree. But… I'm not a social worker."

"You're a public servant, Ms. Stanislaski. So serve." She rapped her gavel. "Next case."

Stunned speechless by the judge's totally unorthodox ruling, Rachel moved to the back of the courtroom. "Good going, champ," her brother muttered in her ear. "Now you've got yourself hooked good."

"How could she do that? I mean, how could she just *do* that?"

"Everybody knows she's a little crazy." Furious, he swung Rachel out in the hall by an elbow. "There's no way in holy hell I'm letting you play babysitter for that punk. Beckett can't force you to."

"No, of course she can't." After dragging a hand through her hair, she shook Alex off. "Stop pulling at me and let me think."

"There's nothing to think about. You've got your own family and your own life. Watching over LeBeck is out of the question. And for all you know, that brother of his is just as dangerous. It's bad enough I have to watch you defend these creeps. No way I'm having you play big sister to one of them."

If he'd sympathized with her predicament, she might not have been quite as hasty. If he'd told her she'd gotten a raw deal, she probably would have agreed and set the wheels in motion to negate it. But...

"You don't have to watch me do anything, Alexi, and I can play big sister to whomever I choose. Now why don't you take that big bad badge of yours and go arrest some harmless vagrant."

His blood boiled every bit as quickly as hers. "You're not doing this."

"I'll decide what I'm going to do. Now back off."

He cupped a hand firmly on her chin just as she poked it out. "I've got a good mind to—"

"The lady asked you to back off." Zack's voice was quiet, like a snake before it strikes. Alex whipped his head around, eyes hot and ready. It took all of his training to prevent himself from throwing the first punch.

"Keep out of our business."

Zack planted his feet and prepared. "I don't think so."

They looked like two snarling dogs about to go for the throat. Rachel pushed her way between them.

"Stop it right now. This is no way to behave outside a courtroom. Muldoon, is this how you're going to show Nick responsibility? By picking fights?"

He didn't even glance at her, but kept his eyes on Alex. "I don't like to see women pushed around."

"I can take care of myself." She rounded on her brother. "You're supposed to be a cop, for heaven's sake. And here you are acting like a rowdy schoolboy. You think about this. The court believes this is a viable solution, so I'm obligated to try it."

"Damn it, Rachel—" Alex's eyes went flat and cold when Zack stepped forward again. "Pal, you mess with me, or my sister, you'll be wearing your teeth in a glass by your bedside."

"Sister?" Thoughtfully Zack examined one face, then the other. Oh, yes, the family resemblance was strong enough when you took a minute to study them. They both had those wild good looks that came through the blood. His anger cooled instantly. That changed things. He gave Rachel another speculative look. It changed a lot of things.

"Sorry. I didn't realize it was a family argument. You go ahead and yell at her all you want."

Alex had to fight to keep his lips from twitching. "All right, Rachel, you're going to listen to me."

She had to sigh. Then she had to take his face in her hands and kiss him. "Since when have I ever listened to you? Go away, Alexi. Chase some bad guys. And I'll have to take a rain check on that movie tonight."

There was no arguing with her. There never was. Changing tactics, Alex stared down Zack. "You watch out for her, Muldoon, and watch good. Because while you're at it, I'm going to be watching you."

"Sounds fair. Come by the bar anytime, Officer. First one's on the house."

Muttering under his breath, Alex stalked away. He turned once when Rachel called something out to him in Ukrainian. With a reluctant smile, he shook his head and kept walking.

"Translation?" Zack asked.

"Just that I would see him Sunday. Did you pay the bond?"

"Yeah, they're going to release him in a minute." Zack took a moment to reevaluate now that he realized she'd been kissing her brother that morning, not a lover. "I take it your brother isn't too thrilled to see you tangled up with me and Nick."

She gave Zack a long, bland look. "Who is, Muldoon? But since that's the court ruling, let's go get started."

"Get started?"

"We're going to pick up our charge, and you're going to move him into your apartment."

After spending the better part of a decade sharing close quarters with a couple hundred sailors, Zack gave one last wistful thought to the dissolution of his privacy. "Right." He took Rachel by the arm—a gesture she tried not to resent. "I don't suppose you've got any rope in that briefcase of yours."

It wasn't necessary to tie Nick up to gain his co-operation. But it was close. He sulked. He argued. He swore. By the time they'd walked out of the courthouse to hail a cab, Zack was biting down on fury and Nick had switched his resentment to Rachel.

"If this is the best deal you could cut, you'd better go back to law school. I've got rights, and the first one is to fire you."

"Your privilege, LeBeck," Rachel said, idly checking her watch. "You're certainly free to seek other counsel, but you can't fire me as your court-appointed guardian. We're stuck with each other for the next two months."

"That's bull. If you and that crazy judge think you can cook up—"

Zack made his move first, but Rachel merely elbowed him out of the way and went toe-to-toe with Nick. "You listen to me, you sorry, spoiled, sulky little jerk. You've got two choices—pretending to be a human being for the next eight weeks or going to prison for three years. I don't give a damn which way you go, but I'll tell you this. You think you're tough? You think you've got all the answers? You go inside for a week, and with that pretty face of yours the cons will be on you like dogs on fresh meat. You'd be willing to deal then, pal. Believe me, you'd be willing to deal."

That shut him up, and Rachel had the added satisfaction of seeing his angry flush die to a sickly pallor. She gestured when a cab swung to the curb. "Your choice, tough guy," she said, and turned to Zack. "I've got work to do. I should be able to clear things up by around seven, then I'll be by to see how things are going."

"I'll keep dinner warm," he said with a smirk, then caught her hand before she could walk away. "Thanks. I mean it." She would have shrugged it off. His hand was hard as rock, calluses over calluses. He grinned. "You're all right, Counselor. For a broad." He climbed into the cab behind his brother, sent her a quick salute as they pulled away. "She's right about you being a jerk,

Nick," Zack said easily. "But you sure as hell picked a lawyer with first-class legs."

Nick said nothing, but he did sneak a look out the rear window. He'd noticed Rachel's legs himself.

When they arrived at Nick's room ten minutes later, Zack had to swallow another bout of temper. It wouldn't do any good to yell at the kid every five minutes. But why in the hell had he picked such a neighborhood?

Hoods loitering on street corners. Drug deals negotiated out in broad daylight. Hookers already slicked up and stalking their prey. He could smell the stench of overripe garbage and unwashed humanity. His feet crunched on broken glass as they crossed the heaving sidewalk and entered the scarred and graffiti-laden brick building.

The smells were worse here, trapped inside, where even the fitful September breeze couldn't reach. Zack maintained his silence as they climbed up three floors, ignoring the shouted arguments behind closed doors and the occasional crash and weeping.

Nick unlocked the door and stepped into a single room furnished with a sagging iron bed, a broken dresser and a rickety wooden chair braced with a torn phone book. A few heavy-metal posters had been tacked to the stained walls in a pitiful attempt to give the room some personality. Helpless against the rage that geysered inside him, Zack let loose with a string of curses that turned the stale air blue.

"And what the hell have you been doing with the money I sent home every month when I was at sea? With the salary you were supposed to be earning from the delivery job? You're living in garbage, Nick. What's worse, you chose to live in it."

Not for a second would Nick have admitted that most
of his money had gone into the Cobra treasury. Nor
would he have admitted the shame he felt at having
Zack see how he lived. "It's none of your damn business," he shot back. "This is my place, just like it's my
life. You were never around, were you? Just because
you got tired of cruising around on some stupid de-
stroyer doesn't give you the right to come back here
and take over."

"I've been back two years," Zack pointed out wearily. "And I spent a year of that watching the old man
die. You didn't bother to come around much, did you?"

Nick felt a fresh wash of shame, and a deep, desperate sorrow that he was certain Zack could never understand. "He wasn't my old man."

Zack's head jerked up. Nick's hands fisted. Violent
temper snapped and sizzled in the room. The slightest
move would have sparked it into flame. Slowly, effort-
fully, Zack forced his body to relax.

"I'm not going to waste my time telling you he did
the best he could."

"How the hell do you know?" Nick tossed back. "You
weren't here. You got out your way, *bro.* I got out mine."

"Which brings us full circle. Pack up what you want,
and let's go."

"This is my place—" Zack moved so quickly that
the snarl caught in Nick's throat. He was up against
the wall, Zack's big hands holding him in place while
his thin body quivered with rage. Zack's face was so
close to his, all Nick could see were those dark, dangerous eyes.

"For the next two months, like it or not, your place
is with me. Now cut the crap and get some clothes to-

gether. Your free ride's over." He released Nick, knowing he had the strength and skill to snap his defiant young brother in half. "You got ten minutes, kid. You're working tonight."

By seven, Rachel was indulging a fantasy about a steamy bubble bath, a glass of crisp white wine and an hour with a good book. It helped ease the discomfort of the crowded subway car. She braced her feet against the swaying, kept her gaze focused on the middle distance. There were a few rough-looking characters scattered through the car whom she'd assessed and decided to ignore. A wino was snoring in the seat behind her, his face hidden under a newspaper.

At her stop, she bulled her way out, then started up the steps into the wet, windy evening. Hunched in her jacket, she fought with her umbrella, then slogged the two blocks to Lower the Boom.

The beveled glass door was heavy. She tugged it open and stepped out of the chill into the warmth, sounds and scents of an established neighborhood bar. It wasn't the dive she'd been expecting, but a wide wood-paneled room with a glossy mahogany bar trimmed in brass. The stools were burgundy leather, and every one was occupied. Neat tables were set around the room to accommodate more customers. There were the scents of whiskey and beer, cigarette smoke and grilled onions. A jukebox played the blues over the hum of conversation.

She spotted two waitresses winding their way through the patrons. No fishnet stockings and cleavage, Rachel mused. Both women were dressed in white slacks with modified sailor tops. There was a great deal of laughter, and she caught snatches of an argument as to whether the Mets still had a chance to make the playoffs.

Zack was in the center of the circular bar, drawing a beer for a customer. He'd exchanged his sweatshirt for a cable-knit turtleneck in navy blue. Oh, yes, she could see him on the deck of a ship, Rachel realized. Braced against the rolling, face to the wind. The bar's nautical theme, with its ship's bells and anchors, suited him.

She conjured up an image of him in uniform, found it entirely too attractive, and blinked it away.

She wasn't the fanciful type, she reminded herself. She was certainly no romantic. Above all, she was not the kind of woman who walked into a bar and found herself attracted to some landlocked sailor with shaggy hair, big shoulders and rough hands.

The only reason she was here was to uphold the court's ruling. However distasteful it might be to be hooked up with Zackary Muldoon for two months, she would do her duty.

But where was Nick?

"Would you like a table, miss?"

Rachel glanced around at a diminutive blonde hefting a large tray laden with sandwiches and beer. "No, thanks. I'll just go up to the bar. Is this place always crowded?"

The waitress's gray eyes brightened as she looked around the room. "Is it crowded? I didn't notice." With a laugh, she moved off while Rachel walked to the bar. She eased her way between two occupied stools, rested a foot on the brass rail and waited to catch Zack's eye.

"Well, darling…" The man on her left had a plump, pleasant face. He shifted on his stool to get a better look. "Don't think I've seen you in here before."

"No." Since he looked old enough to be her father, Rachel granted him a small smile. "You haven't."

"Pretty young girl like you shouldn't be here all alone." He leaned back—his stool creaking dangerously—and slapped the man on her other side on the shoulder. "Hey, Harry, we ought to buy this lady a drink."

Harry, who continued to sip his beer and work a crossword puzzle in the dim light, merely nodded. "Sure thing, Pete. Set it up. I need a five-letter word for the possibility of danger or pain."

Rachel glanced up. Zack was watching her, his blue eyes dark and steady, his bony face set and unsmiling. She felt something hot streak up her spine. *"Peril,"* she murmured, and fought off a shudder.

"Yeah! Hey, thanks!" Pleased, Harry pushed up his reading glasses and smiled at her. "First drink's on me. What'll you have, honey?"

"Pouilly-Fumé." Zack set a glass of pale gold wine in front of her. "And the first one's on the house." He lifted a brow. "That suit you, Counselor?"

"Yes." She let out the breath she hadn't been aware of holding. "Thank you."

"Zack always gets the prettiest ones," Pete said with a sigh. "Tip me another, kid. Least you can do, since you stole my girl." He shot Rachel a wink that had her relaxing with a smile again.

"And how often does he steal your girls, Pete?"

"Once, twice a week. It's humiliating." He grinned at Zack over a fresh beer. "Old Zack did date one of my girls once. Remember that time you were home on leave, Zack, you took my Rosemary to the movies, out to Coney Island? She's married and working on her second kid now."

Zack mopped up the bar with a cloth. "She broke my heart."

"There isn't a female alive who's scratched your heart, much less broken it." This from the blonde waitress, who slapped an empty tray on the bar. "Two house wines, white. A Scotch, water back, and a draft. Harry, you ought to buy yourself one of those little clip-on lights before you ruin what's left of your eyes."

"*You* broke my heart, Lola." Zack put some glasses on the tray. "Why do you think I ran off and joined the navy?"

"Because you knew how good you'd look in dress whites." She laughed, hefted the tray, then glanced at Rachel. "You watch out for that one, sweetie. He's dangerous."

Rachel sipped at her wine and tried to pretend the scents slipping out from the kitchen weren't making her stomach rumble. "Have you got a minute?" she asked Zack. "I need to see where you're living."

Pete let out a hoot and rolled his eyes. "What's the guy got?" he wanted to know.

"More than you'll ever have." Zack grinned at him and signaled to another bartender to cover for him. "I just seem to attract aggressive women. Can't keep their hands off me."

Rachel finished off her wine before sliding from the stool. "I can restrain myself if I put my mind to it. Though it pains me to mar his reputation," she said to Pete, "I'm his brother's lawyer."

"No fooling?" Impressed, Pete took a closer look. "You the one who got the kid out of jail?"

"For the time being. Muldoon?"

"Right this way for the tour." He flipped up a section of the bar and stepped through. Again he took her arm. "Try to keep up."

"You know, I don't need you to hold on to me. I've been walking on my own for some time."

He pushed open a heavy swinging door that led to the kitchen. "I like holding on to you."

Rachel got the impression of gleaming stainless steel and white porcelain, the heavy scent of frying potatoes and grilling meat, before her attention was absorbed by an enormous man. He was dressed all in white, and his full apron was splattered and stained. Because he towered over Zack, Rachel estimated him at halfway to seven feet and a good three-fifty. If he'd played football, he would have been the entire defensive line.

His face was shiny from the kitchen heat, and the color of india ink. There was a scar running from one coal-black eye down to his massive chin. His hamlike hands were delicately building a club sandwich.

"Rio, this is Rachel Stanislaski, Nick's lawyer."

"How-de-do." She caught the musical cadence of the West Indies in his voice. "Got that boy washing dishes like a champ. Only broke him five or six all night."

Standing at a huge double sink, up to the elbows in soapy water, Nick turned his head and scowled. "If you call cleaning up someone else's slop a job, you can just—"

"Now don't you be using that language around this lady here." Rio picked up a cleaver and brought it down with a *thwack* to cut the sandwich in two, then four. "My mama always said nothing like washing dishes to give a body plenty of time for searching the soul. You keep washing and searching, boy."

Nick would have liked to have said more. Oh, he'd have loved to. But it was hard to argue with a seven-foot man holding a meat cleaver. He went back to muttering.

Rio smiled, and noted that Rachel was eyeing the sandwich. "How 'bout I fix you some hot meal? You can eat after you finish your business."

"Oh, I…" Her mouth was watering. "I really should get home."

"Zack, he's going to see you home after you're done. It's too late for a woman to go walking the streets by herself."

"I don't need—"

"Dish her up some of your chili, Rio," Zack suggested as he pulled Rachel toward a set of stairs. "This won't take long."

Rachel found herself trapped, hip to hip with him in a narrow staircase. He smelled of the sea, she realized, of that salty, slightly electric scent that meant a storm was brewing beyond the horizon. "It's very kind of you to offer, Muldoon, but I don't need a meal, or an escort."

"You'll get both, need them or not." He turned, effectively trapping her against the wall. It felt good to have his body brush hers. As good as he'd imagined it would. "I never argue with Rio. I met him in Jamaica about six years ago—in a little bar tussle. I watched him pick up a two-hundred-pound man and toss him through a wall. Now, Rio's mostly a peaceful sort of man, but if you get him riled, there's no telling what he might do." Zack lifted a hand and wound a lock of Rachel's hair around his finger. "Your hair's wet."

She slapped his hand away and tried to pretend her heart wasn't slamming in her throat. "It's raining."

"Yeah. I can smell it on you. You sure are something to look at, Rachel."

She couldn't move forward, couldn't move back, so she did the only thing open to her. She bristled like a cornered cat. "You're in my way, Muldoon. My advice is to move your butt and save the Irish charm for someone who'll appreciate it."

"In a minute. Was that Russian you yelled after your brother today?"

"Ukrainian," she said between her teeth.

"Ukrainian." He considered that, and her. "I never made it to the Soviet Union."

She lifted a brow. "Neither have I. Now can we save this discussion until after I've seen the living arrangements?"

"All right." He started up the steps again, his hand on the small of her back. "It's not much, but I can guarantee it's a large step up from the dump Nick was living in. I don't know why he—" He cut himself off and shrugged. "Well, it's done."

Rachel had a feeling it was just beginning.

Chapter 3

Though it brought on all manner of headaches, Rachel took her new charge seriously. She could handle the inconvenience, the extra time sliced out of her personal life, Nick's surly and continued resentment. What gave her the most trouble was the enforced proximity with Zackary Muldoon.

She couldn't dismiss him and she couldn't work around him. Having to deal with him on what was essentially a day-to-day basis was sending her stress level through the roof.

If only she could pigeonhole him, she thought as she walked from the subway to her apartment after a Sunday dinner with her family, it would somehow make things easier. But after nearly a week of trying, she hadn't even come close.

He was rough, impatient, and, she suspected, potentially violent. Yet he was concerned enough about his stepbrother to shell out money and—much more vital— time and energy to set the boy straight. In his off hours, he dressed in clothes more suited to the rag basket than his tall, muscled frame. Yet when she'd walked through his apartment over the bar, she'd found everything neat as a pin. He was always putting his hands on her—her arm, her hair, her shoulder—but he had yet to make the kind of move she was forever braced to repel.

He flirted with his female customers, but as far as Rachel had been able to glean, it stopped at flirtation. He'd never been married, and though he'd left his family for months, even years, at a time, he'd given up the sea and had landlocked himself when his father became too ill to care for himself.

He irritated her on principle. But on some deeper, darker level, the very things about him that irritated her fanned little flames in her gut that Rachel could only describe as pure lust.

She'd tried to cool them by reminding herself that she wasn't the lusty type. Passionate, yes. When it came to her work, her family and her ambitions. But men, though she enjoyed their companionship and their basic maleness, had never been at the top of her list of priorities.

Sex was even lower than that. And it was very annoying to find herself itchy.

So who was Zackary Muldoon, and would she be better off not knowing?

When he stepped out of the shadows into the glow of a streetlight, she jolted and choked back a scream.

"Where the hell have you been?"

"I— Damn it, you scared me to death." She brought a

trembling hand back out of her purse, where it had shot automatically toward a bottle of Mace. Oh, she hated to be frightened. Detested having to admit she could be vulnerable. "What are you doing lurking out here in front of my building?"

"Looking for you. Don't you ever stay home?"

"Muldoon, with me it's party, party, party." She stalked up the steps and jammed her key in the outer door. "What do you want?"

"Nick took off."

She stopped halfway through the door, and he bumped solidly into her. "What do you mean, took off?"

"I mean he slipped out of the kitchen sometime this afternoon, when Rio wasn't looking. I can't find him." He was so furious—with Nick, with Rachel, with himself—that it took all of his control not to punch his fist through the wall. "I've been at it almost five hours, and I can't find him."

"All right, don't panic." Her mind was already clicking ahead as she walked through the tiny lobby to the single gate-fronted elevator. "It's early, just ten o'clock. He knows his way around."

"That's the trouble." Disgusted with himself, Zack stepped in the car with her. "He knows his way around too well. The rule was, he'd tell me when he was going, and where. I've got to figure he's hanging out with the Cobras."

"Nick's not going to break that kind of tie overnight." Rachel continued to think as the elevator creaked its way up to the fourth floor. "We can drive ourselves crazy running around the city trying to hunt him down, or we can call in the cavalry."

"The cavalry?"

She shoved the gate open and walked into the hallway. "Alex."

"No cops," Zack said quickly, grabbing her arms. "I'm not setting the cops on him."

"Alex isn't just a cop. He's my brother." Struggling to hold on to her own patience, she pried his fingers from her arms. "And I'm an officer of the court, Zack. If Nick's breaking the provisions, I can't ignore it."

"I'm not going to see him tossed back in a cell barely a week after I got him out."

"*We* got him out," she corrected, then unlocked her door. "If you didn't want my help and advice, you shouldn't have come."

Zack shrugged and stepped inside. "I guess I figured we could go out looking together."

The room was hardly bigger than the one Nick had rented, but it was all female. Not flouncy, Zack thought. Rachel wouldn't go for flounce. There were vivid colors in the plump pillows tossed over a low-armed sofa. The scented candles were burned down to various lengths, and mums were just starting to fade in a china vase.

There was a huge bronze-framed oval mirror on one wall. Its glass needed resilvering. A three-foot sculpture in cool white marble dominated one corner. It reminded Zack of a mermaid rising up out of the sea. There were smaller sculptures, as well, all of them passionate, some of them bordering on the ferocious. A timber wolf rearing out of a slab of oak, twisted fingers of bronze and copper that looked like a fire just out of control, a smooth and sinuous malachite cobra ready to strike.

There were shelves of books, and dozens of framed photographs—and there was the unmistakable scent of woman.

Zack felt uncharacteristically awkward and clumsy, and completely out of place. He stuck his hands in his pockets, certain he'd knock over one of those slender tapers. His mother had liked candles, he remembered. Candles and flowers and blue china bowls.

"I'll make coffee." Rachel tossed her purse aside and walked into the adjoining kitchen.

"Yeah. Good." Restless, Zack roamed the room, checked out the view through the cheerful striped curtains, frowned over the photographs that were obviously of her family, paced back to the sofa. "I don't know what I'm doing. What makes me think I can play daddy to a kid Nick's age? I wasn't around for half his life. He hates me. He's got a right."

"You've been doing fine," Rachel countered, taking out cups and saucers. "You're not playing daddy, you're being his brother. If you weren't around for half his life, it's because you had a life of your own. And he doesn't hate you. He's angry and full of resentment, which is a long way from hate—which he wouldn't have any right to. Now stop feeling sorry for yourself, and get out the milk."

"Is that how you cross-examine?" Not sure whether he was amused or annoyed, Zack opened the refrigerator.

"No, I'm much tougher than that in court."

"I bet." He shook his head at the contents of her refrigerator. Yogurt, a package of bologna, another of cheese, several diet soft drinks, a jug of white wine, two eggs, and half a stick of butter. "You're out of milk."

She swore, then sighed. "So we drink it black. Did you and Nick have a fight?"

"No— I mean no more than usual. He snarls, I snarl back. He swears, I swear louder. But we actually had what could pass for a conversation last night, then watched an old movie on the tube after the bar closed."

"Ah, progress..." She handed him his coffee in a dainty cup and saucer that felt like a child's tea set in his hands.

"We get a lot of families in for lunch on Sundays." Zack ignored the china handle and wrapped his fingers around the bowl of the cup. "He was down in the kitchen at noon. I figured he might like to knock off early, you know, take some time for himself. I went into the kitchen around four. Rio didn't want to rat on him, so he'd been covering for him for an hour or so. I hoped he'd just taken a breather, but... Then I went out looking." Zack finished off the coffee, then helped himself to more. "I've been pretty hard on him the last few days. It seemed like the best way. On my first ship, my CO was a regular Captain Bligh. I hated the bastard until I realized he'd turned us into a crew." Zack grinned a little. "Hell, I still hated him, but I never forgot him."

"Stop beating yourself up." She couldn't prevent herself from reaching out, touching his arm. "It isn't as if you hanged him from the yardarm or whatever. Now sit down and try to relax. Let me talk to Alex."

He did sit, though he wasn't happy about it. Because he felt like an idiot trying to balance the delicate saucer on his knee, he set it down on the table. There wasn't an ashtray in sight, so he clamped down on the urge for a cigarette.

He paid little attention to Rachel until her voice rose in frustration. Then he smiled a little. She was certainly full of fire, punching out requests and orders with the aplomb of a seasoned seaman. Lord, he'd gotten so he looked forward to hearing that throaty, impatient voice.

How many times over the past few days had he made up excuses to call her?

Too many, he admitted. Something about the lady had hooked him, and Zack wasn't sure whether he wanted to pry himself loose or be reeled in.

And the last thing he should be doing now was thinking of his libido, he reminded himself. He had to think about Nick.

Obviously Rachel's brother was resisting, but she wasn't taking no for an answer. When she switched to heated Ukrainian, Zack reached over to toy with the spitting cobra in the center of the coffee table. It drove him crazy when she talked in Ukrainian.

"Tak," she said, satisfied that she'd worn Alex down. "I owe you one, Alexi." She laughed, a rich, and full-blooded laugh that sent heat straight to Zack's midsection. "All right, all right, so I'll owe you two." Zack watched her hang up and cross long legs covered in a hunter-green material that was silky enough to whisper seductively when her thighs brushed together. "Alex and his partner are going to cruise around, check out some of the Cobras' known haunts. They'll let us know if they see him."

"So we wait?"

"We wait." She rose and took a fresh legal pad from a drawer. "To pass the time, you can fill me in a little more on Nick's background. You said his mother died when he was about fifteen. What about his father?"

"His mother wasn't married before." Zack reached automatically for a cigarette, then remembered. Recognizing the gesture, Rachel rose again and found a chipped ashtray. "Thanks." Relieved, he lit a cigarette, cupping his fingers around the tip out of habit. "Nadine was about eighteen when she got pregnant, and the guy wasn't interested in family. He took off and left her to fend for herself. So she had Nick and did what she could. One day she came into the bar looking for work. Dad hired her."

"How old was Nick?"

"Four or five. Nadine was barely making ends meet. Sometimes she couldn't get a sitter for him, so Dad told her to bring the kid along and I'd watch him. He was okay," Zack said with a half smile. "I mean, he was real quiet. Most of the time he'd just watch you like he was expecting to get dumped on. But he was smart. He'd just started school, but he could already read, and he could print some, too. Anyway, a couple months later, Nadine and my father got married. Dad was about twenty years older than she was, but I guess they were both lonely. My mother'd been dead for more than ten years. Nadine and the kid moved in."

"How did you...how did Nick adjust?"

"It seemed okay. Hell, I was a kid myself." Restless again, he rose to pace. "Nadine bent over backward trying to please everyone. That's the way she was. My father...he wasn't always easy, you know, and he put a lot of time into the bar. We weren't a Norman Rockwell kind of family, but we did okay." He glanced back at her photographs, surprised at the quick twinge of envy. "I didn't mind the kid hanging around me. Much. Then I joined the navy, right out of high school. It was kind of a family tradition. When Nadine died, it was hard on Nick. Hard on my father. I guess you could say they took it out on each other."

"Is that when Nick started to get into trouble?"

"I'd say he got into his share before that, but it got worse. Whenever I'd get back, my father would be full of complaints. The boy wouldn't do this, he did that.

He was hanging around with punks. He was looking for trouble. And Nick would skulk off or slam out. If I said anything, he'd tell me to kiss his—" He shrugged. "You get the picture."

She thought she did. A young boy unwanted by his father. He begins to admire his new brother, and then feels deserted by him, as well. He loses his mother and finds himself alone with a man old enough to be his grandfather, a man who couldn't relate to him.

Nothing permanent in his life—except rejection.

"I'm not a psychologist, Zack, but I'd say he needs time to trust that you mean to stay part of his life this time around. And I don't think taking a firm hand is wrong. In fact, I think that's just what he'd understand from you, and respect in the long run. Maybe that just needs to be balanced a bit." She sighed and set her notes aside. "Which is where I come in. So far, I've been just as rough on him. Let's try a little good-cop/bad-cop. I'll be the sympathetic ear. Believe me, I understand hotheads and bad boys. I grew up with them. We can start by—" The phone rang and she snagged it. "Hello. Uh-huh. Good. That's good. Thanks, Alex." She could see the relief in Zack's eyes before she hung up. "They spotted him on his way back to the bar."

Relief sparked quickly into anger. "When I get my hands on him—"

"You'll ask, in a very reasonable fashion, where he was," Rachel told him. "And to make certain you do, I'm going with you."

Nick let himself into Zack's apartment. He figured he'd been pretty clever. He'd managed to slip in and out of the kitchen without setting off Rio's radar. The way they were watching him around here, he thought, he might as well be doing time.

Everything was going wrong, anyway. He ducked into the kitchen and, since Zack wasn't around to say any different, opened a beer. He'd just wanted to check in with the guys, see what was happening on the street.

And they'd treated him like an outsider.

They didn't trust him, Nick thought resentfully as he swigged one long swallow, then two. Reece had decided that since he'd gotten out so quickly, he must have ratted. He thought he'd convinced most of the gang that he was clean, but when he'd spilled the whole story—from how he'd been caught to how he'd ended up washing dishes in Zack's bar, they'd laughed at him.

It hadn't been the good, communal laughter he'd shared with the Cobras in the past. It had been snide and nasty, with T.J. giggling like a fool and Reece smirking and playing with his switchblade. Only Cash had been the least bit sympathetic, saying how it was a raw deal.

Not one of them had bothered to explain why they'd left him hanging when the cop showed up.

When he'd left them, he'd gone by Marla's place. They'd been seeing each other steadily for the past couple of months, and he'd been sure he'd find a sympathetic ear, and a nice warm body. But she'd been out—with somebody else.

Looked as though he'd been dumped again, all around. Nothing new, Nick told himself. But the sting of rejection wasn't any easier to take this time.

Damn it, they were supposed to be his family. They were supposed to stick up for him, stand by him, not shake him loose at the first hint of trouble. He wouldn't have done it to them, he told himself, and heaved the

empty beer bottle into the trash, where it smashed satis-
factorily. No, by God, he wouldn't have done it to them.

When he heard the door open, he set his face into
bored lines and sauntered out of the kitchen. He'd expected Zack, but he hadn't expected Rachel. Nick felt
a heat that was embarrassment and something more try
to creep up into his cheeks.

Zack peeled off his jacket, hoping he had a firm grip
on his temper. "I guess you've got a good reason why
you skipped out this afternoon."

"I wanted some air." Nick pulled out a cigarette,
struck a match. "There a law against it?"

"We had an agreement," Zack said evenly. "You were
supposed to check with me before you went out, and
tell me your plans."

"No, man. You had an agreement. Last I looked it
was a free country and people could go for a walk when
they felt like it." He gestured toward Rachel. "You bring
the lawyer to sue me, or what?"

"Listen, kid—"

"I'm not a kid," Nick shot back. "You came and went
as you damn well pleased when you were my age."

"I wasn't a thief at your age." Incensed, Zack took
two steps forward. Rachel snagged his arm.

"Why don't you go down and get me a glass of wine,
Muldoon? The kind you served me the other night will
do just fine." When he tried to shake her off, she tightened her grip. "I want a moment alone with my client,
so take your time."

"Fine." He bit off the word before he stalked to the
door. "Whatever she says, pal, you're on double KP
next week. And if you try to sneak off again, I'll have

Rio chain you to the sink." He gave himself the sweet satisfaction of slamming the door.

Nick took another puff on his cigarette and dropped onto the couch. "Big talk," he muttered. "He's always figured he could boss me around. I've been on my own for years, and it's time he got that straight."

Rachel sat down beside him. She didn't bother to mention that she could smell the beer on his breath and he was underage. Why hadn't Zack seen the raw need in Nick's eyes? Why hadn't *she* seen it before?

"It's tough, having to move in here after having a place of your own."

Her voice was mild, and without censure. Nick squinted through the smoke. "Yeah," he said, cautiously. "I can hack it for a couple of months, I guess."

"When I first moved out, I was a little older than you—not much. I was excited, and scared, and lonely. I wouldn't have admitted to lonely if my life had depended on it. I've got two older brothers. They checked up on me constantly." She laughed a little. Nick didn't crack a smile. "It infuriated me, and it made me feel safe. They still get on my back, but I can usually find a way around them."

Nick stared hard at the tip of his cigarette. "He's not my real brother."

Oh, Lord, he looked young, she thought. And so terribly sad. "I suppose that would depend on your definition of real." She laid a hand on his knee, prepared for him to shrug her off, but he only switched his gaze from his cigarette to her fingers. "It'd be easier for you to believe he doesn't care, but you're not stupid, Nick."

There was a hot ball in his throat that he refused to

believe was tears. "Why should he care? I'm nothing to him."

"If he didn't care, he wouldn't yell at you so much. Take it from me—I come from a family where a raised voice is a sign of unswerving love. He wants to look out for you."

"I can look out for myself."

"And have been," she agreed. "But most of us can use a hand now and again. He won't thank me for telling you all this, but I think you should know." She waited until he raised his eyes again. "He's had to take out a loan to pay for the stolen property and the damages."

"That's bull," Nick shot back, appalled. "Did he lay that trip on you?"

"No, I checked on it myself. It seems old Mr. Muldoon's illness drained quite a bit of his savings, and Zack's. Zack's gotten the bar back on a pretty solid footing again, but he didn't have enough to swing the costs. A man doesn't put himself out like that for someone he doesn't care about."

The sick feeling in Nick's gut had him crushing out the cigarette. "He just feels obligated, that's all."

"Maybe. Either way, it seems to me you owe him something, Nick. At least you owe him a little cooperation over the next few weeks. He was scared when he came looking for me tonight. You probably don't want to believe that, either."

"Zack's never been scared of anything."

"He didn't come right out and say it, but I think he believed you'd taken off for good, that he wasn't going to see you again."

"Where the hell would I go?" he demanded. "There's nobody—" He broke off, ashamed to admit there was no one to go to. "We made a deal," he muttered, "I'm not going to skip."

"I'm glad to hear it. And I'm not going to ask you where you went," she added with a faint smile. "If I did, I'd have to put it in my report to Judge Beckett, and I'd rather not. So we'll just say you went out for some air, lost track of the time. Maybe the next time you feel like you've got to get out, you could call me."

"Why?"

"Because I know how it feels when you need to break loose." He looked so lost that Rachel skimmed a hand through his hair, brushing it back from his face. "Lighten up, Nick. It's not a crime to be friends with your lawyer, either. So what do you say? You give me a break and try a little harder to get along with Zack, and I'll do what I can to keep him off your back? I know all kinds of tricks for handling nosy older brothers."

Her scent was clouding his senses. He didn't know why he hadn't noticed before how beautiful her eyes were. How deep and wide and soft. "Maybe you and I could go out sometime."

"Sure." She saw the suggestion only as a break-through in trust, and she smiled. "Rio's a terrific cook, but once in a while you just got to have pizza, right?"

"Yeah. So I can call you?"

"Absolutely." She gave his hand a quick squeeze. When his hand tightened over hers, she was only mildly surprised. Before she could comment, Zack was pushing the door open again. Nick jumped up as if he were on a string.

Zack passed Rachel her wine, then handed Nick the ginger-ale bottle he had hooked under one finger. Taking his time, he twisted off the top of the beer he had hooked under another. "So, did you two finish your consultation?"

"For now." Rachel sipped her wine and lifted a brow at Nick.

It wasn't easy, especially after what she'd told him Zack had done, but Nick met his brother's eyes. "I'm sorry I took off."

The surprise was so great that Zack had to swallow quickly or choke on his beer. "Okay. We can work out a schedule so you can have more free time." What the hell did he do now? "Uh... Rio could use some help swabbing down the kitchen. Things usually break up early on Sunday nights."

"Sure, no problem." Nick started for the door. "See you, Rachel."

When the door closed, Zack dropped down beside her, shaking his head. "What'd you do, hypnotize him?"

"Not exactly."

"Well, what the hell did you say to him?"

She sighed, tremendously pleased with herself, and settled back. "That's privileged information. He just needs someone to stroke his bruised ego now and again. You two may not be biological brothers, but your temperaments very similar."

"Oh." He settled back, as well, swinging an arm around the top of the couch so that he could play with her hair. "How's that?"

"You're both hotheaded and stubborn—which is easy for me to recognize, as I come from a long line of the same." Enjoying the wine and the quiet, she let her eyes close. "You don't like to admit you made a mistake, and you'd rather punch your way out of a problem than reason it through."

"Are you trying to say those are faults?"

She had to laugh. "We'll just call them personality traits. My family is ripe with passionate natures. And what a passionate nature requires is an outlet. My sister Natasha had dance, then her own business and her family. My brother Mikhail has his art. Alexi has his quest to right wrongs, and I have the law. As I see it, you had the navy, and now this bar. Nick hasn't found his yet."

He brushed a finger lightly over the nape of her neck, felt the quick quiver that ran through her. "Do you really consider the law enough of an outlet for passion?"

"The way I play it." She opened her eyes, but the smile that had started to curve her lips died away. He'd shifted, and his face was close—much too close—and his hands had slipped down to her shoulders. The warning bell that rang in her brain had come too late. "I've got to get home," she said quickly. "I've got a nine-o'clock hearing."

"I'll take you in a minute."

"I know the way, Muldoon."

"I'll take you," he said again, and something in his tone made it quite clear that he wasn't talking about walking her to her door. He tugged the wineglass out of her hand and set it aside. "We were talking about passionate natures." His fingers skimmed up through her hair, fisted in it. "And outlets."

In an automatic defensive gesture, her hand slammed against his chest, but he continued to draw her closer. "I came here to help you, Muldoon," she reminded him as his mouth hovered dangerously above hers. "Not to play games."

"Just testing your theory, Counselor." He nipped lightly at her lower lip, once, twice. When that teasing sample stirred the juices, he crushed his mouth to hers and devoured.

She could stop him. Of course she would stop him, Rachel told herself. She knew how to defend herself against unwanted advances. The trouble was, she hadn't a clue as to how to defend herself against advances she didn't want to want.

His mouth was so…avid. So impatient. So greedy. She wondered if he would swallow her whole. He used lips and tongue and teeth devastatingly. If there was an instant, some fraction of a heartbeat, when she could have resisted, it passed unnoticed, and she was swamped by the hot wave that was his need, or hers. Or what they made together. On one long, throaty moan, she went under for the third time, dragging him with her.

He'd been prepared for her to slap or scratch. And he would have accepted it, would have forced himself to be satisfied with that quick, tempting taste. He was a man with large appetites, but he had never been one to take what wasn't offered willingly.

She didn't offer. She exploded. In that blink of time before his mouth covered hers, he'd seen the fire come into her eyes, that dark, liquid fire that equaled passion. When the kiss had gone from teasing to fevered, she had answered, pulling him far deeper into that hot well of desires than he'd intended to go.

And that moan. It sprinted along his spine, that glorious feline sound that was both surrender and demand. Even as it died away, she was wrapping herself around him, pressing that incredibly lean and limber body against his in a way that had a chain of explosions rioting through his system.

She heard his breathy oath, felt the long cushions of

the couch press into her back as he shifted her. For one wild moment, all she could think was Yes! This was what she wanted, this wild flurry of sensations, this crazed, mindless mating of flesh. As his mouth raced down to savage her throat, she arched against him, craving the possession.

Then he said her name. Groaned it. The shock of hearing it ripped her back to reality. She was grappling on a couch in a strange apartment with a man she barely knew.

"No." His hands were moving over her, and they nearly dragged her back into the whirlwind. Desperate to pull away, she shoved and struggled. "Stop. I said no."

He couldn't get his breath. If someone had held a gun to his head, he wouldn't have moved. But the *no* stopped him. He managed to lift his head, and the reckless light in his eyes had her fighting against a shudder. "Why?"

"Because this is insane." God, she could still taste him on her lips, and the churning for more of him was making her crazy. "Get off me."

He could have strangled her for making him want to beg. "Your call, lady." Because his hands were unsteady, he balled them into fists. "I thought you said you didn't play games."

She was humiliated, furious and frustrated beyond belief. As she saw it, the best disguise was full-blown anger. "I don't. You're the one who pushed yourself on me. The simple fact is, I'm not interested."

"I guess that's why you were kissing me so hard my teeth are loose."

"You kissed me." She jabbed a finger at him. "And you're so damn big I couldn't stop you."

"A simple no did," he reminded her, and lit a cigarette. "Let's keep it honest, Counselor. I wanted to kiss you. I've been wanting to do that, and more, ever since I saw you sitting like a queen in that grubby station house. Now, maybe you didn't feel the same way, but when I kissed you, you kissed me right back."

Sometimes retreat was the best defense. Rachel snatched up her purse and jacket. "It's done, so there's nothing more to discuss."

"Wrong." He was up and blocking her path. "We can finish discussing it while I take you home."

"I don't want you to take me home. I'm not having you take me home." Eyes blazing, she swung her jacket over her shoulders. "And if you insist on following me there, I'll have you arrested for harassment."

He merely grabbed her by the arm. "Try it."

She did something she wished she'd done the first time she laid eyes on him. She punched him in the stomach. He let out a little *whoosh* of air, and his eyes narrowed.

"First one's free. Now, we can walk to the subway, or I can carry you there."

"What's wrong with you?" she shouted. "Can't you take no for an answer?"

His response was to shove her back against the door and kiss the breath out of her. "If I didn't," he said between his teeth, "we wouldn't be walking out of here right now when you've got me so wound up I'm going to have to live in a cold shower for the next week." He yanked open the door. "Now…are you going to walk, or are you going to ride over my shoulder?"

She stuck out her chin and sailed past him.

She'd walk, all right. But she'd be damned if she'd speak to him.

Chapter 4

At the end of a harried ten-hour day, Rachel walked out of the courthouse. She should have been feeling great—her last client was certainly happy with the non-guilty verdict she'd gotten for him. But this time the victory hadn't managed to lift her spirits. The only solution she could see was to pick up a quart of ice cream on the way home and gorge herself into a sugar coma.

It usually worked, and since, as a law-abiding citizen, she couldn't relieve her tension by striding into Lower the Boom and shooting Zackary Muldoon through his thick skull, it was the safest alternative.

She almost tripped over her own feet when she saw him rise from his perch at the bottom of the steps.

"Counselor." He reached out a hand when she teetered. "Steady as she goes."

"What now?" she demanded, jerking away. "Doesn't

it occur to you that—even though I've been appointed by the court as Nick's co-guardian—I'm entitled to an hour of personal time without you in my face?"

He studied that face, noting signs of fatigue, as well as temper, in those big, tawny eyes. "You know, honey, I figured you'd be in a better mood after winning a case like you just did. Let's try these." With a flourish, he brought his other hand from behind his back. It was filled with gold, bronze and rust-colored mums.

Refusing to be charmed, Rachel gave them one long, suspicious glare. "What are those for?"

"To replace the ones that are dying in your apartment." When she made no move to take them, he bit down on his impatience. He'd come to apologize, damn it, and it looked as though she was going to make him go through with it. "Okay, I'm sorry. I got pushy the other night. And after I got over wanting to choke you, I realized you'd gone out of your way to do me a favor, and I'd repaid it by..." Furious all over again, he thrust the flowers at her. "Hell, lady, all I did was kiss you."

All he did? she thought, tempted to toss the flowers down and grind them underfoot. Just kissing didn't jangle a woman's system for better than thirty-six hours. "Why don't you take your flowers, and your charming apology, and—"

"Hold on." He thought it better to stop her before she said something he'd regret. "I said I was sorry, and I meant it, but maybe I should be more specific." To ensure that she'd stay put until he was finished, he wrapped his fingers around the lapel of her plum-colored jacket. "I'm not sorry I kissed you, any more than I'm going to be sorry the next time I kiss you. I am sorry for the way I acted after you put on the brakes."

She lifted a brow. "The way you acted," she repeated. "You mean like a jerk."

It gave her a great deal of pleasure to see a muscle twitch in his jaw.

"Okay."

A smart attorney knew when to accept a compromise. Lips pursed, she studied the flowers. "Are these a bribe, Muldoon?"

The way she said his name, with just a hint of a sneer, told him he'd gotten over the first hurdle. "Yeah."

"All right, I'll take them."

"Gee, thanks." Now that his hands were free, he tucked his thumbs in his front pockets. "I slipped in the courtroom about an hour ago and watched you."

"Oh?" She couldn't tell him how glad she was she hadn't seen him. "And?"

"Not bad. Turning a vandalism charge around on the other guy—"

"The plaintiff," she explained. "My client was justifiably frustrated after he'd exhausted all reasonable attempts to have his landlord live up to the terms of his lease."

"And spray painting The Landlord from Hell all over the guy's brownstone on the Upper West Side was his way of relieving that frustration."

"He certainly made his point. My client had paid his rent on time and in good faith, and the landlord consistently refused to acknowledge each and every request for repair and maintenance. Under the terms of the lease—"

"Hey, babe." Zack raised a hand, palm out. "You don't have to sell me. By the time you got through, I was pulling for him. There were murmurs in the visitors' gallery about lynching the landlord." His mouth was sober enough, but his eyes danced with humor. The contrast was all but irresistible.

Her smile was quick and wicked. "I love justice."

Reaching out, he toyed with the tiny gold links circling her neck. "Maybe you'd like to celebrate your victory for the underdog. Want to go for a walk?"

Mistake. The word popped full-blown into her mind, but she could smell the spicy flowers, and the evening was beautifully balmy. "I guess I would, as long as it's to my apartment. I should put these in water."

"Let me take that." He'd tugged the briefcase out of her hand before she could object. Then—she should have expected it—he took her arm. "What do you carry in here, bricks?"

"The law's a weighty business, Muldoon." His grip on her forced her to slow her pace to his. He strolled when she would have strode. "So, how's it going with Nick?"

"It's better. At least I think it's better. He balked at the idea of Rio teaching him to cook, but the idea of busing tables didn't seem to bother him much. He still won't talk to me—I mean really talk to me. But it's only been a week."

"You've got seven more."

"Yeah." He let go of her arm long enough to reach into his pocket and take out a handful of change. He dropped it into a panhandler's cup in a gesture so automatic that Rachel assumed he made a habit of it. "I figure if they could turn me from a green recruit into a sailor in about the same amount of time, I have a pretty good shot at this."

"Do you miss it?" She tilted her head up to his. "Being at sea?"

"Not so much anymore. Sometimes I still wake up at night and think I'm aboard ship." Then there were the nightmares, but that wasn't something a man shared with a woman. "Once things are stable, I'm planning on buying a boat, maybe taking a couple of months and sailing down to the Islands. Maybe a nice ketch, forty-two feet—not too fancy." He could already see it, a trim little honey, quick to the touch, brass and mahogany gleaming, white sails bulging in the wind. He imagined Rachel would look just fine standing at the bow. "You ever done any sailing?"

"Not unless you count taking the ferry over to Liberty Island."

"You'd like it." He skimmed his fingers lightly down her arm. "It's what you might call an outlet."

Rachel decided it was safer not to comment. When they reached her building, she turned to him, holding out a hand for her briefcase. "Thanks for the flowers, and the walk. I'll probably come by the bar tomorrow after work and look in on Nick."

Instead of giving her the briefcase, he closed his hand over hers. "I took the night off, Rachel. I want to spend it with you."

Her quick jolt of alarm both pleased and amused him. "Excuse me?"

"Maybe I should rephrase that. I'd like to spend the night with you—several nights running, in fact—but I'll settle for the evening." He managed to wind a lock of her hair around his finger before she remembered to bat his hand away. "Some food, some music. I know a place that does both really well. If the idea of a date makes you nervous…"

"I'm not nervous." Not exactly, she thought.

"Anyway, we can consider it a few hours between two people who have a mutual interest. It couldn't hurt if we got to know each other a little better." He pulled out his trump card. "For Nick's sake."

She studied him, much as she had the witness she'd so ruthlessly cross-examined earlier. "You want to spend the evening with me for Nick's sake?"

Giving up, he grinned. "Hell, no. There's bound to be some spillover benefit there, but I want to spend the evening with you for purely selfish reasons."

"I see. Well, since you didn't perjure yourself, I may be able to cut a deal. It has to be an early evening, somewhere I can dress comfortably. And you won't…" How had he phrased it? "Get pushy."

"You're a tough one, Counselor."

"You got it."

"Deal," he said, and gave her the briefcase.

"Fine. Come back in twenty minutes. I'll be ready."

A bar, Rachel thought a half hour later. She should have known Zack would spend his night off on a busman's holiday. Actually, she supposed it was more of a club. There was a three-piece band playing the blues on a small raised stage, and there were a handful of couples dancing on a tiny square of floor surrounded by tables. From the way he was greeted by the waitress, he was obviously no stranger.

Within moments they were settled at a table in a shadowy corner, with a glass of wine for her and a mug of beer for him.

"I come for the music," he explained. "But the food's good, too. That's not something I mention to Rio."

"Since I've seen the way he slices a club sandwich, I can't hold that against you." She squinted at the tiny menu. "What do you recommend?"

"Trust me." His thigh brushed hers as he shifted closer to toy with the stones dangling at her ear. He smiled at her narrowed eyes. "And try the grilled chicken."

She discovered he could be trusted, at least when it came to food. Enjoying every bite, lulled by the music, she began to relax. "You said the navy was a family tradition. Is that why you joined, really?"

"I wanted to get out." He nursed a second beer, appreciating the way she plowed through the meal. He'd always been attracted to a woman with an appetite. "I wanted to see the world. I only figured on the four years, but then I re-upped."

"Why?"

"I got used to being part of a crew, and I liked the life. Looking out and seeing nothing but water, or watching the land pull away when you headed out. Coming into port and seeing a place you'd never seen before."

"In nearly ten years I imagine you saw a lot of places."

"The Mediterranean, the South Pacific, the Indian Ocean, the Persian Gulf. Froze my...fingers off in the North Atlantic and watched sharks feed in the Coral Sea."

Both fascinated and amused, she propped her elbows on the table. "Did you know you didn't mention one land mass? Doesn't one body of water look pretty much like another from the deck of a ship?"

"No." He didn't think he could explain, knew he

wasn't lyrical enough to describe the varying hues of
the water, the subtle degrees of the power of the deep.
What it felt like to watch dolphins run, or whales sound.
"I guess you could say that a body of water has its own
personality, just like a body of land does."

"You do miss it."

"It gets in your blood. How about you? Is the law a
Stanislaski family tradition?"

"No." Under the table, her foot began to tap to the
beat of the bass. "My father's a carpenter. So was his
father."

"Why law?"

"Because I'd grown up in a family who'd known op-
pression. They escaped Ukraine with what they could
carry in a wagon—in the winter through the mountains—eventually reaching Austria. I was born here,
the first of my family to be born here."

"It sounds as though you regret it."

He was astute, she decided. More astute than she'd
given him credit for. "I suppose I regret not being a part
of both sides. They haven't forgotten what it was like
to taste freedom for the first time. I've never known
anything but freedom. Freedom and justice go hand
in hand."

"Some might say you could be serving justice in a
nice, cushy law firm."

"Some might."

"You had offers." When her brows lifted, he
shrugged. "You're representing my brother. I checked
on you. Graduated top of your class at NYCC, passed
the bar first shot, then turned down three very lucra-
tive offers from three very prestigious firms to work

for peanuts as a public defender. I had to figure either you were crazy or dedicated."

She swallowed a little bubble of temper and nodded. "And you left the navy with a chestful of medals, including the Silver Star. Your file includes, along with a few reprimands for insubordination, a personal letter of gratitude from an admiral for your courage during a rescue at sea in a hurricane." Enjoying his squirm of embarrassment, she lifted her glass in toast. "I checked, too."

"We were talking about you," he began.

"No. You were." Smiling, she cupped her chin on her hand. "So tell me, Muldoon, why did you turn down a shot at officer candidate school?"

"Didn't want to be a damn officer," he muttered. Rising, he grabbed her hand and hauled her to her feet. "Let's dance."

She chuckled as he dragged her onto the crowded dance floor. "You're blushing."

"I am not. And shut up."

Rachel tucked her tongue in her cheek. "It must be hell being a hero."

"Here's the deal." Zack held her lightly by the arms on the edge of the dance floor. "You drop the stuff about medals and admirals, and I won't mention that you were class valedictorian."

She thought it over. "Fair enough. But I think—"

He pulled her into his arms. "Stop thinking."

It did the trick, all right. The moment she found herself pressed hard against him, her mind clicked off. She could still hear the music, the low, seductive alto sax, the pulse of the bass, the slow rhythms of the piano notes, but rational thought vanished.

They weren't dancing. Rachel was certain no one would call this locked-hard, swaying embrace a dance. But it would be foolish to try to pull away when there was so little room. Breathing wasn't all that important, after all. Not when you could feel your own heart slamming against your ribs.

She hadn't intended to wind her arms quite so firmly around his neck, but now that they were there, there seemed little point in moving them. Besides, if she skimmed her fingers up just a bit, they could trail through his hair so that she could discover how fascinating that silky contrast was compared to the rock-hard body molded to hers.

"You fit." He bent his head so that his mouth was against her ear. "I was a little too wound up to be sure the other night. But I thought you would."

The subtle movements of his lips against her skin had her shivering before she could prevent it. "What?"

"Fit," he said again, letting his hands follow those curvy lines down to her hips and back again.

"That's only because I'm standing on my toes."

"Honey, height doesn't have a thing to do with it." He rubbed his cheek against her hair, filling himself with the scent, the texture. "You feel right, you smell right, you taste right."

Shaken, she turned her head before his mouth could finish its journey down the side of her face. "I could have you arrested for trying to seduce me in a public place."

"That's all right. I know a good lawyer." He trailed his fingers under the back of her soft wool sweater to the heated skin beneath.

Her breath caught, then released unsteadily. "They'll have us both arrested."

"I'll post bail." There was nothing but Rachel under the sweater, he was sure of it. His mouth went dry as dust. "I want you alone." Biting off a groan, he dipped his head to press his lips to her neck. "Do you know what I'd do to you right now if I had you alone?"

She shook her swimming head. "We should sit down. We shouldn't do this."

"I want to touch you, every inch of you. And taste you. I want to make you crazy."

He already was. If she didn't manage to slow things down, her overcharged system was likely to explode. "Two steps back," she said on a long breath, and took just that. His hands remained at her waist, but at least she could breathe again. At least she managed two gulps of air before she looked into his eyes and the breath backed up in her lungs again. "Too much, too fast, Muldoon. I'm not a spontaneous type of person."

What she *was* was a volcano ready to erupt. He was damn sure going to be there when the ground started to shake. But he didn't intend to scare her off, either. "Hey, you want time. I can give you an hour. Two, if you really want me to suffer."

She shook her head, edging back to the table. "Let's just say I'll let you know if and when I'm ready to take this any further."

"She wants me to suffer," Zack said under his breath. When she didn't sit, he reached for his wallet. "I take it we're leaving."

"An early evening," she reminded him. And she wanted badly to get outside, where the air could cool her blood.

"A deal's a deal." He tossed bills onto the table. "Why don't we walk back? A little exercise might help us both sleep tonight."

A twenty-block hike, Rachel mused. It couldn't hurt.

"Cold?" he asked a short time later.

"No. It's nice." But he slipped an arm around her shoulders anyway. "I don't often get a chance to just walk. Mostly it's a dash from my place to the office, from the office to the courthouse."

"What do you do when you're not dashing?"

"Oh, I go to the movies, window-shop, visit the family. In fact, I was thinking it might be good for Nick to go with me one Sunday. Have some of Mama's home cooking, listen to one of Papa's stories, see how my brothers harass me."

"Just Nick?"

She slanted him a look. "I suppose we could make room for Nick's brother."

"It's been a long time since I—since either of us had a family meal. How about the cop? I can't see him piping us aboard."

"I'll handle Alex." Now that she'd suggested it, her mind began to turn quickly. "You know, Natasha and her family are due to visit in a couple of weeks. Things will be crowded and crazy. It might be the perfect opportunity to toss Nick into your not-so-average-family type of situation. I'll see what I can work out."

"I know I thanked you before, but I don't think I know how to tell you how much I appreciate what you're doing for him."

"The court—"

"That's bilge, Rachel." They reached the steps of her

building, and he turned her to face him. "You're not just filing weekly reports or representing a client. You put yourself out for Nick right from the start."

"Okay, so I've got a weak spot for bad boys. Don't let it get around."

"No, what you've got is class, and a good heart." He liked the way she looked in the shadowy light, the vitality that pulsed from her like breath, the snap of energy and embarrassment in her eyes. "It's a tough combination to beat."

She shrugged under his hands. "Now you're going to make me blush, Muldoon, so let's not get sloppy. If things work out the way we want, you can buy me more flowers at the end of the two months. We'll call it square." He let her back up one step, but then held her firm. She was uneasy, but she wasn't surprised. "Listen, it's been nice, but…"

"I don't figure you're going to ask me in."

"No," she said definitely, remembering how her body had reacted to him in a crowded club. "I'm not."

"So I'll just have to take care of this out here."

"Zack…"

"You know I'm not going to let you go without kissing you, Rachel." To tease them both, he skimmed his lips over her jaw. "Especially when I only have to touch you to know all the want's not on my side."

"This is never going to work," she murmured, but her arms were already sliding around him.

"Sure it will. We just put our lips together, and what happens happens."

This time she knew what to expect, and braced. It made no difference at all. The same heat, the same rush, the same power. The same reckless, unrelenting need.

Had she said it was too much? No, it wasn't enough. She was afraid she could never get enough. How could she have lived her entire life without knowing what it was to be truly needy?

"I'm not getting involved this way," she murmured against his mouth. "Not with you. Not with anyone."

"Okay. Fine." Ruthlessly, he dragged her head back and plundered. A flash fire erupted between them until he felt singed down to the bone. He all but whimpered when she nipped impatiently at his lower lip. Images began to cartwheel in his head—him scooping her up and carrying her inside, falling with her into a big, soft bed. Making love with her on some white, deserted beach, with the sun beating down on her naked, golden skin. Waves pounding against the shore as she cried out his name.

"Hey, buddy."

The voice behind him was nothing more than an irritating buzzing in his head. Zack would cheerfully have ignored it, but he felt the slight prick of a knife at his back. Keeping Rachel behind him, he turned and looked into the pale, sooty-eyed face of the mugger.

"How about I let you keep the babe, and you hand over your wallet? Hers, too." The mugger turned the knife so that the backwash of the streetlight caught the steel. "And let's make it fast."

Blocking Rachel with his body, Zack reached in his back pocket. He could hear Rachel's unsteady breathing as she unzipped her bag. It wasn't impulse, but instinct. The moment the mugger's eyes shifted, Zack lunged.

With a scream in her throat and the Mace in her hand, Rachel watched them struggle. She saw the knife flash, heard the awful crunch of fist against bone before the blade clattered to the sidewalk. Then the mugger was racing off into the dark, and she and Zack were as alone as they'd been seconds before.

He turned back to her. She noted that he wasn't even breathing hard, and that the gleam in his eyes had only sharpened. "Where were we?"

"You idiot." The words were little more than a whisper as she fought to get them out over the lump of fear in her throat. "Don't you know any better than to jump someone holding a knife? He could have killed you."

"I didn't feel like losing my wallet." He glanced down at the can in her hand. "What's that?"

"Mace." Disgusted by the fact she hadn't even popped off the safety top, she dropped it back in her purse. "I'd have given him a faceful if you hadn't gotten in the way."

"Next time I'll step aside and let you handle it." He frowned down at the trickle of blood on his wrist and swore without much heat. "I guess he nicked me."

She went pale as water. "You're bleeding."

"I thought it was his." Annoyed more than hurt, he poked a finger through the rip in the arm of his sweater. "I got this on Corfu, my last time through. Damn it." Eyes narrowed, he stared down the street, wondering if he had a chance of catching up with the mugger and taking the price of the sweater, if not its sentimental value, out of his hide.

"Let me see." Her fingers trembled as she pushed the sleeve up to examine the long, shallow slash. "Idiot!" she said again, and began to fumble in her purse for her keys. "You'll have to come inside and let me fix it. I can't believe you did something so stupid."

"It was the principle," he began, but she cut him off

with a stream of Ukrainian as she stabbed her key at the lock.

"English," he said, pressing a hand to his stomach as it began to knot. "Use English. You don't know what it does to me when you talk in Russian."

"It's not Russian." Snatching his good arm, she pulled him inside. "You were just showing off, that's all. Oh, it's just like a man." Still pulling him, she stalked into the elevator.

"Sorry." He was fighting off a grin, trying to look humble. "I don't know what got into me." He certainly wasn't going to admit he'd had worse scratches shaving.

"Testosterone," she said between her teeth. "You can't help it." She kept her hand on him until she'd gotten them inside her apartment. "Sit," she ordered, and dashed into the bathroom.

He sat, making himself at home by propping his feet on her coffee table. "Maybe I should have a brandy," he called out. "In case I'm going into shock."

She hurried back out with bandages and a small bowl of soapy water. "Do you feel sick?" Scared all over again, she pressed a hand to his brow. "Are you dizzy?"

"Let's see." Always willing to take advantage of an opportunity, he grabbed a fistful of her hair and pulled her mouth to his. "Yeah," he said when he let her go. "You could say I'm feeling a little light-headed."

"Fool." She slapped his hand aside, then sat down to clean the wound. "This could have been serious."

"It was serious," he told her. "I hate having someone poke me in the back with a knife when I'm kissing a woman. Honey, if you don't stop shaking, I'm going to have to get *you* a brandy."

"I'm not shaking—or if I am, it's just because I'm

mad." She tossed her hair back and glared at him. "Don't you ever do that again."

"Aye, aye, sir."

To pay him back for the smirk, she dumped iodine over the wound. When he swore, it was her turn to smile. "Baby," she said accusingly, but then took pity on him and blew the heat away. "Now hold still while I put a bandage on it."

He watched her work. It was very pleasant to feel her fingers on his skin. It seemed only natural that he should lean over to nibble at her ear.

Fire streaked straight up her spine. "Don't." Shifting out of reach, she pulled his sleeve down over the fresh bandage. "We're not going to pick things up now. Not here." Because if they did, she knew there would be no backing off.

"I want you, Rachel." He caught her hand in his before she could stand. "I want to make love with you."

"I know what you want. I have to know what I want."

"Before we were interrupted downstairs, I think that was pretty clear."

"To you, maybe." After a deep breath, she pulled her hand free and stood. "I told you, I don't do things spontaneously. And I certainly don't take a lover on impulse. If I act on the attraction I feel for you, I'll do so with a clear head."

"I don't think I've had a clear head since I laid eyes on you." He stood, as well, but because it suddenly seemed important to both of them he kept his distance. "I realize how the saying goes about guys like me and women in every port. That's not reality—not my reality, anyway. I'm not going to tell you I spent every liberty curled up with a good book, but..."

"It's not my business."

"I'm beginning to think it is, or could be." The look in his eyes kept her from arguing. "I've been on land for two years, and there hasn't been anybody important." He couldn't believe what he was saying, what he felt compelled to say, but the words just tumbled out. "I'll be damned if there's ever been anyone like you in my life."

"I have priorities..." she began. The words sounded weak to her. "And I don't know if I want this kind of complication right now. We have Nick to think about, as well, and I'd rather we just take it slow."

"Take it slow," he repeated. "I can't give you any promises on that. I *can* promise that the first chance I get, when it's just you and me, I'm going to do whatever it takes to shake up those priorities of yours."

She jammed nervous hands in her pockets. "I appreciate the warning, Muldoon. And here's one for you. I don't shake easily."

"Good." His grin flashed before he walked to the door. "Winning's no fun if it's easy. Thanks for the first aid, Counselor. Lock your door." He shut it quietly behind him and decided to walk home.

At this rate, he was never going to get any sleep.

Chapter 5

She wasn't avoiding him. Exactly. She was busy, that was all. Her caseload didn't allow time for her to drop by Zack's bar night after night and chat with the regulars. It wasn't as if she were neglecting her duty. She had slipped in a time or two to talk with Nick in the kitchen. If she'd managed to get in and out without running into Zack, it was merely coincidence.

And a healthy survival instinct.

If she let her answering machine screen her calls at home, it was simply because she didn't want to be disturbed unnecessarily.

Besides, he hadn't called. The jerk.

At least she was making some progress where Nick was concerned. He had called her, twice. Once at her office, and once at home. She found his suggestion that they catch a movie together a hopeful sign. After all, if he spent an evening with her, he wouldn't be hanging out with the Cobras, looking for trouble.

After ninety minutes of car chases, gunplay and the assorted mayhem of the action-adventure he'd chosen, they settled down in a brightly lit pizzeria.

"Okay, Nick, so tell me how it's going." His answer was a shrug, but Rachel gave his arm a squeeze and pressed. "Come on, you've had two weeks to get used to things. How are you feeling about it?"

"It could be worse." He pulled out a cigarette. "It's not so bad having a little change in my pocket, and I guess Rio's not so bad. It's not like he's on my case all the time."

"But Zack is?"

Nick blew out a stream of smoke. He liked to watch her through the haze. It made her look more mysterious, more exotic. "Maybe he's laid off a little. But it's like tonight. I got the night off, right? But he wants to know where I'm going, who I'm going with, when I'll be back. That kind of sh—" He caught himself. "That kind of stuff. I mean, hey, I'm going to be twenty in a couple of months. I don't need a keeper."

"He's a pushy guy," Rachel said, trying to strike a balance between sympathy and sternness. "But he's not only responsible for you in the eyes of the law—he cares about you." Because his answering snort seemed more automatic than sincere, she smiled. "His style's a little rough, but I'd have to say his intentions are good."

"He's going to have to give me some room."

"You're going to have to earn it." She squeezed his hand to take the sting out of her words. "What did you tell him about tonight?"

"I said I had a date, and he should butt out." Nick

grinned, pleased when he saw the answering humor in Rachel's eyes. He'd have been very disappointed if he'd realized she was amused at the term *date*. "It's like he's got his life and I got mine. You know what I'm saying?"

"Yes." She drew a deep appreciative breath as their pizza arrived. "And what do you want to do with your life, Nick?"

"I figure I'll take what comes."

"No ambitions?" She took the first bite, watching him. "No dreams?"

Something flickered in his eyes before he lowered them. "I don't want to be serving drinks for a living, that's for sure. Zack can have it." After crushing out his cigarette, he applied himself to the pizza. "And no way I'm going into the damn navy, either. He swung that one by me the other day, and I shot it down big-time."

"Well, you seem to know what you don't want. That's a step."

He reached out to toy with the little silver ring on her finger. "Did you always want to be a lawyer?"

"Pretty much. For a while I wanted to be a ballerina, like my sister. That's when I was five. It only took about three lessons for me to figure out it wasn't all tutus and toe shoes. Then I thought I might be a carpenter, like the men in my family, so I asked for a tool set for my birthday. I think I was eight. I managed to build a pretty fair book rack before I retired." She smiled, and his heart rate accelerated. "It took me a while to come to the conclusion that I couldn't be what Natasha was, or Papa or Mama or anyone else. I had to find my own way." She said it casually, hoping the concept would take root.

"So you went to law school."

"Mmm…" Her eyes brightened as she studied him. "Can you keep a secret?"

"Sure."

"Perry Mason." Laughing at herself, she scooped up another slice. "I was fascinated by those old reruns. You know, how there would always be this murder, and Perry would take the case when his client looked doomed. Lieutenant Tragg would have all this evidence, and Perry would have Della and Paul Drake out looking for clues to prove his client's innocence. Then they'd go to court. Lots of objections, and 'Your Honor, as usual the counsel for the defense is turning this proceeding into a circus.' It would look bad for Perry. He'd be up against that smug-faced DA."

"Hamilton Berger," Nick said, grinning.

"Right. Perry would play it real close to the vest, dropping little hints to Della, but never spilling the whole thing. You just knew he had all the answers, but he would string it out. Then, always at the eleventh hour, he'd get the real murderer up on the witness stand, and he'd just hammer the truth out of him, until the poor slob would crumble like a cookie and confess all."

"Then he'd explain how he'd figured it all out in the epilogue," Nick finished for her. "And you wanted to be Perry Mason."

"You bet," Rachel agreed over a bite of pizza. "By the time I realized it wasn't that black-and-white, and it certainly wasn't that tidy, I was hooked."

"Ray Charles," Nick said, half to himself.

"What?"

"It just made me think how listening to Ray Charles made me want to play the piano."

Rachel rested her chin on her folded hands and tried to ease the door open a little farther. "Do you play?"

"Not really. I used to think it would be pretty cool. Sometimes I'd hang around this music store and fiddle around until they kicked me out." The twinge of embarrassment made him brush the rest aside. "I got over it."

But once she had a purpose, Rachel wasn't easily shaken. "I always wished I'd learned. Tash got my mother a piano a few months ago—when we found out she'd always wanted to play. All those years we were growing up, she never mentioned it. All those years…" Her words trailed off, and then she shook herself back to the matter at hand. "My sister married a musician. Spencer Kimball."

"Kimball?" Nick's eyes widened before he could prevent it. "The composer?"

"You know his work?"

"Yeah." He struggled to keep it cool. A guy couldn't admit he listened to longhair music—unless it was heavy metal. "Some."

Delighted with his reaction, Rachel continued, just as casually. "At one of our visits down to see Tash and her family, we caught Mama at the piano. She got all flustered and kept saying how she was too old to learn, and how foolish it was. But then Spence sat down with her to show her a few chords, and you could see, you could just see, how much she wanted to learn. So on Mother's Day, we worked out this big, elaborate plan to get her out of the house for a few hours. Anyway, when she came back, the piano was in the living room. She cried." Rachel blinked the mist out of her own eyes and sighed. "She takes lessons twice a week now, and she's practicing for her first recital."

"That's cool," Nick murmured, obscurely touched.

"Yeah, it's pretty cool." She smiled at him. "I guess it proves it's never too late to try." When she offered a hand, she wanted him to take it as a gesture of friendship and support. "What do you say we walk off some of this pizza?"

"Yeah." His fingers closed around hers, and Nicholas LeBeck was in heaven.

He was content to listen to her talk, to have her laugh shiver over him. Even the shadows of the girls who had weaved in and out of his life faded away. They were nothing compared to the woman who walked beside him, slim and soft and fragrant.

She listened when he talked. And she was interested in what he had to say. When she smiled up at him, those exotic eyes flashing with humor, his stomach tied itself into slippery knots.

He could have walked with her for hours.

"This is it."

Nick pulled up short, standing in almost the exact spot his brother had a few nights before. As his gaze skimmed over the building at her back, he imagined what it would be like if she asked him in. They'd have coffee, and she'd slip off her shoes and curl those long legs up as they talked.

He'd be careful with her, even gentle. Once his nerves settled.

"I'm glad we could do this," she was saying, already taking out her keys. "I hope if you're feeling restless again, or just need to talk to someone, you'll call me. When I file my report with Judge Beckett tomorrow, I think she'll be pleased with the way things are working out."

"Are you?" His eyes locked on hers as he lifted a hand to her hair. "Pleased with the way things are working out?"

"Sure." A little alarm shrilled in Rachel's head, but she dismissed it as absurd. "I think you've taken a step in the right direction."

"Me too."

The alarm continued to beep as she backed up. "We'll have to do this again soon, but I've got to get in now. I have an early meeting."

"Okay. I'll call you."

She blinked as his hand slipped around to cup her neck. "Ah, Nick…"

His mouth closed over hers, very warm, very firm. Her eyes stayed open, registering shock, as her hand flew up to press against his shoulder. His fingers tensed against her neck, and she had the impression of a very lean, very hard body before she managed to pull away.

"Nick," she said again, groping.

"It's okay." He smiled, tucked her hair behind her ear in a gesture that reminded her vividly of his brother. "I'll be in touch."

He strolled away. No…good Lord, he was swaggering, Rachel thought as she stared after him. With her mind whirling, she let herself in. "Oh, boy," she sighed as she paced the elevator.

What now? What now? How could she have been so stupid? Cursing herself, she stomped off the elevator and toward her apartment. This was great, just great. Here she'd been trying to make friends with Nick, and all the while he'd been thinking…

She didn't want to think about what he'd been thinking. Without taking off her jacket, she paced the apartment. There had to be a reasonable, diplomatic way to handle this, she told herself. He was only nineteen, he just had a crush, she was overreacting.

Then she remembered those limber fingers on the back of her neck, the firm press of those lips, the smooth and practiced way he'd drawn her against him.

Wrong, Rachel thought, and closed her eyes. She wasn't dealing with a child's puppy love, but with a full-grown man's desire.

Dropping down onto the arm of the couch, she dragged her hands through her hair. She should have seen it coming, she told herself. She should have stopped it before it started. She should have done a lot of things.

After twenty minutes of kicking herself, she snatched up the phone. She might be hip-deep in quicksand, but she wasn't going to sink alone.

"Lower the Boom."

"Let me talk to Muldoon," Rachel snapped, scowling at the sound of laughter and bar chatter that hummed through the receiver. "It's Rachel Stanislaski."

"You got it. Hey, Zack, phone for you. It's the babe."

Babe? Rachel thought, narrowing her eyes. "Babe?" she repeated out loud the moment Zack had answered.

"Hey, sugar, I'm not responsible for the opinions of my bartenders." He took a swallow of mineral water. "So you finally realized you couldn't keep away from me."

"Stuff it, Muldoon. We need to talk. Tonight."

He stopped grinning and shifted the phone. "Is there a problem?"

"Damn right."

"Nick breezed through a couple of minutes ago. He seemed fine when he headed upstairs."

"He's upstairs?" she said, calculating. "Just make

sure he stays up there. I'm coming right over." She hung up before he could ask any questions.

It wasn't exactly the way he'd planned it, Zack thought as he mixed a couple of stingers. His strategy had been to lie back for a few days, let Rachel simmer. Until she came to a boil—and came looking for him.

She hadn't sounded lonely or aroused or vulnerable over the phone. She'd sounded mad as a hornet.

He cast his eyes up at the ceiling, picturing the apartment overhead, as he automatically added a twist to a glass of club soda. Obviously it had to do with Nick. Where the hell had the boy been all evening? he wondered.

What kind of trouble had he gotten himself into this time? With half an ear, Zack took an order for two drafts, a margarita on the rocks and a coffee, black. Damned if he'd thought the boy was in trouble, Zack reflected. Nick had looked relaxed, calm, even approachable, when he'd checked in. Zack remembered thinking that the date had been a rousing success. And he'd hoped to be able to ease the girl's name out of his brother—along with a bit more salient information.

He didn't figure Nick needed a course in the birds and bees, but he hoped to drop a few hints about responsibility, protection and respect.

A steady girl, a steady job, a stable home. They all seemed to be coming together. So what the hell...

His thoughts broke off as he looked up. Rachel walked in, cheeks flushed from the chilly evening, eyes snapping. As she crossed the room, she peeled off her jacket to reveal one of those soft sweaters she often wore. This one was the color of a good burgundy, with a wide cowl neck that draped softly over the swell of her breasts. It rode her hips, and under it she wore snug black leggings that showed off those first-class legs.

Zack checked to make sure his tongue wasn't hanging out.

She stopped at the bar only long enough to glare at him. "In your office." Without waiting for a response, she strode off.

"Well, well…" Lola watched Rachel swing Zack's office door open, then shut it behind her with a loud click. "Looks like the lady's got something on her mind."

"Yeah." Zack set the last glass on Lola's tray. All he could think was, there was definitely a fire in the hole. "If Nick comes back down, tell him I'm…tied up."

"You're the boss."

"Right." And he intended to remain the boss. He swung through the bar and, taking one bracing breath, marched into his office.

Rachel had tossed her jacket and purse aside, and was pacing. When the door opened, she stopped, swung her hair back and leveled a killing gaze at him.

"Don't you ever talk to him?" she demanded. "Aren't you making any effort to find out what's going on in his head? What kind of a guardian are you, anyway?"

"What the hell is this?" He threw up his hands in disgust. "I don't see or hear from you in days, then you come stalking in here just so you can yell at me. Just simmer down, Counselor, and remember I'm not some felon on the witness stand."

"Don't tell me to simmer down," she tossed back. It felt good, really good, to assuage her guilt and frustration with a pitched battle. "I'm the one who's going to have to deal with him. And if you were any kind of a brother, you would have known. You could have warned me."

Because his confidence as a brother was still at low tide, he hissed out an oath. Rachel echoed it as he shoved her into a chair. "Just sit down and take it from the top. I assume we're talking about Nick."

"Of course we're talking about Nick." She popped up again, and was pushed right back down. "I don't have anything else to discuss with you."

"We'll bypass that for now. Just what is it I should have known and warned you about?"

"That he'd...he'd..." She blew out a breath, struggling for the proper phrase. "That he'd started to think of me as a woman."

"How the hell is he supposed to think of you? As a tuna?"

"I mean as a *woman*," she said between her teeth. "Do I have to spell it out?"

His brows shot up, then settled again as he reached for a cigarette. "Don't be stupid, Rachel. He's nineteen. I'm not saying he's blind and wouldn't appreciate the way you look. But he's got a girl. He was out with her tonight."

"You idiot." She sprang up again, and this time she thumped a fist on his chest. "He was out with *me* tonight."

"Out with you?" With a frown, Zack studied her. "What for?"

"We went to the movies, had a pizza. I wanted to get him to talk a little—informally—so when he called I said sure."

"One step at a time. Nick called you and asked you out on a date."

"It wasn't a date. I didn't think it was a damn date." Since she didn't see anything handy to kick other than Zack's shin, she stalked a circle around his office again.

"It seemed to me if we could develop a relationship—A friendship," she corrected hastily. "It would make things easier all around."

Considering, Zack took a drag of his cigarette. "Sounds reasonable. So you took in a flick and had a pizza. What's the problem? Did he get into a fight, give you a hard time?" He stopped, alarmed. "You didn't run into any of the Cobras?"

"No, no, no…" Incensed, she whirled around the room. "Aren't you listening to me? I said he was thinking about me as a woman…as a date. As a… Oh, boy." She let out a long breath. "He kissed me."

Zack's eyes turned into dark, dangerous slits. "Define *kiss*."

"You know damn well what a kiss is. You smack your lips up against somebody's." She spun away, then back. "I should have seen it coming, but I didn't. Then, before I realized what he was thinking, wham!"

"Wham," Zack repeated, trying to stay calm. He took his own turn around the room, bumping his shoulders against hers. "Okay, listen, I think you're making a big deal out of nothing. He kissed you good-night. It's a gesture. He's just a kid."

"No," Rachel said, and her tone had Zack turning back to her. "He's not."

Temper was clawing to gain freedom. As a result, Zack's voice was deadly calm. "Did he try to—"

"No." Recognizing the signs, she cut him off. "Of course he didn't. He just kissed me. But it was the way… Listen, Zack, I know the difference between a casual kiss good-night between friends and—and, well, a move. And I can tell you Nick has a very smooth move."

"Glad to hear it," Zack said between his teeth.

Suddenly drained, she dropped down onto the corner of his desk. "I don't know what to do."

"I'll straighten him out."

"How?"

"I don't know how," he shot back, crushing out his cigarette. "I'll be damned if I'm going to be competing with my kid brother."

The muttered aside had her narrowing her eyes. "I'm not a trophy, Muldoon."

"I didn't mean—" With a shake of his head, he leaned on the desk beside her. "Look, this throws me off course, okay? I figured Nick was out making time with some pretty little teenager whose daddy would want her home by midnight, and now I find out he's coming on to you. If he wasn't my brother, I'd go knock him around a little."

"Typical," she muttered.

He ignored that and tried to think. "It's probably normal for him to develop—or think he's developed—feelings for you. Don't you think?"

"Maybe." She tilted her head to slant Zack a look. "I don't want to hurt him."

"Me either. You could back off, stay unavailable—the way you've tried to be with me."

"I've been busy." All dignity, she lifted her chin. "And we're not talking about you. In any case, I considered that, but I'm supposed to be his co-guardian. I can't do that long-distance. Besides, he talked to me tonight. He really talked, and relaxed, and showed me a little of what's underneath all that defiance. If I cut him off now, just when he's beginning to open up and trust me, I don't know what damage I might do."

"You can't string him along, Rachel."

"I know that." She wanted to lay her head on Zack's shoulder, just for a minute. She looked down at her hands instead. "I need to find a way to let him know I want to be his friend—just his friend—without crushing his ego."

Zack took her hand, and when she didn't pull it away he twined his fingers in hers. "I'll talk to him. Calmly," he added when Rachel frowned at him.

"Actually, I wanted to dump the whole business in your lap, but the more I think about it, the more I'm sure he'd only resent it coming from you. How can you tell him I'm not interested without letting him know we discussed his feelings behind his back?" She shut her eyes. "And I'm not feeling very good about that, either."

"You had to tell me."

"Yeah, I think I did, just like I think I'm going to have to figure out what to do."

He ran his thumb over her knuckles. "We're in this together, remember?"

"How can I forget? But you and Nick are just getting your balance. This is bound to tilt the scales, Zack. I think it's best if I try to handle it." A smile played around the corners of her mouth. "I guess I should apologize for coming here and jumping on you."

"At least it got you here. We'll handle it." He brought her hand to his lips, enjoying the way her eyes darkened and became cautious. "You let him down easy, and I'll let him take it out on me. After all, I can't blame the kid for trying, when I'm doing the same myself."

"One has nothing to do with the other." She pushed away from the desk, but he continued to hold her hand.

"I'm glad to hear it. Feeling better?"

Her lips quirked. "Fighting always makes me feel better."

"Then, sugar, by the time we're through with each

other, you should be feeling like a million bucks. I don't suppose you'd like to hang around for a couple of hours until I can close the bar."

"No." Her heart picked up a beat at the thought. A dark, empty bar, blues on the juke, the world locked outside. "No, I have to go."

"I'm shorthanded tonight, or I'd see you home. I'll put you in a cab."

"I can put myself in a cab."

"Okay. In a minute." He caught her by the hips, lifted her, then set her on the desk. "I've missed you," he murmured, nuzzling her neck.

Without thinking—he certainly had a way of making her stop thinking—she tilted her head to give him more access to her skin. "I've been busy."

"I don't doubt you've been busy." He moved up to nip at her earlobe. "But you've been stubborn. I like that about you, Rachel. Right now I can't think of a damn thing I don't like about you."

This was a mistake. Any minute she'd remember why it was a mistake. She was sure of it. "You just want to talk me into bed."

His lips curved before they came down on hers. "Oh, yeah…" He fisted his hands in her hair, and a deep sound of pleasure came from his throat when she arched against him. "How'm I doing?"

"You're making things very difficult for me."

"Good. That's good." He was very close to pressing her back on the desk and doing all the things he'd fantasized about during those long, dark nights he'd lain alone in bed, thinking of her. And she sighed. The soft, broken sound of it seemed to rip something inside his gut. Grinding out an oath, he buried his face in her hair.

"I sure pick my spots," he muttered. "On the sidewalk with a mugger, in my office with a barful of customers outside the door. Every time I'm around you I start acting like a kid in the back seat of a parked car."

She had to concentrate just to breathe. As he continued to hold her, just hold her, she found herself stroking his hair, counting his heartbeats, warming toward him in a way that was entirely different from the flash heat of a moment before.

She'd been right about the quicksand, she realized. And she'd been right about not sinking alone. "We're not kids," she murmured.

"No, we're not." Not quite sure he could trust himself, he drew back, taking both her hands in his. "I know it's moving fast, and I know it's complicated, but I want you. There's no getting around it."

"I knew this would happen if I came here tonight. I came anyway." Muddled, she shook her head. "I don't know what that says about me, or about us. I do know it's not smart, and I'm usually smart. The best thing for me to do is walk out the door and go home."

He tugged on her hands, bringing her off the desk and close to him again. "What are you going to do?"

She wavered, caught on the thin edge between temptation and common sense. Images of what could be swam giddily through her head and left her throat dry. Repercussions…she couldn't quite see them clearly, but she knew they existed. And she was afraid they would be severe indeed.

"I'm going to walk out the door and go home." She let out an unsteady breath when he said nothing. "For now."

She grabbed up her jacket, her purse. When she reached the door, his hand closed over hers on the knob.

A quick thrill of panicked excitement raced through her at the thought that he would simply turn the lock.

She wouldn't permit it. Of course she wouldn't permit it.

Would she?

"Sunday" was all he said.

Her scattered thoughts scrambled to make sense of the word. "Sunday?"

"I can shift things around and take the day off. Spend it with me."

Relief. Confusion. Pleasure. She had no idea which emotion was uppermost. "You want to spend Sunday with me."

"Yeah. You know, take in a couple of museums, maybe an art gallery, a walk in the park, have a fancy lunch somewhere. I figure most of the time we've spent together so far's been after dark."

Odd…that hadn't occurred to her before. "I guess it has."

"Why don't we try a Sunday afternoon?"

"I…" She couldn't think of a single reason why not. "All right. Why don't you come by around eleven?"

"I'll be there."

She turned the knob, then glanced back at him. "Museums?" she said on a laugh. "Is this on the level, Muldoon?"

"I happen to appreciate art," he told her, leaning forward to touch his lips to hers in a quiet kiss that rocked her back on her heels. "And beauty."

She slipped out quickly. As she walked up to the corner to hail a cab, it occurred to her she hadn't yet decided how best to handle Nick. And she sure as hell hadn't figured out how to handle Nick's big brother.

Chapter 6

Rachel was cursing when her buzzer sounded promptly at eleven o'clock Sunday morning. Securing an earring, she pressed the intercom. "Muldoon?"

"You sound out of breath, sugar. Should I take that as a compliment?"

"Come on up," she said shortly. "And don't call me sugar."

After snapping off the intercom, she flipped off her three security locks, then gave herself one last look in the mirror. She'd forgotten her second earring. Grumbling, she went on a quick search until she found it lying on the kitchen counter beside her empty coffee cup.

It was her day off, damn it. And she resented having it interrupted for work. Not because she'd been looking forward to spending it with Zack. Particularly. It was just that it had been a long time since she'd had a

day to wander through museums and galleries, and—
She broke off her silent complaining at the knock on
the door.

"Come in, it's open."

"Anxious?" Zack commented as he walked in. Then
he lifted a brow and took one long look. She was standing in the center of the room, slim and lovely in a bronze-
toned suede jacket and short skirt set off by a slightly
mannish silk blouse in a flashy blue. She was barefoot,
and he found his mouth watering as he watched her perform the feminine and oddly intimate task of securing a
shiny gold knot to her ear. "You look nice."

"Thanks. You, too." No, what he looked was sexy,
she thought, damn sexy, in snug black jeans, a midnight-
blue sweater, and a bomber jacket in soft black leather.
But *nice* would have to do. "Listen, Zack, I tried to catch
you before you left the bar. I'm sorry I missed you."

"Is there a problem?" He watched as she wiggled
one foot into a bronze-colored pump. By the time she'd
wiggled into the second, his palms were sweaty and he'd
missed what she'd said. "Sorry, what?"

"I said my boss called, about a half hour ago. I've got
an attempted murder I have to deal with."

That cut his fantasy off as quickly as a faceful of ice
water. "A what?"

"Attempted murder. Alexi's precinct. I can probably
plead down to assault with a deadly weapon, but I have
to see him today so I can meet with the DA in the morning." She spread her hands. "I'm really sorry I didn't
catch you before you came all the way over."

"No problem. I'll go with you."

"With me?" She liked the idea, a little too much.

"You don't want to spoil your day off spending it at a police station."

"I'm taking the day off to be with you," he reminded her, and picked up her coat where she'd tossed it over the back of the couch. "Besides, it won't take all day, will it?"

"No, probably no more than an hour, but—"

"So let's get started." He walked to her, then turned her around so that he could slip the coat slowly on one arm, then the other. Lowering his head, he sniffed at her neck. "Did you spray that stuff on for the felon, or for me?"

She shivered once before cautiously stepping away. "For me." Picking up her briefcase, she held it between them like a shield. "I have to go by the office first. We already have a file on the guy. He's been around."

"Okay." He tugged the briefcase away, took her hand. "Let's go, Counselor."

Alex spotted his sister the moment she walked into the station. Since he wasn't any happier than she to be spending his Sunday morning at work, he immediately brightened. Giving Rachel a hard time always lifted his spirits.

Grinning, he strolled over, a greeting on his lips. When he spotted the man hovering around her, the humor in his eyes turned instantly to suspicion. "Rach."

Still clipping her visitor's badge to her lapel, she glanced up. "Alex. They got you, too, huh?"

"Looks like. Muldoon, isn't it?"

"That's right." Zack returned the steady stare and nodded. "Nice to see you again, Officer."

"Detective," Alex corrected. "I didn't hear anything about LeBeck being pulled in."

"I'm not here about Nick." Rachel recognized Alex's unfriendly, aggressive stance. He'd assumed it with every boy and man she'd dated since she'd turned fifteen. "I'm representing Victor Lomez."

"Now that's real slime." But Alex wasn't nearly as concerned about Rachel's client as he was with the reason the big Irishman was carrying her briefcase. "So, did you two run into each other outside?"

"No, Alexi." Rachel commandeered the coffee he was carrying. Though she knew it was worthless, she shot him a warning glance. "Zack and I had plans for the day."

"What kind of plans?"

"The kind that aren't any of your business." She kissed his cheek as an excuse to get close enough to his ear to whisper, "Knock it off." Leaning back, she smiled at Zack. "Grab a seat, Muldoon, and some of this horrible coffee. Like I said, this shouldn't take too long."

"I got all day," he told her as she walked off to a conference room. He turned back to Alex and said blandly, "So, you want to take me down to interrogation?"

Alex told himself he wasn't particularly amused, and gestured with a jerk of his head. "In here'll do." It pleased him to be behind his desk while Zack sat in the chair used to grill witnesses. "What's the story, Muldoon?"

Casually Zack took out a cigarette. He offered one to Alex and lit up when Alex shook his head. "You want to know what I'm doing with your sister." He blew out a stream of smoke, considering. "If you're any kind of detective, you should be able to figure that one out. She's beautiful, she's smart. She's a soft heart in a tough, sexy shell." Taking another drag, he watched Alex's eyes narrow. "Listen, you want it straight, or do you want me to tell you I'm just interested in her legal services?"

"Watch your step."

Because he understood the need to protect what he loved, Zack leaned forward. "Stanislaski, if you know Rachel, you know *she's* been watching my step. Nobody, but nobody, pushes her into something she doesn't want."

"You figure you got her pegged?"

"Are you kidding?" Zack's smile came quickly, and was friendly enough to make Alex's shoulders relax. "There isn't a man alive who really understands a woman. Especially a smart one." When he saw Alex's eyes shift over his shoulder, Zack glanced around. He saw a short, wiry, oily-skinned man being hauled toward the conference room by a uniformed cop. "Is that the one?"

"Yeah, that's Lomez."

Zack hissed smoke through his teeth and swore roundly. Alex could only agree.

At the conference table, Rachel looked up. Though she'd represented Lomez on his last count of assault, she was going over his file. "Well, Lomez, we meet again."

"You took your sweet time getting here." He dropped down in the seat and ignored the hovering cop. But he was sweating. Bungling the mugging meant he'd missed his connection. He hadn't had a fix in fourteen hours. "You bring me a smoke this time?"

"No. Thank you, Officer." Rachel waited until she was alone with her client, then folded her hands over his paperwork. "Well, you really pulled a prize this time out. The woman you attacked was sixty-three. I called the hospital this morning. You should be relieved to know they've bumped her condition up from critical to fair."

Lomez shrugged, his small black eyes gleaming at Rachel. He couldn't keep his hands still. He began to beat a tattoo on the table with his fingertips as he tapped his feet. His system was skidding to a much wilder rhythm. "Hey, if she'd handed over her purse like I told her, I wouldn't have had to get rough, you know?"

God, he sickened her, Rachel thought, fighting to remember she was a public servant. And Lomez, however revolting, was the public. "Knifing a senior citizen isn't going to win you the key to the city. It's sure as hell going to buy you a lock. Damn it, Lomez, she had twelve dollars."

His mouth was dry, and his skin was cold. "Then it wouldn't have cost her a lot to hand it over. You just get me out. That's your job." And the minute he was back on the street, he'd pressure one of the other Hombres to score for him. "I had to sit in that stinking cell all night."

"You're charged with attempted murder," Rachel said flatly.

Lomez tapped his damp hands against his thighs. Even his bones were screaming. "I didn't kill the old bitch."

Rachel wished she hadn't finished the coffee. At least she could have used it to wash some of the disgust out of her mouth. "You stuck a knife in her, three times. The officer responding pursued you as you fled the scene—with the knife and the victim's purse. They've got you cold, Lomez, and your priors aren't going to make the judge think leniency. Your repertoire includes assault, assault and battery, breaking and entering and two counts of possession."

"I don't need a list. I need bail."

"Odds are slim the DA's going to agree to bail, and if he does, it'll be well out of your range. Now I'm going to do what I can to get him to toss the attempted murder. You plead guilty to—"

"Guilty, my butt."

"It's going to be your butt," she said evenly. "You're not going to walk away from this one, Lomez. No matter how many rabbits I pull out of my hat, you're not going to do short time this turn around. Plead guilty to assault with a deadly weapon, it's likely I can swing the judge for seven to ten."

Sweat popped cold on his brow, on his lips. "The hell with that."

Because she was fast running out of patience, she slapped his file closed. "It won't get any sweeter. You cooperate, and I should be able to keep you from spending the next twenty years in a cage."

He screamed at her, then leaped across the table and struck before she had a chance to dodge. The backhanded blow knocked her out of her chair and onto the floor, where he fell on her. "You get me out!" He squeezed his hands on her throat, too wired even to feel her nails rake his wrist. "You bitch, you get me out or I'll kill you!"

At first she could only see his face, the sick rage in it. Then it faded as red dots swam in front of her eyes. Choking, she struck out, smashing the heel of her hand against the bridge of his nose. His blood splattered over her, but his hands tightened.

A roaring filled her ears, buzzing over the wild

curses he shouted at her. The red dots faded to gray as she bucked under him.

Then her windpipe was free and she was sucking air down her burning throat. Someone was calling her name, desperately, and she was being lifted, held tight. She thought she smelled the scent of the sea before she fell limply into it.

Cool fingers on her face. Wonderful. Strong hands clasped hard over hers. Comforting. A sigh before waking. Agony.

Rachel blinked her eyes open. Two faces were looming over hers, equally grim, with eyes that held both rage and fear. Woozily she lifted a hand to Zack's cheek, then Alex's. "I'm all right." Her voice was husky, bruises already forming on her throat.

"Just lie still," Alex murmured in Ukrainian, stroking her head with a hand that still throbbed from where it had connected with Lomez's face. "Can you drink some water?"

She nodded. "I want to sit up." As she focused on the room, she realized she was lying on the faded couch in the captain's office. Murmuring her thanks to her brother, she sipped from the paper cup he held to her lips. "Lomez?"

"In a cage, where he belongs." Fighting off the tremors of reaction, Alex lowered his brow to hers. He continued to speak in Ukrainian, kissing her brow, her cheeks, then sitting back on his heels to hold her hand. "You just relax. An ambulance is on the way."

"I don't need an ambulance." Reading the argument in his eyes, she shook her head. "I don't." She glanced down to see that her blouse was gaping open. It was ruined, of course, she thought in disgust. That and her suede skirt were spotted with blood. "His blood, not mine," she pointed out.

"You broke his slimy low-life nose," Alex snapped.

"I'm glad my self-defense class wasn't wasted." When he began to swear, she caught his hand. "Alexi," she began, her voice low, intense. "Do you know what it is for me to accept that you risk your life every day, every night? Do you know I accept only because I love you so much?"

"Don't turn this around on me," he said furiously. "That bastard nearly killed you. He was so far gone it took three of us to drag him off."

She didn't want to think about that just yet. She couldn't. "I played it wrong."

"You—"

"I did," she insisted. "But the point is, we can't change what we are. I won't change, not even for you. Now cancel the ambulance and do something for me."

He called her a name, a rude one, in their native language. It made her smile. "I'm no more of a horse's ass than you. I need to contact my office and explain. I won't be able to represent Lomez under the circumstances."

"Damn right you won't." It was small satisfaction, but he could hope for little more. Gently he touched his fingers to the bruise on her cheekbone. "He's going down, Rachel. I'll make damn sure he goes down for this, if nothing else. There's nothing you or anyone else can do."

"That's for the courts to decide." She got shakily to her feet. "And you will not call Mama and Papa." When he said nothing, she lifted a brow. "If you do, I'll have to tell them about your last undercover assignment. The one where you went through the second-story window."

"Go home," he said, giving up. "Get some rest." He turned away from her to study Zack. His opinion of him had changed a bit, since Zack had been one of the three who'd hauled Lomez off Rachel. Alex had been a cop long enough to recognize murder in a man's eyes, and it had shone darkly in Zack's. He assumed, correctly, that Zack would have dealt with Lomez himself, regardless of cops, if he hadn't been so busy cradling Rachel in his arms. "You'll get her there." It wasn't a question.

"Count on it." He said nothing else as Alex left them.

Unsteady, and far from sure of herself, Rachel tried to smile. "Some date, huh?"

A muscle jumped in his jaw as he studied her spattered blouse. "Can you walk?"

"Of course I can walk." She hoped. The little seed of annoyance his terse question planted helped her get across the room. "Look, I'm sorry things got messed up this way. You don't have to—"

"Do me a favor," he said as he took her arm and led her through the squad room. "Just shut up."

She obliged him, though she was sorely tempted to tell him how foolish it was to indulge in a cab for the few blocks to her building. It was better if she didn't talk, she realized. Not only did it hurt, but she was also afraid her voice would begin to shake as much as her body wanted to.

She'd be alone in a few minutes, she reminded herself. Then she'd be able to indulge in a nice bout of trembling and weeping if she wanted to. But not in front of Zack. Not in front of anybody.

With a drunk's exaggerated care, she stepped out of the cab and onto the sidewalk. Mild shock, she deduced. It would pass. She'd make it pass.

"Thanks," she began. "I'm sorry…"

"I'm taking you up."

"Look, I've already ruined your morning. It isn't necessary to—" But he was already half carrying her to the door.

"Didn't I tell you to shut up?" He pulled open her briefcase to look for her keys himself. White-hot rage had his fingers fumbling. Didn't she know how pale she was? Couldn't she understand what it did to him inside to hear the way her voice rasped?

He pulled her through the door, into the elevator, and jabbed his finger on the button.

"I don't know what you're so mad about," she muttered, wincing a little as she swallowed. "You lost a couple of hours, sure, but do you know what I paid for this suit? And I've only worn it twice." Tears sprang to her eyes, and she blinked them back furiously as he dragged her down the hall to her apartment. "A PD's salary isn't exactly princely." She rubbed ice-cold hands together as he unlocked her door. "I had to eat yogurt for a month to afford it, even on sale. And I don't even like yogurt."

The first tear spilled out. She dashed it away as she walked inside. "Even if I could get it cleaned, I wouldn't be able to wear it after—" She broke off and made an enormous effort to pull herself back. She was babbling about a suit, for God's sake. Maybe she was losing her mind.

"Okay." She let out what she thought was a slow,

careful breath. It hitched as it came out. "You got me home. I appreciate it. Now go away."

He merely tossed her briefcase aside, then tugged the coat from her shoulders. "Sit down, Rachel."

"I don't want to sit down." Another tear. It was too late to stop it. "What I want is to be alone." When her voice broke, she pressed her hands to her face. "Oh, God, leave me alone."

He picked her up, moving to the couch to hold her in his lap. Stroking her back through the tremors, feeling her tears hot and damp on his neck. He forced his hands to be gentle, even as the rage and fear worked inside him. As she curled up against him, he closed his eyes and murmured the useless words that always seemed to comfort.

She cried hard, he realized. But she didn't cry long. She trembled violently, but the trembling was soon controlled. She didn't try to push away. If she had, he wouldn't have allowed it. Perhaps he was comforting her. But holding her, knowing she was safe, and with him, brought him tremendous comfort.

"Damn it." When the worst was over, she let her head lie weakly on his shoulder. "I told you to go away."

"We had a deal, remember? You're spending the day with me." His hands tightened once, convulsively, before he managed to gentle them again. "You scared me, big-time."

"Me, too."

"And if I go away, I'm going to have to go back down there, find a way to get to that son of a bitch, and break him in half."

It was odd how a threat delivered so matter-of-factly could seem twice as deadly as a shout. "Then I guess you'd better hang around until the impulse fades. I'm really all right," she told him, but she left her head cuddled against his shoulder. "This was just reaction."

There was still an ice floe of fury in his gut. That was his reaction, and he'd deal with it later. "It may be his blood, Rachel, but they're your bruises."

Frowning, she touched fingers gingerly to her cheek. "How bad does it look?"

Despite himself, he chuckled. "Lord, I didn't know you were that vain."

She bristled, pulling back far enough to scowl at him. "It has nothing to do with vanity. I have a meeting in the morning, and I don't need all the questions."

He cupped her chin, tilted her head to the side. "Take it from someone who's had his share of bruises, sugar. You're going to get the questions. Now forget about tomorrow." He touched his lips, very gently, to the bruise, and made her heart stutter. "Have you got any tea bags? Any honey?"

"Probably. Why?"

"Since you won't go to the hospital, you'll have to put up with Muldoon first aid." He shifted her from his lap and propped her against the pillows. Their vivid colors only made her appear paler. "Stay."

Since the bout of weeping had tired her, she didn't argue. When Zack came out of the kitchen five minutes later, tea steaming in the cup in his hands, she was out like a light.

She awakened groggy, her throat on fire. The room was dim and utterly quiet, disorienting her. Pushing herself up on her elbows, she saw that the curtains had

been drawn. The bright afghan her mother had cro-
cheted years before had been tucked around her.

Groaning only a little, she tossed it aside and stood
up. Steady, she thought with some satisfaction. You
couldn't keep a Stanislaski down.

But this one needed about a gallon of water to ease
the flames in her throat. Rubbing her eyes, she padded into the kitchen, then let out a shriek that seared
her abused throat when she spotted Zack bending over
the stove.

"What the hell are you doing? I thought you were
gone."

"Nope." He stirred the contents of the pot on the
stove before turning to study her. Her color was back,
and the glazed look had faded from her eyes. It would
take a great deal longer for the bruises to disappear. "I
had Rio send over some soup. Do you think you can
eat now?"

"I guess." She pressed a hand to her stomach. She
was starving, but she wasn't sure how she was going
to manage getting anything down her throbbing throat.
"What time is it?"

"About three."

She'd slept nearly two hours, she realized, and found
the idea of her dozing on the couch while Zack puttered
in the kitchen both embarrassing and touching. "You
didn't have to hang around."

"You know, your throat would feel better sooner if
you didn't talk so much. Go in and sit down."

Since the scent of the soup was making her mouth
water, she obliged him. After tugging the curtains open,
she sat at the little gateleg table by the window. With
some disgust, she shrugged out of her stained jacket

and tossed it aside. As soon as she'd indulged herself with some of Rio's soup, she would shower and change.

Obviously Zack had found his way around her kitchen, Rachel mused as he came in carrying bowls and mugs on a tray.

"Thanks." She saw his gaze light briefly on the jacket, heat, then flatten.

"I pawed through some of your records while you were out." It pleased him that he could speak casually when he wanted to break something. Someone. "Mind if I put one on?"

"No, go ahead."

Watching the steam, she stirred her soup while he put an old B.B. King album on her stereo. "And they said we had nothing in common."

Relieved that he wasn't going to bring the incident up, she smiled. "I stole it from Mikhail. He has very eclectic taste in music." Once Zack was seated across from her, she spooned up soup and swallowed gingerly. Sighed. It soothed her fevered throat the way a mother soothes a fretful child. "Wonderful. What's in it?"

"I never ask. Rio never tells."

With a murmur of acknowledgment, she continued to eat. "I'll have to figure out how to bribe him. My mother would love the recipe for this." She switched to tea. After the first sip, her eyes opened wide.

"You didn't have honey," Zack said mildly. "But you had brandy."

She took another, more cautious sip. "It ought to dull the nerve endings."

"That's the idea." Reaching across the table, he took her hand. "Feel any better?"

"Lots. I really am sorry you had your Sunday wrecked."

"Don't make me tell you to shut up again."

She only smiled. "I'm starting to think you're not such a bad guy, Muldoon."

"Maybe I should have brought you soup before."

"The soup helped." She spooned up some more. "But not making me feel like an idiot when I was crying all over you did the trick."

"You had pretty good cause. Being tough's not always the answer."

"It usually works." She sipped more of the brandy-laced tea. "I didn't want to let go in front of Alex. He worries enough." Her lips curved. "You know how it is to have a younger sibling who refuses to see things the way you do."

"You mean so you'd like to rap their head against the wall? Yeah, I know."

"Well, whether Alex likes to believe it or not, I can handle my own life. Nick will, too, when the time comes."

"He's not like that creep today," Zack said softly. "He never could be."

"Of course not." Concerned, she pushed her bowl aside. This time she took his hand. "You mustn't even think like that. Listen to me. For two years I've seen them come in and go out. Some are twisted beyond redemption, like Lomez. Others are desperate and confused, either battered by the streets or part of the streets. Working with them, it gets to the point that if you don't burn out or just scab over, you learn to recognize the nuances. Nick's been hurt, and his self-esteem is next to zero. He turned to a gang because he needed to be part of something, anything. Now he has you. No matter how much he might try to shake you loose, he wants you. He needs you."

"Maybe. If he ever starts to trust me, he might be able to turn a corner." He hadn't realized how much it was weighing on him. "He won't talk to me about my father, about what it was like when I was gone."

"He will, when he's ready."

"The old man wasn't so bad, Rachel. He'd never have made father of the year, but—hell." He let out a breath in disgust. "He was a hard-nosed, hard-drinking Irish son of a bitch who should never have given up the sea. He ran our lives like we were green crewmen on a sinking ship. All shouts and bluster and the back of his hand. We never agreed on a damn thing."

"Families often don't."

"He never got over my mother. He was in the South Pacific when she died."

Which meant Zack would have been alone. A child, alone. Her fingers tightened on his.

"He came back, mad as hell. He was going to make a man out of me. Then Nadine and Nick came along, and I was old enough to go my own way. You could say I abandoned ship. So he tried to make a man—his kind of man—out of Nick."

"You're beating yourself up again over something you can't change. And couldn't have changed."

"I guess I keep remembering how it was that first year I came back. The old man was so fragile. He couldn't remember things, kept wandering out and getting lost. Damn it, I knew Nick was running wild, but I didn't have my legs under me. Having to put the old man in a home, watching him die there, trying to keep the bar going. Nick got lost in the shuffle."

"You found him again."

He started to speak again, then sat back with a sigh. "Hell of a time to be dumping this on you."

"It's all right. I want to help."

"You've already helped. Do you want more soup?"

Subject closed, Rachel realized. She could press, or she could give him room. One favor deserved another, she decided, and smiled. "No, thanks. It really did the job."

He wanted to say more, a whole lot more. He wanted to hold her again, and feel her head resting on his shoulder. He wanted to sit and watch her sleep on the couch again. And if he did any one of those things, he wouldn't make it to the door.

"I'll clear it up and get out of your hair. I imagine you'd like some time alone."

She frowned after him as he walked into the kitchen. She had wanted time alone, hadn't she? So why was she trying to think of ways to stall him, keep him from walking out the door.

"Hey, look." She pushed away from the table to wander in after him. He was already pouring the remaining soup in a container. "It's still early. We might be able to salvage some of the day."

"You need rest."

"I had rest." Feeling awkward, she ran water over the bowls he'd stacked in the sink. "We could probably make at least one museum, or catch a matinee. I don't want to think you spent your whole day off mopping up after me."

"Will you quit worrying about my day off?" Zack

slapped the container on a shelf in the refrigerator. "I'm the boss, remember? I can take another."

"Fine." She slammed the water off. "See you around."

"Man, you've got a short fuse." Amused, he put his hands on her shoulders and rubbed. "Don't get yourself worked up, sugar. All in all, I had a very eventful day."

She closed her eyes, feeling those rough fingers through the silk of her blouse. "Any time, Muldoon."

He could smell her hair, and he had to fight the urge to bury his face in it. It wouldn't be possible to stop there. "You going to be all right alone? I could call the cop to come stay with you."

"No. I'm fine." Gripping the edge of the counter, she stared hard at the wall. "Thanks for the first aid."

"My pleasure." Damn it, he was stalling when he should be out the door. Away from her. "Maybe we can have an early dinner one night this week."

She pressed her lips together. The way his hands were rubbing up and down her arms made her want to whimper. "Sure. I'll check my schedule."

He turned her around. He couldn't be sure if she moved into his arms or if he'd pulled her there, but he was holding her. Her lips were parting for his. "I'll call you."

"Okay." Her eyes fluttered closed as the kiss deepened.

"Soon." He felt the breath backing up in his lungs as she molded against him.

"Um-hmm…" As his tongue danced over hers, she gave a quick sigh that caught in the middle.

He tore his mouth away to nibble along her jaw. "One more thing."

"Yes?"

"I'm not leaving."

"I know." Her arms curled around his neck as he lifted her. "It's just chemistry."

"Right." Struggling to remember her bruises, he rained soft kisses over her face.

"Nothing serious." She shuddered, nipping at his neck. "I can't afford to get involved. I have plans."

"Nothing serious," he agreed, blood pounding in his head, in his loins. He jerked open a door and found himself facing a closet. "Where's the damn bedroom?"

"What?" She focused, realized he'd carried her out of the kitchen. "This is it. The couch…" She nipped his ear. "It pulls out. I can…"

"Never mind," he managed, and settled for the rug.

Chapter 7

He ripped her blouse. It wasn't only passion that made him grab and tear. He couldn't bear to see her wear it another moment, to see that vivid blue stained with spots of blood.

Yet the sound of it, of the silk rending beneath his fingers, and her gasp of shocked excitement, spread fire through his gut.

"The first time I saw you..." His breath was already short and fast when he tossed the mangled blouse aside. "From the first minute, I wanted this. Wanted you."

"I know." She reached for him, amazed at how deep and ripe a need could be. "Me, too. It's crazy," she said against his mouth. "Insane." Her skin trembled as he tugged the straps of her chemise from her shoulders to replace them with impatient lips. "Incredible."

Glorying in it, she arched against him when he took

her breasts in those greedy, rough-palmed hands. Then his mouth—oh, his mouth, hot and seeking—closed over her to tug and suckle. *Hurry,* was all she could think, *hurry, hurry,* and her nails scraped heedlessly up his sides as she dragged his sweater over his head.

Flesh to flesh was what she wanted. Skin already hot, already damp. The feel of his lips against her thundering heart had her locking her fists in his hair, pressing him closer. She fretted for more. Even as the storm built to a crisis point inside her, she met, she ached, and she demanded.

Her fingers dug into his broad shoulders when he slid down, setting off hundreds of tiny eruptions by streaking hungry, openmouthed kisses down her torso. Then back, quickly back, to drown her in desire with his lips on hers.

He couldn't stop himself from taking. No matter that he had once imagined making slow, tortuously slow, love to her on some huge, soft bed. The desperation of what was overpowered any fantasy of what might have been.

She possessed him. Obsessed him. No mystical siren could have stolen his mind and soul more completely.

A button popped from her skirt as he fought to drag it down her hips. He thought he might go mad if he didn't rip aside all obstacles, if he didn't see her. All of her.

Half-crazed, he peeled off her stockings, and the delicate lace that had secured them. Somewhere through the roaring in his brain he heard her throaty cry when his fingers brushed against her thigh. Fighting to hold back, he knelt between her legs, filling himself with the sight of her, slim and golden and naked, her hair tousled around her face, her eyes dark and heavy.

She reared up, too desperate to wait even another moment. Her mouth closed avidly over his, and her fingers tore at the snap of his jeans.

"Let me," she said in a husky whisper.

"No." He slipped a hand behind her back to support her, and brought the other down to cover the source of heat. "Let me."

The volcano he'd imagined erupted at the first touch. Her body shuddered, quaked. And he watched, impossibly aroused, as her head fell back. Not surrender. Even in his own delirium, he understood that she was not surrendering. It was abandonment, the pure, unleashed quest for pleasure. He gave her more, and gave to himself, stroking that velvet fire, letting his tongue slide over hers in a delicious, matching rhythm.

How could she have known that desire could be dark and deadly? Or that she, always so sure, always so cautious, would throw reason to the winds for more of the dangerous delights? No, not just more. All of them, she thought dizzily. All of him. She would have all. Locking her legs around his hips, she took him into her.

She heard his gasp—the first one ended with a groan. She saw his eyes, cobalt now, and fixed on hers as he shifted to fill her. A sword to the hilt. Then he moved, and she with him. Lost in the whirlwind, she heard nothing but the screaming of her own heart.

"The bigger they are," Rachel murmured some time later.

"Hmm?"

Smiling to herself, she lifted one of Zack's hands, let it go and watched it drop limply to the rug. "The harder they fall." She rolled over and propped her elbows on his chest so that she could study him. If she hadn't known better, she would have thought he was sleeping—or unconscious. His breathing had slowed—somewhat—but his eyes were still closed. It had been some time since he'd moved a single muscle.

"You know, Muldoon, you look like you went ten rounds with the champ."

His lips curved. It was about all he had the energy for. "You pack a hell of a punch, sugar."

As a matter of principle, she bit his shoulder. "Don't call me 'sugar.' But, since you mention it, you didn't do too badly yourself."

He opened one eye. "Too badly? I melted you down to a gooey puddle."

True enough, she admitted, but she wouldn't stroke his ego by agreeing. "I'll say that you have a certain un-refined style that is strangely appealing." She trailed a fingertip down his chest. "But the simple fact is, I had to carry you." That got his other eye open, she thought with satisfaction. "Not that I minded. I didn't have any-thing else pressing to do this afternoon."

"You carried me?"

"Metaphorically speaking."

His opinion of that was short and rude. "Want to take me on again? Champ?"

She fluttered her lashes. "Any time. Any place."

"Here and now." She was laughing as he rolled her over, but the laughter ended on a hiss of pain when he bumped her bruised cheek. "Klutz," she said as he jerked back and swore.

"I'm sorry."

"Come on, Zack." She smiled, wanting to lighten

the concern in his eyes and bring back the laughter. "I was only kidding."

Ignoring that, he turned her head for a closer look at the mark on her cheek. "I should have put ice on that. He didn't break the skin, but it's..."

She could feel the tension hardening his shoulders. Instead of trying to stroke it away, she pinched him. "Listen, Buster, I come from tough stock. I got worse than that wrestling with my brothers."

"If he ever gets out—"

"Stop it." Very firmly she put her hands on either side of his face. "Don't say anything you might regret. Remember, I'm an officer of the court."

"I wouldn't regret it." He tugged her upward until she was sitting beside him. They were circled, he realized, by the tattered remains of her clothes. "And I don't regret this—except for the unrefined style."

She let out an impatient breath. "Look, if you can't take a joke, learn to."

"Wait until I'm finished before you swipe at me, okay? I swear, you come on faster than a typhoon." He tucked her hair back and kissed her once, hard. "I wasn't going to stay. Not today. I figured a bout of hot sex wasn't the best encore after you'd been strangled."

"I wasn't—"

He interrupted her. "Close enough. You know that I wanted you however I could get you, Rachel. I sure as hell didn't make a secret of it. But it occurs to me that you were upset and vulnerable and I took advantage of that."

She had to wait nearly a full minute before she could speak. "Don't make me mad at you, Muldoon. And don't insult me."

"All I'm trying to say is... I don't know what the hell I'm trying to say," he muttered, and tried again. "Except—well, maybe I could have pulled that stupid couch out instead of using the floor."

Eyes narrowed, she leaned her face close to his. Her eyes were the color of gold doubloons, and just as exotic. "I like the floor. Get it?"

He was starting to feel better. Zack knew that tending to fragility was out of his league. But this tough, hardheaded woman was just his style. Watching her, he picked up her ruined blouse. "I ripped your clothes off."

"Proud of yourself?"

He tossed it aside. "Yeah. I can wait, if you want to put some more on. Then I can rip them off you again."

She bit the inside of her lip, but didn't quite defeat the smile. "Those were ruined anyway. Next time I'll have to bill you for damages. I'm on a budget."

Chuckling, he flicked her earring with his finger. "I'm crazy about you."

Her heart did a fast skip and shudder. The statement was as romantic as a whispered endearment to her. "Hey, don't get sloppy on me."

"Crazy," he said again, amazed and delighted at the faint blush that stole into her cheeks. "And did I mention that your body makes me wild?"

She was a great deal more comfortable with that. "No." She tilted her head. "Why don't you?"

"From stem to stern," he said, letting his hand speak more eloquently. "Forward and aft. Port and starboard."

"Oh, God." She gave an exaggerated sigh and shiver. "Salty talk. I just love a man out of uniform." More than willing to be aroused, she nuzzled her lips against his. "Tell me something, sailor."

"You bet."

"Which part is the stern?"

"I'll show you." Very gently, he touched his lips to her bruised throat. "Honey, we better pull that couch out before this gets out of hand again."

"Okay." There was something unspeakably erotic about a callused finger stroking the underside of her breast. "If you want."

Though the idea had merit, the couch seemed entirely too far away. "Or we could do it later. Tell you what, if you'd say something in Ukrainian, I'd forget we were on the floor. And I promise to make you forget it, too."

"Why should I say something in Ukrainian?"

"Because it drives me insane."

She tilted her head back. "Are you putting me on?"

"Uh-uh." His tongue traced a slow, teasing circle on her lips. "Go ahead. Say anything."

After a little sigh, she twined her arms around his neck. Against his ear, she murmured the words, then chuckled when he groaned.

"What did it mean?" he demanded, busying himself by nibbling his way along her shoulder.

"Loosely translated? I said you were a big, pigheaded fool."

"Mmm…are you sure you didn't say how much you wanted my body?"

"No. This is how you say that."

She told him, but by the time she was finished, he was already obliging her.

In the dark, he drew her close. They had managed, finally, to pull out the bed. Now they were tangled in her sheets. The afternoon had become evening, and evening night.

"I'd like to stay," he said quietly.

"I know." It was silly, she thought, to be unhappy that he would go. She'd always jealously prized her nights alone. "But you can't. It's too soon to trust Nick overnight."

"If things were different…" Damn, he hadn't expected it to be so frustrating. "I'd like to take you back home with me. I'd like to have you in my bed tonight, wake up with you tomorrow."

"He's not ready for that, either." She wasn't sure she was ready herself. "Until I have a chance to smooth things out with him, and make him understand, it's probably best if he doesn't know we're…"

What were they? The question ran through both their heads. Neither of them voiced it.

"You're right." The mattress creaked as he shifted. "Rachel, I want to be with you again. It doesn't just have to be in bed." He traced the curve of her cheek. "Or on the floor."

"I want to be with you." She touched her fingers to the back of his hand. "It's good. And that's enough."

"Yeah." He was nearly sure it was. "I can take some time Wednesday. How about an early dinner?"

"I'd like that." They fell into silence again, until she sighed. "You'd better go."

"I know."

"Maybe Sunday you and Nick could come to dinner at my parents'. We talked about it before, remember?"

"That would be good." He kissed her again, and the kiss went on and on. "Just once more."

"Yes." She enfolded him. "Just once more."

* * *

Rachel shifted the phone to her other ear, scribbled on a legal pad and stared dubiously at the stack of files on her desk.

"Yes, Mrs. Macetti, I understand. What we need are a couple of good character witnesses for your son. Your priest, perhaps, or a teacher." As she listened to the rapid-fire broken English, she wondered if she could catch the attention of any of her harried co-workers and hope that they'd feel sorry enough for her to bring her a cup of coffee. "I can't tell you that, Mrs. Macetti. Our chances are very good for a suspended sentence and probation, since Carlo wasn't driving. But the fact is, he was riding in a stolen car, and…"

She trailed off, carefully folding the page she'd written on. "Uh-huh. Well, as I explained before, it would be rather difficult to convince anyone he didn't know the car was stolen, since the locks had been sprung and the engine hot-wired." Satisfied with the shape of her paper airplane, she shot it out her door. It was as good as a note in a bottle.

"I'm sure he's a good boy, Mrs. Macetti." Rachel rolled her eyes. "Bad companions, yes. Let's hope that this experience will have him keeping his distance from the Hombres. Mrs. Macetti. Mrs. Macetti," Rachel said, trying to be firm, "I'm doing everything I can. Try to be optimistic, and I'll see you in court next week. No—no, really. I'll call you. Yes, I promise. Goodbye. Yes, absolutely. Goodbye."

Rachel hung up the phone, then dropped her head on her desk. Ten minutes of trying to deal with the frantic mother of six was as exhausting as a full day in court.

"Tough day?"

Lifting her head, Rachel spotted Nick in her doorway. He had her paper airplane in one hand, and a large paper cup in the other.

"Tough month." Her gaze locked on the steaming cup. "Tell me that's coffee."

"Light, no sugar." He stepped in and offered it. "Your note sounded desperate." As she took the first sip, he grinned. "I was coming down the hall, and it hit me in the chest. Nice form."

"I find they make excellent interoffice memos." Another sip and she felt the caffeine begin to pump through her system. "Since you saved my life, what can I do for you?"

"I was just kicking around. Thought maybe we could grab some lunch."

"I'm sorry, Nick." She gestured to the clutter on her desk. "I'm swamped."

"They don't let you eat?" Because he found he enjoyed seeing her here, entrenched in the business of justice, he eased a hip down on the corner of the desk.

"Oh, they throw us some raw meat now and again." Lord, he was flirting with her, she realized. Rachel gauged the files piled in front of her, calculated how much time she had before her meeting with the DA to bargain on a half a dozen cases. It was going to be close. "Actually, I would like to talk to you, if you have a few minutes."

"I'm on six to two tonight, so I've got plenty of minutes."

"Good." She stood, easing by him to close the door. The moment she turned back, she realized he'd taken that gesture the wrong way. His hands went to her waist. She had a moment to think that in a few years that combination of smooth moves and rough manners would devastate hordes of women. Then she managed to slip aside.

"Nick," she began, then hesitated. "Sit down." When he settled in her battered office chair, she sat behind the desk. "We're going on three weeks. I'd like to know how you're feeling."

"I'm cool."

"What I mean is, when we go back in front of Judge Beckett, it's very likely she'll give you probation—unless you make a big mistake in the meantime."

"I don't plan on mistakes." The chair creaked rustily as he leaned back. "Going to jail isn't high on my list these days."

"Glad to hear it. But she may also ask about your plans. This might be the time to start thinking about that, whether you'd like to make the situation with Zack more permanent."

"Permanent?" He gave a quick laugh. "Hey, I don't know about that. I'll probably want my own place, you know. Zack and me...well, maybe we're getting on a little better, but he cramps my style. Kind of hard to have a lady over when big brother can walk in any time." He flicked his green eyes over her face. "Know what I mean?"

An opening, she thought, and dived in. "Do you have a girl?"

His smile was very male and very attractive. "I'm more interested in women. Women with big brown eyes."

"Nick—"

"You know, when I was walking over here, I started to think how getting busted turned out to be a pretty lucky break." He lifted her hand, brushing his thumb over her knuckles before toying with her fingers. His eyes never left hers. "Otherwise, I wouldn't have needed such a great-looking lawyer."

"Nick, I'm twenty-six." It wasn't what she'd meant to say, or how she'd meant to say it, but he only tilted his head.

"Yeah? So?"

"And I'm your court-appointed guardian."

"Kind of an interesting situation." His smile spread. "It'll be over in about five weeks."

"I'll still be seven years older than you."

"More like six," he said easily. "But who's counting?"

"I am." Frustrated, she started to rise, then realized it would be best if she stayed in the position of authority behind the desk. "Nick, I like you, very much. And I meant what I said when I told you I wanted to be your friend."

"You can't let the age thing bother you, babe." When he rose, she realized she'd miscalculated by staying behind the desk. When he came around to sit on the edge of it, she was trapped between him and the wall.

"Of course I can. I was in college when you were starting puberty."

"Well, I've finished now." He grinned and traced his finger down her cheek. And his eyes narrowed. "Is that a bruise?"

"I ran into something," she said, and tried again. "The bottom line is, I'm too old for you."

He frowned at the bruise another minute, then lifted his eyes to hers. "I don't think so. Let me put it this way.

Do you figure a woman shouldn't get tangled up with a guy six years older than she is?"

"That's entirely different."

"Sexist," he said clucking his tongue. "Here I figured you'd be all for equal rights."

"Of course I am, but—" She broke off with a hiss of breath.

"Gotcha."

"Regardless of age—" since that wasn't working, she thought "—I'm your guardian, and it would be wrong, certainly unethical, for me to encourage or agree to anything beyond that. I care about what happens to you, and if I've given you the impression that I'm interested in anything more than friendship, I'm sorry."

He considered. "I guess you take your work pretty seriously."

"Yes, I do."

"I can dig it. No pressure, right?"

Relief made her sigh. "Right." She rose, giving his hand a quick squeeze. "You're all right, Nick."

"You too." They both looked around when her phone began to shrill. "I'll let you get back to serving justice," he told her, then had her mouth dropping open as he brought her hand to his lips. "Five weeks isn't so long to wait."

"But—"

"Catch you later." He strolled out, leaving Rachel wondering if it would help to beat her head against the wall.

Nick was feeling great. He had the whole day ahead of him, money in his pocket, and a gorgeous woman planted in his heart. He had to grin when he thought about the way he'd flustered her. He hadn't realized it could be so satisfying to make a woman nervous.

And imagine a knockout like Rachel worrying about her age. Shaking his head, he jogged down to the subway. Maybe he'd thought she was a couple of years younger, but it didn't matter one way or the other. Everything about her was dead-on perfect.

He wondered how Zack would react when he saw Nick LeBeck strut into the bar one night with Rachel on his arm. He didn't imagine Zack would think of him as a kid when everybody saw he'd bagged a babe like Rachel Stanislaski.

Wrong, he told himself as he hopped on a car that would take him to Times Square. That was no way to talk about a classy lady. What they'd have was a relationship. As the subway car rattled and squeaked, he occupied himself by daydreaming about what they'd do together.

There would be dinners and long walks, quiet talks. They'd go listen to music, and dance. Now and again they'd have a lazy evening snuggled up in front of the television.

Nick considered it a sign of his commitment that he hadn't put sex at the top of the list.

On top of the world, he came out into the bustle and blare of Times Square and decided to use some of his loose change for a little pinball.

The arcade was noisy, and there was a loud rock backbeat blasting over the metallic sounds of beeps and buzzes. Though he'd missed the freedom of being able to breeze into an arcade any time he chose, he had to admit it felt good to be able to spend money he'd earned.

No sneaking around, no vague sense of guilt. Maybe

he didn't have the gang to hang around with, but he didn't feel nearly as lonely as he'd thought he would.

It wasn't something he'd admit out loud, but he was getting a kick out of working in the kitchen with Rio. The big cook had plenty of stories, many of them about Zack. When he listened to them, Nick almost felt as though he'd been part of it.

Of course, he hadn't, Nick reminded himself, using expert body English to play out the ball. There was no possible way he could explain how miserable he'd been when Zack shipped out. Then he'd had no one again. His mother had tried, he supposed, but she'd always been more shadow than substance in his life.

It had taken all her energy to put food on the table and clothes on his back. She'd had little of herself left over once that was done.

Then there had been Zack.

Nick could still remember the first time he'd seen his stepbrother. In the kitchen of the bar. Zack had been sitting at the counter, gobbling potato chips. He'd been tall and dark, with an easy grin and a casually generous manner. Once Nick had gotten up the courage to follow him around, Zack hadn't tried to shake him off.

It was Zack who'd brought him into an arcade the first time, propped him up and shown him how to make the silver balls dance.

It was Zack who'd taken him to the Macy's parade. Zack who had patiently taught him to tie his shoes. Zack who'd clobbered him when he chased a ball into traffic.

And it was Zack who, barely a year later, had left him with a sick mother and an overbearing stepfather. Postcards and souvenirs hadn't filled the hole.

Maybe Zack wanted to make up for it, Nick thought

with a shrug, then swore when the ball slipped by the flipper. And maybe, deep down, Nick wanted to let him.

"Hey, LeBeck." The slap on his shoulder nearly made Nick lose the next ball. "Where you been hiding?"

"I've been around." Nick sliced a quick glance at Cash before concentrating on his game. He wondered if Cash would make any comment about him not wearing his Cobra jacket.

"Yeah? Thought you'd dropped down the sewer." Cash leaned against the machine, as always, appreciating Nick's skill. "Haven't lost your touch."

"I've got great hands. Ask the babes."

Cash snorted and lighted a crushed cigarette. His last. Since Reece had copped less than ten cents on the dollar for the stolen merchandise, Cash's share was long gone. "Man, the chicks see that ugly face and you never get a chance to use your hands."

"You've got your butt mixed up with my face." Nick eased back on his heels, satisfied with his score and the free game he'd finessed. "Want to take this one?"

"Sure." After stepping behind the machine, Cash began to bull his way through the game. "You still hanging with your stepbrother?"

"Yeah, got a few more weeks before we go back to court."

Cash lost the first ball and pumped up another. "You got a tough break, Nick. I mean that, man. I feel real bad about the way it went down."

"Right."

"No, man. Really." In his sincerity, Cash lost track of the ball and let it slip away. "We screwed up, and you took the heat."

Slightly mollified, Nick shrugged. "I can handle it."

"Still sucks. But hey, it can't be so bad working a bar. Plenty of juice, right?"

Nick smiled. He wasn't about to admit he'd downed no more than two beers in the past three weeks. And if Zack got wind of that much, there'd be hell to pay. "You got it, bro."

"I guess the place does okay, right? I mean, it's popular and all."

"Does okay."

"Must be plenty of sexy ladies dropping in, looking for action."

The neighborhood bar ran more to blue-collar workers and families, but Nick played along. "The place is lousy with them. It's pick and choose."

Cash laughed appreciatively even as he blew his last ball. "Want to go doubles?"

"Why not?" Nick dug in his pocket for more tokens. "So what's going on with the gang?"

"The usual. T.J.'s old man kicked him out, so he's bunking with me. Jerk snores like a jackhammer."

"Man, don't I know it. I put up with him a couple of nights last summer."

"Couple of the Hombres crossed over to our turf. We handled them."

Nick knew that meant fists, maybe chains and bottles. Occasionally blades. It was odd, he thought, but all that seemed so distant to him, distant and useless. "Yeah, well…" was all he could think of to say.

"Some people never learn, you know. Got a cigarette? I'm tapped."

"Yeah, top pocket." Nick racked up another ten thousand points while Cash lit up.

"Hey, I got a connection at this strip joint downtown. Could get you in."

"Yeah?" Nick answered absently as he sent the ball bouncing.

"Sure. I'd like to make that other business up to you. Maybe I'll drop by one night and we'll hang out."

"Forget it."

"No, man, really. I'll spring for the brew, too. Don't tell me slippery LeBeck can't slip out."

"I can get out when I want. Just walk out the kitchen."

"Around the back?"

"Yeah. Zack's usually tied up at the bar until three. Two on Sundays. I can get around Rio when I want to, or take the fire escape."

"You got a place upstairs?"

"Mmm… Your ball."

When they switched positions, Cash continued to question him, making it casual. The cash went in a safe in the office. Business usually peaked by one on Wednesdays. There were three ways in. The front door, the back and through the upstairs apartment.

By the time Nick had trounced him three games in a row, Cash had all he needed. He made his excuses and wandered out to meet with Reece.

He didn't feel good about conning Nick. But he *was* a Cobra.

Chapter 8

Zack stepped out of the shower, grateful the endless afternoon was over. He didn't mind paperwork. Or at least he didn't hate it. Well, the truth was, he hated it, but accepted that it was a necessary evil.

He'd made his orders, paid his invoices and tallied his end-of-the-month figures. Well, maybe he was a week or so behind the end of the month, but still, he figured he was doing pretty well.

And so was the business.

It looked as though he'd finally pulled it out of the hole his father's illness and the resulting expenses had dug. Paying off the loan he'd taken to square things for Nick would pinch a little, but in another year he'd be able to do more than look at boats in catalogs.

He wondered how Rachel would feel about taking a month off and sailing down to the Caribbean. He liked to imagine her lying out on the polished deck, wearing some excuse for a bikini. He liked the idea of watching her hair blow around her face when it caught the wind.

Of course, he'd have to take some time to check the boat out, test the rigging. He thought he'd be able to talk Nick into a day sail, or maybe a weekend. He wanted the two of them to be able to get away—away from the bar, the city, and the memories that tied them to both.

With a towel slung around his hips, he walked to the bedroom to dress. He hoped, sincerely, that the Sunday dinner at the Stanislaskis' would crack the kid's defenses a little more. Whenever Rachel spoke about her family, it made him think of what they—of what Nick—had missed.

All the kid needed was a little time to see how things could be. They were nearly halfway through the trial run, and apart from a few skirmishes, it had gone smoothly enough.

He had Rachel to thank for that, Zack thought as he tugged on a pair of jeans. He had Rachel to thank for a lot of things. Not only had she given him a second chance with Nick, but she'd added something incredible to his life. Something he'd never expected to have. Something he'd—

On a long breath, he stared hard into the mirror. When a man was going down for the third time, he recognized the signs.

Don't be an idiot, Muldoon, he told his reflection. Keep it steady as she goes. The lady wants to keep it simple, and so do you.

It wouldn't do to forget it.

"Hot date?" Feigning disinterest, Nick slouched

against the doorjamb. He'd been passing and had caught the way Zack was staring blindly into the mirror.

"Huh? Yeah, I guess you could say that." Zack dragged a hand through his wet hair and scattered drops of water. "I didn't know you were back."

"I'm on at six." For reasons Nick couldn't understand, he was swamped by the memory of the times he'd stood in the bathroom watching Zack shave. How it had made him feel when Zack slapped shaving cream on his face. "Rio's got beef stew on special tonight. Too bad you'll miss it."

Zack grabbed a shirt. "You take my share or Rio'll make me eat it for breakfast."

Nick grinned, then remembered himself and smirked. "You take a lot of crap from him."

"He's bigger than I am."

"Yeah, right."

Watching Nick in the mirror, Zack buttoned his shirt. "He likes to think he's looking out for me. It doesn't cost me anything to let him. He ever tell you about how he got that scar down the side of his face?"

"He said something about a broken bottle and a drunk marine."

"The drunk marine was going for my throat with that broken bottle. Rio got in his way. The way I see it, I owe Rio a lot more than putting up with his nagging." Tucking in his shirt, Zack turned, grinned. "And you're getting paid to put up with it."

"He's okay." Nick would have liked to ask more, like why a drunk marine had wanted to slice Zack's throat, but he was afraid Zack would just shrug it off. "Listen, if you get lucky tonight, don't worry about coming back."

Zack's fingers paused on the snap of his jeans. Tucking his tongue in his cheek, he wondered how Rachel would take his brother's turn of phrase. "Thanks for the thought, but I'll be home."

"For bed check," Nick muttered.

"Call it what you want," Zack shot back, then bit off an oath. Come hell or high water, they were going to get through one conversation without raised voices. "Listen, I don't figure you're going to climb out the window. Hell, you could do that while I'm here. It could be the lady won't want company overnight."

Mollified, Nick hooked his thumbs in his pockets. "They didn't teach you a hell of a lot in the navy, did they, bro?"

In an old gesture they'd both nearly forgotten, Zack rubbed his knuckles over Nick's head. "Kiss my butt." With his jacket slung over his shoulder, he headed out. "And don't wait up. I'm feeling lucky."

Long after the door shut behind Zack, Nick was still grinning.

Rachel was just unlocking the outside door when Zack strode up behind her. "Good timing," he said, and pressed a kiss to the back of her neck.

"For you, maybe. Everything ran over today. I was hoping to get back and soak in the tub before you got here."

"You want to soak?" The minute they were in the elevator, he had her against the wall. "Go ahead. I'll scrub your back."

"What a guy." When his mouth closed over hers, it hurt, somewhere deep, reminding her just how much she'd wanted to be with him again. "You smell good."

"Must be these." He pulled a paper cone filled with roses from behind his back.

Her heart wanted to sigh, but she resisted. "Another bribe?" She couldn't resist the urge to bury her face in the blooms.

"There was a guy selling them a couple of blocks down. He looked like he could use a couple bucks."

"Softy." She handed him her keys so that he could unlock her door and she could continue to sniff the roses.

"Keep it to yourself."

"It'll cost you." After kicking the door closed with her foot, she dumped her briefcase and laid the spray of roses on a table. "Pay up, Muldoon," she demanded, tossing her arms around him.

There was such joy in it. Heat, yes. And the sweet, sharp ache of need. But the joy was so unexpected, so fast and full, that she laughed against his mouth as he twirled her around.

"I missed you." He continued to hold her, inches off the floor.

"Oh, yeah?" With her hands linked comfortably around his neck, she smiled. "Maybe I missed you, too. Some. How long are you going to hold me up here?"

"This way I can look right at you. You're beautiful, Rachel."

It wasn't the words so much as the way he said them that brought a lump to her throat. "You don't have to soften me up."

"I don't know how to tell you how beautiful—except that sometimes when I look at you, I remember how the sea looks, right at sunrise, when all that color spills out of the sky, kind of seeps over the horizon and falls into the water. Just for a few minutes, everything's so vivid, so... I don't know, special. When I look at you, it's like that."

Her eyes had darkened with an emotion she couldn't begin to analyze. All she could do was rest her cheek against his. "Zack." His name was a sigh, and she knew she would cry any minute if she didn't lighten the mood. "Roses and poetry, all in one day. I don't know what to say to you."

Enchanted, he buried his face in her hair. "That's a first."

"We're not going to get—"

"Sloppy," he finished for her, laughing. "Us? Are you kidding?" But when he sat on the couch, he kept her cuddled in his lap. "Let me see that bruise."

"It's nothing," she said, even as he tilted her head for a closer inspection. "The worst of it was that the word got out and I had to deal with all this sympathy and advice. If those cops had kept their mouths shut, I could have said I'd walked into a door."

"Take off the jacket and sweater."

She arched a brow. "You're such a romantic, Muldoon."

"Can it. I want to see your neck."

"It's fine."

"Which is why you're wearing a sweater that comes up to your chin."

"It's very fashionable."

"Peel it off, babe, or I'll have to do it for you."

Her eyes lit. "Ah, threatening a public official." After kicking off her shoes, she tossed up her chin. "Try it, Buster. Let's see how tough you are."

She didn't put up much of a fight, but the initial wres-

tling was enough to arouse them both. By the time he
had her pinned to the couch, her arms over her head and
her wrists cuffed in his hand, they were both breathing hard.

"I took it easy on you," she told him.

"I could see that." Her jacket was crumpled on the
floor beside them. Smiling, Zack began to inch her
sweater upward, letting his fingers skim over the silky
material beneath.

Her breath caught, and released unsteadily. "That's
not my neck," she managed as his hand cupped and
molded her breast.

"Just checking." Watching her, always watching her,
he teased the nipple until it was hot and hard. "You're
quick to the touch, Rachel."

His touch, she thought, trembling. Only his.

Slowly, determined to savor every moment, he
slipped the sweater up. He released her wrists to tug it
off, then clasped them again.

"Zack."

He ignored her flexing hands. "My turn at the helm,"
he said quietly. "I told you once I wanted to drive you
crazy. Do you remember?"

He was. He already was. "I want to touch you."

"You will." He skimmed a fingertip over her neck
first, carefully studying the bruises. They were fading
to yellow. "I don't want to see you hurt again." Gently
he lowered his head to trail a necklace of kisses over
the marks. "Not ever again."

"It doesn't hurt." Her pulse jackhammered under his
nuzzling lips. "I don't need to be seduced."

"Yes, you do. But you're afraid to be, which makes
the whole idea damn near irresistible. You're just going

to have to trust me." He shifted so that he could unzip her skirt and slip it off. "I have places to take you." His mouth lowered to hers, rubbing, then nibbling. "Strange, wonderful places." Then diving deep.

The journey wasn't calm, but she had no choice but to go where he took her. This eagerness for pleasure, this immediacy of need, was still so new that she had no defense against it. His hand slid over her, lingering here, exploiting there, while his mouth devoured hers with a relentless hunger.

No escape, she thought desperately as he brought her close, painfully close, to that first tumultuous release. She was trapped in him, utterly lost in a tangled maze of sensations. She writhed beneath his hand, too steeped in her own needs to know how deliciously wanton her movements were.

"I didn't have time to appreciate these last time." Zack trailed his fingers up the sheer stocking to the pristine white garter. She would think them practical, he knew. He thought them erotic.

With an expert flick of his fingers that had her moaning, he released one stocking, then the other, before tormenting them both by peeling them, inch by lazy inch, down her legs.

He had to kneel on the floor to taste her calves, the backs of her knees, the glorious satin skin of her thighs. She cried out when he slid his tongue beneath her panties to sample the hot, sensitive flesh underneath. Fighting impatience, he tugged them off to give himself the freedom to taste more of her.

As the first wave swamped her, she arched like a bow, leaping into Ukrainian when the aftershocks shuddered through her. Freed, her hands groped for him until they were struggling together to strip off his clothes. Heat to heat, she pressed against him, overbalancing him, until she straddled him and her mouth could merge hotly with his.

"Now" was all he said, all he *could* say, as he gripped her hips.

"I really did mean to take you out," Zack said when they lay on the couch in a tangle of limbs.

"I bet."

He smiled, recognized the sleepy satisfaction in her voice. "Really. We can get dressed and try again."

With a half laugh, she pressed her lips to his chest. His heart was still thundering. "You're not going anywhere, Muldoon. Not till I'm finished with you."

"If you insist."

"That's what free delivery's for. How about Chinese?"

"You're on. Who's going to get up and call?"

She shifted for the pleasure of rubbing her cheek against his skin. "We'll flip for it."

He lost, and Rachel took advantage of the moment to grab a quick, bracing shower. When she came back, her hair damp and curly, a plain white terry-cloth robe skimming her knees, he was pouring them both a glass of wine.

"I think I'm repeating myself," he said, offering her a glass. "But you sure look good wet."

He'd tugged on his jeans, but hadn't bothered with his shirt. Rachel trailed a finger down his chest. "You could have joined me."

"We'd have missed the delivery boy."

"Since he's bringing egg rolls, you have a point." She

moved to the kitchen to get some plates, then set them on the table by the window. "And I do have to refuel. I only had time for a candy bar at lunch." Because the mood seemed right, she lit candles. "Nick dropped by the office."

"Oh."

"I wish I had had more time...." She touched match to wick and watched the candle flare. "He caught me between phone calls and before a plea-bargaining meeting."

He watched her move around the room in her practical terry-cloth robe, turning the light into romance with her candles. He wondered if she realized how compelling that contrast was. "You don't have to explain to me, Rachel."

She shook out a match, struck another. It wasn't that she was superstitious, but there was no use taking chances with three on a match. "I have to explain to myself. He wanted to go to lunch, and I just couldn't swing it. I did talk to him about...the situation."

"About the fact that he's fallen in lust with you."

"I wouldn't put it like that." She sighed heavily when the intercom buzzed. After flipping it on, she released the security lock for the delivery boy. "He's simply misinterpreted gratitude and friendship."

Zack took one long look at her in the candleglow. "Whatever you say."

Disgusted, she went back to the table and sat. "You're buying, Muldoon."

He took out his wallet agreeably. He had the tab and the tip ready when the delivery arrived. After carrying three bulging bags to the table, he unpacked the little white cartons. In moments the air was filled with exotic aromas.

"Do you want to tell me the rest?"

"Well..." Rachel wound some noodles around her chopsticks. "I started off explaining the difference in our ages. Umm..." She chewed appreciatively. "He didn't buy it," she said over a mouthful. "He had a very convincing argument, and since I couldn't override it, I changed tactics."

"I've seen you in court," he reminded her.

"I explained the ethics of my being his guardian, and how it wasn't possible for us to go beyond those terms." Thoughtful, she scooped up some sweet and sour pork. "He seemed to understand that."

"Good."

"I thought it was. I mean, he agreed with me. He was very mature about it. Then, when he was leaving, he said how it wasn't so hard to wait five more weeks."

Zack said nothing for a moment. Then, with a half laugh, he picked up his wine. "You've got to give the kid credit."

"Zack, this is serious."

"I know. I know. It's sticky for both of us, but you have to admire the way he turned it around on you."

"I told you he was smooth." After peeking in another carton, she nibbled on some chilled chicken and bean sprouts. "Don't you know any nice teenage girls you could nudge in his direction?"

"Lola's got one," Zack said, considering. "I think she's sixteen."

"Lola has a teenager?"

"Three of them. She likes to say she started young

so that she could lose her mind before she turned forty. I can feel her out about it."

"It couldn't hurt. I'm going to try again, though I'm hoping the feeling will pass in another week or two."

"I wouldn't count on it." Reaching across the table, he linked his fingers with hers. "You stick in a man's mind."

"Does that mean you're thinking of me when you're mixing drinks and flirting with the customers?"

"I never flirt with Pete."

She laughed. "I was thinking more of those two 'babes' who drop in. The blonde and the redhead. They always order stingers."

"You are observant, Counselor."

"The redhead's got her big green eyes on you."

"They're blue."

"Aha!"

He shook his head, amazed he'd fallen so snugly into the trap. "It pays to know your regulars. Besides, I like brown eyes—especially when they lean toward gold."

She let his lips brush hers. "Too late." With her head close to his, she laughed again. "It's all right, Muldoon. I can always borrow Rio's meat cleaver if you notice more than her eyes."

"Then I'm safe. I've never paid any attention to those cute little freckles over her nose. Or that sexy dimple in her chin."

Eyes narrowed, Rachel bit his lip. "Get any lower, and you'll be in deep water."

"That's okay. I'm a strong swimmer."

Hours later, when Zack crawled into a cold, empty bed, he warmed himself by thinking of it. It had been nice, just nice, to laugh together over the cardboard boxes and chopsticks. They'd sampled each other's choices, talking while the candles had burned low. Not about Nick, not about work, but about dozens of other things.

Then they'd made love again, slowly, sweetly, while the night grew late around them.

He'd had to leave her. He had responsibilities. But as he settled his body toward sleep, he let his mind wander, imagining what it could be like.

Waking up with her. Feeling her stretch against him as the alarm rang. Watching her. Smiling to himself as she hurried around the apartment, getting dressed for work.

She'd be wearing one of those trim suits while they stood in the kitchen sharing coffee, talking over their plans for the day.

Sometimes they'd steal a quick lunch together, because they both hated to have a whole day pass without touching. When he could, he'd slip away from work so that he could walk home with her in the evening. When he couldn't, he'd look forward to seeing her come through the door, slide onto a stool at the bar, where she'd eat Rio's chili and flirt with him.

Then they would go home together.

One balmy weekend they would set sail together. He'd teach her how to man the tiller. They'd glide out over blue water, with the sails billowing....

The waves were high as mountains, rearing up to slap viciously at the ship. The bellow of the wind was like a thousand women screaming. Burying a fear that he knew could be as destructive as the gale, he scrambled over the pitching deck, clinging to the slippery rail as he shouted orders.

The rain was lashing his face like a whip, blinding him. His red-rimmed eyes stung from the salt water. He knew the boat was out there—radar had it—but all he could see was wall after wall of deadly water.

The next wave swamped the deck, sucking at him. Lightning cracked the sky like a bullet through glass. The ship heeled. He saw the seaman tumble, heard the shout as his hands scrambled on the deck for purchase. Zack leaped, snagging a sleeve, then a wrist.

A line. For God's sake, get me a line.

And he was dragging the dead weight back from the rail.

Wind and water. Wind and water.

There, in a flash of lightning, was the disabled boat. Lower the tow line. Make it fast. As the lightning stuttered against the dark, he could see three figures. They'd lashed themselves on—a man to the wheel, a woman behind him, a young girl to the mast.

They were fighting, valiantly, but a forty-foot boat was no match for the fury of a hurricane at sea. It was impossible to send out a launch. He had to hope one of them could hold the boat steady while another secured the tow.

Signal lights flashed instructions through the storm.

It happened fast. Another spear of lightning, and the mast cracked, falling like a tree under an ax. Horrified, he watched the young girl being dragged with it into the swirling water.

No time to think. Pure instinct had Zack grabbing a flotation device and diving into the face of the storm.

Falling, falling, endlessly, while the gale tumbled

his body like dice in a gambler's hand. Black, pitch-black, then the white flare of lightning. Hitting a wall of water that felt like stone. Having it close relentlessly over your head. Like death.

Zack awoke gasping for air and choking against the nightmare water. Sweat had soaked through to the sheets, making him shiver in the chill. With a groan, he let his head fall back and waited for the first grinding ache of nausea to pass.

The room tilted once as he staggered to his feet. From past experience, Zack knew to close his eyes until it righted again. Moving through the dark, he went into the bathroom to splash the cold sweat from his face.

"Hey, you okay?" Nick was hovering in the doorway. "You sick or something?"

"No." Zack cupped a hand near the faucet, catching enough water to ease his dry throat. "Go back to bed."

Nick hesitated, studying Zack's pale face. "You look sick."

"Damn it, I said I'm fine. Beat it."

Nick's eyes darkened with angry hurt before he swung away.

"Hey, wait. Sorry." Zack let out a long breath. "Nightmare. Puts me in a lousy mood."

"You had a nightmare?"

"That's what I said." Embarrassed, Zack snatched up a towel to dry off.

It was hard for Nick to imagine big, bad Zack having a nightmare, or anything else that would make him sweat and go pale. "Uh, you want a drink?"

"Yeah." Steadier now, Zack lowered the towel. "There's some of the old man's whiskey in the kitchen."

After a moment, Zack followed Nick out. He sat on

the arm of a chair while Nick splashed three fingers of whiskey into a tumbler. He took it, swallowed, then hissed. "I can't figure out how he had a liver left at the end."

Nick wished he'd pulled pants over his briefs. At least he'd have had pockets to dip his hands into. "I think when he started to forget stuff, it helped him to blame it on the whiskey instead of—you know."

"Alzheimer's. Yeah." Zack took another swallow, let it lie on his tongue a moment so that his throat could get used to the idea.

"I heard you thrashing around in there. Sounded pretty bad."

"It was pretty bad." Zack tilted the glass, watched the whiskey lap this way and that. "Hurricane. One mean bitch. I never understood why they started naming them after guys, too. Take it from me, a hurricane's all woman." He let his head fall back again, let his eyes close. "It's been nearly three years, and I haven't been able to shake this lady."

"You want to—" Nick cut himself off. "That should help you sleep."

Zack knew what Nick had wanted to ask. And he did want to. It might be best for both of them if they talked it through. "We were off of Bermuda when we got the distress call. We were the closest ship, and the captain had to make a choice. We turned back into the hurricane. Three civilians in a pleasure boat. They'd been thrown off course and hadn't been able to make it to shore before the storm hit."

Saying nothing, Nick sat on the arm of the couch so that he was facing his brother.

"Seventy-five knot winds, and the seas—they must

have been forty feet. I've been through a hurricane after it's made landfall. It can be bad, real bad, but it's nothing like it is when it's at sea. You don't know scared until you see something like that. Hear something like that. The lieutenant took a rap on the head, it put him out. We came close to losing some of the crew over the side. Sometimes it was black, so black you couldn't see your own hands—but you could see that water rising up. Then the lightning would hit, and blind you."

"How were you supposed to find them in all that?"

"We had them on radar. The quartermaster could've slipped that ship through the crack of dawn. He was good. We spotted them, thirty degrees off to starboard. They'd tied the kid—little girl—to the main mast. The man and woman were fighting to keep it afloat, but they were taking on water fast. We had time. I remember thinking we could pull it off. Then the mast cracked. I thought I heard the girl scream, but it was probably the wind, because she went under pretty quick. So I went in."

"You went in?" Nick repeated, wide-eyed. "You jumped in the water?"

"I was over the side before I thought about it. I wasn't being a hero, I just didn't think. Believe me, if I had..." He let the words trail off, then swallowed the rest of the whiskey. "It was like jumping off a skyscraper. You don't think you're ever going to stop falling. It was end over end, forever, giving you plenty of time to realize you've just killed yourself. It was stupid—if the wind had been wrong it would have just smashed me against the side of the ship. But I was lucky, and it tossed me toward the boat. Then I hit. God, it was like ramming full-length into concrete."

He hadn't known until later that he'd snapped his collarbone and dislocated his left shoulder.

"I couldn't get my bearings. The water kept heaving me around, sucking me down. It was so black, the searchlight barely cut through. There I was, drowning, and I couldn't even remember what I was doing. It was blind luck that I found the mast. She was all tangled up in the line. I don't know how many times we went under while I was trying to get her loose. My hands were numb, and I was working blind. Then I had her, and I managed to get the flotation on her. They said I got the tow line secured, but I don't remember. I just remember hanging on to her and waiting for the next wave to finish us off. Next thing, I was waking up in the infirmary. The kid was sitting there, wrapped in a blanket and holding my hand." He smiled. It helped to think about that part. Just that part. "She was one tough little monkey. A damn admiral's granddaughter."

"You saved her life."

"Maybe. For the first couple of months, I jumped off that deck every time I closed my eyes. Now it's only once or twice a year. It still scares the breath out of me."

"I didn't think you were scared of anything."

"I'm scared of plenty," Zack said quietly as he met his brother's eyes. "For a while I was scared I wouldn't be able to stand on deck and look out at the water again. I was scared to come back here, knowing that once I did, my whole life was going to change. And I'm scared of ending up like the old man, sick and feeble and used up. I guess I'm scared you're going to walk out that door in a few weeks, feeling the same about me you did when you walked in."

Nick broke the gaze first, staring over Zack's shoul-

der at the shadowy wall. "I don't know how I feel. You
came back because you had to. I stayed because there
was no place else to go."

There was no arguing with the truth. As far as Zack
could see, Nick had summed it up perfectly. "We never
had much of a shot before."

"You didn't hang around very long."

"I couldn't get along with the old man—"

"You were the only one he cared about," Nick blurted
out. "Every day I'd have to hear about how great you
were, how you were making something out of yourself.
What a hero you were. And how I was nothing." He
caught himself, swallowed the need. "But that's cool.
You were his blood, and I was just something that got
dumped on him when my mother died."

"He didn't feel that way. He didn't," Zack insisted.
"For God's sake, Nick, when I lived with him, he was
never satisfied with me, either. I was here, and my
mother wasn't. That was enough to make him miserable every time he looked at me. Hell, he didn't mean
it." Zack closed his eyes and missed the flicker of surprise that passed over Nick's face. "It was just the way
he was. It took me years to realize he was always on
my back because it was the only way he knew to be a
father. It was the same with you."

"He wasn't my..." But this time Nick trailed off without finishing the sentence, or the thought.

"Toward the end, he asked for you. He really wanted
to see you, Nick. Most of the times he came around like
that, he thought you were still a little kid. And sometimes—most times, really—he just got the two of us
mixed up together. Then he'd yell at me for both of us."
He said it with a smile—a smile that Nick didn't return.

"I'm not blaming you for staying away, or for holding all those years of criticism and complaints against him. I understand that it was too late for him, Nick. It doesn't have to be too late for you."

"What does it matter to you?"

"You're all the family I've got." He rose and laid a hand on Nick's shoulder, relaxing when it wasn't shoved off. "Maybe, when it comes right down to the bottom line, you're all the family I've ever had. I don't want to lose that."

"I don't know how to be family," Nick murmured.

"Me either. Maybe we can figure it out together."

Nick glanced up, then away. "Maybe. We're stuck with each other a few more weeks, anyway."

It would do, Zack thought as he gave Nick's shoulder a quick squeeze. It would do for now. "Thanks for the drink, kid. Do me a favor and don't mention the nightmare business to anyone."

"I can dig it." Nick watched Zack start back toward the bedroom. "Zack?"

"Yeah."

He didn't know what he wanted to say—just that it felt good, that he felt good. "Nothing. Night."

"Good night." Zack eased back into bed with a sigh, certain he'd sleep like a baby.

Chapter 9

Something had changed. Rachel couldn't put her finger on it, but as she sat between Zack and Nick on the subway to Brooklyn she knew there was something going on between them. Something different.

It made her nerves hum. It made her wonder if she'd made a mistake in bringing the problems of the men who flanked her into her parents' home.

And her problem, as well, she admitted. After all, she wouldn't deny she cared about both of them more than what could be considered professional. She felt a kinship with Nick—the younger-sibling syndrome, she supposed. Added to that, she'd been telling the simple truth when she confessed to Zack that she had a weakness for bad boys.

She wanted to do more for Nick LeBeck than help him stay out of jail.

As for Nick's big brother, she'd long since crossed all professional boundaries with him, into what could only be termed a full-blown affair. Even sitting beside him in the rumbling car, she thought about the last time they'd been together, alone. And it took no effort at all to imagine what it would be like the next time they could steal a few hours.

Her mother was bound to sense it, Rachel mused. Nothing got past Nadia Stanislaski when it came to her children. She wondered what her mother would think of him. What she would think of the fact that her baby girl had taken a lover.

For two people who had vowed not to complicate matters, she and Zack had done a poor job of it, Rachel decided. She'd been so certain she could keep her priorities well in line, accept the physical aspects of a relationship with a man she liked and respected without dwelling on the thorny issue of what-happens-next.

But she was thinking about Zack too much, already slotting herself as part of a couple when she'd always been perfectly content to go along single.

Now, when she imagined moving along without him, the picture turned dull and listless.

Her problem, Rachel reminded herself. After all, they had made a pact, and she never went back on her word. It was something she would have to deal with when the time came. Much more immediate was the nagging sensation that the relationship of the men beside her had taken a fast turn without her being aware of it.

To offset the feeling, she kept up a steady stream of conversation until they reached their stop.

"It's only a few blocks," Rachel said, dragging her

hair back as a brisk autumn wind swirled around them. "I hope you don't mind the walk."

Zack lifted a brow. "I think we can handle it. You seem nervous, Rachel. She seem nervous to you, Nick?"

"Pretty jumpy."

"That's ridiculous." She headed into the wind, and the men fell in beside her.

"It's probably the thought of having a criminal type sit down to Sunday dinner," Zack commented. "Now she's going to have to count all the silverware."

Shocked at the statement, Rachel started to respond, but Nick merely snorted and answered for himself. "If you ask me, she's worried about inviting some Irish sailor. She has to worry if he'll drink all the booze and pick a fight."

"I can handle my liquor, pal. And I don't plan on picking a fight. Unless it's with the cop."

Nick crunched a dry leaf as it skittered across the sidewalk. "I'll take the cop."

Why, they're *joking* with each other, Rachel realized. Like brothers. Very much like brothers. Delighted, she linked arms with both of them. "If either of you takes on Alex, you'll be in for a surprise. He's meaner than he looks. And the only thing I'm nervous about is that I won't get my share of dinner. I've seen both of you eat."

"This from a woman who packs it away like a linebacker."

Rachel narrowed her eyes at Zack. "I merely have a healthy appetite."

He grinned down at her. "Me too, sugar."

She was wondering how to control the sudden leap of her heart rate when a car skidded to a halt in the street beside them. "Hey!" the driver called out.

"Hey back." Rachel broke away to walk over to greet her brother and sister-in-law. Bending into the tiny window of the MG, she kissed Mikhail and smiled at his wife. "Still keeping him in line, Sydney?"

Cool and elegant beside her untamed-looking husband, Sydney smiled. "Absolutely. Difficult jobs are my forte."

Mikhail pinched his wife's thigh and nodded toward the sidewalk. "So what's the story there?"

"They're my guests." She gave Mikhail a long, warning look that she knew was wasted on him before calling to Nick and Zack. "Come meet my brother and his long-suffering wife. Sydney, Mikhail, this is Zackary Muldoon and Nicholas LeBeck."

His eyes shielded by dark glasses, Mikhail took a careful survey. He had a brother's natural lack of faith in his sister's judgment. "Which is the client?"

"Today," Rachel said, "they're both guests."

Sydney leaned over and jammed her elbow sharply in Mikhail's ribs. "It's very nice to meet you, both of you. You're in for quite a treat with Nadia's cooking."

"So I hear." Zack kept his eyes on Mikhail as he answered, and lifted a proprietary hand to Rachel's shoulder.

Mikhail's fingers drummed on the steering wheel. "You own what? A bar?"

"No, actually, I'm into white slavery."

That got a chuckle from Nick before Rachel shook her head. "Go park your car."

As they retreated to the sidewalk, Nick smiled over at Rachel. "I see what you mean now about older brothers. Being a pain must go with the position."

"Responsibility," Zack told him. "We just pass on the benefit of our experience."

"No," Rachel said, "what you are is nosy." Amused, she gestured toward the sound of voices and laughter. Mikhail and Sydney were already at the door of the row house, hugging and being hugged. "This is it." When Rachel spotted Natasha, she gave a cry of pleasure and dashed up the steps.

Hanging back a little, Zack watched Rachel embrace her sister. Natasha was slighter, more delicately built, with rich brown eyes misted with tears, and tumbled raven curls raining down her back. Zack's first thought was that this could not be the mother of three Rachel had described to him. Then a young boy of six or seven squeezed between the women and demanded attention.

"You let in the cold!" This was bellowed from inside the house in a rumbling male voice that carried to the sidewalk and beyond. "You are not born in barn."

"Yes, Papa." Her voice sounded meek enough, but Rachel winked at her nephew as she lifted him up for a kiss. "My sister, Natasha," she continued, as they stood in the open doorway. "And my boyfriend, Brandon. And," she said when a toddler wandered up to hang on Natasha's legs, "Katie."

"You pick me up," Katie demanded, homing in on Nick. "Okay?" She was already holding up her arms, smiling flirtatiously. Nick cleared his throat and glanced at Rachel for help. When he only got a smile and a shrug, he bent down awkwardly.

"Sure. I guess."

An expert at such matters, Katie settled herself on his hip and wound an arm around his neck.

"She enjoys men," Natasha explained. When her father bellowed again, she rolled her eyes. "Come inside, please."

Zack was struck by the sounds and the scents. Home, he realized. This was a home. And stepping inside made him realize he'd never really had one himself.

The scents of ham and cloves and furniture polish, the clash of mixed voices. The carpet on the stairway leading to the second floor was worn at the edges, testimony to the dozens of feet that had climbed up or down. The furniture in the cramped living room was faded with sun and time, crowded now with people. A gleaming piano stood against one wall. Atop it was a bronze sculpture. He recognized the faces of Rachel's family, melded together, cheek to cheek, flanked by two older, proud faces that could only be her parents'.

He didn't know much about art, but he understood that this represented a unity that could not be broken.

"So you bring your friends, then leave them in the cold." Yuri sat in an armchair, cuddling a sprite of a girl. His big workingman's arms nearly enveloped the pretty child, who had a fairy's blond hair and curious eyes.

"It's only a little cold." Rachel bent to kiss her father, then the girl. "Freddie, you get prettier every time I see you."

Freddie smiled and tried to pretend she wasn't staring at the young blond man who was holding her little sister. But she had just turned thirteen, and whole worlds were opening up to her.

Rachel went through another round of introductions. Freddie turned the name Nick LeBeck over in her head while Yuri shouted out orders.

"Alexi, bring hot cider. Rachel, take coats upstairs.

Mikhail, kiss your wife later. Go tell Mama we have company."

Within moments, Zack found himself seated on the couch, scratching the ears of a big, floppy dog named Ivan and discussing the pros and cons of running a business with Yuri.

Nick felt desperately self-conscious with a baby on his knee. She didn't seem to be in any hurry to get down. And the little blond girl named Freddie kept studying him with solemn gray eyes. He glanced away, wishing their mother would come along and do something. Anything. Katie snuggled up and began to toy with his earring.

"Pretty," she said, with a smile so sweet he couldn't help but respond. "I have earrings, too. See?" To show off her tiny gold hoops, she turned her head this way and that. "'Cause I'm Daddy's little gypsy."

"I bet." Unconsciously he lifted a hand to stroke her hair. "You kind of look like your Aunt Rachel."

"I can take her." Freddie had worked up her courage and now she stood beside the couch smiling down at Nick. "If she's bothering you."

Nick merely moved his shoulders. "She's cool." He struggled to find something to say. The girl was china-doll pretty, he thought, and as foreign to him as Rachel's Ukraine. "Uh…you don't look a whole lot like sisters."

Freddie's smile bloomed warm and her fledgling woman's heart tapped a little faster. *He'd noticed her.* "Mama's my stepmother, technically. I was about six when she and my father got married."

"Oh." A *step,* he thought. That was something he knew about, and sympathized with. "I guess it was a little rough on you."

Though she was baffled, Freddie continued to smile. After all, he was talking to her, and she thought he looked like a rock star. "Why?"

"Well, you know…" Nick found himself flustered under that steady gray stare. "Having a stepmother—a stepfamily."

"That's just a word." Gathering her nerve, she sat on the arm of the couch beside him. "We have a house in West Virginia—that's where Dad met Mama. He teaches at the university and she owns a toy store. Have you ever been to West Virginia?"

Nick was still stuck on her answer. *It's just a word.* He could hear in the easy tone of her voice that she meant just that. "What? Oh, no, never been there."

Inside the warm, fragrant kitchen, Rachel was laughing with her sister. "Katie certainly knows how to snag her man."

"It was sweet the way he blushed."

"Here." Nadia thrust a bowl into her eldest daughter's hands. "You make biscuits. The boy had good eyes," she said to Rachel. "Why is he in trouble?"

Sniffing a pot of simmering cabbage, Rachel smiled. "Because he didn't have a mama and papa to yell at him."

"And the older one," Nadia continued, opening the oven to check her ham. "He has good eyes, too. And they're on you."

"Maybe."

After smacking her daughter's hand away, Nadia replaced the lid on the pot. "Alex grumbles about them."

"He grumbles about everything."

Natasha cut shortening in the bowl and grinned. "I

think it's more to the point that Rachel has her eye on
Zack every bit as much as he has his on her."

"Thanks a lot," Rachel said under her breath.

"A woman who doesn't look at such a man needs
glasses," Nadia said, and made her daughters laugh.

When her curiosity got to be too much for her, Rachel opened the swinging door a crack and peeked out.
There was Sydney, sitting on the floor and keeping
Brandon entertained with a pile of race cars. The men
were huddled together, arguing football. Freddie was
perched on the arm of the sofa, obviously in the first
stages of infatuation with Nick. As for Nick, he seemed
to have forgotten his embarrassment and was bouncing
Katie on his knee. And Zack, she noted with a smile,
was leaning forward, entrenched in the hot debate over
the upcoming game.

By the time the table was set and groaning under the
weight of platters of food, Zack was thoroughly fascinated with the Stanislaskis. They argued, loudly, but
without any of the bitterness he remembered from his
own confrontations with his father. He discovered that
Mikhail was the artist who had crafted the sculpture
on the piano, as well as all the passionate pieces in Rachel's apartment. Yet he talked construction and building codes with his father, not art.

Natasha handled her children with a deft hand. No
one seemed to mind if Brandon created a racket imitat-
ing race cars or if Katie climbed all over the furniture.
But when it was time to stop, they did so at little more
than a word from their mother or father.

Alex didn't seem like such a tough cop when he was
being barraged by his family's teasing over his latest

lady friend—a woman, Mikhail claimed, who had the I.Q. of the cabbage he was heaping on his plate.

"Hey, I don't mind. That way I can do the thinking for her."

That earned an unladylike snort from Rachel. "He wouldn't know how to handle a woman with a brain."

"One day one will find him," Nadia predicted. "Like Sydney found my Mikhail."

"She didn't find me." Mikhail passed a bowl of boiled potatoes to his wife. "I found her. She needed some spice in her life."

"As I recall, you needed someone to knock the chip off your shoulder."

"It was always so," Yuri agreed, shaking his fork. "He was a good boy, but— What is the word?"

"Arrogant?" Sydney suggested.

"Ah." Satisfied, Yuri dived into his meal. "But it's not so bad for a man to be arrogant."

"This is true." Nadia kept an eagle eye on Katie, who was concentrating on cutting her meat. "So long as he has a woman who is smarter. Is not hard to do."

Female laughter and male catcalls had Katie clapping her hands in delight.

"Nicholas," Nadia said, pleased that he was going back for seconds, "you will go to school, yes?"

"Ah…no, ma'am."

She urged the basket of biscuits on him. "So you know what work you want."

"I… Not exactly."

"He is young, Nadia," Yuri said from across the table. "Time to decide. You're skinny." He pursed his lips as he studied Nick. "But have good arms. You need work, I give you job. Teach you to build."

Speechless, Nick stared. No one had ever offered to give him anything so casually. The big, broad-faced man who was plowing through the glazed ham didn't even know him. "Thanks. But I'm sort of working for Zack."

"It must be interesting to work in a bar. Brandon, eat your vegetables, or no more biscuits. All the people you meet," Natasha continued, saving Katie's glass from tipping on the floor without breaking rhythm.

"You don't meet a whole lot of them in the kitchen," Nick muttered.

"You have to be twenty-one to tend bar or serve drinks," Zack reminded him.

Noting Nick's mutinous expression, Rachel broke in. "Mama, you should see Zack's cook. He's a giant from Jamaica, and he makes the most incredible food. I've been trying to charm some recipes out of him."

"I will give you one to trade."

"Make it the glaze for this ham, and I guarantee he'll give you anything." Zack sampled another bite. "It's great."

"You will take some home," Nadia ordered. "Make sandwiches."

"Yes, ma'am." Nick grinned.

Rachel bided her time, waiting until dinner was over and three of the four apple pies her mother had baked had been devoured. With just a little urging, Nadia was persuaded to play the piano. After a time, she and Spence played a duet, the music flowing out over the sound of clattering dishes and conversation.

She saw the way Nick glanced over, watching, listening. As cleverly as a general aligning his troops, she dropped down on the bench when Spence and Nadia took a break. She held out a hand, inviting Nick to join her.

"I shouldn't have had that second piece of pie," she said with a sigh.

"Me either." It was difficult to decide how to tell her the way the afternoon had made him feel. He wouldn't have believed people lived this way. "Your mom's great."

"Yeah, I think so." Very casually, she turned and began to noodle with the keys. "She and Papa love these Sundays when we can all get together."

"Your dad, he was saying how the house would get bigger when the kids left home. But now he thinks they'll have to add on a couple of rooms to hold everyone. I guess you get together like this a lot."

"Whenever we can."

"They didn't seem to mind you brought me and Zack along."

"They like company." She tried a chord, wincing at the clash of notes. "This always looks so easy when Spence or Mama does it."

"Try this." He put his hand over hers, guiding her fingers.

"Ah, better. But I don't see how anyone can play different things with each hand. At the same time, you know."

"You don't think about it that way. You just have to let it happen."

"Well…"

She trailed off and, unable to resist, he began to improvise blues. When the music moved through him, he forgot he was in a room crowded with people and let it take over. Even when the room fell silent, he continued, wrapped up in the pleasure of creating sound and feeling from the keys. When he played, he wasn't Nick LeBeck, outcast. He was someone he didn't really understand yet, someone he couldn't quite see and yearned desperately to be always.

He eased into half-remembered tunes, filling them out with his own interpretation, letting the music swing with his mood from blues to boogie-woogie to jazz and back again.

When he paused, grinning to himself from the sheer pleasure it had given him to play, Zack laid a hand on his shoulder and snapped him back to reality.

"Where'd you learn to do that?" The amazement in Zack's voice was reflected in his eyes. "I didn't know you could do that."

With a shrug, Nick wiped his suddenly nervous hands on his thighs. "I was just fooling around."

"That was some fooling around."

Cautious, trying to put a label on the tone of Zack's voice, Nick glanced back. "It's no big deal."

Grinning from ear to ear, Zack shook his head. "Man, to somebody who can't play 'Chopsticks,' that was one whale of a big deal." Pride was bubbling through the amazement. "It was great. Really great."

The pleasure working its way into him made Nick almost as uneasy as the criticism he'd expected. It was then he realized that everyone had stopped talking and was looking at him. Color crept into his cheeks. "Look, I said it was no big deal. I was just banging on the keys."

"That was some very talented banging." With Katie on his hip, Spencer moved to the piano. "Ever think about studying seriously?"

Flabbergasted, Nick stared down at his hands. It had been one thing to sit across the table from Spencer Kimball, and another entirely to have the renowned composer discussing music with him. "No... I mean, not really. I just fool around sometimes, that's all."

"You've got the touch, and the ear." Catching Rachel's eye, he passed her Katie and changed positions with her so that he sat with Nick on the edge of the piano bench. "Know any Muddy Waters?"

"Some. You dig Muddy Waters?"

"Sure." He began to play the bass. "Can you pick it up?"

"Yeah." Nick laid his hands on the keys and grinned. "Yeah."

"Not too shabby," Rachel murmured to Zack.

He was still staring at his brother, dumbfounded. "He never told me. Never a word." When Rachel reached for his hand, he gripped hard. "I guess he did to you."

"A little, enough to make me want to try this. I didn't know he was that good."

"He really is, isn't he?" Overwhelmed, he pressed his lips to Rachel's hair. Nick was too involved to notice, though several pairs of eyes observed the gesture. "Looks like I'm going to have to get my hands on a piano."

Rachel leaned her head against his shoulder. "You're all right, Muldoon."

It took him nearly a week to arrange it, but taking another deep dip into his savings, Zack bought an upright piano. With Rachel's help, he dragged furniture around the apartment to make room for it.

Puffing a bit, her hands on her hips, she surveyed the

space they had cleared under the window. "I wonder if it wouldn't be better against that wall there."

"You've already changed your mind three times. This is it." He took a long pull from a cold beer. "For better or worse."

"You're not marrying the stupid piano. You're arranging it. And I really think—"

"Keep thinking, and I'll pour this over your head." He caught her chin to tilt her head up for a kiss. "And it's not a stupid piano. The guy assured me it was the best for the money."

"Don't get started on that again." She eased closer to link her arms around his neck. "Nick doesn't need a baby grand."

"I'd just like to have done a little better for him."

"Muldoon." She pressed her mouth to his. "You did good. When's it supposed to get here?"

"Twenty minutes ago." Wound up, he began to pace. "If they blow this after I went through all that business to get Nick out for a few hours—"

Rachel interrupted him, amused and touched. "It's going to be fine. And I think it was inspired of you to use beer nuts to get him out of the way."

"He was steaming." With a grin, Zack dropped down on the couch. "Argued with me for ten minutes about why the hell he had to go check on a missing delivery of beer nuts when he was getting paid to wash dishes."

"I think he'll forgive you when he gets back."

"Hey up there." Rio's musical voice echoed up the stairway. "We got us one fine piano coming in. Best you come down and take a look."

Rachel tried to stay out of the way—though several times, as they muscled and maneuvered the piano up those steep stairs, she wanted to offer advice. The best part was watching Zack, which she did the entire time the instrument was hauled, set into place and tuned. He worried over the piano like a mother hen, wiping smudges from the surface, opening and closing the lid on the bench.

"That looks real fine." Rio folded his massive arms over his chest. "Be good to have music when I cook. You do right by that boy, Zack. He's going to make himself somebody. You'll see. Now I'm going to fix us something special." He grinned at Rachel. "When you going to bring that mama of yours by here so we can talk food?"

"Soon," Rachel promised. "She's going to bring you an old Ukrainian recipe."

"Good. Then I give her my secret barbecue sauce. I think she must be a fine woman." He started out just as Nick came clattering up the steps. "What's your hurry, boy? Got a fire in your pocket?"

"Damn beer nuts" was all Nick said as he pushed by. He swung into the apartment, ready for a fight. "Listen, bro, the next time you want somebody to—" Everything went out of his mind when he spotted the piano standing new and shiny under the window.

"Sorry about the wild-goose chase." Nervous, Zack jammed his hands in his pockets. "I wanted to get you out so we could get this in." He shifted back on his heels when Nick remained silent. "So, what do you think?"

Nick swallowed hard. "What did you do, rent it or something?"

"I bought it."

Because his fingers itched to feel the keys, he, too, stuck them in his pockets. Rachel nearly sighed. They looked like two stray dogs that didn't know whether to fight or make friends.

"You shouldn't have done that." The strain in Nick's voice made it come out curt and sharp.

"Why the hell not?" Zack shot back. His hands were now balled into fists and straining against denim. "It's my money. I thought it would be nice to have some music around here. So, do you want to try it out or not?"

There was an ache spreading, twisting in his gut and burning the back of his throat. He had to get out. "I forgot something," he muttered, and strode stiffly out the door.

"What the hell was that?" Zack exploded. He snatched up his beer, then set it down again before he gave in to the temptation to hurl the bottle against the wall. "If that little son of a—"

"Hold it." Rachel's order snapped out as she thumped a fist against Zack's chest. "Oh, the pair of you are a real prize. He doesn't know how to say thank you, and you're too stupid to see he was so overwhelmed he was practically on the verge of tears."

"That's bull. He all but tossed it back in my face."

"Idiot. You gave him a dream. It's very possibly the first time anyone ever understood what he wanted, deep down, and gave him a shot at it. He didn't know how to handle it, Zack, any more than you would."

"Listen, I—" He broke off and swore, because it made sense. "What am I supposed to do now?"

"Nothing." Cupping his face in her hands, she pulled it toward hers to kiss him. "Nothing at all. I'm going to go talk to him, okay?" She pulled back and started for the door.

"Rachel." He took a deep breath before crossing to

her. "I need you." He watched surprise come into her eyes as he took her hands and brought them to his lips. "Maybe I don't know how to handle that, either."

Something fluttered around her heart. "You're doing all right, Muldoon."

"I don't think you understand." He didn't, either. "I really need you."

"I'm right here."

"But are you going to stay here, once your obligation to Nick is over?"

The fluttering increased. "We've got a couple of weeks before we have to think about that. It's…" Steady, Rachel, she warned herself. Think it through. "It's not just Nick I care about." She tightened her fingers on his briefly before drawing away. "Let me go find him. We'll talk about the rest of this later."

"Okay." He stepped back from her, and from what he was feeling. "But I think we are going to have to talk about it. Soon."

With a quick nod, she hurried down the steps. Rio merely gestured toward the front of the bar, and, grateful she didn't have to talk for a moment, she went out to look.

She found him standing on the sidewalk with his hands balled in his pockets, staring at the late-afternoon traffic. Oh, she knew a portion of what he was feeling. How Zackary Muldoon could get inside you and pull your emotions apart before you had a chance to defend yourself.

Later, she promised herself, she would think about what he'd done to *her* emotions. For now, she would concentrate on Nick.

She stepped up beside him and brushed at the hair on his shoulders. "You doing okay?"

He didn't look at her, just continued to watch the fits and starts of traffic. "Why did he do that?"

"Why do you think?"

"I didn't ask him for anything."

"The best gifts are the ones we don't ask for."

He shifted, meeting her eyes for the barest of moments. "Did you talk him into it?"

"No." Trying to be patient, she took him by the arms so that he had to face her. "Open your eyes, Nick. You saw the way he reacted when he heard you play. He was so proud of you he could barely talk. He wanted to give you something that would matter to you. He didn't do it so you'd be obligated to him, but because he loves you. That's what families do."

"Your family."

She gave him a quick shake. "And yours. Don't try to con me with that bull about not being real brothers. You care just as much about him as he does about you. I know how much it meant to you to walk in there and see that piano. Mama had the same look on her face on Mother's Day, but it was easier for her to show what she was feeling. You just need a little practice."

Closing his eyes, he laid his brow against hers. "I don't know what to say to him. How to act. Nobody's ever… I've never had anybody. When I was a kid, I just wanted to hang around him. Then he took off."

"I know. Try to remember he wasn't much more than a kid himself when he did. He's not going anywhere now." Rachel kissed both his cheeks, as her mother might have done. "Why don't you go back inside, Nick, and do what you do best?"

"What's that?"

She smiled at him. "Play it by ear. Go on. He's dying for you to try it out."

"Yeah. Okay." He took a step back. "You coming?"

"No, I've got some things to do." Some things to think about, she thought, correcting herself. "Tell Zack I'll see him later."

But she waited after he'd gone in. Standing on the sidewalk, she watched the window. And after a while, very faintly, she heard the sound of music.

Chapter 10

"Yo, Rachel." Pete straightened on his stool and sucked in some of his comfortable stomach when he spotted Rachel swinging through the front door of the bar. "How 'bout I buy you a drink?"

"I might just let you do that." But her smile was for Zack as she hung her coat on one of the hooks by the door. As she crossed the room, she shot a meaningful glance at the blonde who was seductively wrapped around a bar stool, purring an order for another drink while she walked her fingers up Zack's arm. "Busy night?"

Lola juggled a tray as she passed. "That one's on her third stinger," she said to Rachel under her breath. "And those big blue eyes of hers have been crawling all over the boss for two hours."

"That's all she'll do—unless she wants those eyes black-and-blue."

Lola gave a snap of appreciative laughter. "Atta girl. Hey, hold on a minute." With a skill Rachel admired, Lola served a full tray of drinks, emptied ashtrays and replaced an empty basket of chips. "See the brunette by the juke?"

With her lips pursed, Rachel studied the slim jean-clad hips and the waterfall of honey-brown hair. "Don't tell me I have to worry about her, too?"

"No, *I* do. That's my oldest."

"Your daughter? She's gorgeous."

"Yeah. That's why I have to worry. Anyway, Zack's been hinting around about how he'd like Nick to meet some people closer to his own age, so I talked her into coming in, having one of Rio's burgers."

"And?"

"Nick looked. Actually, he was pretty enthusiastic about busing tables tonight. But he didn't make a move in her direction."

"Looking's good," Rachel mused. "It wouldn't bother you if he was interested enough to ask her out?"

"Nick's okay. Besides, my Terri can take care of herself." Lola winked. "Takes after her mom. Keep your pants on," she shouted to the table of four that was signaling to her. "Catch you later."

"Well, now…" Rachel eased onto the stool between Harry and Pete. A glass of white wine was already waiting for her. "What's the latest?"

"Seven-letter word for rapture," Harry told her. "Ending in 'y'."

Rachel smiled into her wine. *"Ecstasy,"* she said, watching Zack.

"Okay!" Pleased with that, he skimmed over the

blank spaces in his puzzle. "Here's another seven. Characterized by a lack of substance."

"Perfect," she murmured, shifting her gaze to the blonde, who was leaning her cleavage over the bar. "Try *vacuous.*"

"Damn, you're good."

"Harry," she gave him a smile that had him going beet red, "I'm terrific. Keep an eye on things for me. I want to talk to Nick."

Pete watched her go, sighed. "If I was twenty years younger, thirty pounds lighter, didn't have a wife who'd slit my wrists and still had all my hair…"

"Yeah. Keep dreaming." Harry signaled for another round.

The minute she passed into the kitchen, Rachel took a deep breath. It always smelled like heaven. "Okay, Rio, what's good tonight?"

"Everything's always good." He grinned, wiping his big hands on his apron. "But tonight my fried chicken's number one."

"There must be a drumstick with my name on it. Hey, Nick." Now as at home here as she was in her mama's kitchen, she eased against the counter where he was stacking the dishes. "How's it going?"

"By last count, I've washed six thousand and eighty-two plates." But he smiled when he said it. "Zack mentioned you might be coming by tonight. I've been looking for you."

Rio handed her a plate heaped with fried chicken, creamed potatoes and coleslaw. "If I came by any more often, they'd have to roll me in and out the door."

"You eat." Rio gestured with his spatula before he flipped burgers. "I like to see a woman with hips."

"You're about to." Her willpower was nonexistent when she was faced with Rio's extra-spicy chicken. Rachel began to eat where she stood. "Definitely number one," she said with her mouth full. Rio grinned. "So, did you want to see me about anything in particular?" she asked Nick.

"No." He brushed a hand down her hair. "I just wanted to see you."

Whoops. "Nick, I really think—"

"We've only got a couple of weeks to go."

"I know." She shifted slightly, putting the plate between them. "In fact, I was able to speak to the DA, tell him about your progress. He doesn't plan on making an objection to the suspended sentence and probation we expect from Judge Beckett."

"I knew I could count on you, but I wasn't just thinking about that."

She knew very well what he was thinking of, and she'd put off dealing with it long enough. "Rio—" she set the plate aside "—I need to talk to Nick for a minute. Can you handle things without him if we go upstairs?"

"No problem. He just wash twice as fast when he come back."

She would be calm, Rachel promised herself as they started upstairs. She would be logical, and she would be in control. "Okay, Nick," she said the minute they stepped into the apartment. And that was all she said, because she found herself being thoroughly kissed. "Stop." Her voice was muffled, but it was firm, and the hands she shoved against his shoulders did the rest.

"I've missed you, that's all." He gentled his grip, then released her completely when she stepped back. "It's been a long time since we had a chance to be alone."

Pressing her hands to her temples, she sighed. "Oh, Nick. I've made a mess of this." The confused churning of emotion was clear in her eyes as she stared at him. "I kept telling myself it would resolve itself, even though I knew it wouldn't." In a gesture that mirrored the helplessness she was feeling, she let her hands drop to her sides. "I don't want to hurt you."

There was a quick warning twist in his gut. People only said that stuff about not hurting you in that particular tone of voice when they were about to. "What are you talking about?"

"About you and me—about you thinking there's a you and me." She turned away, hoping she could find the right words. "I tried to explain it to you before, but I did a poor job of it. You see, initially I was so surprised that you would think of me that way. I didn't—" With a sound of disgust, she turned to face him again. "I'm not handling it any better now."

"Why don't you just say what you mean?"

"I care about you, not only as my client, but as a person."

That all-too-familiar light came into his eyes. "I care about you, too."

When he took a step toward her, she lifted her hands, palms out. "But not that way, Nick. Not…romantically."

His eyes narrowed, and she watched, hurting, as he absorbed the rejection. "You're not interested in me."

"I am interested in you, but not the way you think you'd like me to be."

"I get the picture." Trying to tough it out, he hooked his thumbs in his front pockets. "You think I'm too young."

She thought about the way she'd just been kissed, and

let out a long breath. "That argument doesn't seem altogether valid. It should, but you're not a typical teenager."

"So what is it? I'm just not your type?"

When she thought of how much he and Zack had in common, she had to block a quick laugh. "That doesn't work either." Sorry that she was going to hurt him, knowing she had to, Rachel did her best with the truth. "What I feel for you is the same sort of thing I feel for my brothers. I'm sorry it's not what you want, Nick, but it's all I can give." She wanted to reach out, touch his arm, but she was afraid he'd shrug her off. "I'm sorry, too, that I didn't put it just that way weeks ago. I didn't seem to know how."

"I feel like an idiot."

"Don't." She couldn't keep herself from reaching out now, taking his hand in hers. "There's nothing for you to feel like an idiot about. You were attracted, and you were honest about it. And underneath all my confusion and dismay," she added, trying out a smile, "I was very flattered."

"I'd rather you said you were tempted."

"Maybe." Her smile warmed, squeezing his battered heart. "For a moment. I hope it doesn't hurt you to have me say it, but I do want to be your friend."

"Well, you gave it to me straight." And he supposed he would have to accept it. A babe was just a babe, he tried to tell himself. But he knew there was no one else like Rachel. "No hard feelings."

"Good." She wanted to kiss him, but figured it was best not to push her luck. Or his. She did take his other hand. "I always wanted a younger brother."

He wasn't quite ready to take that position. "Why?"

"For the purest of reasons," she told him. "To have

somebody I could push around." When he smiled, she
felt the first genuine tug of relief. "Come on, get back
to work."

She walked down with him, certain they had progressed to the next stage. To reassure herself, she stayed
in the kitchen for a few minutes, pleased when she felt
no lingering tension from Nick's direction.

When she slipped out, she looked immediately for
Zack.

"In the office," Pete told her, grinning. "You should
go right on in."

"Thanks." She was puzzled by the chuckles that rumbled around the bar, but when she glanced back, everyone looked busy and innocent. Too innocent, Rachel
thought as she pushed open Zack's office door.

He was there all right, big as life, standing in front of
his shipshape desk. There was a curvy blonde wrapped
around him, clinging like cellophane.

With one brow arched, Rachel took in the scene. The
blonde was doing her best to crawl up Zack's body. She
nearly had him pinned to the desk, and Zack was tugging at the arms that roped his neck. The expression on
his face, Rachel mused—a kind of baffled embarrassment—was worth the price of admission all by itself.

"Listen, honey, I appreciate the offer. Really. But I'm
not—" He broke off when he spotted Rachel.

That expression, she decided, was even better. This
one had traces of shock, chagrin and apology, all seasoned with a nice dollop of fear.

"Oh, God." He managed to pry one arm from around
his neck, and he tried to shake her off, but she trans-
ferred her grip to his waist.

"Excuse me," Rachel said, her tongue firmly in her cheek. "I can see you're busy."

"Damn it, don't shut the door." His eyes widened when the blonde shifted to give his bottom a nice, intimate squeeze. "Give me a break, Rachel."

"You want a break?" She glanced back to where the regulars had moved closer, craning their necks to catch the show. "He wants a break," she told them. Very casually, she strolled across the threshold. "Which leg would you like me to break, Muldoon? Or would you prefer an arm? Maybe your neck."

"Have a heart." The blonde was giggling now as she tugged at his sweater. "Help me get her off. She's plowed."

"I'd think a big strong man like you could handle that all by yourself."

"She moves like a damn eel," he muttered. "Come on, Babs, let go. I'll call you a cab."

She was slithering over him, Rachel noted, and with a sigh she took charge. Gripping the blonde's artfully tangled mane in one hand, she tugged. Hard. The quick squeal of pain was very satisfying. Following up on it, Rachel shoved her face close. "You're trespassing, dear."

Babs weaved, gave a glazed-eyed grin. "I didn't see any signs."

"Consider yourself lucky I don't make you see stars." Using the hair as a leash, Rachel pulled the squeaking blonde to the door. "This way out."

"I'll take it from here." Lola slipped an arm around the blonde's waist. "Come on, sweetie, you're looking a little green."

"He's just so damn cute," Babs sighed as she stumbled toward the ladies' room with Lola.

"Call her a cab," Zack shouted. After one heated glare at the grinning faces of his customers, he slammed the door shut. "Listen, Rachel…" Besides being mortified, he was out of breath, and he took a moment to steady himself. "It wasn't the way it looked."

"Oh?" The situation was too entertaining to resist. She sauntered over to his desk, scooted onto the edge and crossed her legs. "How did it look, Muldoon?"

"You know damn well." He blew out a breath, tucked his useless hands in his pockets. "She got herself wasted on a couple of stingers. I came in to call her a cab, and she followed me." His brows drew together when Rachel lifted a hand to examine her nails. "She attacked me."

"Want to press charges?"

"Don't get cute with me." As embarrassing moments went, Zack considered this in the top ten. "I was trying to…defend myself."

"I could see it was a pitched battle. You're lucky you came out of it alive."

"What was I supposed to do, knock her cold?" He paced from one wall to the other. "I told her I wasn't interested, but she wouldn't back off."

"You're just so damn cute," Rachel said, fluttering her lashes.

"Funny," he tossed over his shoulder. "Really funny. You're going to play this one out all the way, aren't you?"

"Bingo." She picked up a letter opener from his desk, tested the point, thoughtfully. "As counsel for the defense, I have to ask if you feel that strutting behind the bar in those snug black jeans—"

"I don't strut."

"I'll rephrase the question." She flicked the tip of

the letter opener with her thumb. "Can you say—and I remind you, Mr. Muldoon, you're under oath—can you tell this court you haven't done anything to entice the defendant, to make her believe you were available? Even willing?"

"I never… Well, I might have before you…" As a man of the sea, Zack knew when to cut line. He crossed his arms over his chest. "I take the Fifth."

"Coward."

"You bet." He eyed the letter opener warily. "You don't plan to use that on any particularly sensitive part of my anatomy?"

Letting her gaze skim down, Rachel touched her tongue to her upper lip. "Probably not."

His smile came slowly and was full of relief. "You're really not mad, are you, sugar?"

"That I walked in and found you in a compromising position with a blonde bombshell?" After a quick laugh, she shifted her grip on the letter opener. "Why should I be mad, sugar?"

"You may have saved my life." He thought he'd gauged her mood correctly, but his approach was still cautious. "You don't know what she said she was going to do to me." He gave a mock shudder, and slipped his arms around her, as if for support. "She's a yoga instructor."

"Oh, my." Biting back a grin, Rachel patted his back. "What did she threaten you with?"

"Well, I think it went something like…" He leaned close to her ear, whispering. He heard Rachel's surprised chuckle. "And then…"

"Oh, *my*" was all she could say. She swallowed once. "Do you think that's anatomically possible?"

"I think you'd have to be double-jointed, but we could give it a try."

Wicked laughter gleaming in her eyes, she tilted her head back. "I don't care what you say, Muldoon. I think you liked being pawed."

"Uh-uh." He nuzzled her neck. "It was degrading. I feel so…cheap."

"There, there. I saved you."

"You were a regular Viking."

"And you know what they say about Vikings…" she murmured as she turned her mouth to his.

"Go ahead," he said invitingly. "Use me."

"Oh, I plan to."

The kiss was long and satisfying, but as it began to heat he tore his mouth from hers to bury his face in her hair.

"Rachel, you don't know how good you feel. How right."

"I know this feels right." Eyes shut tightly, she held him close.

"Do you?"

"Yes. I think…" She let her words trail off into a sigh. She'd been doing a great deal of thinking over the past few days. "I think sometimes people just fit. The way you told me once before."

He drew back, cupping her face in his hands. His eyes were very dark, very intense, on hers. She wasn't entirely sure what she was reading in them, but it made her heart trip-hammer into her throat. "We fit. I know you said you didn't want to get involved. That you have priorities."

She linked her fingers around his wrists. "I said a lot of things."

"Rachel, I want you to move in with me." He saw the surprise in her eyes and hurried on before she could answer. "I know you wanted to keep it simple. So did I. This doesn't have to be a complication. You'd have time to think about it. We have to wait until everything's straightened out with Nick. But I need for you to know how much I want to be with you—not just snatching time."

She let out an unsteady breath. "It's a big step."

"And you don't do things on impulse." He lowered his lips to brush hers. "Think about it. Think about this," he whispered, and took the kiss deep, deep, fathoms deep, until thinking was impossible.

"Zack, I need to—" Nick burst into the office, and froze. He saw Rachel pressed against his brother, her hands fisted in his hair, her eyes soft and clouded.

They cleared quickly enough, and now there was alarm there, and apology. But as Nick stared at them, all he could see was the red mist of betrayal.

She shouted his name as Nick leaped. Zack saw the blow coming, and he let it connect. It rocked him back on his heels. He tasted blood. Instinct had him gripping Nick's wrists to prevent another punch, but Nick twisted away, agile as a snake, and braced for the next round.

"Stop it!" Heedless that the next fist could fly any second, Rachel stepped furiously between them, shoving them apart. "This isn't the way."

Clamping down on his own temper, Zack merely lifted her up and set her aside. "Stay clear. You want to go a round in here?" he said to Nick. "Or take it outside?"

"Of all the—"

"Anywhere you say," Nick snapped, cutting Rachel

off. "You son of a bitch. It was always you." He shoved, but the bright hurt in his eyes kept Zack from striking back. "You always had to come out on top, didn't you?" His breathing was labored as he rammed Zack back against the wall. "All this crap about family. Well, you know where you can stick it, *bro*."

"Nick, please." Rachel lifted a hand, but let it drop when he turned those furious eyes on her.

"Just shut up. That whole line of bull you handed me upstairs. You've got real talent, lady, because I was buying it. You knew how I felt, and all the time you're making it with him behind my back."

"Nick, it wasn't like that."

"You lying bitch."

His head snapped back when Zack clipped him with a backhand. There was blood on both sides now. "You want to take a swing at me, go ahead. But you don't talk to her like that."

Teeth gritted, Nick wiped the blood from his lip. He wanted to hate. Needed to. "The hell with you. The hell with both of you."

He swung on his heel and darted out.

"Oh, God." Rachel covered her face, but it did nothing to erase the image of the hurt she'd seen in Nick's eyes. The damage, she thought miserably, that she had done. "What a mess. I'm going after him."

"Leave him alone."

"It's my fault," she said, dropping her arms to her sides. "I have to try."

"I said leave him alone."

"Damn it, Zack—"

"Excuse me." There was a rap on the door, which

Nick had left hanging open. Rachel turned and bit back a groan.

"Judge Beckett."

"Good evening, Ms. Stanislaski. Mr. Muldoon, I dropped in for one of your famous manhattans. Perhaps you could mix one for me while I have a conference with your brother's attorney."

"Your Honor," Rachel began, "my client…"

"I saw your client as he roared out of here. Your mouth's bleeding, Mr. Muldoon." She turned and shot a look at Rachel. "Counselor?"

"Perfect timing," Rachel said under her breath. "I'll handle this," she said to Zack. "Don't worry. And once Nick works off a little steam—"

"He'll come back smiling?" Zack finished. His temper was fading, but guilt was moving full steam ahead. "I don't think so. And it's not your fault." He wished he had more than his own empty sense of failure to give her. "He's my brother. I'm responsible." He shook his head before she could speak. "Let me go fix the judge her drink."

He brushed by her. Rachel reached out to stop him, then let her hand fall away. There was nothing she could say to ease the hurt. But she had a chance to minimize the damage with Judge Beckett.

She found the judge looking attractive and relaxed at a table on the far side of the bar. Yet the aura of power the woman had when wearing black robes on the bench wasn't diminished in the least by the trim blue slacks and white sweater she wore tonight.

"Have a seat, Counselor."

"Thank you."

Beckett smiled, tapping rose-tipped nails on the edge

of the table. "I can see the wheels turning. How much do I tell her, how much do I evade? I always enjoy having you in my courtroom, Ms. Stanislaski. You have style."

"Thank you," Rachel said again. Their drinks arrived, and she took the time while they were served to gather her thoughts. "I'm afraid you might, understandably, misinterpret what you saw tonight, Your Honor."

"Are you?" With a smile, Beckett sampled her drink. She shifted her gaze to meet Zack's and sent him an approving smile. "And what would you consider my interpretation?"

"Obviously, Nick and his brother were arguing."

"Fighting," Beckett corrected, stirring the cherry around in her drink before biting it from its stem. "Arguing involves words. And, while words may leave scars, they don't draw blood."

"You don't have brothers, do you, Your Honor?"

"No, I don't."

"I do."

With a lift of a brow, Beckett sipped again. "All right, I'll sustain that. What were they arguing about?"

Rachel eased around the boggy ground. "It was just a misunderstanding. I won't deny both of them are hotheaded, and that with their type of temperament a misunderstanding can sometimes evolve into…"

"An argument?" Beckett suggested.

"Yes." Needing to make her point, Rachel leaned forward. "Judge Beckett, Nick has been making such incredible progress. When I was first assigned to his case, I very nearly dismissed him as just another street punk. But there was something that made me reevaluate him."

"Haunted eyes do that to a woman."

Surprised, Rachel blinked. "Yes."

"Go on."

"He was so young, and yet he'd already started to give up on himself, and everyone else. After I met Zack, and found out about Nick's background, it was easy to understand. There's never been anyone permanent in his life, anyone he felt he could count on and trust. But with Zack…he wanted to. No matter how tough and disinterested he tried to act, the longer he was with Zack, the more you could see that they needed each other."

"Just how involved are you with your co-guardian?"

With her face carefully blank, Rachel sat back in her seat. "I believe that's irrelevant."

"Do you? Well." She gestured with her hand. "Continue."

"For nearly two months, Nick has stayed out of trouble. He's been handling the responsibilities Zack has given him. He's developing outside interests. He plays the piano."

"Does he?"

"Zack bought him one when he found out."

"That doesn't seem like something that would make fists fly." A faint smile played around her mouth as she gestured with her manhattan. "You're dodging the point, Counselor."

"I want you to understand that this probationary period has been successful. What happened tonight was simply a product of misunderstandings and hot tempers. It was the exception rather than the rule."

"You're not in court."

"No, Your Honor, but I don't want you to hold this against my client when I am."

"Agreed." Pleased with what she saw in Rachel, what

she heard, and what she sensed, Beckett rattled the ice in her glass. "Explain tonight."

"It was my fault," Rachel said, pushing her wine aside. "It was poor judgment on my part that caused Nick to feel, to believe he felt...something."

Beckett pursed her lips. "I begin to see. He's a healthy young man, and you're an attractive woman who's shown an interest in him."

"And I blew it," Rachel said bitterly. "I thought I'd handled it. I was so damn sure I was on top of everything."

"I know the feeling." Beckett sampled a beer nut thoughtfully. "Off the record. Start at the beginning."

Hoping her own culpability would lighten Nick's load, even if it got her thrown off the case, Rachel explained. Beckett said nothing, only nodding or making interested noises now and again. "And when he walked into the office and saw Zack and me together," she concluded, "all he saw was betrayal. I know I had no right to become involved with Zack. Excuses don't cut it."

"Rachel, you're an excellent attorney. That doesn't preclude your having a private life."

"When it endangers my relationship with a client—"

"Don't interrupt. I'll grant that you may have exercised poor judgment in this instance. I'll also grant that one can't always choose the time, place or circumstances for falling in love."

"I didn't say I was in love."

Beckett smiled. "I noticed that. It's easier to beat yourself up about it if you tell yourself love had nothing to do with it." Her smile widened. "No rebuttal, Counselor? Just as well, because I haven't finished. I could tell you you've lost your objectivity, but you already know that. I, for one, am not entirely sure objectivity is always the answer. There are so many shades between right and wrong. Finding the one that fits is something we struggle with every day. Your client is trying to find his. You may not be able to help."

"I don't want to let him down."

"Better you should do what's possible to prevent him from letting himself down. Sometimes it works, sometimes it doesn't. You'll discover how often it doesn't when it's your turn to sit on the bench."

The understanding in Beckett's eyes had Rachel reaching for her wine again. "I didn't know I was that transparent."

"Oh, to one who's been there, certainly." Amused, Beckett tapped her glass against Rachel's. "A few more years of seasoning, Counselor, and you'll make quite a competent judge. That *is* what you want?"

"Yes." She met Beckett's eyes levelly. "That's exactly what I want."

"Good. Now, since I've had a drink and I'm feeling rather mellow, I'll tell you something—off the record. It was almost thirty years ago that I was you. So very close to who and what you are. Things were more difficult for women in our position than they are now. They're far from perfect now," she added, setting her glass aside, "but some of the battles are over. I had to make choices. Those professional-versus-personal choices that men rarely have to make. Do I have a family or do I have a career? I don't regret choosing my career."

She glanced back at the bar, at Zack, and sighed. "Or only rarely. But times change, and even a professionally ambitious woman doesn't have to make an either-or decision. She can have both, if she's clever. You strike me as a clever woman."

"I like to think so," Rachel murmured. "But it doesn't make it any less terrifying."

"That kind of terror makes life worthwhile. I don't think nerves will stop you, Counselor. I don't think anything will. In the meantime, see that you and your client are prepared for the hearing."

When Beckett rose, Rachel was instantly on her feet. "Judge Beckett, about tonight—"

"I came in for a drink. It's a nice bar. Clean, friendly. As for my decision, that will depend on what I see and hear in my courtroom. Understood?"

"Yes. Thank you."

"Tell Mr. Muldoon he makes an excellent manhattan."

With her emotions still in a state of upheaval, Rachel watched Beckett stroll out.

"How bad is it?" Zack asked from behind her.

Rachel merely shook her head, reaching back to take his hand. "She likes the way you mix a drink." Turning to him, she comforted him with a hug. "And I think I've just met another intelligent woman with a weakness for bad boys. It's going to be all right."

"If Nick doesn't come back…"

"He'll be back." She needed to believe it. Needed to make Zack believe it. "He's mad, and he's hurt, but he's not stupid." She gave his hand another quick squeeze and smiled up at him. "He's too much like you."

"I shouldn't have hit him."

"Intellectually, I agree. Emotionally…" Because passion was a part of her life, she shrugged it off. "I've seen my brothers pound on each other too often to believe it's the end of the world. I've got to go." She touched a gentle kiss to his swollen lip. "When he comes back, it's probably best if I'm not here. But I want you to call me when he shows up, no matter what time it is."

"I don't like you going home alone," he said as he walked with her to where her coat was hanging.

"I'll take a cab." The fact that he didn't argue made her realize just how distracted he was. "We're going to work this out, Zack. Trust me."

"Yeah. I'll call you."

She stepped outside and headed down to the corner to hail a cab. Trust me, she'd told him. She could only hope she deserved that trust.

Chapter 11

She nearly called Alex when she got home, but she was afraid that if her brother put out feelers, even unofficially, Nick would only be more furious.

All she could do was wait. And wait alone.

An odd triangle they made, she thought as she wandered restlessly around her apartment with a rapidly cooling cup of tea. Nick, young and defiant, seeing rejection and betrayal everywhere, even as he looked so desperately for his place in the world. And Zack, so innately generous, so fueled by passion and so vulnerable to his brother. And herself, the objective, logical and ambitious attorney who'd fallen in love with them both.

Maybe she should be writing soap operas, she thought as she dropped down on the couch. She curled up her legs, cupping her mug in both hands. If she had the imagination for that, at least she might be able to write herself out of this situation.

Oh, how had it happened? she wondered, and closed her tired eyes. She was the one who had had things aligned so clearly. Hadn't she always known exactly where she was going and how she was going to get there? Every obstacle that could possibly block her path had been considered and weighed. All the options, all the ways of going around or through those obstacles, had been calculated.

All of them.

Except Zackary Muldoon.

By becoming involved with him, by letting her emotions rule her head, she'd made a mess of everything. It was entirely possible that Nick, pumped by hurt and frustration, would race headlong into trouble before the night was over. However understanding and compassionate Judge Beckett was, if Nick broke his probation, she would have no choice but to sentence him.

Even if the sentence was light, how could she forgive herself? How could Zack forgive her for failing? And, worst of all, how could Nick rebound from that final rejection when society put him behind bars?

She wanted to believe he'd go back to Zack. Angry, yes…defiant, certainly…maybe even spoiling for a fight. All those things could be dealt with, if only he went back.

But if he didn't…

The sound of her buzzer had her jolting. Well aware that it was after midnight, she unfolded herself, hoping it was Zack coming by to tell her Nick was safe and sound.

"Yes?"

"I want to come up." It was Nick's voice, edgy and demanding. Rachel had to bite back a cry of relief.

"Sure." She kept her tone light as she released the lock. "Come ahead."

She pressed her fingers against her eyes to push back the tears that filled them. It was stupid to get so emotional. Hadn't logic told her he'd have to come back? Hadn't she said as much to Zack?

But when the knock rapped sharply at her door, she was swinging it open, and the words were tumbling out. "I was so worried. I was going to go after you, but I didn't know where to start to look. Oh, Nick, I'm sorry. I'm so sorry."

"Sorry it blew up in your face?" He shoved the door closed behind him. He hadn't intended to come here, but he'd been walking, walking. Then it had seemed like the only place to go. "Sorry I came in and found you with Zack?"

It was far from over, Rachel realized. What she saw in his eyes was just as dangerous as what had been in them when he'd leaped across the office at Zack. "I'm sorry I hurt you."

"You're sorry I found out what you really are. You're nothing but a liar."

"I never lied to you."

"Every time you opened your mouth." He hadn't moved away from the door, and his hands were balled into fists, white-knuckled, at his side. "You and Zack. The whole time you were pretending to care about me, acting as if you liked being with me, you were making it with him."

"I do care—" she began, but he cut her off.

"I can see what a kick the two of you must've gotten

out of it. Poor, pathetic Nick, mooning around, trying to make something of himself because he had a case on the sexy lawyer. I guess the two of you lay in bed and laughed yourself sick."

"No. It was never like that."

"Are you going to tell me you didn't go to bed with him?"

He saw the truth in her eyes before her own temper kicked in. "You're out of line. I'm not going to discuss—"

His hands shot out, snatching the lapels of her robe and swinging her around. Her back rammed hard into the door. The first bubble of fear evaporated in her throat as Nick pushed his face close to hers. All she could see was his eyes, sharp green and glinting with fury.

"Why did you do it? Why did you have to make a fool out of me? Why did it have to be my brother?"

"Nick." She had his wrists now, and she tried to drag them away. But rage had added weight to his sinewy strength.

"Do you know how it makes me feel to know that while I was imagining us you were with him? And he knew. He knew."

Her breath was hitching, but she fought to control it. "You're hurting me."

She thought the statement would come out calm, even authoritative. Instead, it was shaky, and the fear underneath it clear even in his reckless state. His eyes went blank for a moment, then focused on his hands. They were digging into her shoulders. Appalled, he pulled them away and stared at her.

"I'm going."

Sometimes all you had was impulse. Rachel went with it and pressed her back against the door. "Don't. Please. Don't go like this."

There was a churning in his stomach that was pure self-loathing. "I never pushed a woman around before. It's as low as it gets."

"You didn't hurt me. I'm okay."

What she was, he noted, was deathly pale. "You're shaking."

"Okay, I'm shaking. Can we sit down?"

"I shouldn't have come here, Rachel. I shouldn't have jumped on you that way."

"I'm glad you came. Let's leave it at that for a minute. Please, let's sit down."

Because he was afraid she'd stay pressed against the door trembling until he agreed, he nodded. "You've got some things to toss back at me. I figure I owe you that." As he sat, his shoulders slumped. "I guess you'll ask to be taken off the case."

"That has nothing to do with this. But no." She thought about picking up her cold tea, but she was afraid her hands weren't steady enough. "This is personal, Nick. I'm the one who screwed up by blurring the lines. I knew better. There's no excuse." Inhaling deeply, she linked her fingers in her lap. "What happened between Zack and me wasn't planned, and it certainly wasn't professional."

He gave a quick snort. "Now you're going to tell me you couldn't help yourself."

"No," she said quietly. "I could have. There's always a choice. I didn't want to help myself."

Her answer, and the tone of it, had him frowning.

He'd been certain she would try to find an easy way out. "So, you chose him."

"What happened was immediate, and maybe a little overwhelming..." She wasn't certain there were words to describe what had happened between her and Zack. "In any case, I could have stopped it. Or at least postponed it. I didn't, and that fault lies with me. The fact that we were both your guardians made it a poor call, but—" She shook her head. "No buts. It was a poor call." Her eyes met his, pleaded for trust. "We never thought of you as poor or pathetic. We never laughed at you. Whatever you think of me, don't let it ruin what you've started to get back with Zack."

"He moved in on me."

"Nick." Her voice held both patience and compassion. "He didn't. You know he didn't."

He did know, wondered if he had always known, that his relationship with Rachel had never been anything more than a fantasy. But knowing it didn't ease the raw wounds of rejection.

"I cared about you."

"I know." Her eyes filled again, and spilled over before she could prevent it. "I'm sorry."

"God, Rachel. Don't." He didn't think he could stand it. First he'd terrified her, and now he was making her cry. "Don't do that."

"I won't." But as quickly as she swiped at the tears, more fell. "I just feel so lousy about it all. When I look back, I can see a dozen ways I should've handled things. I'm usually in control." Her breath hitched as she fought for composure. "I hate, I really hate, that I've come between the two of you."

"Hey, come on." He was totally at a loss. When he

rose to cross to her, he was surprised he didn't leave a trail of slime on her rug. "Listen, take it easy, okay?" He patted her shoulder awkwardly. "I've been dumped before."

All that did was force her to fumble in the pocket of her robe for a tissue. "Don't hate him because of this."

"Don't ask for miracles."

"Oh, Nick, if you could only see through all the mistakes to what you mean to him."

"No lectures." Since her tears seemed to be drying up, he felt he could take a stand on that. "You carry on like you're in love with him." He was stunned when he saw the look in her eyes, the miserable, heartsick look, before they filled again. "Oh, man." While she crumpled into sobs, he readjusted his thinking. "You mean it's not just sex?"

"It was supposed to be." His arm went around her tentatively, and she leaned into it. "Oh, God, how did I get into all this? I don't want to be in love with anybody."

"That's rough." It occurred to Nick that he was holding her close but there weren't any tingles or tugs. The hell of it was, he was feeling almost brotherly. No one had ever cried on his shoulder before, or looked to him for support. "How about him? Is he stuck in the same groove?"

"I don't know." She sniffled, blew her nose. "We haven't talked about it. We aren't going to talk about it. The whole thing's ridiculous. I'm ridiculous." Thoroughly ashamed, she eased back. "Let's just say it's been an emotional night all around. Please, don't say anything to him about this."

"I figure that's up to you."

"Good. I appreciate it." Still shaky, she wiped at a stray tear with the back of her hand. "Don't hate me too much."

"I don't hate you." He leaned back, suddenly exhausted. "I don't know what I feel. Maybe I thought I could come up here tonight and prove to you I was the better man. Pretty stupid."

"You're both pretty special," she told him. "Why else would a nice, sensible woman like me fall for both of you?"

He turned his head to give her a weak smile. "You sure can pick 'em."

"Yeah." She touched his cheek. "I sure can. Tell me you're going back."

His lips flattened. "Where else would I go?"

That didn't satisfy her. "Tell me you're going back to talk things through with him, to work things out."

"I can't tell you that."

When he started to stand, she took his hand. "Let me go back with you. I want to help. I need to feel as though I've made some of this up to the two of you."

"You didn't do anything but fall for the wrong guy."

She took a great deal of comfort from the familiar smirk. "You may be right. Let me come anyway."

"Suit yourself. You might want to wash your face. Your eyes are red."

"Great. Give me five minutes."

Rachel could feel Nick start to tense up half a block from Lower the Boom. His shoulders were hunched, his brows were lowered, his hands were jammed in his pockets.

Typical, she thought. The male animal ruffles his

fur and bares his teeth to show the opposing male how tough he is.

She kept the observation to herself, knowing neither of these males would appreciate it.

"Here's the idea," she said, pausing by the door. "It was a pretty slow night, and it's already after one. We'll wait until the bar closes, and you two can say your piece. I'll be mediator."

Nick wondered if she had any idea how hard it was for him to face what was on the other side of that door. "Whatever."

"And if there are any punches thrown," she added as she pulled the door open, "I'll throw them."

That brought the ghost of a smile to his face. It faded as soon as they stepped in.

Rachel had been right. It was a slow night, as it often was in the middle of the week. Most of the regulars had already headed off to home and hearth. A few diehards lingered at the bar, which Zack was manning alone. Lola was busy wiping down the tables. She glanced up, shot Rachel a satisfied look, then went back to work.

Zack took a pull from a bottle of mineral water. Rachel saw his eyes change, recognized the relief in them before the shutters came down.

"Hey, barkeep—" Rachel slid onto a stool "—got any coffee?"

"Sure."

"Make it two," she said, sending a meaningful glance in Nick's direction.

He said nothing, but he did sit beside her.

"There's an old Ukrainian tradition," she began when Zack set the cups on the bar. "It's called a family meeting. Are you up for it?"

"Yeah." Zack inclined his head toward his brother. "I guess I can handle it. What about you?"

"I'm here," Nick muttered.

"Hey." A man, obviously well on his way to being drunk, leaned heavily on the bar a few stools away. "Am I going to get another bourbon over here?"

"Nope." Carrying the pot, Zack crossed over. "But you can have coffee on the house."

The man scowled through red-rimmed eyes. "What the hell are you, a social worker?"

"That's me."

"I said I want a damn drink."

"You're not going to get another one here."

The drunk reached out and grabbed a handful of Zack's sweater. Considering Zack's size, Rachel took this to be a testament to the bourbon already in his system.

"This a bar or a church?"

Something flickered in Zack's eyes. Rachel recognized it, and was slipping out of her seat when Nick clamped a warning hand on hers.

"He'll handle it," he said simply.

Zack lowered his gaze to the hands on his sweater, then shifted it back to the irate customer's face. When he spoke, his voice was surprisingly mild. "Funny you should ask. I knew this guy once, down in New Orleans. He favored bourbon, too. One night he went from bar to bar, knocking them back, then staggering back out on the street. Story goes that he got so blind drunk he wandered into a church, thinking it was another bar. Weaved his way up to the front—you know, where the altar is? Slammed his fist down and ordered himself a double. Then he dropped dead. Stone dead." Zack pried the fingers from his sweater. "The way I figure it, if you drink enough bourbon so you don't know where you are, you could wake up dead in church."

The man swore and snatched up the coffee. "I know where the hell I am."

"That's good news. We hate hauling out corpses."

Rachel heard Nick's muffled chuckle and grinned. "Truth or lie?" she whispered.

"Probably some of both. He always knows how to handle the drunks."

"He wasn't doing very well with the blonde earlier."

"What blonde?"

"Another story," Rachel said, and smiled into her coffee. "Another time. Listen, would you be more comfortable doing this upstairs, or—" She broke off when she heard a crash from the kitchen. "Lord, it sounds like Rio knocked over the refrigerator." She started to rise and go check. Then froze. The kitchen door swung open. Rio staggered out, blood running down his face from a wound on his forehead. Behind him was a man in a stocking mask. He was holding a very large gun to Rio's throat.

"Party time," he snarled, then shoved the big man forward with the butt of the gun.

"Jumped me," Rio said in disgust as he staggered against the bar. "Come in front upstairs."

There was a quick giggle as two more armed men, their features distorted by their nylon masks, stepped in. "Don't anybody move." One of them accentuated the order by blasting away at the ship's bell over the bar. It clanged wildly.

"Lock the front door, you jerk." The first man gestured furiously. "And no shooting unless I say so. Everybody empty their pockets on the bar. Make it fast." He gestured the third man into position so that the whole bar was covered. "Wallets, jewelry, too. Hey, you." He lifted the barrel of the gun toward Lola. "Dump out those tips, sweetheart. You look like you'd earn plenty."

Nick didn't move. Couldn't. He knew the voice. Despite the distorted features, all three gunmen were easy for him to recognize. T.J.'s giggle and shambling walk. Cash's battered denim jacket. The scar on Reece's wrist where an Hombre blade had caught him.

These were his friends. His family.

"What the hell are you doing?" he demanded as T.J. pranced around the bar, scooping the take into a laundry bag.

"Empty them," Reece demanded.

"You've got to be crazy."

"Do it!" He swung the barrel toward Rachel. "And shut the hell up."

Nick kept his eyes on Reece as he complied. "This is the end, man. You crossed the line."

Behind the mask, Reece only grinned. "On the floor!" he shouted. "Facedown, hands behind your heads. Not you," he said to Zack. "You empty out the cash register. And you—" he grabbed Rachel's arm "—you look like mighty fine insurance. Anybody gets any ideas, I cash her in."

"Leave her the hell—"

"Nick!" Zack's quick and quiet order cut him off. "Back off." As he emptied the till, he watched Reece. "You don't need her."

"But I like her."

Rachel swallowed as the hand tightened on her arm, squeezing experimentally.

"Fresh meat," he called out, smacking his lips. T.J. erupted into giggles. "Maybe we'll take you along with us, sweet thing. Show you a real good time."

The furious retort burned the tip of her tongue. Rachel gritted her teeth against it. The heel of her foot on his instep, she thought. An elbow to his windpipe. She could do it, and the idea of taking him out had her blood pumping fast. But if she did, she knew the other two would open fire.

When Nick strained forward, Reece locked his arm around Rachel's throat. "Try it, dishwasher." His teeth flashed in a brutal challenge. "Do it, man. Take me on."

"Cool it." Reece's attitude toward the woman was making Cash nervous. "Come on, we came for the money. Just the money."

"I take what I want." He watched as T.J. scooped the contents of the till into his sack. "Where's the rest?"

"Slow night," Zack told him.

"Don't push me, man. There's a safe in the office. Open it."

"Fine." Zack moved slowly, passing through the opening of the bar. He had to control the urge to fight, to grab the little sneering-voiced punk and pound his face to pulp. "I'll open it as soon as you let her go."

"I got the gun," Reece reminded him. "I give the orders."

"You've got the gun," Zack agreed. "I've got the combination. You want what's in the safe, you let her go."

"Go on," Cash urged. His hands were sweating on the gun he held. "We don't need the babe. Shake her loose."

Reece felt his power slipping as Zack continued to

watch him with cold blue eyes. He wanted to make them tremble. All of them. He wanted them to cry and beg. He was the head of the Cobras. He was in charge. Nobody was going to tell him any different.

"Open it," he said between his teeth. "Or I'll blow a hole in you."

"You won't get what's inside that way." Out of the corner of his eye, Zack saw Rio shift from his prone position. The big man was braced for whatever came. "This is my place," Zack continued. "I don't want anyone hurt in my place. You let the lady go, and you can take what you want."

"Let's trash the dump," T.J. shouted, and swung his gun at the glasses hanging over the bar. Shards went flying, amusing him enough to have him breaking more. "Let's kick butt and trash it." He grabbed up a vodka on the rocks and slurped it down. Then, howling, he hurled the glass to the floor.

The sound of the wreckage, and the muffled cries of the hostages on the floor, pumped Reece full of adrenaline. "Yeah, we'll trash this dump good." Over Cash's halfhearted objections, he fired at the overhead television, blasting out the screen. "That's what I'm going to do to the safe. I don't need a damn woman." He shoved Rachel aside, and she overbalanced, landing on her hands and knees. "And I don't need you."

He swung the gun toward Zack, savoring the moment. He was about to take a life, and that was new. And darkly exciting.

"This is how I give orders."

Even as Zack braced to jump, Nick was springing to his feet. Like a sprinter off the mark, he lunged, hurling full force into Zack as Reece's gun exploded.

There were screams, dozens of them. Rachel swung out with a chair, unaware that one of them was her own. She felt the chair connect, heard a grunt of pain. She caught a glimpse of the mountain that was Rio whiz past. But she was already scrambling over to where Zack and Nick lay limp on the floor.

She saw the blood. Smelled it. Her hands were smeared with it.

The room was like a madhouse around her. Shouts, crashes, running feet. She heard someone weeping. Someone else being sick.

"Oh, God. Oh, please." She was pressing her hands against Nick's chest as Zack sat up, shaking his head clear.

"Rachel. You're—" Then he saw his brother, sprawled on the floor, his face ghostly pale. And the blood seeping rapidly through his shirt. "*No!* Nick, no!" Panicked, Zack grabbed for him, fighting Rachel off as she tried to press her hands to the wound.

"Stop! You have to stop! Listen to me—keep your hands there. Keep the pressure on. I'll get a towel." With prayers whirling in her head, she scrambled up to her feet and dashed behind the bar. "Call an ambulance," she shouted. "Tell them to hurry." Because terror left no room for fumbling, she clamped down on it. Kneeling by Zack, she pushed his hands aside and pressed the folded towel on Nick's wound. "He's young. He's strong." The tears were falling even as she felt frantically for Nick's pulse. "We're not going to let him go."

"Zack." Rio crouched down. "They got away from me. I'm sorry. I'll go after them."

"No." Revenge glittered in his eyes. "I'll go after

them. Later. Get me a blanket for him, Rio. And more towels."

"I've got some." Lola passed them to Rachel, then dropped a hand on Zack's head. "He's a hero, Zack. We don't let our heroes die."

"He got in the way," Zack said as grief welled into his throat. "Damn kid was always getting in the way." He looked at Rachel, then covered her hands with his over his brother's chest. "I can't lose him."

"You won't." She heard the first wail of sirens and shuddered with relief. "We won't."

Endless hours in the waiting room, pacing, smoking, drinking bitter coffee. Zack could still see how pale Nick had been when they rushed him through Emergency and into an elevator that snapped shut in Zack's face.

Helpless. Hospitals always made him feel so helpless. Only a year had passed since he'd watched his father die in one. Slowly, inevitably, pitifully.

But not Nick. He could cling to that. Nick was young, and death wasn't inevitable when you were young.

But the blood. There had been so much blood.

He looked down at the hands that he'd scrubbed clean, and could still see his brother's life splattered across them. In his hands. That was all he could think. Nick's life had been in his hands.

"Zack." He stiffened when Rachel came up behind him and rubbed his shoulders. "How about a walk? Some fresh air?"

He just shook his head. She didn't press. It was useless to suggest he try to rest. She couldn't. Her eyes were burning, but she knew that if she closed them she would see that last horrible instant. The gun swinging toward Zack. Nick leaping. The explosion. The blood.

"I'm going to find food." Rio pushed himself off the sagging sofa. The white bandage gleamed against his dark brow. "And you're going to eat what I bring you. That boy's going to need tending soon. You can't tend when you're sick." With his lips pressed tightly together, he marched out into the hallway.

"He's crazy about Nick," Zack said, half to himself. "It's eating at him that he didn't round up three armed men all by himself."

"We'll find them, Zack."

"I thought he would hurt you. I saw it in his eyes. That kind of sickness can't be disguised by a mask. He was going to hurt somebody, wanted to hurt somebody, and he had you. I never even thought about Nick."

"It's not your fault. No," she said sharply when he tried to pull away. "I won't let you do that to yourself. There were a lot of people in that bar, and you were doing your best to protect all of them. What happened to Nick happened because he was trying to protect you. You're not going to turn an act of love into blame."

This time, when she put her arms around him, he went into them. "I need to talk to him. I don't think I could handle it if I don't get to talk to him."

"You're going to have plenty of time to talk."

"I'm sorry." Alex hesitated at the doorway. His heart was thumping, as it had been ever since he'd gotten the news. "Rachel, are you all right?"

"I'm fine." She kept one arm firm around Zack's waist as she turned. "It's Nick…"

"I know. When the call came in, I asked to handle

it. I thought it would be easier on everybody." His eyes shifted to Zack's, held. "Is that okay with you?"

"Yeah. I appreciate it. I've already talked to a couple of cops."

"Why don't we sit down?" He waited while Zack sat on the edge of a chair and lit another cigarette. "Any news on your brother's condition?"

"They took him into surgery. They haven't told us anything."

"I might be able to find something out. Why don't you tell me about these three creeps?"

"They wore stocking masks," Zack began wearily. "Black clothes. One of them wore a denim jacket."

Rachel reached for Zack's hand. "The one who shot Nick was about five-eight or nine," she added. "Black hair, brown eyes. There was a scar on his left wrist. On the side, about two inches long. He wore engineer's boots, worn down at the heel."

"Good girl." Not for the first time, Alex thought that his sister would have made a damn good cop. "How about the other two?"

"The one who wanted to trash the place had a high-pitched giggle," Zack remembered. "Edgy. Skinny guy."

"About five-ten," Rachel put in. "Maybe a hundred and thirty. I didn't get a good look at him, but he had light hair. Sandy blond, I think. The third one was about the same height, but stockier. At a guess, I'd say the guns made him nervous. He was sweating a lot."

"How about age?"

"Hard to say." She looked at Zack. "Young. Early twenties?"

"About. What are the chances of catching them?"

"Better with this." Alex closed his notebook. "Look,

I won't con you. It won't be easy. Now if they left prints, and the prints are on file, that's one thing. But we're going to work on it. *I'm* going to work on it," he added. "You could say I've got a vested interest."

"Yeah." Zack looked at Rachel. "I guess you do."

"Not just for her," Alex said. "I've got a stake in the kid, too. I like to see the system work, Muldoon."

"Mr. Muldoon?" A woman of about fifty dressed in green scrubs came into the room. When Zack started to rise, she gestured to him to stay where he was. "I'm Dr. Markowitz, your brother's surgeon."

"How—" He had to pause and try again. "How is he?"

"Tough." As a concession to aching feet and lower back pain, she sat on the arm of a chair. "You want all the technical jargon so I can show off, or you want the bottom line?"

The next lick of fear had his palms damp. "Bottom line."

"He's critical. And he's damn lucky, not only to have had me, but to have taken a bullet at close range that missed the heart. I put his chances now at about seventy-five percent. With luck, and the constitution of youth, we'll be able to bump that up within twenty-four hours."

The coffee churned violently in his stomach. "Are you telling me he's going to make it?"

"I'm telling you I don't like to work that hard and long on anyone and lose them. We're going to keep him in ICU for now."

"Can I see him?"

"I'll have someone come down and let you know when he's out of Recovery." She stifled a yawn and noted that she'd spent yet another sunrise in an operating room. "You want all the crap about how he'll be out for several more hours, won't know you're there, and how you should go home and get some rest?"

"No thanks."

She rubbed her eyes and smiled. "I didn't think so. He's a good-looking boy, Mr. Muldoon. I'm looking forward to chatting with him."

"Thanks. Thanks a lot."

"I'll be checking in on him." She rose, stretched, and narrowed her eyes at Alex. "Cop."

"Yes, ma'am."

"I can spot them a mile away," she said, and walked out.

Chapter 12

The pain was a thin sheet of agony layered under dizziness. Every time Nick surfaced, he felt it, wondered at it, then slipped away again into a cocoon of comforting unconsciousness. Sometimes he tried to speak, but the words were disjointed and senseless even to him.

He heard a disconcerting beeping, annoying and consistent, that he didn't recognize as his heartbeat on the monitor. The squeak of crepe-soled shoes against tile was muffled by the nice, steady humming in his ears. The occasional prodding and poking as his vital signs were checked and rechecked was only a minor disturbance in the huge, dark lack of awareness that covered him.

Sometimes there was a pressure on his hand, as if someone were holding it. And a murmuring—someone speaking to him. But he couldn't quite drum up the energy to listen.

Once he dreamed of the sea in a hurricane, and watched himself leap off the deck of a pitching ship into blackness. But he never hit bottom. He just floated away.

There were other dreams. Zack standing behind him at a pinball machine, guiding his hands, laughing at the whirl of bells and whistles.

Then Cash was there, leaning on the machine, the smoke from his crooked cigarette curling up in front of his face.

He saw Rachel, smiling at him in a brightly lit room, the smell of pizza and garlic everywhere. And her eyes were bright, interested. Beautiful.

Then they were drenched with tears. Overflowing with apologies.

The old man, shouting at him. He looked so sick as he stumbled to the top of the stairs. *You'll never amount to anything. Knew it the first time I laid eyes on you.* Then that blank, slack look would come over his face, and he could only whine, *Where have you been? Where's Zack? Is he coming back soon?*

But Zack was gone, hundreds of miles away. There was no one to help.

Rio, frying potatoes and cackling over one of his own jokes. And Zack, always back to Zack, coming through the kitchen. *You going to eat all the profits, kid?* An easy grin, a friendly swipe as he went out again.

The gleaming piano—that polished dream—and Zack standing beside it, grinning foolishly. Then the glitter of the overhead light on the barrel of a gun. And Zack—

With a grunt, he threw off sleep, tried to struggle up.

"Hey, hey…take it easy, kid." Zack sprang up from

the chair beside the bed to press a gentle hand on Nick's shoulder. "It's okay. You got no place to go."

He tried to focus, but the images around him kept slipping in and out like phantoms in shadows. "What?" His throat was sand-dry and aching. "Am I sick?"

"You've been better." And so have I, Zack thought, fighting to keep his hand from shaking as he lifted the plastic drinking cup. "They said you could suck on this if you came around again."

Nick took a pull of water through the straw, then another, but didn't have the energy for a third. At least his vision had cleared. He took a long, hard look at Zack. Dark circles under tired eyes in a pale face prickled by a night's growth of beard.

"You look like hell."

Grinning, Zack rubbed a hand over the stubble. "You don't look so hot yourself. Let me call a nurse."

"Nurse." Nick shook his head, almost imperceptibly, then frowned at the IV. "Is this a hospital?"

"It ain't the Ritz. You hurting?"

Nick thought about it and shook his head. "Can't tell. Feel…dopey."

"Well, you are." Swamped with relief, Zack laid a hand on Nick's cheek, left it there until embarrassment had it dropping away. "You're such a jerk, Nick."

Nick was too bleary to hear the catch in Zack's voice. "Was there an accident? I…" And then it came flooding back, a tidal wave of memory. "At the bar." His hand fisted on the sheets. "Rachel? Is Rachel all right?"

"She's fine. Been in and out of here. I had Rio browbeat her into getting something to eat."

"You." Nick took another long look to reassure himself. "He didn't shoot you."

"No, you idiot." His voice broke, then roughened. "He shot you."

When his legs went watery, Zack sat again, buried his face in his hands. The hands were trembling. Nick stared, utterly amazed, as this man he'd always thought was the next best thing to superhuman struggled for composure.

"I could kill you for scaring me like this. If you weren't flat on your back already, I'd damn well put you there."

But insults and threats delivered in a shaky voice held little power. "Hey." Nick lifted a hand, but wasn't sure what to do with it. "You okay?"

"No, I'm not okay," Zack tossed back, and rose to pace to the window. He stared out, seeing nothing, until he felt some portion of control again. "Yeah, yeah, I'm fine. Looks like you're going to be that way, too. They said they'd move you down to a regular room sometime soon, if you rated it."

"Where am I now?" Curious, Nick turned his head to study the room. Glass walls and blinking, beeping machines. "Wow, high tech. How long have I been out?"

"You came around a couple times before. They said you wouldn't remember. You babbled a lot."

"Oh, yeah. About what?"

"Pinball machines." Steadier now, Zack walked back to the bed. "Some girl named Marcie or Marlie. Remind me to pump you on that little number later." It pleased him to see a faint smile curve Nick's lips. "You asked for french fries."

"What can I say? It's a weakness. Did I get any?"

"No. Maybe we'll sneak some in later. Are you hungry?"

"I don't know. You didn't tell me how long."

Zack reached for a cigarette, remembered, and sighed. "About twelve hours since they finished cutting you up and sewing you back together. I figure if he'd shot you in the head instead of the chest, you'd have walked away whistling." He tapped his knuckles on Nick's temple. "Hard as a rock. I owe you one, a big one."

"No, you don't."

"You saved my life."

Nick let his heavy lids close. "It's kind of like jumping off a ship in a hurricane. You don't think about it. Know what I mean?"

"Yeah."

"Zack?"

"Right here."

"I want to talk to a cop."

"You've got to rest."

"I need to talk to a cop," Nick said again as he drifted off. "I know who they were."

Zack watched him sleep and, since there was no one to see, brushed gently at the hair on his brother's forehead.

"I told you his condition is good," Dr. Markowitz repeated. "Go home, Mr. Muldoon."

"Not a chance." Zack leaned against the wall beside the door to Nick's room. He was feeling a great deal better since they'd brought his brother out of ICU, but he wasn't ready to jump ship.

"God save me from stubborn Irishmen." She aimed a hard look at Rachel. "Mrs. Muldoon, do you have any influence with him?"

"I'm not Mrs. Muldoon, and no. I think we might

pry him away once he checks in on Nick. My brother shouldn't be with him much longer."

"Your brother's the cop?" She sighed and shook her head. "All right. I'll give you five minutes with my patient, then you're out of here. Believe me, I'll call Security and have them toss you out if necessary."

"Yes, ma'am."

"That goes for that giant who's been lurking around the corridors, too."

"I'll take them both home," Rachel promised. She looked around quickly as the door opened. "Alexi?"

"We're finished." He couldn't keep the satisfied gleam out of his eyes. "I've got some rounding up to do."

"He identified them?" Zack demanded.

"Cold. And he's raring to testify."

"I want—"

"No chance," Alex said quickly, noting Zack's clenched fists. "The kid figured out how to do it the right way, Muldoon. Take a lesson. Keep him in line, Rach."

"I'll try," she murmured as her brother hurried off. "Zack, if you're going in there to talk to him, pull it together."

"That son of a bitch shot my brother."

"And he'll pay for it."

With a curt nod, Zack walked by her and into Nick's room. He stood at the foot of the bed, waiting. "How are you feeling?"

"Okay." He was exhausted after his interview with Alex, but he wasn't finished. "I need to talk to you, to tell you. Explain."

"It can wait."

"No. It was my fault. The whole thing. They were Cobras, Zack. They knew when to come in and how, because I told them. I didn't know… I swear to God I didn't know what they were going to do. I don't expect you to believe me."

Zack waited a moment until he got his bearings. "Why shouldn't I believe you?"

Nick squeezed his eyes tight. "I messed up. Like always." He poured out the entire story of how he'd run into Cash at the arcade. "I thought we were just talking. And all the time he was setting me up. Setting you up."

"You trusted him." Zack came around the side of the bed to put a hand on Nick's wrist. "You thought he was your friend. That's not messing up, Nick, it's just trusting people who don't deserve it. You're not like them." When Nick's eyes opened again, Zack took a firm hold of his hand. "If you messed up anything, it was yourself by trying to be like them. And that's done."

"I won't let them get away with it."

"*We* won't," Zack told him. "We're in this together."

"Yeah," Nick said on a long breath. "Okay."

"They're going to kick me out of here so you can get some rest. I'll be back tomorrow."

"Zack," Nick called out as his brother hit the door. "Don't forget the fries."

"You got it."

"Okay?" Rachel asked when Zack came out.

"Okay." Then he gathered her up, held her hard and close. She was slim and small, and as steady as an anchor in a storm-tossed sea. "Come home with me, please," he murmured against her hair. "Stay with me tonight."

"Let's go." She pressed a kiss to his cheek. "I can buy a toothbrush on the way."

* * *

Later, when he fell into an exhausted sleep, she lay beside him and kept watch. She knew it was the first time he'd done more than nod off in a chair in nearly forty-eight hours. Odd, she thought as she watched his face in the faint, shadowy light that sneaked through the windows. She'd never considered herself the nurturing type. But it had been very satisfying to simply lie beside him and hold him until the strain and fatigue of the past few days had toppled him into sleep.

The bigger they are, she thought again, pressing a light kiss to his forehead.

Still, as tired as she was, and as relieved, she couldn't find escape in sleep herself. How daunting it was to realize she'd come to a point in her life where she wasn't sure of her moves.

Love didn't run on logic. It didn't follow neat lines or a list of priorities. Yet, in a matter of days, the bond that had brought them together would be broken. They would go into court, and it would be resolved one way or the other.

Now was the time to face the what-happens-next.

He'd asked her to move in with him. Rachel shifted to watch the pattern of shadows on the ceiling. It could be enough. Or much too much. Her problem now was to decide what she could live with, and what she could live without.

She was very much afraid that the one thing she couldn't live without was sleeping beside her.

He shuddered once, made a strangled sound in his throat before ripping himself awake. Instantly she moved to soothe.

"Shh…" She touched a hand to his cheek, to his shoulder, stroking. "It's all right. Everything's all right."

"Hurricanes," he murmured, groggy. "I'll tell you about it sometime."

"Okay." She rested a hand on his heart, as if to slow its rapid pace. "Go back to sleep, Muldoon. You're worn out."

"It's nice that you're here. Real nice."

"I like it, too." One brow arched as she felt his hand slide up her thigh. "Don't start something you won't be able to finish."

"I just want my T-shirt back." He moved his hand up her makeshift nightie until her warm, soft breast filled his palm. Comfort. Arousal. Perfection. "Just as I thought. This is a completely nonregulation body."

The stirring started low and deep, working its way through her. "You're pushing your luck."

"I was having this dream about the navy." His fatigue had everything moving in slow motion, making it all the more erotic when he slipped the shirt up and off. Her arms seemed to flow over her head and down again like water. "It makes me remember what it was like being at sea for months without seeing a woman." He lowered his mouth to flick his tongue over her. "Or tasting one."

She sighed luxuriously, and even that slight movement heightened his need. "Tell me more." His mouth met hers, so soft, so sweet.

"When I woke up just now, I could smell your hair, your skin. I've been waking up wanting you for weeks. Now I can wake up and have you."

"Just that easy, huh?"

"Yeah." He lifted his head and smiled down at her. "Just that easy."

She trailed a finger down his back as she considered. "I've got only one thing to say to you, Muldoon."

"What?"

"All hands on deck." With a laugh, she rolled on top of him.

And it was very, very easy.

"You're not being sensible," she said to Nick as she walked up the courthouse steps beside him, supporting his arm. "It's the simplest thing in the world to get a postponement under the circumstances."

"I want it over," he repeated, and glanced over at Zack.

"I'm with you."

"Far be it from me to fight the pair of you," she said in disgust. "If you keel over—"

"I'm not an invalid."

"You're two days out of the hospital," she pointed out.

"Dr. Markowitz gave him the green light," Zack put in.

"I don't care what Dr. Markowitz gave him."

"Rachel." A little winded from the climb, but still game, Nick shook off her hand. "Stop playing mother."

"Fine." She tossed up her hands, then lowered them again to fuss with Nick's tie, brush the shoulders of his jacket. She caught Zack's grin over Nick's shoulder and scowled. "Shut up, Muldoon."

"Aye, aye, sir."

"He thinks he's so cute with the nautical talk." She stood back to study her client. He was still a little pale, but he would do. "Now, are you sure you remember everything I explained to you?"

"Rachel, you went over the drill a dozen times." Letting out a huff of breath, he turned to his brother. "Can I have a minute with her?"

"Sure." Zack tossed a look over his shoulder. "Hands off."

"Yeah, yeah." The smirk was back, but it was good-natured rather than nasty. "Listen, Rachel, first I want to tell you how… Well, it was really nice of your family to come by the hospital the way they did. Your mom—" he pushed restless hands in his pockets, then pulled them out again "—bringing me cookies, and all the other stuff. Your father, coming by to hang out and play checkers."

It should have sounded corny, he reflected. But it didn't.

"They came to see you because they wanted to."

"Yeah, but…well, it was nice. I even got a card from Freddie. And the cop—he was okay."

"Alex has his moments."

"What I'm trying to say is, whatever happens today, you've done a lot for me. Maybe I don't know where I'm going, but I know where I'm not. I owe that to you."

"No, you don't." Worried she might cry, she made her tone brisk. "A little, sure, but most of it was right here." She tapped a finger on his heart. "You're okay, LeBeck."

"Thanks. One more thing." He glanced over to be sure Zack was out of earshot. "I know I made things a little sticky before. Zack's been making noises that you might be moving in. I just wanted you to know that I wouldn't be in the way."

"I haven't decided what I'm going to do. Regardless, you wouldn't be in the way. You're family. Got it?"

His lips curved. "I'm getting it. If you decide to throw him over, I'm available."

"I'll keep it in mind." She gave his jacket one last tug. "Let's go."

There was no reason to be nervous, she told herself as she led Nick to the defense table. Her statement was well prepared, and she had a sympathetic judge on the bench.

She was terrified.

She rose with the rest of the court when Judge Beckett came in. Ignoring the twisting in her gut, she gave Nick a quick, confident smile.

"Well, well, Mr. LeBeck," Beckett began, folding her hands. "How time flies. I hear through the grapevine that you ran into a bit of trouble recently. Are you quite recovered?"

"Your Honor..." Puzzled by the break in courtroom routine, Rachel rose.

"Sit, sit, sit." Beckett gestured with the back of her hand. "Mr. LeBeck, I asked how you're feeling."

"I'm okay."

"Good. I'm also informed that you identified the three desperadoes who broke into Mr. Muldoon's bar. Three members of the Cobras—an organization with which you were associated, I believe—who are now in custody awaiting trial."

Rachel tried again. "Your Honor, in my final report—"

"I read it, thank you, Counselor. You did an excellent job. I'd prefer to hear from Mr. LeBeck directly.

My question is, why did you identify these men, who a relatively short time ago you chose to protect?"

"Stand up," Rachel hissed under her breath.

Frowning, Nick complied. "Ma'am?"

"Was the question unclear? Shall I repeat it?"

"No, I got it."

"Excellent. And your answer?"

"They messed with my brother."

"Ah." As if she were a teacher congratulating a much-improved student, Beckett smiled. "And that changes the complexion of things."

Forgetting all Rachel's prompting, he took the natural stance. The aggressive one. "Listen, they broke in, busted Rio's head open, shoved Rachel around and waved guns all over the place. It wasn't right. Maybe you think turning them in makes me a creep, but Reece was going to shoot my brother. No way he was going to walk from that."

"What I think it makes you, LeBeck, is a clear-thinking, potentially responsible adult who has grasped not only the basic tenets of right and wrong, but also of loyalty, which is often more valuable. You will likely make more mistakes in your life, but I doubt you will make the kind that will bring you back into my courtroom. Now, I believe the district attorney has something to say."

"Yes, Your Honor. The state drops all charges against Nicholas LeBeck."

"All *right!*" Rachel said, springing to her feet.

"Is that it?" Nick managed.

"Not quite." Beckett pulled the attention back to the bench. "I get to do this." She slapped the gavel down. "Now that's it."

With a laugh, Rachel threw her arms around Nick's neck. "You did it," she murmured to him. "I want you to remember that. You did it."

"I'm not going to jail." He hadn't been able to allow anyone, even himself, to see how much that had terrified him. He gave Rachel one last squeeze before turning to Zack. "I'm going home."

"That's right." Zack held out a hand. Then, with an oath, he dragged Nick into a hug. "Play your cards right, kid, I'll even give you a raise."

"Raise, my butt. I'm working my way up to partner."

"If you gentlemen will excuse me, I have other clients." She gave each of them a highly unprofessional kiss.

"We have to celebrate." Zack caught her hands. There was nothing he could say. Too much that needed to be said. "Seven o'clock, at the bar. Be there."

"I wouldn't miss it."

"Rachel," Nick called out, "you're the best."

"No." She tossed a laugh over her shoulder. "But I will be."

She was a little late. It couldn't be helped. How could she have known she'd get a case of criminal assault tossed at her at six o'clock?

Two years with the PD's office, she reminded herself, grinning a little, as she pushed open the door of the bar.

When the cheer went up, she stopped cold. There were streamers, balloons, and several people in incredibly stupid party hats. A huge banner hung across the back wall.

Next to Rachel, Perry Mason is a Wimp.

It made her laugh, even as Rio hauled her onto his

shoulders and carried her to the bar. He set her down, and someone thrust a glass of champagne in her hand.

"Some party."

Zack tugged at her hair until she turned her face for a kiss. "I tried to make them wait for you, but they got caught up."

"*I'll* catch up…" she began. Then her mouth dropped open. "Mama?"

"We're already eating Rio's short ribs," Nadia informed her. "Now your papa is going to dance with me."

"Maybe I dance with you later," Yuri informed his daughter as he swept Nadia off for what was surely to be a polka.

"You invited my parents. And—" She shook her head in wonder. "That's Alex stuffing meatballs in his face."

"It's a private party." Zack clinked his glass against hers. "Nick made up the list. Take a look."

She craned her neck and spotted him at a table. "Isn't that Lola's daughter?"

"She's really impressed that he's been shot."

"It's one of the top ten ways to impress a woman."

"I'll keep it in mind. Want to dance?"

She took another sip of champagne. "I'd bet a week's pay you don't know how to polka."

"You lose," he said, and grabbed her hand.

It went on for hours. Rachel lost track of the time as she sampled the enormous spread Rio had prepared and washed it down with champagne. She danced until her feet went numb and ultimately collapsed to sing Ukrainian folk songs with her slightly snookered father.

"Good party," Yuri said, swaying a bit, while his wife helped him into his coat.

"Yes, Papa."

He grinned as he leaned toward Rachel. "Now I go home and make your mama feel like a girl."

"Big talk. You'll snore in truck on the way home."

He leered at his wife. "Then you wake me up."

"Maybe." She kissed her daughter. "You make me very proud."

"Thank you, Mama."

"You're a smart girl, Rachel. I'll tell you what you should already know. When you find a good man, you lose nothing by taking hold, and everything by letting go. You understand me?"

"Yes, Mama." Rachel looked over at Zack. "I think I do."

"This is good."

Rachel watched them walk out, arm in arm.

"They're pretty great," Nick said from behind her.

"Yes, they are."

"And your brother's not so bad—for a cop."

"I'm pretty fond of him, all in all." With a sigh, she brushed a streamer from her hair. "Looks like the party's over."

"This one is." Smiling to himself, he turned away to help Rio gather up some of the mess. If Nick knew his brother—and he was beginning to believe he did—Rachel was in for another surprise before the evening was over.

Zack tolerated the cleanup crew for nearly twenty minutes before ordering Rio home and Nick to bed. If he didn't get Rachel to himself, he was going to explode. "We'll get the rest tomorrow."

"You're the boss." Rio gave Rachel a wink as he shrugged into his coat. "For the time being."

Zack shook a nearly empty bottle. "There's a little champagne left. How about it?"

"I think I could choke it down." She settled at the bar and, aiming her best provocative look at him, held out her glass. "Buy me a drink, sailor?"

"Be my pleasure." After filling her glass, he slid the bottle aside. "There's nothing I can say or do to repay you."

"Don't start."

"I want you to know how much I appreciate everything. You made all the difference."

"I was doing my job, and following my conscience. No one needs to thank me for that."

"Damn it, Rachel, let me explain how I feel."

Nick swung in from the kitchen. "If that's the best you can do, bro, you need all the help you can get."

The single glance Zack shot in his direction was explosive. "Go to bed."

"On my way." But he walked to the juke and popped in a few quarters. After punching some buttons, he turned back to them. "You two are a real case. Take it from someone who knows you both have weaknesses, and cut to the chase." With a shake of his head, he dimmed the lights and walked out.

"What the hell was that?" Zack demanded.

"Don't ask me. Weaknesses? I don't have any weaknesses."

Zack grinned at her. "Me either." He came around the bar. "But it's nice music."

"Real nice," she agreed, going willingly into his arms to sway there.

"Things have been a little hectic."

"Hmm... Just a little."

"I'd like to talk to you about what I asked you a while back. About moving in."

She shut her eyes. She'd already decided the answer was no. As hard as it was to resist a half a loaf, she would hold out for the whole one. "This may not be the time to go into it."

"I can't think of a better one. The thing is, Rachel, I don't want you to move in."

"You—" She stiffened, then shoved away, nearly toppling him over. "Well, that's just fine."

"What I want—"

"Stuff what you want," she tossed back at him. "Isn't that just typical? After I clean up the mess for you, you brush me off."

"I'm not—"

"Shut up, Muldoon. I'll have my say."

"Who could stop you?" he muttered.

Her heels slapped the floor as she tried to walk off her anger. "You're out of order, Buster. You're the one who kept pushing your way in, pushing your way in." She demonstrated by making shoving motions with her hands. "Just wouldn't take no for an answer."

"You didn't say no," he reminded her.

"That's irrelevant." Facing him, she fisted her hands on her hips. "So, you don't want me to move in. Fine. My answer was an unqualified no anyway."

"Great." He stepped closer so that he had to lean over to shout in her face. "Because I'm not settling for you packing up a few things and coming by to play house. I want you to marry me."

"And if you think— Oh, God." She swayed back, forward, then pressed a hand to his chest for balance. "I have to sit down."

"So sit." He nipped her around the waist and plopped her down on the bar. "And just listen. I know we said no long-term commitments. You didn't want them, and neither did I. But we're turning the page here, Rachel, and there's a whole new set of rules."

"Zack, I—"

"No. You're not going to get me tangled up in an argument." She was too good at winning those, and he'd be damned if he was going to lose this time. "I've thought this through. You've got your priorities, and that's fine." He grabbed her hands, hard. Rachel decided she'd check for broken fingers later. Right now, she couldn't feel anything but amazement. "All you have to do is add one to the list. Me. I didn't plan on falling in love with you, but that's the way it is, so deal with it."

"Me either," she murmured, but he plowed on.

"Maybe you think you don't have room…" His grip tightened, and he ignored her quick yelp. "What did you say?"

"I said, 'Me either.'"

"'Me either' what?"

"You said, 'I didn't plan on falling in love with you,' and I said, 'Me either.'" She let out a long, shaky sigh when his hands slid limply from hers. "But that's the way it is, so deal with it."

"Oh, yeah?"

"Yeah." Perched on the bar, she linked her arms around his neck, lowered her brow to his. Amazing, she thought. He was as scared as she was. "You beat me to it, Muldoon. I was going to turn you down because I love you too much, and I wasn't going to settle for anything less with you than everything. It's had me going in circles for days."

"Weeks." He brought his mouth to hers. "I was going to try to ease you into it, but I couldn't wait. I even talked to your father about my intentions tonight."

Unsure whether to laugh or groan, she drew back. "You did not."

"I plied him with vodka first, just in case. He told me he wanted more grandchildren."

She felt her heart swell. "I'd like to accommodate him."

Something caught in his chest, then broke beautifully free. "No kidding?"

And here it was, she thought, looking down into his eyes. A whole new set of rules. A whole new life for the taking. "No kidding. I want a family with you. I want it all with you. That's my choice."

He cupped her face in his hands. "You're everything I've wanted and never thought I'd have."

"You're everything I wanted," she repeated. "And pretended not to." When she lowered her lips to his, she felt the sting of tears in her throat. "We're not going to get sloppy, are we, Muldoon?"

"Who, us?" He grinned as she slid off the bar and into his arms. "Not a chance."

* * * * *

CONVINCING ALEX

For Pat Gaffney, to even things out

Chapter 1

The curvy blonde in hot-pink spandex tottered on sti-letto heels as she worked her corner. Her eyes, heavily painted with a sunburst of colors, kept a sharp watch on her associates, those spangled shadows of the night. There was a great deal of laughter on the street. After all, it was springtime in New York. But beneath the laughter there was a flat sheen of boredom that no amount of glitter or sex could disguise.

For these ladies, business was business.

After popping in some fresh gum, she adjusted the large canvas bag on her bare shoulder. Thank God it was warm, she thought. It would be hell to strut around half-dressed if the weather was ugly.

A gorgeous black woman in red leather that barely covered the essentials languidly lit a cigarette and cocked her hip. "Come on, baby," she said to no one in particular, in a voice husky from the smoke she exhaled. "Wanna have some fun?"

Some did, Bess noted, her eyes skimming the block. Some didn't. All in all, she thought, business was pretty brisk on this spring night. She'd observed several transactions, and the varied ways they were contracted. It was too bad boredom was the byword here. Boredom, and a defiant kind of hopelessness.

"You talking to yourself, honey?"

"Huh?" Bess blinked up into the shrewd eyes of the black goddess in red leather who had strolled over. "Was I?"

"You're new?" Studying Bess, she blew out smoke. "Who's your man?"

"My... I don't have one."

"Don't have one?" The woman arched her ruthlessly plucked brows and sneered. "Girl, you can't work this street without a man."

"That's what I'm doing." Since she didn't have a cigarette, Bess blew a bubble with her gum. Then snapped it.

"Bobby or Big Ed find out, they're going to mess you up." She shrugged. After all, it wasn't her problem.

"Free country."

"Girl, ain't nothing free." With a laugh, she ran a hand down her slick, leather-covered hip. "Nothing at all." She flicked her cigarette into the street, where it bounced off the rear fender of a cab.

There were dozens of questions on Bess's lips. It was in her nature to ask them, but she remembered that she had to go slow. "So who's *your* man?"

"Bobby." With her lips pursed, the woman skimmed her gaze up and down Bess. "He'd take you on. A little skinny through the butt, but you'd do. You need protection when you work the streets." And she could use the extra money Bobby would pass her way if she brought him a new girl.

"Nobody protected the two girls who got murdered last month."

The black woman's eyes flickered. Bess considered herself an excellent judge of emotion, and she saw grief, regret and sorrow before the eyes hardened again. "You a cop?"

Bess's mouth fell open before she laughed. That was a good one, she thought. Sort of flattering. "No, I'm not a cop. I'm just trying to make a living. Did you know either of them? The women who were killed?"

"We don't like questions around here." The woman tilted her head. "If you're trying to make a living, let's see you do it."

Bess felt a quick ripple of unease. Not only was the woman gorgeous, she was big. Big and suspicious. Both qualities were going to make it difficult for Bess to hang back on the fringes and observe. But she considered herself an agile thinker and a quick study. After all, she reminded herself, she'd come here tonight to do business.

"Sure." Turning, she strutted slowly along the sidewalk. Her hips—and she didn't for a minute believe that her butt was skinny—swayed seductively.

Maybe her throat was a little dry. Maybe her heart was pounding a bit too quickly. But Bess McNee took a great deal of pride in her work.

She spotted the two men half a block away and licked her lips. The one on the left, the dark one, looked very promising.

"Look, rookie, the idea's to take one, maybe two."
Alex scanned the sidewalk ahead. Hookers, drunks,

junkies and those unfortunate enough to have to pass through them to get home. "My snitch says that the tall black one—Rosalie—knew both the victims."

"So why don't we just pick her up and take her in for questioning?" Judd Malloy was anxious for action. His detective's shield was only forty-eight hours old. And he was working with Alexi Stanislaski, a cop who had a reputation for moving quickly and getting the job done. "Better yet, why don't we go roust her pimp?"

Rookies, Alex thought. Why were they always teaming him up with rookies? "Because we want her cooperation. We're going to pick her up, book her for solicitation. Then we're going to talk to her, real nice, before Bobby can come along and tell her to clam up."

"If my wife finds out I spent the night picking up hookers—"

"A smart cop doesn't tell his family anything they'd don't need to know. And they don't need to know much." Alex's dark brown eyes were cool, very cool, as they flicked over his new partner's face. "Stanislaski's rule number one."

He spotted the blonde. She was staring at him. Alex stared back. Odd face, he thought. Sharp, sexy, despite the makeup she'd troweled on. Beneath all the gunk, her eyes were a vivid green. The face itself was all angles, some of them wrong. Her nose was slightly crooked, as if it had been broken. Some john or pimp, he figured, then skimmed his eyes down to her mouth.

Full, overfull, and a glossy red. It didn't please him at all that he felt a reaction to it. Not knowing what she was, what she did. Her chin came to a slight point, and with her prominent cheekbones it gave her face a triangular, foxlike look.

The clinging tube top and spandex capri pants showed every inch of her curvy, athletic little body. He'd always been a sucker for the athletic type—but he reminded himself just where this particular number got her exercise.

In any case, she wasn't the one he was looking for.

Now or never, Bess told herself, feeling her new acquaintance's eyes on her.

"Hey, baby…" Though she hadn't smoked since she'd been fifteen, her voice was husky. Saying a prayer to whatever gods were listening, she veered in on Alex. "Want to party?"

"Maybe." He hooked a finger in the top of her tube, and was surprised when she flinched. "You're not quite what I had it mind, sweetie."

"Oh?" What next? Combining instinct with her observations, she tossed her head and leaned into him. She had the quick impression of pressing against steel—hard, unyielding and very cool. "Just what *did* you have in mind?"

Then, for a moment, she had nothing at all on hers. Not with the way those dark eyes cut into her, through her. His knuckles were brushing her skin, just above the breasts. She felt the heat from them, from him. As she continued to stare, she was struck by a vivid image of the two of them, rolling on a narrow bed in some dark room.

And it had nothing to do with business.

It was the first time Alex had ever seen a hooker blush. It threw him off, made him want to apologize for the fantasy that had just whipped through his brain. Then he remembered himself.

"Just a different type, babe."

In her heels, they were eye-to-eye. It made him want to rub off the powders and paints to see what was beneath.

"I can be a different type," Bess said, delighted with her inspired response.

"Hey, girlfriend." Rosalie strutted over and slipped a friendly arm around Bess's shoulders. "You're not going to be greedy and take both of these boys, are you?"

"I—"

Pay dirt, Alex thought, and shifted his attention to Rosalie. "You two a team?"

"We are tonight." She glanced from Alex to his partner. "How 'bout you two?"

Judd searched for his voice. He'd rather have been facing a gunman in an alley. And he simply couldn't put his hands on this big, beautiful woman, when a picture of his wife's trusting face was flashing in his head like a neon light.

"Sure." He let out a long breath and tried to emulate some of Alex's cocky confidence.

Rosalie threw back her head and laughed before she stepped forward, bumping bodies with Judd. He gave way instinctively as a dark red flush crept up his neck. "I believe you're new at this, honey. Why don't you let Rosalie show you the ropes?"

Because his partner seemed to have developed laryngitis, Alex took over. "How much?"

"Well…" Rosalie didn't bother to look over at Bess, who had gone dead pale. "Special rate tonight. You get both of us for a hundred. That's the first hour." She leaned down and whispered something in Judd's ear that had him babbling. "After that," she continued, "we can negotiate."

"I don't—" Bess began, then felt Rosalie's fingers dig into her bare shoulder like sharp little knives.

"I think that'll do it," Alex said, and pulled out his badge. "Ladies, you're busted."

Cops, Bess realized on a wave of sweet relief. While Rosalie expressed her opinion with a single vicious word, Bess struggled not to burst into wild laughter.

Perfect, Bess thought as she was bumped along into the squad room. She'd been arrested for solicitation, and life couldn't be better. Trying to take everything in at once, she grinned as she scanned the station house. She'd been in one before, of course. As she always said, she took her work seriously. But not in this precinct. Not downtown.

It was dirty—grimy, really, she decided, making mental notes and muttering to herself. Floors, walls, the barred windows. Everything had a nice, picturesque coat of crud.

It smelled, too. She took a deep breath so that she wouldn't forget the ripe stench of human sweat, bitter coffee and strong disinfectant.

And it was noisy. With every nerve on sensory alert, she separated the din into ringing phones, angry curses, weeping, and the clickety-clack of keyboards at work.

Man, oh, man, she thought. Her luck was really in.

"You're not a tourist, sweetheart," Alex reminded her, adding a firm nudge.

"Sorry."

The vibrant excitement in her eyes was so out of place that he stared. Then, with a shake of his head, he jabbed a finger toward a chair. He was letting the rookie get his feet wet getting the vitals from Rosalie. Once they had her booked, he'd take over himself, using charm or threats or whatever seemed most expedient to make her talk to him about her two murdered associates.

"Okay." He took his seat behind his battered and overcrowded desk. "You know the drill."

She'd been staring at a young man of about twenty with a face full of bruises and a torn denim jacket. "Excuse me?"

Alex just sighed as he rolled a form onto his typewriter. "Name?"

"Oh, I'm Bess." She held out her hand in a gesture so natural and friendly he nearly took it.

Instead, he swore softly. "Bess what?"

"McNee. And you're?"

"In charge. Date of birth."

"Why?"

His eyes flicked up, arrowed hers. "Why what?"

"Why do you want to know?"

Patience, never his strong suit, strained. He tapped a finger on the form. "Because I've got this space to fill."

"Okay. I'm twenty-eight. A Gemini. I was born on June the first."

Alex did the math and typed in the year. "Residence."

Natural curiosity had her poking through the folders and papers on his desk until he slapped her hand. "You're awfully tense," she commented. "Is it because you work undercover?"

Damn that smile, he thought. It was sassy, sexy, and far from stupid. That, and those sharp, intelligent green eyes, might have fooled him. But she looked like a hooker, and she smelled like a hooker. Therefore...

"Listen, doll, here's the way this works. I ask the questions, you answer them."

"Tough, cynical, street-smart."

One dark brow lifted. "Excuse me?"

"Just a quick personality check. You want my address, right?" she rattled off an address that made both of Alex's brows raise.

"Let's get serious."

"Okay." Willing to oblige, Bess folded her hands on the edge of his desk.

"Your address," he repeated.

"I just gave it to you."

"I know what real estate goes for in that area. Maybe you're good." Thoughtful, he scanned her attributes one more time. "Maybe you're better than you look. But you don't make enough working the streets to pop for that kind of rent."

Bess knew an insult when it hit her over the head. What made it worse was that she'd spent over an hour on her makeup. And she happened to know that her body was good. Lord knew, she sweated to keep it that way by working out three days a week. "That's where I live, cop." Her temper, which had a habit of flaring quickly, had her upending her enormous canvas tote onto his desk.

Alex watched, fascinated, as she pawed through the pile of contents. There were enough cosmetics to supply a small department store. And they weren't the cheap kind. Six lipsticks, two compacts, several mascara sticks and pots of eye shadow. A rainbow of eyeliner pencils. Scattered with them were two sets of keys, a snowfall of credit-card receipts, rubber bands, paper clips, twelve pens—he counted—a few broken pencils, a steno pad, two paperback books, matches, a leather address book embossed with the initials *ELM,* a stapler—he didn't even pause to wonder why she would carry one—tissues and crumpled papers, a tiny micro-cassette recorder. And a gun.

He whipped it out of the pile and stared at it. A water gun.

"Careful with that," she warned as she found her overburdened wallet. "It's full of ammonia."

"Ammonia?"

"I used to carry Mace, but this works fine. Here." Pleased with herself, she pushed the open wallet under his nose.

It might have been her in the picture. The hair was short and curly and chic, a deep chestnut rather than a brassy blonde. But that nose, that chin. And those eyes. He frowned over the driver's license. The address was right.

"You got a car?"

She shrugged and began to dump things back into her purse. "So?"

"Women in your position usually don't."

Because it made sense, Bess stalled. "I've got a license. Everybody who has a license doesn't have to have a car, do they?"

"No." He jerked the wallet out of her reach. "Take off the wig."

Pouting a little, she patted it. "How come?"

He reached across the desk and yanked it off himself. She scowled at him while she ran her fingers through short, springy red curls. "I want that back. It's borrowed."

"Sure." He tossed it onto his desk before he leaned back in his squeaky chair for a fresh evaluation. If this lady was a hooker, he was Clark Kent. "What the hell *are* you?"

It was time to come clean. She knew it. But something about him egged her on. "I'm just a woman trying to make a living, Officer." That was how Jade would handle it, Bess was sure. And since Jade was her creation, Bess was determined to do right by her.

He opened the wallet, skimmed through the bills. She was carrying around what would be for him more than two weeks' pay. "Right."

"Can you do that?" she demanded, more curious than annoyed. "Go through my personal property?"

"Honey, right now *you* are *my* personal property." There were pictures in the wallet, as well. Snapshots of people, some with her, some without her. And the lady was a card-carrying member of dozens of groups, including Greenpeace, the World Wildlife Federation, Amnesty International and the Writers' Guild. The last brought him back to the tape recorder. When he picked up the little toy, he noted that it was running. "Let's have it, Bess."

God, he was cute. The thought passed through her head as she smiled at him. "Have what?"

"What were you doing hanging around with Rosalie and the rest of the girls?"

"My job." When his eyes narrowed that way, Bess thought, he was downright irresistible. Impatient, a little mean, with a flash of recklessness just barely under control.

Fabulous.

"Really." All honesty and cheap perfume, she leaned forward. "You see, it all has to do with Jade, and how she's having this problem with a dual personality. By day, she's a dedicated lawyer—a real straight arrow, *you* know—but by night she hits the streets. She's blocking what happened between her and Brock, and coupled with a childhood memory that's begun to resurface, the strain's been too much for her. She's on a path of self-destruction."

The frown in his eyes turned them nearly black. "Who the hell is Jade?"

"Jade Sullivan Carstairs. Don't you watch daytime TV?"

His head was beginning to buzz. "No."

"You don't know what you're missing. You'd probably really enjoy the Jade-Storm-Brock story line. Storm's a cop, you see, and he's falling in love with Jade. Her emotional problems, and the hold Brock has on her, complicate things. Then there was a miscarriage, and the kidnapping. Naturally, Storm has problems of his own."

"Naturally. What's your point?"

"Oh, sorry. I get offtrack. I write for 'Secret Sins' daytime drama."

"You're a soap-opera writer?"

"Yeah." Unlike many in the trade, she wasn't bothered by that particular label. "And I like to get the feel of the situations I put my characters into. Since Jade is a special pet of mine, I—"

"Are you out of your mind?" Alex barked the question as he leaned over into her face. "Do you have any idea what you were doing?"

She blinked, at once innocent and amused. "Research?"

He swore again, and Bess found she liked the way he raked impatient fingers through his thick black hair. "Lady, just how far were you intending to take your research?"

"How—? Oh." Her eyes brightened with laughter. "Well no, not quite that far."

"What the hell would you have done if I hadn't been a cop?"

"I'd have thought of something." She continued to

smile. He had a fascinating face—golden skin, dark eyes, wonderful bones. And that mouth, so beautifully sculpted, even if it did tend to scowl. "It's my job to think of things. And when I spotted you, I thought you looked safe. What I mean is, you didn't strike me as the kind of man who'd be interested in…" What was a delicate way of putting it? she wondered. "Paying for pleasure."

He was so angry he wanted to yank her up and toss her over his lap. The idea of administering a few good whacks to that cute little butt was tremendously appealing. "And if you'd guessed wrong?"

"I didn't," she pointed out. "For a minute there, I was worried, but it all worked out. Better than I expected, really, because I had a chance to ride in a— Do you still call them paddy wagons?"

He'd been so sure he'd seen everything. Heard everything. With his temper straining at the bit, he spoke through clenched teeth. "Two hookers are dead. Two who worked that area."

"I know," she said quickly, as if that explained it all. "That was one of the reasons I chose it. You see, I plan to have Jade—"

"I'm talking about you," he interrupted in a voice that had her wincing. "You. Some bubbleheaded hack writer who thinks she can strut around in spandex and a half a ton of makeup, then go home to her nice neighborhood and wash it all off."

"Hack?" It was the only thing she took offense to. "Look, cop—"

"*You* look. You stay out of my territory, and out of those slut clothes. Do your research out of a book."

Her chin shot out. "I can go where I want, wearing what I want."

"You think so?" There was a way to teach her a lesson. A perfect way. "Fine." He rose, tugged the tote out of her hands, then took a firm grip on her arm. "Let's go."

"Where?"

"To holding, babe. You're under arrest, remember?"

She stumbled in the three-inch heels and squawked, "But I just explained—"

"I hear better stories before breakfast every day."

"You're not going to put me in a cell." Bess was sure of it. Positive. Right up until the moment the bars closed in her face.

It took about ten minutes for the shock to wear off. When it did, Bess decided it wasn't such a bad turn. She could be furious with the cop—whoever he was—but she could appreciate and take advantage of the unique opportunity he'd given her. She was in a holding cell with several other women. There was atmosphere to be absorbed, and there were interviews to be conducted.

When one of her cellmates informed her that she was entitled to a phone call, she demanded one. Pleased with the progress she was making, she settled back on her hard cot to talk to her new acquaintances.

It was thirty minutes later when she looked up and spotted her friend and cowriter Lori Banes, standing beside a uniformed policeman.

"Bess, you look so natural here."

With a grin, Bess popped up as the guard unlocked the door. "It's been great."

"Hey!" one of her cellmates called out. "I'm telling you that Vicki's a witch, and Jeffrey should boot her out. Amelia's the right woman for him."

Bess sent back a wink. "I'll see what I can do. Bye, girls."

Lori didn't consider herself long-suffering. She didn't consider herself a prude or a stuffed shirt. And she said as much to Bess as they walked through the corridors, up the stairs and back into the lobby area outside the squad room. "But," she added, pressing fingers to her tired eyes. "There's something that puts me off about being woken up at 2:00 a.m. to come bail you out of jail."

"Sorry, but it's been great. Wait until I tell you."

"Do you know what you look like, dear?"

"Yep." Unconcerned, Bess craned her neck. The chair behind Alex's desk was empty. "I had no idea that so many of the working girls watched the show. But they do work nights, mostly. Uh, excuse me..." She caught the sleeve of one of New York's finest as he walked by. "The officer who uses that desk?"

The cop swallowed the best part of a bite of his pastrami sandwich. "Stanislaski?"

"Whew. That's a mouthful. Is he still around?"

"He's in Interrogation."

"Oh. Thanks."

"Come on, Bess, we've got to pick up your things."

Bess had signed for her purse and its contents, still keeping an eye out for Alex. "Stanislaski," she repeated to herself. "Is that Polish, do you think?"

"How the hell do I know?" Out of patience, Lori steered her toward the door. "Let's get out of here. The place is lousy with criminals."

"I know. It's fabulous." With a laugh, she tucked an arm around Lori's waist. "I got ideas for the next three years. If we decide to have Elana arrested for Reed's murder..."

"I don't know about having Reed murdered."

With a sigh, Bess looked around for a cab. "Lori, we both know Jim isn't going to sign another contract. He wants to try the big leagues. Having his character offed is the perfect way to beef up Elana's story line."

"Maybe."

Bess slyly pulled out her ace. "'Our Lives, Our Loves' picked up two points in the ratings last month."

Lori only grunted.

"Word is Dr. Amanda Jamison is going to have twins."

"Twins?" Lori shut her eyes. Soap diva Ariel Kirkwood, who played the long-suffering psychiatrist on the competing soap, was daytime's most popular star. "It had to be twins," Lori muttered. "Okay, Reed dies."

Bess allowed herself one quick victory smile, then hurried on.

"Anyway, while I was in there, I was picturing the elegant, cool Dr. Elana Warfield Stafford Carstairs in prison. Fabulous, Lori. It'd be fabulous. I wish you'd seen the cop."

They'd walked to the corner, and there wasn't a cab in sight. "What cop?"

"The one who arrested me. He was incredibly sexy."

Lori only had the energy to sigh. "Leave it to you to get busted by a sexy cop."

"Really. All this thick black hair. His eyes were nearly black, too. Very intense. He had all those hollows and planes in his face, and this beautiful mouth. Nice build, too. Sort of rough-and-ready. Like a boxer, maybe."

"Don't start, Bess."

"I'm not. I can find a man sexy and attractive without falling in love."

Lori shot her a look. "Since when?"

"Since the last time. I've sworn off, remember?" Her smile perked up when she spotted a cab heading their way. "I'm interested in this Stanislaski for strictly professional reasons."

"Right." Resigned, Lori climbed in when the cab swung to the curb.

"I swear." She lifted her right hand to add impact to the oath. "We want to get into Storm's head more, into his background and stuff. So I pick this cop's brain a little." She gave a cabbie both her address and Lori's. "After Jade gets attacked by the Millbrook Maniac, Storm isn't going to be able to hold back his feelings for her. More has to come out about who and what he is. If we do have Elana arrested for Reed's murder, that's going to complicate his life—you know, family loyalty versus professional ethics. And once he confronts Brock—"

"Hey." At a red light, the cabbie turned, peering at them from under his fading Mets cap. "You talking about 'Secret Sins'?"

"Yeah." Bess brightened. "Do you watch it?"

"The wife tapes it every day. You don't look familiar."

"We're not on it," Bess explained. "We write it."

"Gotcha." Satisfied, he punched the accelerator when the light changed. "Let me tell you what I think about that two-timing Vicki."

As he proceeded to do just that, Bess leaned forward, debating with him. Lori closed her eyes and tried to catch up on lost sleep.

Chapter 2

"My wife went nuts." Judd Malloy munched on his cherry Danish while Alex swung in and out of downtown traffic. "She's a big fan of that soap, you know? Tapes it every day when she's in school."

"Terrific." Alex had been doing his best to forget his little encounter with the soap queen, but his partner wasn't cooperating.

"Holly figures it was just like meeting a celebrity."

"You don't find many celebrities turning tricks."

"Come on, Alex." Judd washed down the Danish with heavily sugared coffee. "She wasn't, really. You said so yourself, or the charges wouldn't have been dropped."

"She was stupid," Alex said between his teeth. "Carrying a damn water pistol in that suitcase of hers. I guess she figured if a john got rough, she'd blast him between the eyes and that would be that."

Judd started to comment on how it might feel to get a blast of ammonia in the eyes, but didn't think his partner wanted to hear it. "Well, Holly was impressed, and we got some fresh juice out of Rosalie, so we didn't waste our time."

"Malloy, you'd better get used to wasting time. Stanislaski's rule number four." Alex spotted the building he was looking for and double-parked. He was already out of the car and across the sidewalk before Judd found the NYPD sign and stuck it in the window. "We sure as hell could be wasting it here with this Domingo."

"Rosalie said—"

"Rosalie said what we wanted to hear so we'd spring her," Alex told him. His cop's eyes were already studying the building, noting windows, fire escapes, roof. "Maybe she gave us the straight shot on Domingo, and maybe she pulled it out of a hat. We'll see."

The place was in good repair. No graffiti, no broken glass or debris. Lower-middle-income, Alex surmised. Established families, mostly blue-collar. He pulled open the heavy entrance door, then scanned the names above the line of mailboxes.

"J. Domingo. 212." Alex pushed the buzzer for 110, waited, then hit 305. The answering buzz released the inner door. "People are so careless," he commented. He could feel Judd's nerves shimmering as they climbed the stairs, but he could tell he was holding it together. He'd damn well better hold it together, Alex thought as he gestured Judd into position, then knocked on the door of 212. He knocked a second time before he heard the cursing answer.

When the door opened a crack, Alex braced his body against it to keep it that way. "How's it going, Jesús?"

"What the hell do you want?"

He fit Rosalie's description, Alex noted. Right down to the natty Clark Gable moustache and the gold incisor. "Conversation, Jesús. Just a little conversation."

"I don't talk to nobody at this hour."

When he tried to shove the door to, Alex merely leaned on it and flipped open his badge. "You don't want to be rude, do you? Why don't you ask us in?"

Swearing in Spanish, Jesús Domingo cracked the door a little wider. "You got a warrant?"

"I can get one, if you want more than conversation. I can take you down for questioning, get the paperwork and do the job before your shyster lawyer can tap-dance you out. Want a team of badges in here, Jesús?"

"I haven't done nothing." He stepped back from the door, a small man with wiry muscles who was wearing nothing but a pair of gym shorts.

"Nobody said you did. Did I say he did, Malloy?"

Enjoying himself, Judd stepped in behind Alex. "Nope."

The building might be lower-middle-class, but Domingo's apartment was a small high-tech palace. State-of-the-art stereo equipment, Alex noted. A big-screen TV with some very classy video toys. The wall of tapes ran mostly to the X-rated.

"Nice place," Alex commented. "You sure know how to make your unemployment check stretch."

"I got a good head for figures." Domingo plucked up a pack of cigarettes from a table, lighted one. "So?"

"So, let's talk about Angie Horowitz."

Domingo blew out smoke and scratched at the hair on his chest. "Never heard of her."

"Funny, we got word you were one of her regulars, and her main supplier."

"You got the wrong word."

"Maybe you don't recognize the name." Alex reached into his inside jacket pocket, and his fingers brushed over his leather shoulder harness as he pulled out a manila envelope. "Why don't you take a look?" He stuck the police shot under Domingo's nose and watched his olive complexion go a sickly gray. "Look familiar?"

"Man." Domingo's fingers shook as he brought his cigarette to his lips.

"Problem?" Alex glanced down at the photo himself. There hadn't been much left of Angie for the camera. "Oh, hey, sorry about that, Jesús. Malloy, didn't I tell you not to put the dead shot in?"

Judd shrugged, feigning casualness. He was thinking he was glad he didn't have to look at it again himself. "Guess I made a mistake."

"Yeah." All the while he spoke, Alex held the photo where Domingo could see it. "Guy's a rookie," he explained. "Always screwing up. You know. Poor little Angie sure got sliced, didn't she? Coroner said the guy put about forty holes in her. You can see most of them. Poor Malloy here took one look and lost his breakfast. I keep telling him not to eat those damned greasy Danishes before we go check out a stiff, but like I said…" Alex grinned to himself as Domingo made a dash for the bathroom.

"That was cold, Stanislaski," Judd said, grinning.

"Yeah, I'm that kind of guy."

"And I didn't throw up my breakfast."

"You wanted to." The sounds coming from the bathroom were as unpleasant as they get. Alex tapped on the door. "Hey, Jesús, you okay, man? I'm really sorry about that." He passed the photo and envelope to Judd. "Tell you what, let me get you some nice cold water, okay?"

The answer was a muffled retch that Alex figured anyone could take for assent. He moved into the kitchen and opened the freezer. The two kilos were exactly where Rosalie had said he'd find them. He took one out just as Domingo rushed in.

"You got no warrant. You got no right."

"I was getting you some ice." Alex turned the frozen cocaine over in his hands. "This doesn't look like a TV dinner to me. What do you think, Malloy?"

By leaning a shoulder against the door jamb, Judd blocked the doorway. "Not the kind my mother used to make."

"You son of a bitch." Domingo wiped his mouth with a clenched fist. "You violated my civil rights. I'll be out before you can blink."

"Could be." Taking an evidence bag out of his pocket, Alex slipped both kilos inside. "Malloy, why don't you read our friend his rights while he's getting dressed? And, Jesús, try some mouthwash."

"Stanislaski," the desk sergeant called out when Alex came up from seeing Domingo into a cell. "You got company."

Alex glanced over toward his desk, seeing that several cops were huddled around it. There was quite a bit of laughter overriding the usual squad room noise. Curiosity had him moving forward even before he saw the legs. Legs he recognized. They were crossed at the knee and covered almost modestly in a canary-yellow skirt.

He recognized the rest of her, too, though the tough little body was clad in a multihued striped blazer and a scoop-necked blouse the same color as the skirt. Half a dozen slim columns of gold danced at her ears as she laughed. She looked better, sexier, he was forced to admit, with her mouth unpainted, her freckles showing, and those big green eyes subtly smudged with color. Her hair was artfully tousled, a rich, deep red that made him think of a mahogany statue his brother had carved for him.

"So I told the mayor we'd try to work it in, and we'd love for him to come on the show and do a cameo." She shifted on the desk and spotted Alex. He was frowning at her, his thumbs tucked into the pockets of a leather bomber jacket. "Officer Stanislaski."

"McNee." He inclined his head, then swept his gaze over his fellow officers. "The boss comes in and finds you here, I might have to tell him how you didn't have enough work and volunteered to take some of mine."

"Just entertaining your guest, Stanislaski." But the use of the squad room's nickname for their captain had the men drifting reluctantly away.

"What can I do for you?"

"Well, I—"

"You're sitting on a homicide," he told her.

"Oh." She scooted off the desk. Without the stilettos, she was half a head shorter than he. Alex discovered he preferred it that way. "Sorry. I came by to thank you for straightening things out for me."

"That's what they pay me for. Straightening things out." He'd been certain she would rave a bit about being tossed into a cell, but she was smiling, friendly as a kindergarten teacher. Though he couldn't recall ever having a teacher who looked like her. Or smelled like her.

"Regardless, I appreciate it. My producer's very tolerant, but if it had gone much further, she would have been annoyed."

"Annoyed?" Alex repeated. He stripped off his jacket and tossed it onto his chair. "She'd have been annoyed to find out that one of her writers was out soliciting johns down at Twenty-third and Eleventh Avenue."

"Researching," Bess corrected, unoffended. "Darla—that's my producer—she gets these headaches. I gave her a whopper when I went on a job with a cat burglar."

"With a…" He let his words trail off and eased down on the spot on the desk she'd just vacated. "I don't think you want to tell me about that."

"Actually, he was a former cat burglar. Fascinating guy. I just had him show me how he'd break into my apartment." She frowned a little, remembering. "I guess he was a little rusty. The alarm—"

"Don't." Alex held up a hand. He was beginning to feel a headache coming on himself.

"That's old news, anyway." She waved it away with a cheerful gesture of her hands. "Do you have a first name, or do I just call you Officer?"

"It's Detective."

"Your first name is Detective?"

"No, my rank." He let out a sigh. "Alex."

"Alex. That's nice." She ran a fingertip over the strap of his harness. She wasn't being provocative; she wanted to know what it felt like. Once she knew him better, she was sure, she'd talk him into letting her try it on. "Well, Alex, I was wondering if you'd let me use you."

He'd been a cop for more than five years, and until this moment he hadn't thought anything could surprise him. But it took him three seconds to close his mouth. "I beg your pardon?"

"It's just that you're so perfect." She stepped closer. She really wanted to get a better look at his weapon—without being obvious about it.

She smelled like sunshine and sex. As he drew it in, Alex thought that combination would baffle any man. "I'm perfect?"

"Absolutely." She looked straight into his eyes and smiled. Her gaze was frank and assessing. She was studying him, the way a woman might study a dress in a showroom window. "You're exactly what I've been looking for."

Her eyes were pure green. No hint of gray or blue, no flecks of gold. There was a small dimple near her mouth. Only one. Nothing about that odd, sexy face was balanced. "What you're looking for?"

"I know you're busy, but I'd try not to take up too much of your time. An hour now and then."

"An hour?" He caught himself echoing her, and shook himself loose. "Listen, I appreciate—"

"You're not married, are you?"

"Married? No, but—"

"That makes it simpler. It just came to me last night when I was getting into bed."

God. He'd learned to appreciate women early. And he'd learned to juggle them skillfully—if he said so himself. He knew how to dodge, when to evade and when to sit back and enjoy. But with this one, all bets were off.

"Is this heavy?" she asked, fiddling with his harness.

"You get used to it. It's just there."

Her smile warmed, making him think of sunlight again. "Perfect," she murmured. "I'd be willing to compensate you for your time, and your expertise."

"You'd be—" He wasn't certain if he was insulted or embarrassed. "Hold on, babe."

"Just think about it," Bess said quickly. "I know it's a lot to ask, but I have this problem with Matthew."

A brand-new emotion snuck in under his guard, and it was as green as her eyes. "Matthew? Who the hell is Matthew?"

"We call him Storm, actually. Lieutenant Storm Warfield, Millbrook PD."

Now he definitely had a headache. Alex rubbed his fingers against his temple. "Millbrook?"

"The fictional town of Millbrook, where the show's set. It's supposed to be somewhere in the Midwest. Storm's a cop. Personally, his life's a mess, but professionally, he's focused and intense and occasionally ruthless. In this new story line I'm working on, I want to concentrate on his police work, the routine, the frustrations."

"Wait." He'd always been quick, but it was taking him a minute to change gears. "You want me to help you with a story line?"

"Exactly. If you could just tell me how you think, how you go about solving a case, working with the system or around it. TV cops have to work around the system quite a bit, you know. It plays better than by-the-book."

He swore under his breath and rubbed his hands over his face. Damn it, his palms were sweaty. "You're a real case, McNee."

"You don't have to decide right now." She was also persistent. And she wondered if he had a spare gun strapped to his calf. One of those sexy-looking little chrome jobs. She'd seen that ploy in several movies. Still, she thought if she asked him that, she'd lose her edge. "I'm having a thing tonight." As she spoke, she dug into her huge bag for her notebook. "Eight o'clock until whenever. Bring a friend, if you like. Your partner, too. He seemed very sweet."

"He's adorable."

"Yeah." She ripped off the page and handed it to him. "I'd really like you to stop by."

He took the sheet, not bothering to remind her he already had her address. "Why?"

"Why not?" She beamed at him again.

Before he could list the reasons, he heard his name called.

"Alexi."

Alexi. Bess was already enchanted with the sound as she rolled the name over in her head. Different, exotic. Sexy. She was certain it suited him much more than the casual *Alex*.

Bess studied the woman bearing down on them. This wasn't one who'd be lost in a crowd, she mused. She was stunning, totally self-assured and very pregnant. Beside Bess, Alex pushed off the desk and sighed.

"Rachel."

"A moment of your time, Detective," Rachel said, flipping a glance over Bess before pinning Alex with a tawny stare. "To reacquaint you with civil rights."

"Your sister?" Bess surmised, beaming at both of them.

Alex sent her a considering frown. "How did you know that?"

"I'm really good with faces. Same bone structure, same coloring, same mouth. You have to be brother and sister, or first cousins."

"Guilty," Rachel admitted. Though she would have liked to know what Alex was doing with the sharp-eyed redhead, she wasn't about to be swayed from her duties as a public defender. "Jesús Domingo, Alexi. Illegal search and seizure."

"Bull." Alex crossed his arms and leaned back against the desk.

"You had a search warrant?"

"Didn't need one. He invited us in."

"And invited you to poke through his belongings, I suppose."

"Nope." Alex grinned while Bess watched them bounce the verbal ball as though they were champion tennis players. "Jesús got sick. I offered to get him some water. He didn't object. I opened the freezer to get the poor guy some ice, and there it was. Two kilos. It'll all be in my report."

"That's lame, Alexi. You'll never get a conviction."

"Maybe. Maybe not. Talk to the DA."

"I intend to." Rachel shifted her briefcase and began to rub her belly in circular motions to soothe the baby, who seemed to be doing aerobics in her womb. "You had no probable cause."

"Sit down."

"I don't want to sit down."

"The baby does." He yanked over a chair and all but shoved her into it. "When are you going to knock this off?"

It did feel better to sit. Indescribably better. But she wasn't about to admit it. "The baby's not due for two months. I have plenty of time. We were discussing..."

"Rach." He laid a hand on her cheek, very gently. A shouted curse wouldn't have stopped her, but the small gesture did. "Don't make me worry about you."

"I'm perfectly fine."

"You shouldn't be here."

"I'm having a baby. It's not contagious. Now, about Domingo."

Alex gave a brief, pithy opinion on what could be done with Domingo. "Talk to the DA," he repeated. "Sitting down."

"She looks pretty strong to me," Bess commented. Two pair of eyes turned to her, one furious, the other thoughtful.

"Thank you. The men in my life are coddlers," Rachel explained. "Sweet, but annoying."

"Muldoon should take better care of you," Alex insisted.

"I don't need Zack to take care of me. And the fact is, between him and Nick, I'm barely allowed to brush my own teeth." She held out a hand to Bess. "Since my brother is too rude to introduce me, I'm Rachel Muldoon."

"Bess McNee. You're a lawyer?"

"That's right. I work for the public defender's office."

"Really?" Bess's thoughts began to perk. "What's it like to—"

Alex held up a hand. "Don't get her started. She'll pick your brain clean before you know she's had her fingers in it. Look, McNee—" he turned to Bess, determined not to be charmed by her easy smile "—we're a little busy here."

"Of course you are. I'm sorry." Obligingly she swung her huge purse onto her shoulder. "We'll talk tonight. Nice to meet you, Rachel."

"Same here." Rachel ran her tongue over her teeth, and both she and Alex watched Bess weave her way out of the squad room. "Well, that was rude."

"It's the only way to handle her. Believe me."

"Hmm… She seems like an interesting woman. How did you meet her?"

"Don't ask." He sat back down on his desk, irked that the scent of sunshine and sex still lingered in the air.

"I can't believe we're doing this." Holly, Judd's pretty wife of eight months, was all but hopping out of her party shoes. "Wait until I tell everyone in the teachers' lounge where I spent the evening."

"Take it easy, honey." Judd tugged at the tie she'd insisted he wear. "It's just a party."

"Just a party?" As the elevator rode up, she fussed with her honey-brown hair. "I don't know about you two, but it isn't every day I get to eat canapés with celebrities."

Ominously silent, Alex stayed hunched in his leather jacket. He didn't know what the hell he was doing here. His first mistake had been mentioning the invitation to Judd. No matter how insouciant Judd pretended to be, he'd been bursting at the seams when he called his wife. Alex had been swept along in their enthusiasm.

But he wasn't going to stay. Holly's sense of decorum might have insisted that she and Judd couldn't attend without him, but he'd already decided just how he'd play it. He'd go in, maybe have a beer and a couple of crackers. Then he'd slip out again. He'd be damned if he'd spend this rare free evening playing soap-opera groupie.

"Oh, my" was all Holly could say when the elevator doors opened.

The walls of the private foyer were splashed with a mural of the city. Times Square, Rockefeller Center, Harlem, Little Italy, Broadway. People seemed to be rushing along the walls, just as they did the streets below. It was as if the woman who lived here didn't want to miss one moment of the action.

The wide door to the main apartment was open, and music, laughter and conversation were pouring out, along with the scents of hot food and burning candles.

"Oh, my," Holly said again, dragging her husband along as she stepped inside.

From behind them, Alex scanned the room. It was huge, and it was packed with people. Draped in silk or cotton, clad in business suits and lush gowns, they stood elbow to elbow on the hardwood floor, lounged hip to hip on the sapphire cushions of the enormous circular conversation pit, sat knee to knee on the steps of a bronze circular staircase that led to an open loft where still more people leaned against a railing decked with naked cherubs.

Two huge windows let the lights of the city in. More partygoers sat on the pillow-plumped window seats, balancing plates and glasses on their laps.

Paintings were scattered over the ivory-toned walls. Vivid, frenetic modern art, mind-bending surrealism. There was enough color to make his head swim. Yet, through the crowd and the clashing tones, he saw her.

Dancing seductively with a distinguished-looking man in a gray pin-striped suit.

She wore an excuse for a dress, the color of crushed purple grapes. He wondered, irritated, if she owned anything that covered those legs. This number certainly didn't. Nor did it cover much territory at all, the way it dipped to the waist in the back, skimmed above mid-thigh and left her shoulders bare, but for skinny, glittery straps. Multihued gemstones fell in a rope from her earlobes to those nicely sloped shoulders. Her feet were bare.

She looked, Alex thought as his stomach muscles twisted themselves into nasty knots, outrageously alluring.

"Oh, Lord, there's Jade. Oh, and Storm and Vicki. Dr. Carstairs, too." Holly's fingers dug into her husband's arm. "It's Amelia."

"Who?"

"'Secret Sins,' dummy." She gave Judd a playful punch. "The whole cast's here."

"That's not all." Because he remembered in time he was supposed to be jaded, Judd stopped himself from pointing and inclined his head. "That's Lawrence D. Strater dancing with our hostess. *The* L.D. Strater, of Strater Industries. The *Fortune 500*'s darling. The mayor's over in that corner, talking with Hannah Loy, the grand old lady of Broadway." His excitement began to hum in his voice as he continued to scan the room. "Man, there are enough luminaries in this room to light every borough in New York."

But Alex hadn't noticed. Furthermore, he didn't give a damn. His attention was focused on Bess. She'd stopped dancing, and had leaned up to whisper something in her partner's ear that made him laugh before he kissed her. Smack on the lips.

She kissed him back, too, her hands lightly intimate at his waist, before she turned and spotted the new arrivals. She waved, made her excuses, then scooted and dodged her way through the crowd toward them.

"You made it." She gave both Alex and Judd a friendly peck on the cheek before holding out both hands to Holly. "Nice to meet you."

"My wife, Holly, this is Bess McNee."

"Thanks for asking us." Holly caught herself starting to stutter, as she had the first time she faced a classroom of ten-year-olds. She flushed.

"My pleasure." Bess gave her hands a reassuring squeeze. "Let's get you something to eat and drink." She gestured toward a long table by the wall. Instead of the useless finger food and fancy, unrecognizable dishes Alex had expected, it was laden with big pots of spaghetti, mountains of garlic bread, and generous trays of antipasti.

"It's Italian night," she explained, grabbing a plate and heaping it high. "There's plenty of wine and beer, and a full bar." She handed the plate to Holly and began to dish up another. "The desserts are on the other side of the room. They're unbelievable." As she passed Judd a plate, she noted the gleam in Holly's eyes. "Would you like to meet some of the cast?"

"Oh, I…" The hell with sophistication. "Yes. I'd love it."

"Great. Excuse us. Help yourself, Alexi."

"This is really something," Judd said over a mouthful of spaghetti.

"Something," Alex agreed. Deciding to make the best of it, he fixed himself a plate.

He wasn't going to stay. But the food was great. In any case, he didn't have anything else to do. It didn't hurt to hang around and rub elbows with the fast and famous while he was helping himself to a good hot meal. It certainly made a change from his daily routine of wading through misery and bitterness.

After washing down spaghetti with some good red wine, he found himself a spot on a window seat where he could sit back and watch the show.

Bess dropped down beside him, clinked her glass against his. "Best seat in the house."

"Some house."

"Yeah, I like it. I'll show you the rest later, if you want." She broke off a tiny piece of the pastry on his plate and sampled it. "Great stuff."

"Yeah. You got a little…here." Before his good sense could take over, he rubbed a bit of the rich cream from her lip. Watching her, he licked it from the pad of his thumb. And tasted her. "It's not bad."

For a moment she wondered if the circuits in her brain had crossed. Something certainly had sent out a spark. She managed a small sound of agreement as she flicked her tongue to the corner of her mouth. And tasted him.

"Your, ah, partner's wife. Holly." Small talk, any talk, had always come easily to her. She wasn't sure why she was laboring now.

"What about her?"

"Who? Oh, right. Holly. She's nice. I can't imagine what it would be like to teach fifth-graders."

"I'm sure you'll ask her."

"I already did." At ease again, she smiled at him. Something about that sarcastic edge to his voice made her relax and enjoy. "Come on, Alexi. We may be in different professions, but both of them require a certain amount of curiosity about human nature. Aren't you sitting here right now wondering about all of these people, and what they're doing at my party?"

"Not as much as I'm wondering what *I'm* doing at your party." He swirled the wine in his glass before sipping. When he drank, his eyes stayed on hers. Watchful.

She liked that. She liked that very much, the way he could sit so still, energy humming from every pore, while he watched. While he waited. Bess was willing to admit that one of her biggest failings was being unable to wait for anything.

"You were curious," she told him.

"Some."

Her skirt hitched up another inch when she curled her legs up on the seat. "I'd be happy to tell you whatever you want to know, in exchange for your help. You see that guy over there, the gorgeous one with the blonde hanging on his biceps?"

Alex scanned, homed in. "Yeah. I wouldn't say he was gorgeous."

"You're not a woman. That's my detective, Storm Warfield, the black sheep of the snooty, disgustingly rich Warfield clan, the rebel, the volatile brother of the long-suffering Elana Warfield Stafford Carstairs. He's recently pulled himself out of the destructive affair with the wicked, wily Vicki. The blonde crawling up his chest. They're an item off-camera, but on, Storm is madly in love with the tragedy-prone and ethereal Jade, who is, of course, torn between her feelings for him and her misplaced loyalty to the maniacally clever and dastardly Brock Carstairs—half brother to Elana's stalwart husband Dr. Maxwell Carstairs. Max was once married to Jade's formerly conniving but now repentant sister, Flame, who was killed in a Peruvian earthquake soon after the birth of her son—who may or may not be her husband's child. Naturally, the body was never recovered."

"Either I've had too much wine, or you're making me dizzy."

Bess smiled and gave him a companionable pat on the thigh that sent his blood pressure soaring. "It's really not that complicated, once you know the players. But I want you for Storm."

Alex sent the actor a considering look. "I don't think he's my type."

"Your professional expertise, Detective. I need an informal technical advisor. My producer'd be happy to compensate you for your time—particularly since we've been number one in the ratings for the past nine months." Someone called her name, and Bess sent a quick wave. "Looks like it's going to start to thin out. Listen, can you hang around until I've finished playing hostess?"

She popped up and was gone before he could answer. After a moment, Alex set the rest of the dessert aside and rose. If he was going to see the party through, he might as well enjoy himself.

As she saw to the rest of her guests, Bess kept an eye on him. Once he decided to relax, she noted, he made the most of it. It didn't surprise her that he knew how to flirt, or that several women in the room made a point of wandering in his direction. Not even Lori—no pushover in the men department—was unaffected.

"So, that's the one who busted you?" Lori asked her, popping a plump olive into her mouth.

"What do you think?"

Lori chewed, savored, swallowed. "Yum-yum."

With a laugh, Bess chose a wedge of cheese. "I assume that's a comment on the man, not my buffet."

"You bet. And the best part is, he's not an actor."

"Still sore?" Bess murmured.

Lori shrugged, but her gaze cut over to Steven Marshall, alias Brock Carstairs. "I never give him, or his weenie little brain, a thought. No sensible woman would spend her life competing with an actor's ego for attention."

"Sense has nothing to do with it."

Lori looked away, because it hurt, more than she could bear to admit, to watch Steven while he was so busy ignoring her. "This from the queen of the bungled relationships."

"I don't bungle them, I enjoy them."

"I hasten to remind you that two of your former fiancés are in this room."

"It's a big party. Besides, I wasn't engaged to Lawrence."

"He gave you a ring with a rock the size of a Buick."

"A token of his esteem," Bess said blithely. "I never agreed to marry him. And Charlie and I…" She waved to Charles Stutman, esteemed playwright. "We were only engaged for a few months. We both agreed Gabrielle was perfect for him and parted the closest of friends."

"It was the first time I'd heard of a woman being

best man at her former fiancé's wedding," Lori admitted. "I don't know how you do it. You don't angst over men, and they never toss blame your way when things fall apart."

"Because I end up being a pal." Bess's lips curved. For the briefest of moments, there was something wistful in the smile. "Not always a position a woman craves, but it seems to suit me."

"Going to be pals with the cop?"

Once again Bess found herself searching the remaining guests for Alex. She found him, dancing slow and close with a sultry brunette. "It would help if he'd bring himself to like me a little. I think it's going to take some work."

"I've never known you to fail. I've got to go. See you Monday."

"Okay." Bess was astute enough to glance over in Steven's direction as Lori left. She was also clear-sighted enough to see the expression of misery in his eyes as he watched Lori walk to the elevator.

People were much too hard on themselves, she thought with a sigh. Love, she was certain, was a complicated and painful process only if you wanted it to be. And she should know, she mused as she took another sip of wine. She had slipped painlessly in and out of love for years.

As she set the glass aside, Alex caught her eye. There was a quick, surprising tremor around her heart. But it was gone quickly as someone swept her up into a dance.

Chapter 3

"How often do you have one of these *things?*" Alex asked when he took Bess up on her offer of a last cup of cappuccino in her now empty and horribly cluttered apartment.

"Oh, when the mood strikes." The after-party wreckage didn't concern her. She and the cleaning team she'd hired would shovel it out sooner or later. Besides, she enjoyed this—the mess and debris, the spilled wine, the lingering scents. It was a testament to the fact that she, and a good many others, had enjoyed themselves.

"Want some cold spaghetti?" she asked him.

"No."

"I do." She unfolded herself from the corner section of the pit and wandered over to the buffet. "I didn't get a chance to eat much earlier—just what I could steal off other people's plates." She came back to stretch out on the cushions and twine pasta on her fork. "What did you think of Bonnie?"

"Who?"

"Bonnie. The brunette you were dancing with. The one who stuck her phone number in your pocket."

Remembering, Alex patted his shirt pocket. "Right. Bonnie. Very nice."

"Mmm…she is." As she agreed, Bess twined more pasta. She propped her feet on the coffee table, where they continued to keep the beat of the low-volume rock playing on the stereo. "I appreciate your staying."

"I've got some time."

"I still appreciate it. Let me run this by you, okay?" She continued to eat, rapidly working her way through a large plate full of food. "Jade's got a split personality due to an early-childhood trauma, which I won't go into."

"Thank God."

"Don't be snide—millions of viewers are panting for more. Anyway, Jade's alter ego, Josie, is the hooker—or will be, once we start taping that story line. Storm's nuts about Jade. It's difficult for him, as he's a very passionate sort of guy, and she's fragile at the moment."

"Because of Brock."

"You catch on. Anyway, he's wildly in love and miserably frustrated, and he's got a hot case to solve. The Millbrook Maniac."

"The—" Alex shut his eyes. "Oh, man."

"Hey, the press is always giving psychotics catchy little labels. Anyway, the Maniac's going around strangling women with a pink silk scarf. It's symbolic, but we won't get into that right now, either."

"I can't tell you how grateful I am."

She offered him a forkful of cold pasta. After a moment, he gave in and leaned closer to take it. "Now, the press is going to start hounding Storm," Bess continued. "And the brass will be on his case, too. His emotional life is a wreck. How does he separate it? How does he go about establishing a connection between the three— so far—victims? And when he realizes Jade may be in danger, how does he keep his personal feelings from clouding his professional judgement?"

"That's the kind of stuff you want?"

"For a start."

"Okay." He propped his feet beside hers. "First, you don't separate, not like you mean. The minute you have to think like a cop, that's what you are, that's how you think, and you've got no personal life until you can stop thinking like a cop again."

"Wait." Bess shoved the plate into his lap, then bounded up and hunted through a drawer until she came up with a notebook. She dropped onto the sofa again, curling up her legs this time, so that her knee lay against the side of his thigh. "Okay," she said, scribbling. "You're telling me that when you start on a case, or get a call or whatever, everything else just clicks off."

Since she seemed to be through eating, he set the plate on the coffee table. "It better click off."

"How?"

He shook his head. "There is no how. It just is. Look, cop work is mostly monotonous. It's routine, but it's the kind of routine you have to keep focused on. Make a mistake in the paperwork, and some slime gets bounced on a technicality."

"What about when you're on the street?"

"That's a routine, too, and you'd better keep your

head on that routine, if you want to go home in one piece. You can't start thinking about the fight you had with your woman, or the bills you can't pay, or the fact that your mother's sick. You think about now, right now, or you won't be able to fix any of those things later. You'll just be dead."

Her eyes flashed up to his. He said it so matter-of-factly. When she studied him, she saw that he thought of it that way. "What about fear?"

"You usually have about ten seconds to be afraid. So you take them."

"But what if the fear's for someone else? Someone you love?"

"Then you'd better put it aside and do what you've been trained to do. If you don't, you're no good to yourself or your partner, and you're a liability."

"So, it's cut-and-dried?"

He smiled a little. "Except on TV. You're asking me for feelings, McNee, intangibles."

"A cop's feelings," she told him. "I'd think they would be very tangible. Maybe a cop wouldn't be allowed to show his emotions on the job. An occasional flare-up, maybe, but then you'd have to suck it in and follow routine. And no matter how good you are, an arrest isn't always going to stick. The bad guy isn't always going to pay. That has to cause immeasurable frustration. And repressing that frustration…" Considering, she tapped her pencil against the pad. "See, I think of people as pressure cookers."

"Sure you do."

"No, really." That quick smile, the flash of the single dimple. "Whatever's inside, good or bad, has to have some means of release, or the lids blows." She shifted again, and her fingers nearly brushed his neck. She talked with them, he'd noted. With her hands, her eyes, her whole body. The woman simply didn't know how to be still. "What do you use to keep the lid on, Alexi?"

"I make sure I kick a couple of small dogs every morning."

She smiled with entirely too much understanding. "Too personal? Okay, we'll come back to it later."

"It's not personal." Damn it, she made him uncomfortable. As if he had an itch in the small of his back that he couldn't quite scratch. "I use the gym. Beat the crap out of a punching bag a few days a week. Lift too many weights. Sweat it out."

"That's great. Perfect." Grinning now, she cupped a hand over his biceps and squeezed. "Not too shabby. I guess it works." She flexed her own arm, inviting him to test the muscle. It was the gesture of a small boy on a playground, but Alex couldn't quite think of her that way. "I work out myself," she told him. "I'm addicted to it. But I can't seem to develop any upper-body strength."

He watched her eyes as he curled a hand over her arm and found a tough little muscle. "Your upper body looks fine."

"A compliment." Surprised that a reaction had leapt straight into her gut at the casual touch, she started to move her arm. He held on. It took some work to keep her smile from faltering. "What? You want to arm-wrestle, Detective?"

Her skin was like rose petals—smooth, fragrant. Experimenting, he skimmed his hand down to the curve of her elbow. She was smiling, he noted, and her eyes were lit with humor, but her pulse was racing. "A few years back I arm-wrestled my brother for his wife. I lost."

The idea was just absurd enough to catch her imagination. "Really? Is that how the Stanislaskis win their women?"

"Whatever works." Because he was tempted to explore more of that silky, exposed skin, he rose. He reminded himself that the uncomplicated Bonnie was more his style than the overinquisitive, oddly packaged Bess McNee. "I have to go."

Whatever had been humming between them was fading now. As Bess walked him to the door, she debated with herself whether she wanted to let those echoes fade or pump up the volume until she recognized the tune. "Stanislaski. Is that Polish, Russian, what?"

"We're Ukrainian."

"Ukrainian?" Intrigued, she watched him pull his jacket on. "From the southwest of the European Soviet Union, with the Carpathian Mountains in the west."

"Yeah." And through those mountains his family had escaped when he was no more than a baby. He felt a tug, a small one, as he often did when he thought of the country of his blood. "You've been there?"

"Only in spirit." Smiling, she straightened his jacket for him. "I minored in geography in college. I like reading about exotic places." She kept her hands on the front of his jacket, enjoying the feel of leather, the scent of it, and of him. Their bodies were close, more casual than intimate, but close. Looking into his eyes, those dark, uncannily focused eyes, she discovered she wanted to hear that tune again after all.

"Are you going to talk to me again?" she asked him.

His fingers itched to roam along that tantalizingly bare skin on her back. For reasons he couldn't have named, he kept his hands at his sides. "You know where to find me. If I've got the time and the answers, we'll talk."

"Thanks." Her lips curved as she rose on her toes so that their eyes and mouths were level. She leaned in slowly, an inch, then two, to touch her mouth to his. The kiss was soft and breezy. Either of his sisters might have said goodbye to him in precisely the same manner. But that cool and fleeting taste of her didn't make him feel brotherly.

She heard the humming in her head. A nice, quiet sound of easy pleasure. He tasted faintly of wine and spices, and his firm lips seemed to accept the gesture as it was meant—as one of affection and curiosity. Her lips were still curved when she dropped back on her heels.

"Good night, Alexi."

He nodded. He was fairly sure he could speak, but there was no point in taking the chance. Turning, he walked into the foyer and punched the elevator button. When he glanced back, she was still standing in the doorway. Smiling, she waved another goodbye and started to close the door.

It surprised them both when he whirled around and slapped a hand on it to keep it open. The fact that she took an automatic step in retreat surprised her further. But it was the look in his eyes, she thought, that made her feel like a rabbit caught in a rifle's cross hairs.

"Did you forget something?"

"Yeah." Very slowly, very deliberately, he slid his arms around her waist, ran his hand up her back, so that her eyes widened and her skin shivered. "I forgot I like to make my own moves."

Bess braced for the kind of wild assault that was in his eyes, and was surprised for the third time in as many minutes. He didn't swoop or crush, but eased her closer, degree by degree, until she was molded to him. His fingers cruised lazily up her back until they reached the nape of her neck, where they cupped and held. Still his mouth hovered above her.

His hand moved low, intimately, where skin gave way to silk. "Stand on your toes," he murmured.

"What?"

"Stand on your toes." This time, it was his lips that curved.

Dazed, she obeyed, then gave a strangled gasp when he increased the pressure on her back and pressed them center to center. His eyes stayed open as he moved his mouth to hers, brushing, nipping, then taking, in a dreamy kind of possession that had her own vision blurring.

The humming in her brain increased until it was a wall of sound, unrecognizable. She was deaf to everything else, even her own throaty moan as he dipped his tongue between her lips to seduce hers.

It was all slow-motion and soft-focus, but that didn't stop the heat from building. She could feel the little flames start to flare where she was pressed most intimately against him, then spread long, patient fingers of fire outward. Everywhere.

He never pushed, he never pressured, he savored, as a man might who had enjoyed a satisfying meal and was content to linger over a tasty dessert. Even knowing she was being sampled, tested, lazily consumed, she couldn't protest. For the first time in her life, Bess understood what it was to be helplessly seduced.

He hadn't meant to do this. He'd been thinking about doing just this for hours. However much pleasure it gave him to feel her curvy body melt against his, to hear those small, vulnerable sounds vibrating in her throat, to taste that dizzy passion on her lips, he knew he'd made a mistake.

She wasn't his type. And he was going to want more.

The instinct he'd been born with and then honed during his years on the force helped him to hold back that part of himself that, if let loose, could turn the evening into a disaster for both of them. Still, he lingered another moment, taking himself to the edge. When his system was churning with her, and his mind was clouded with visions of peeling her out of that swatch of a dress, he stepped back. He supported her by the elbows until her eyes fluttered open.

They were big and dazed. He clenched his teeth to fight back the urge to pull her to him again and finish what he'd started. But, however stunned and fragile she looked at the moment, Alex recognized a dangerous woman. He'd been a cop long enough to know when to face danger, and when to avoid it.

"You, ah…" Where was all her glib repartee? Bess wondered. It was a little difficult to think when she wasn't sure her head was still on her shoulders. "Well," she managed, and settled for that.

"Well." He let her go and added a cocky grin before he walked back to the elevator. Though his stance was relaxed, he was praying the elevator would come quickly, before he lost it and crawled back to her door. She was still there when the elevator rumbled open. Alex let out a quiet, relieved breath as he stepped inside and leaned against the back wall. "See you around, McNee," he said as the doors slid shut.

"Yeah." She stared at the mural-covered walls. "See you around."

"Holly hasn't been able to stop talking about that party." Judd was scarfing down a blueberry muffin as Alex cruised Broadway. "It made her queen of the teachers' lounge."

"I bet." Alex didn't want to think about Bess's party. He especially didn't want to think about what would be after the party. Work was what he needed to concentrate on, and right now work meant following up on the few slim leads they'd hassled out of Domingo.

"If Domingo's given it to us straight, Angie Horowitz was excited about a new john." Alex tapped his fingers against the steering wheel. "He'd hired her two Wednesdays running, dressed good, tipped big."

Judd nodded as he brushed muffin crumbs from his shirt. "And she was killed on a Wednesday. So was Rita Shaw. It's still pretty thin, Alex."

"So we make it thick." It continued to frustrate him that they'd wasted time interrogating the desk clerks at the two fleabag hotels where the bodies had been found. Like most in their profession, the clerks had seen nothing. Heard nothing. Knew nothing.

As for the ladies who worked the streets, however nervous they were, they weren't ready to trust a badge.

"Tomorrow's Wednesday," Judd said helpfully.

"I know what the hell tomorrow is. Do you do anything but eat?"

Judd unwrapped another muffin. "I got low blood sugar. If we're going to go back and look at the crime scene again, I need energy."

"What you need is—" Alex broke off as he glanced past Judd's profile and into the glaring lights of an all-night diner. He knew only one person with hair that shade of red. He began to swear, slowly, steadily, as he searched for a parking place.

* * *

"You really write for TV?" Rosalie asked.

Bess finished emptying a third container of nondairy product into her coffee. "That's right."

"I didn't think you were a sister." Interested as much in Bess as in the fifty dollars she'd been paid, Rosalie blew out smoke rings. "And you want to know what it's like to turn tricks."

"I want to know whatever you're comfortable telling me." Bess shoved her untouched coffee aside and leaned forward. "I'm not sitting in judgment or asking for confidences, Rosalie. I'd like your story, if you want to tell it. Or we can stick with generalities."

"You figure you can find out what's going on on the streets by putting on spandex and a wig, like you did the other night?"

"I found out a lot," Bess said with a smile. "I found out it's tough to stand in heels on concrete for hours at a time. That a woman has to lose her sense of self in order to do business. That you don't look at the faces. The faces don't matter—the money does. And what you do isn't a matter of intimacy, not even a matter of sex—for you—but a matter of control." She scooted her coffee back and took a sip. "Am I close?"

For a moment, Rosalie said nothing. "You're not as stupid as you look."

"Thanks. I'm always surprising people that way. Especially men."

"Yeah." For the first time, Rosalie smiled. Beneath the hard-edged cosmetics and the lines life had etched in her face, she was a striking woman, not yet thirty. "I'll tell you this, girlfriend, the men who pay me see

a body. They don't see a mind. But I got a mind, and
I got a plan. I've been on the streets five years. I ain't
going to be on them five more."

"What are you going to do? What do you want to
do?"

"When I get enough saved up, I'm going South.
Going to get me a trailer in Florida, and a straight job.
Maybe selling clothes. I look real fine in good clothes."
She crushed out her cigarette and lit another. "Lots of
us have plans, but don't make it. I will. I'm clean," she
said, and lifted her arms, turning them over. It took
Bess a minute to realize Rosalie was saying she wasn't
a user. "One more year, I'm gone. Less than that, if I
hook onto a regular john with money. Angie did."

"Angie?" Bess flipped through her mental file.
"Angie Horowitz? Isn't that the woman who was murdered?"

"Yeah." Rosalie moistened her lips before sucking in
smoke. "She wasn't careful. I'm always careful."

"How can you be careful?"

"You keep yourself ready," Rosalie told her. "Angie,
she liked to drink. She'd talk a john into buying a bottle. That's not being careful. And this guy, the rich one?
He—"

"What the hell do you think you're doing?"

Both Rosalie and Bess looked up. Standing beside
the scarred table was a tall man with thin shoulders.
There was a cheroot clamped between his teeth, and a
diamond winked on his finger. His face was moon-pale,
with furious blue eyes. His hair was nearly as white,
and slicked back, ending in a short ponytail.

"I'm having me a cup of coffee and a smoke, Bobby,"

Rosalie told him. But beneath the defiance, Bess recognized the trickle of fear.

"You get back on the street where you belong."

"Excuse me." Bess offered her best smile. "Bobby, is it?"

He cast his icy blue eyes on her. "You looking for work, sweetheart? I'll tell you right now, I don't tolerate any loafing."

"Thank you, but no, I'm not looking. Rosalie was just helping me with a small problem."

"She doesn't solve anyone's problems but mine." He jerked his head toward the street. "Move it."

Bess slid out of the booth but held her ground. "This is a public place, and we're having a conversation."

"You don't talk to anybody I don't tell you to talk to." Bobby gave Rosalie a hard shove toward the door.

Bess didn't think, simply reacted. If she detested anything, it was a bully. "Now just a damn minute." She grabbed his sleeve. He rounded on her. Other patrons put on their blinders when he pushed her into the table. Bess came up, fists clenched, just as Alex slammed through the door.

"One move, Bobby," he said tightly. "Just one move toward her."

Bobby brushed at his sleeve and shrugged. "I just came in for a cup of coffee. Isn't that right, Rosalie?"

"Yeah." Rosalie closed her hand over the business card Bess had slipped her. "We were just having some coffee."

But Alex's eyes were all for Bess. She didn't look pale and frightened. Her eyes were snapping, and her cheeks were flushed with fury. "Tell me you want to press charges."

"I'm sorry." With an effort, Bess relaxed her hands. "We were just having a conversation. Nice talking to you, Rosalie."

"Sure." She swaggered out, blowing smoke in Alex's face for effect.

"Take off."

Bobby moved his shoulders again, smirked. "The coffee's lousy here, anyway." He flicked a glance at Bess. "Next time, sweetheart."

Alex waited ten humming seconds after the door swung shut. Without a word, he stalked over to Bess and grabbed her by the arm and hustled her out the door.

"Look, if this is a knight-in-shining-armor routine, I appreciate it, but I don't need rescuing."

"You need a straitjacket."

With murder in his heart, he dragged her half a block.

"In the car," he snapped, opening the back door of the patrol car.

"A cab would be—"

He swore, put a hand on her head and shoved her into the back seat.

Resigned, Bess settled back. "Hi, Judd," she said as he took his place in the passenger seat in front. "How's Holly?"

"Great, thanks." He slanted a look toward his partner. "Ah, she really had a good time at your place."

"I'm glad. We'll have to do it again." Alex whipped out into traffic with enough force to have her slamming back against the seat. Without missing a beat, Bess crossed her legs. "Am I allowed to ask where we're going, or is this another bust?"

"I should be taking you to Bellevue, where you belong," Alex responded. "But I'm taking you home."

"Well, thanks for the lift."

His eyes flashed to hers in the rearview mirror. Her face was still flushed, and her irises were a sharp enough jade to slice to the bone, but she looked more miffed than upset. *Miffed,* he thought with a snort. Stupid word. It fit her perfectly.

"You're an idiot, McNee. And, like most idiots, you're dangerous."

"Oh, really?" She scooted up in the seat so that she could lean between him and Judd. "Just how do you figure that, smart guy?"

"Not only do you go back down to an area you have no business even knowing about—"

"Give me a break."

"But," he continued, "you sit there drinking coffee with a hooker, then pick a fight with her pimp. The kind of guy who'd as soon give a woman a black eye as wish her good-morning."

Bess poked a finger at his shoulder. "I didn't pick a fight with anyone, and if I had, it would be my business."

"That's why you're an idiot."

"Hey, Alex, ease off."

"Keep out of this," Alex and Bess snarled in unison.

"I'm not even here," Judd mumbled, scooting down in his seat.

"It so happens I was conducting an interview." Bess folded her arms on the seat so that she wouldn't give in to the nasty urge to twist Alex's ear. "In a public place," she added. "And you had no right to come bursting in and ruining everything before I'd finished."

"If I hadn't come bursting in, babe, you'd have had your nose broken again."

She scowled, wrinkling her undeniably crooked nose. "I can defend my nose, and anything else, just fine."

"Yeah, anyone can see you're a regular amazon. Ow!" He slapped at her hand and swore the air blue when she gave in and twisted his ear. "The minute I get you out of this car, I'm going to—"

"Uh, Alex?"

"I told you to keep out of it."

"I'm out," Judd assured him. "But you might want to take a look at the liquor store coming up at nine o'clock."

Still steaming, Alex did, then let out a heavy sigh. "Perfect. This makes it perfect. Call it in."

Bess watched, wide-eyed, as Judd radioed in an armed robbery in progress, gave their location and requested backup. Before she could shut her gaping mouth, Alex was swinging to the curb.

"You," he said, stabbing a finger in her face. "Stay in the car, or I swear I'll wring your neck."

"I'm not going anywhere," Bess assured him after she managed to swallow the large ball of fear lodged in her throat. But before the words were out, he and Judd were out of the car and drawing their weapons.

He'd already forgotten her, she realized as she stared at his profile. Before he and Judd had crossed the street, he'd put on his cop's mind and his cop's face. She'd seen hundreds of actors try to emulate that particular look. Some came close, she realized, but this was the real thing. It wasn't grim or fierce, but flat, almost blank.

Except for the eyes, she thought with a quick shudder. She'd had only one glimpse of his eyes, but it had been enough.

Life and death had been in them, and a potential for violence she would never have guessed at.

In the darkened car, she gripped her hands together and prayed.

He hadn't forgotten her. It infuriated him that he had to fight to tuck her into some back corner of his mind. There were innocent people in that store. A man and a woman. He could smell the fear while he was still three yards away.

But he broke his concentration long enough to glance back and make certain she was staying put.

He gestured Judd to one side of the door while he took the other. He didn't have time to worry that the rookie might freeze. Right now they were just two cops, and he had to believe Judd would go with him through the door.

The 9 mm felt warm in his hand. He'd already identified the weapons of the two perpetrators. One had a sawed-off shotgun, the other a wicked-looking .45. He could hear the woman crying, pleading not to be hurt. Alex ignored it. They would wait for backup as long as they could.

He shifted just enough to look inside.

Behind the counter, a woman of approximately sixty stood with her hands at her throat, weeping. A man of about the same age was emptying the cash register as fast as his trembling hands allowed. One of the gunmen grabbed a bottle off a shelf. He ripped off the top and guzzled. Swearing at the old man, he smashed the bottle on the counter and jabbed the broken glass toward his face.

Alex had seen the look before, and he knew they wouldn't be content with the money. "We're going in," he whispered to Judd. "You go low, go for the one on the right."

Pale, Judd nodded. "Say when."

"Don't fire your weapon unless you have to." Alex sucked in his breath and went through the door. "Police!" In the back of his mind he heard the sirens from the backup as the first gunman swung the shotgun in his direction. "Drop it!" he ordered, knowing it was useless. The woman was already screaming before the first shots were fired.

The shotgun blew out a bank of fluorescent lights as the force of Alex's bullet sent the man slamming backward. Alex was getting the second man in his sights when a bullet from the .45 slammed into a bottle inches above his head, spraying alcohol and glass. Judd fired, and stopped being a rookie.

Slowly, with the same blank look on his face, Alex came out of his crouch and studied his partner. Judd wasn't pale now. He was green. "You okay?"

"Yeah." After replacing his weapon, Judd rubbed the back of his hand over his mouth. There was a greasy knot in his stomach that was threatening to leap into his throat. "It was my first."

"I know. Go outside."

"I'm okay."

Alex gave him a nudge on the shoulder. His hand remained there a moment, surprisingly gentle. "Go outside anyway. Tell the backup to call an ambulance."

Bess was waiting beside the car when Alex came out some twenty minutes later. He looked the same, she thought. Just the same as he'd looked when he walked in. Then he lifted his head and looked at her, and she saw she was wrong.

His eyes hadn't looked so tired, so terribly tired, twenty minutes before.

"I told you to stay in the car."

"I did."

"Then get back in."

Gently she laid a hand on his arm. "Alexi, you made your point. I'll take a cab. You have things to do."

"I've done them." He skirted the car and yanked open the passenger door. She could almost feel his body vibrating, but when he spoke, his voice was firm, sharp. "Get in the damn car, Bess."

She didn't have the heart to argue, so she crossed over and complied. "What about Judd?"

"He's heading to the cop shop to file the report."

"Oh."

He let the silence hang for three blocks. It hadn't been his first, but he hadn't told Judd that the bright, shaky sickness didn't fade. It only turned inward, becoming anger, disgust, frustration. And you never stopped asking yourself why.

"Aren't you going to ask how it felt? What went through my mind? What happens next?"

"No." She said it quietly. "I don't have to ask when I can see. And it's easy enough to find out what happens next."

It wasn't what he wanted. He didn't want her to be understanding, or quietly agreeable, or to turn those damned sympathetic eyes on him. "Passing up a chance for grist for your mill? McNee, you surprise me. Or can't your TV cop blow away a couple of stoned perps?"

He was trying to hurt her. Well, she understood that,

Bess thought. It often helped to lash out when you were in pain. "I'm not sure I can fit it into any of our scheduled story lines, but who knows?"

His hands clenched on the wheel. "I don't want to see you down there again, understand? If I do, I swear I'll find a way to lock you up for a while."

"Don't threaten me, Detective. You had a rough night, and I'm willing to make allowances, but don't threaten me." Leaning back, she shut her eyes. "In fact, do us both a favor and don't talk to me at all."

He didn't, but when he pulled up at her building, the smoke from his anger was still hanging in the air. Satisfied, she slammed out of the car. She'd taken two steps when he caught up with her.

"Come here," he demanded, and hauled her against him. She tasted it, all the violence and pain and fury of what he'd done that night. What he'd had to do. There was no way for her to comfort. She wouldn't have dared. There was no way for her to protest. She couldn't have tried. Instead, she let the sizzling passion of the kiss sweep over her.

Just as abruptly, he let her go. He'd be trembling in a minute, and he knew it. God, he needed...something from her. Needed, but didn't want.

"Stay off my turf, McNee." He turned on his heel and left her standing on the sidewalk.

Chapter 4

"When it comes to murder," Bess mused, "I like a nice, quick-acting poison. Something exotic, I think."

Lori pursed her lips. "If we're going to do it, I really think he should be shot. Through the heart."

Shifting in her seat at the cluttered table, Bess scooped up a handful of sugared almonds. "Too ordinary. Reed's a sophisticated, sensuous cad. I think he should go out with more than just a bang." She munched and considered. "In fact, we could make it a slow, insidious poison—milk a few weeks of him wasting away."

"Nagging headaches, dizzy spells, loss of appetite," Lori put in.

"And chills. He really should have chills." Bess steepled her hands and imagined. "He gives this big cocktail party, see. You know how he likes to flaunt his power and money in the faces of all the people he's dumped on over the years."

Lori sighed. "That's why I love him."

"And why millions of viewers love to hate him. If we're going to take him out, let's do it big. They're all there at Reed's mansion.... Jade, who's never forgiven him for using her sister for his own evil ends. Elana, who's agonizing over the fact that Reed will use his secret file, distorting the information to discredit Max."

"Mmm..." Getting into the spirit, Lori gestured with her watered-down soft drink. "Brock, who's furious that with one phone call Reed can upset the delicate balance of the Tryson deal and cost Brock a fortune. And Miriam, of course."

"Of course. We haven't seen nearly enough of her lately. Reed's self-destructive ex-wife, who blames him for all her problems."

"Justifiably," Lori pointed out.

"Then there's Vicki, the woman scorned. Jeffrey, the cuckolded husband." She grinned. "And the rest of the usual suspects."

"Okay. What kind of poison?"

"Something rare," Bess mused. "Maybe Oriental. I'll work on it." She scribbled a reminder on a notepad. "So they all have a motive for killing him. Even the housekeeper, because he seduced her naive, innocent daughter, then cast her aside. Sometime during the party, we see a glass of champagne. The room's in shadows. Close-up on a small black vial. A hand pours a few drops into the glass."

"We'll see if it's a man or woman."

"The hand's gloved," Bess decided, then realized how ridiculous it would be to wear gloves at a cocktail party. "Okay, okay, we don't see it at the party. Before. There's this box, see? This ornately carved wooden box."

"And the gloved hand opens it. Candlelight flickers off the glass vial as the hand removes it from the bed of velvet."

"That's the ticket. We'll cut to that kind of thing three or four times during the week of the party. Let the audience know it's bad business for somebody."

"Meanwhile, Reed's playing everyone like puppets. Handing out his personal brand of misery, building the pressure to the boiling point, until it explodes on the night of the party."

"It'll be great," Bess assured her. "Throughout the evening, Reed's enjoying himself stirring up old fires, poking at sores. Miriam has too much to drink and gets sloppy and shrill. This provides the perfect distraction for our killer to doctor Reed's champagne. Because it's slow-acting, the symptoms don't begin to show right away. We have some fatigue, a little dizziness, some minor pain. Maybe a rash."

"I like a good rash," Lori agreed.

"By the time he kicks off, it'll be difficult for the cops to pinpoint the time and place when the poison was administered. We just might have the perfect crime."

"There is no perfect crime."

Both Bess and Lori glanced toward the doorway. Alex stood there, his hands tucked in his pockets. There was a half smile on his face, a result of his enjoyment at listening to them plotting a murder. "Besides, if your TV cop didn't figure it out, your viewers would be pretty disappointed."

"He'll figure it out." Bess reached for another almond

as she watched him, her bare feet propped on the chair beside her. Alex discovered that the baggy slacks she wore effectively hid her legs but didn't stop him from thinking about them. "Did somebody call a cop?" she asked Lori.

"Not me." Well aware that three was most definitely a crowd, Lori rose. "Listen, I've got to make a call, and I think I'll run up and peek in on the taping. Nice to see you, Detective."

"Yeah." He shifted so that Lori could get through the door, but he didn't step inside. Instead, he glanced around, annoyed with himself for feeling so awkward. "Some place," he said at length.

Bess's lips curved. The room was hardly bigger than a closet and windowless. The table where she and Lori worked was covered with books, folders and papers, and dominated by a word processor that was still humming. Besides the table, there was one overstuffed chair, a small couch and two televisions.

"We call it home," Bess said, and tilted her head. "So, what brings you down to the dungeons, Alexi?"

The description was fairly apt. They were in the basement of the building that held the studios and production offices for "Secret Sins" and its network. He shrugged off her question with one of his own. "How long are you in for?"

"The duration, I hope." Casually she rubbed the ball of one foot over the instep of the other. "After the last Emmy, they did offer us an upstairs office with a view, but Lori and I are creatures of habit. Besides, who's going to come down here and peek over our shoulders while we write?" She recrossed her ankles. "Are you off-duty?"

"I took a couple hours' personal time."

"Oh." She drew the word out, thinking he looked very appealing when he was embarrassed. "Should I consider this a personal visit?"

"Yeah." He stepped inside, then regretted it. There wasn't enough room to wander around. "Listen, I just wanted to apologize."

It was probably very small of her, Bess thought, but, oh, she was enjoying this. "Generally or specifically?"

"Specifically." He shook his head when she held out the bowl of almonds. "After the robbery attempt, when I took you home. I was out of line."

"Okay." She set the bowl down and smiled at him. "We're dealing with your behavior during the last half hour of the evening."

His brows drew together. "Everything I said before that sticks. You had no business doing what you were doing, where you were doing it."

"Get back to the apology. I like that better."

"I took what I was feeling out on you, and I'm sorry." Figuring the worst was over, he sat on the edge of the table. "You didn't react the way I expected."

"Which was?"

"Scared, outraged, disgusted." He shrugged again. "I don't usually take women to armed robberies."

Now things were getting interesting. "Where *do* you take them?"

His gaze locked on hers. He knew when he was being teased, and he knew when it was good-natured. "To dinner, to the flicks, dancing. To bed."

"Well, armed robbery is probably more exciting. At least than the first three." She rose, placed her hands on his shoulders and kissed him lightly on the mouth.

"No hard feelings." When his hands came to her hips and held her in place, she lifted a brow. "Was there something else?"

"I've been thinking about you."

"That could be good."

His lips twitched. "I haven't decided that yet. Maybe we could start with dinner."

"Start what?"

"Working our way to bed. That's where I want you."

"Oh." Her breath came out a little too quickly and not quite steady. It didn't help that his eyes were calm, amused and very confident. How, she wondered, had their positions been so neatly reversed? "That's certainly cutting to the chase."

"You said once that people in our professions observe people. What I've observed about you, McNee, is that you'd probably see through any flowers and moonbeams I might toss at you."

Slowly she ran her tongue over her teeth. "Depends on your pitching arm. The idea isn't without its appeal, Alexi, but I prefer taking certain aspects of my life— sex being one of them—in a cautious, gradual manner."

He grinned at her. "That could be good."

She had to laugh. "Meanwhile—" But he didn't let her scoot back.

"Meanwhile," he echoed, keeping his hands firm. "Have dinner with me. Just dinner."

Hadn't she told herself she wasn't going to get involved again, fall in love again? Oh, well. "I often enjoy just dinner."

"Tomorrow. I'm on tonight."

"Tomorrow's fine."

He nudged her an inch closer. "I'm making you nervous."

"No, you're not." Yes, he was.

"You're wriggling." He grinned again, surprised at how satisfying it was to know he'd unsettled her.

"I've got work, that's all."

"Me too. Why don't I come by about seven-thirty? My brother-in-law's got this place. I think you'll get a kick out of it."

"Lady clothes or real clothes?"

"What are you wearing now?"

She glanced down at her sweater and slacks. "Real ones."

"That'll do." He stood, then tilted her chin with a finger until they were eye-to-eye. "You have the oddest face," he said half to himself. "You should be ugly."

She laughed, unoffended. "I was. I've burned all pictures of me before the age of eighteen." Her dimple winked out as she smiled at him. "I imagine you were always gorgeous."

He winced, though he knew he should be used to having that term applied to him. "My sisters were gorgeous," he told her. "Are. My brother and I are ruggedly attractive."

"Ah, manly men."

"You got it."

"And you grew up surrounded by flocks of adoring females."

"We started with flocks and moved on to hordes."

Her eyes lit with amusement and curiosity. "What was it like to—"

He cut her off the most sensible way. He liked the quick little jolt her body gave before she settled into him. And the way her mouth softened, accepted. No pretenses here, he thought as she gave a quiet sigh and melted into the kiss. It was simple and easy, as basic as breathing.

If his system threatened to overcharge, he knew how to control it. Perhaps he drew the kiss out longer than he'd intended to, deepened it more than he had planned. But he was still in control. Maybe, for just a moment, he imagined what it would be like to lock the door, to sweep all those papers off the table and take her, fast and hot, on top of it.

But he wasn't a maniac. He reminded himself of that, even as his blood began to swim. A slow and gentle touch brought pleasure to both, and let a woman see that she was appreciated for everything she was.

"Dangerous," he murmured in Ukrainian as he slid his mouth from her. "Very dangerous woman."

"What?" She blinked at him with eyes that were arousingly unfocused and heavy. "What does that mean?"

He had to make a conscious effort to keep his hands gentle at her shoulders. "I said I have to go. Keep off the streets, McNee."

She called to him as he reached the doorway. "Detective." Her heart was thumping, her head was reeling, but she really hated not having the last word. For lack of anything better, she dredged up an old line from "Hill Street Blues." "Let's be careful out there."

Alone, she lowered herself into a chair, as carefully as an elderly aunt. Five minutes later, Lori found her in exactly the same spot, still staring into space.

"Uh-oh." One look had Lori dropping down beside her. With a shake of her head, she handed Bess a fresh soft drink. "I knew it. I knew this was going to happen the minute I saw that gorgeous cop at your party."

"It hasn't happened yet." Bess took a long drink. Funny, she hadn't realized how dry her throat had become. "I'm afraid it's going to, but it hasn't happened yet."

"You had that same look on your face when you fell for Charlie. And for Sean. And Miguel. Not to mention—"

"Then don't." Frowning, she focused on Lori. "Miguel? Are you certain? I was sure I had better taste."

"Miguel," Lori said ruthlessly. "Granted, you came to your senses within forty-eight hours, but the day after he took you to the opera you had the same stupid look on your face."

"We saw *Carmen,*" Bess pointed out. "I don't think the look had anything to do with him. Besides, I'm not in love with Alexi, I'm just having dinner with him tomorrow."

"That's what you always say. Like with George."

Bess's shoulders straightened. "George was the sweetest man I've ever known. Being engaged to him taught me a lot about understanding and compassion."

"I know. You were understanding enough to be godmother to his firstborn."

"Well, after all, I did introduce him to Nancy."

"And he promptly dumped you and ran off with her."

"He didn't dump me. I wish you wouldn't hold that against him, Lori. Breaking our engagement was a mutual decision."

"And the best thing to happen to you. George was a wimp. A whiny wimp."

Because it was precisely true, Bess sighed. "He just needed a lot of emotional support."

"At least you never slept with him."

"He was saving himself."

They looked at each other and burst out laughing. Once she caught her breath, Bess shook her head. "I should never have told you that. It was indiscreet."

"Observation," Lori announced, and Bess gestured a go-ahead. "The cop isn't going to save himself."

"I know." Bess felt the warning flutter in her stomach. Thoughtfully she drew her finger down through the moisture on the bottle. "I'll cross that bridge when I come to it."

"Bess, you don't cross bridges, you burn them." Lori gave her hand a quick squeeze. "Don't get hurt."

There was a touch of regret in Bess's smile. "Do I ever?"

Alex liked the way she looked. It took a certain panache, he supposed, to be able to wear the jade-toned blouse with bright blue slacks, particularly if you were going to add hot-pink high-tops. But Bess pulled it off. Everything about her was vivid. He supposed that was why he'd gone into her office to apologize and ended up asking her out.

It was probably why he hadn't been able to get her, or the idea of taking her to bed, out of his mind since he'd met her.

For herself, Bess took one look at Zackary Muldoon's bar, Lower the Boom, and knew she had a relaxed, enjoyable evening in store. There was music from the juke box, a babble of voices, a medley of good, rich scents. The tangle of pear-shaped gemstones at her ears swung as she turned to Alex. "This is great. Is the food as good as it smells?"

"Better." He gave a wave in the general direction of the bar as he found them a table.

As usual, the bar was cluttered with people and thick with noise. Since his sister had married Zack, Alex had made a habit of dropping in once a week or so, and he knew most of the regulars by name. He grinned at the waitress who stopped at their table. "Hey, Lola. How's it going?"

"It'll do, cutie." Resting her tray on her hip, Lola gave Bess the once-over. Though less than ten years Alex's senior, Lola had taken a maternal interest in him. It wasn't often Alex brought a date into the bar, and Lola made it her business to check out his current lady. "So, what can I get you?"

"Tequila." Bess dropped her bag in the empty chair beside her with a thunk. "Straight up."

Alex only lifted a brow at Bess's choice. "Give me a beer, Lola. Rachel around?"

"Upstairs. And she better have her feet up." She gave the ceiling a scowl. "She'll probably sneak down here before the night's over. Can't keep her away from the boss."

"What's Rio's special tonight?"

"Paella." Her eyes lit with appreciation. She'd sampled some herself. "He's been driving Nick crazy, making him shell shrimp."

"You game for that?" Alex asked Bess.

"You bet." As Lola wandered off, Bess propped her chin on her hands. "So, who's the boss, who's Rio, and who's Nick?"

"Zack's the boss." He gestured toward the tall, broad-shouldered man working the bar. "Rio's the cook, this Jamaican giant who'll fix you the best meal this side of heaven. Nick's Zack's brother."

Bess nodded. She liked to know the players. "And Rachel's married to Zack." After a long study of the man behind the bar, she smiled. "Impressive. How'd she meet him?"

"She was Nick's PD after I busted him for attempted burglary."

Bess didn't blink or look shocked, she simply leaned a little closer. "What was he stealing?"

Alex was vaguely disappointed that he hadn't gotten a reaction. "Electronics—and doing a poor job of it. He was tangled up with a gang at the time. This was about a year and a half ago." Absently he toyed with the square-cut aquamarine on her finger, watching it catch the light. "Nick had some problems. Actually, he's Zack's stepbrother. Nick was still a kid when Zack went off and joined the navy and his mother died. Anyhow, when Zack came back a few years ago, his father was dying, and the kid was chin-deep in trouble."

"This is great." Bess beamed up at Lola as their drinks were served. "Thanks."

The smile did it. Lola sent Alex a look of approval before she swung by the bar to report to Zack.

"Don't stop now."

Alex lifted his mug of beer. He knew very well that Lola was giving Zack a sotto voce rundown of her impressions and opinions of his choice of companion. "You want to hear the whole thing?"

"Of course I do." Bess sprinkled salt on her wrist, licked it, then tossed back the tequila with all the flair of a Mexican bandit. While she sucked on the lime wedge

Lola had brought with the drink, she grinned at Zack. "I like the zing."

"How many times can you do that and live?"

"I haven't tested it that far." The liquor left a nice trail of heat down her throat and into her stomach. "I did ten once, but I was younger then, and stupid. So keep going." She leaned forward again. "Zack came back after sailing the seven seas and found his brother in trouble."

"Well, Nick was tangled up with the Cobras..." Alex began. By the time their paella was served, he was enjoying himself. It always polished a man's ego to have a woman's complete and fascinated attention. "So that's how I ended up on the point of having an Irish-Ukrainian niece or nephew."

"Terrific. You've got a flair for storytelling, Alexi. Must be some Gypsy blood in there."

"Naturally."

She smiled at him. All he needed was a hoop of gold in one ear and a violin, she thought—but she was sure he wouldn't want to hear it. "It doesn't hurt that you have this wisp of an accent that peeks out now and then. Of course, your material's first-rate, too. I'm a sucker for happy endings. I can't have many of them in my field. Once we tie things up, we have to unravel them again, or we lose the audience."

"Why? I thought most people went for the happy ending."

"They do. But in soaps, a character loses the edge if he or she isn't dealing with some crisis or tragedy." She sampled the paella and sighed her satisfaction. "That's why Elana's been married twice, had amnesia, was sexually assaulted, had two miscarriages and a nervous breakdown, went temporarily blind, shot a former lover in self-defense, overcame a gambling addiction, had twins who were kidnapped by a psychotic nurse—and recovered them only after a long, heartrending and perilous search through the South American jungles." She took another glorious bite. "Not necessarily in that order."

Before Alex could ask who Elana was, Lola was setting down fresh drinks. "You watch 'Secret Sins'?" she asked Bess.

"Religiously. You?"

"Well, yeah." She shrugged, knowing there were several patrons in the bar who'd rag her about it. "I got hooked when I was in the hospital having my youngest. He's ten now. That was back when Elana was a first-year resident at Millbrook Memorial and in love with Jack Banner. He was a great character."

"One of the best," Bess agreed. "Brooding and self-destructive."

"I was really sorry when he died in that warehouse fire. I didn't think Elana would ever get over it."

"She's a tough lady," Bess commented.

"Had to be." When someone called her, Lola waved to them to wait. "If it hadn't been for her, Storm would never have gotten himself together and become the man he is today."

"You like Storm?"

"Oh, man, who wouldn't?" With a chuckle, Lola rolled her eyes. "The guy's every woman's fantasy, you know? I'm really pulling for him and Jade. They deserve some happiness, after everything they've been through. Jeez, all right, Harry, I'm on my way. Enjoy your dinner," she said to Bess, and hurried off.

Bess turned to Alex with a smile. "You look confused."

He only shook his head. "You two were talking about those characters as though they were real people."

"But they are," Bess told him, and scooped up some shrimp. "For an hour a day, five days a week. Didn't you ever believe in Batman, or Sam Spade? Scarlett O'Hara, Indiana Jones?"

"It's fiction."

"Good fiction creates its own reality. That's entertainment." Picking up the saltshaker, she grinned. "Come on, Alexi, even a cop needs to fantasize now and then."

He looked at her long enough to make her pulse dance. "I do my share."

Bess swallowed the tequila, but its zing paled beside the one that Alex's quiet statement had streaking through her. "You'll have to tell me about that sometime." She glanced around at the sound of piano music.

Against the far wall was a huge upright. A slimly built, sandy-haired young man was caressing blues out of the keys.

"That's Nick," Alex told her.

"Really?" Bess angled her chair around for a better look. "He's very good."

"Yeah. He talked Zack into putting a piano in the bar about a year ago. Rachel and Muldoon tried to get him to go back to school, get more training, but no dice."

"Some things can't be taught," Bess murmured.

"Looks like. Anyway, he still works in the kitchen with Rio, and comes out and plays when the mood strikes."

"And has every female in the joint mooning over him."

"He's just a kid," Alex said quickly—too quickly.

With her tongue in her cheek, Bess turned back. "Younger men have their own appeal to the experienced woman. In fact, right now Jessica is embroiled in a passionate affair with Tod—who's ten years her junior. The mail is running five to one in favor."

"We were talking about you."

She only smiled. "Were we?"

Zack walked over to slap Alex on the back. "How's the meal?"

"It's terrific." Bess held out a hand. "You're Zack? I'm Bess."

"Nice to see you." Zack kept a hand on Alex's shoulder after giving Bess's a quick squeeze. "You must be the Bess Rachel ran into down at the station."

"I must be. You have a great place here. Now that I've found it, I'll be back."

"That's what we like to hear." His blue eyes sparkled with friendly curiosity. "Alex doesn't bring his ladies around very often. He likes to keep us guessing."

She couldn't help but respond to the humor in Zack's eyes. "Is that so?"

"Ease off, Muldoon," Alex muttered.

"He's still sore at me for stealing his baby sister."

Alex sent him an arched look. "I just figured she had better taste." He lifted his beer. "Speaking of which." He gestured with the mug.

Bess saw Zack's eyes change and, recognizing love, her heart sighed. It didn't surprise her when Rachel came to the table.

"What's this?" Rachel demanded. "A party, and nobody invited me?"

"Sit," Zack and Alex said in unison.

"I'm tired of sitting." Ignoring them both, she turned to Bess. "Nice to see you again." She took a deep, appreciative sniff. "Rio's paella. Incredible, isn't it?"

"Yes, it is. Alex was just telling me how the two of you met."

"Oh?" Rachel's brow lifted.

"Why don't you join us and give me your side of it?"

Twenty minutes later, Alex was forced to admit that Bess's casual friendliness had gotten Rachel to sit down and relax in a way neither he nor Zack would have been able to with their demanding concern.

For a woman who was so full of energy and verve, she had a knack for putting people at ease, he noted.

A gift for listening to details and asking just the right question. And for entertaining, he mused—effortlessly.

It didn't surprise him that she was able to talk music with Nick when he was called over to join them, or food with Rio when she asked to go back into the kitchen to compliment him on the meal. He wasn't surprised when she and Rachel made a date to meet for lunch the following week.

"I like your family," Bess stated as they settled into a cab.

"You've only met a fraction of it."

"Well, I like the ones I've met. How much more do you have?"

"My parents. Another sister, her husband, their three kids. A brother, his wife, and their kid. What about you?"

"Hmm?"

"Family."

"Oh. I was an only child. Do they all live in New York?"

"All but Natasha." He toyed with the curls at the nape of her neck. "You don't talk about yourself."

"Are you kidding?" She laughed, though she wanted

to curl like a cat into the fingers brushing her skin. "I never stop talking."

"You ask questions. You talk about things, other people, your characters. But you don't talk about Bess."

She should have known a cop would notice what most people didn't. "We haven't had that many conversations," she pointed out. When she turned her head, her mouth was close to his. She wanted to kiss him, Bess thought. It wasn't merely to distract him. After all, she had nothing to hide. But she didn't speak, only moved her lips to his.

The fingers at the back of her neck tensed as he changed the angle of the kiss and the mood of it. It was light and friendly only for an instant. Then it darkened, deepened, lengthened. Mixed with the taste, the texture, were hints of what was to come.

There's a storm brewing, Bess thought dizzily. And, oh, she'd never been able to resist a storm.

Her heart was knocking by the time his lips moved to her temple. "You know how to change the subject, McNee."

"What subject?"

His hand slid to her throat, cupped there. He felt the pigeon beat of her rapid pulse. The rhythm of it was as seductive as jungle drums. "You. Now I'm only more curious."

"There's not that much to tell." Uneasy and confused by the sensation, she drew back as the cab pulled to the curb. "Looks like we're here." She slid across the seat while Alex paid the driver. Her knees were a little weak, she realized. Another first. Alexi Stanislaski was going to require some thought. "You don't have to walk me up," she said, surprised that it unnerved her to see the cab pull away and leave the two of them alone on the shadowy sidewalk.

"Which means you're not going to ask me in."

"No." She smiled a little, running her fingers up and down the strap of her bag. But she wanted to. It was amazing to her just how much she wanted to. "I think it would be smarter if I didn't."

He accepted that, because the choice had to be hers. And the prospect of changing her mind along the way was tremendously appealing. "We'll do this again."

"Yes."

He closed a hand over her restless one, brought it to his lips. "Soon."

She felt something, a small, vague ache centered in her heart. Confused by it, she slipped her hand away. "All right. Soon. Good night."

"Hold it." Before she could turn away, he took her face in his hands, held it there for a moment before lowering his mouth to hers.

The pressure was whisper-light, persuasive, invasive. Even as she responded, the kiss had that odd ache spreading. Helpless, she brought her hands to his wrists, clinging to them for balance. Though his mouth remained beautifully gentle, the pulse she felt beneath her fingers raced in time with her own.

Then he let her go, stepped back. His eyes stared into hers. "Good night," he said.

She managed a nod before hurrying inside.

There was something about Bess, Alex thought as he waited patiently for the light in her apartment to come on. Something. He'd just have to find out what it was.

Chapter 5

The last person Bess expected to see when she left her office a few days later was Rosalie. Even in the bustling crowds of midtown, the woman stood out. After a moment of blank surprise, Bess smiled and crossed the sidewalk.

"Hi. Were you waiting for me?"

"Yeah."

"You should have come in." Bess adjusted the weight of her bag and briefcase.

"I figured it would be better for you if I waited out here."

"Don't be silly..." Her words trailed off as she tried to see through and around Rosalie's huge tinted glasses. Those sunburst colors around the left eye weren't all cosmetics. Bess's friendly smile faded. "What happened to you?"

Rosalie shrugged. "Bobby. He was a little ticked off about the other night."

"That's despicable."

"I've had worse."

"Bastard." She said it between her teeth, but overlying her fury was a terrible sense of guilt. "I'm sorry. I'm so sorry. It was my fault."

"Ain't nobody's fault, girlfriend. Just the way things are."

"It's not the way they should be. And if I hadn't…" She let that go, knowing you could only go back and change things in scripts. "Do you want to go to the police? I'll go with you. We could—"

"Hell, no." Rosalie let out what passed for a laugh. "I'd get a lot worse than a sore eye if I tried that. And if you think there's a cop alive who gives a damn about a hooker with a black eye, you *are* as dumb as you look."

Alex would care, Bess thought. She refused to believe otherwise. "We'll do whatever you want."

Rosalie pulled out a cigarette, cocking her hip as she lit it. "Listen, you said you'd pay me to talk. I figure I can use the extra money. And I'm on my own time."

"All right." Ideas were beginning to stir. "How much do you average a night?"

As a matter of course, Rosalie started to inflate it, but found the lie stuck in her throat. "After Bobby takes his cut, about seventy-five. Maybe a hundred. Business isn't as good as it used to be."

"We'll talk." Distracted, Bess searched for a cab. "We'll never get a taxi at this hour," she mumbled. "I live uptown about twenty blocks. Do you mind walking?"

This time Rosalie laughed full and long. "Girl, walking the streets comes natural to me."

Once they reached Bess's apartment, Rosalie tipped down her shaded glasses and whistled. Unable to resist, she walked to one of the wide windows. She could see a swatch of the East River through other buildings. The sound of traffic was so muted, it was almost musical. A far cry from the clatter and roar she lived with every day.

"My, oh, my, you do live high."

"How about dinner?" Automatically Bess stepped out of her shoes. "We'll order in." Red meat, Bess thought. At the moment, she could have eaten it raw. "Sit down, I'll get us some wine."

Wine, Rosalie thought as she stretched out on the plump cushions of the pit. She figured that sounded just dandy. "You pay for all this just writing stuff?"

"Mostly." On impulse, Bess chose one of the best bottles in her wine rack. "You're not a vegetarian, are you?"

Rosalie snorted. "Get real."

"Good. I want a steak." After handing Rosalie a glass, she picked up the phone to order dinner.

"I can't pay for that."

"I'm buying," Bess assured her, and curled up on the couch. "I need a consultant, Rosalie." It was a risk, but so was breathing, she decided. "I'll give you five hundred a week."

Rosalie choked on the wine. "Five hundred, just to tell you about turning tricks?"

"No. I want more. I want why. I want you to tell me about the other women. What draws them in. What you're afraid of, what you're not. When I ask you a question, I'll want an answer." Her voice was brisk now, all business. "I'll know if you lie."

Rosalie's eyes were shrewd and steady. "You need all that for a TV show?"

"You'd be surprised." It had gone well beyond the show. The bruise on Rosalie's face grated on her. She had caused it, Bess reflected. She would find a way to fix it. "I'm buying a lot of your time for five hundred a week, Rosalie. You might want to take a little vacation from Bobby."

"What I do after I talk to you is for me to say."

"Absolutely. But if you decided you wanted to take a break from the streets, and if you needed a place to stay while you did, I could help you."

"Why?"

Bess smiled. "Why not? It wouldn't cost me any more."

Intrigued, Rosalie considered. "I'll think about it."

"Fine. We can get started right away." She rose to gather up pads, pencils, her tape recorder. "Remember, this is daytime TV, and we can only do so much. I'll have to filter down a great deal of what you tell me. Why don't I fill you in on the story line?"

Rosalie merely shrugged. "It's your nickel."

"Yes, it is." She settled down again, and was weaving the complex and overlapping relationships of Millbrook—to Rosalie's confusion and fascination—when she heard the buzzer for her private elevator. Still talking, she walked over to release the security lock. "So, anyway, the Josie personality is dynamically opposed to Jade. The stronger she gets, the more confused and frightened Jade becomes. She doesn't remember where she's been when Josie comes out. And the lapses are getting longer."

"Sounds like the lady needs a shrink."

"Actually, she'll go to Elana—she's a psychiatrist—but that's down the road a bit. And under hypnosis—Ah, here's the food." At the elevator's ding, Bess opened the door. The smile froze on her face.

"Alexi."

"Don't you bother to ask who it is before you let someone come up?" He shook his head before he caught her chin in his hand and kissed her.

"Yes—that is, not when I'm expecting someone. What are you doing here?"

"Kissing you?" And, at that moment, she wasn't as responsive as he'd come to expect. Then it occurred to him that she'd said she was expecting someone. A man? A date? A lover? His eyes cooled as he stepped back. "I guess I should have called first."

"No. I mean, yes. That is…are you off tonight?"

"I go back on in a couple hours."

"Oh. Well." The buzzer sounded again.

"You could always tell him I'm the plumber."

Baffled, she stepped back inside to release the elevator. "Tell who what?"

"The guy on his way up."

"Why should I tell the delivery boy you're a plumber?"

"Delivery boy?" A sound inside the apartment had him edging closer. He wasn't jealous, damn it, he was just curious. "I guess you've already got company," he began, and pushed the door wider.

"Actually, I do." Giving up, Bess gestured him inside. "We were just about to have some dinner."

He looked over at the couch just as Rosalie stood. Caught between them, Bess felt herself battered by double waves of hostility.

"What the hell is she doing here?"

"You called the cops," Rosalie said accusingly before Bess could answer. "You called the damn cops."

"No. No, I didn't."

Rosalie was already striding across the room. Bess knew that if the woman made it to the door she would have lost her chance. "Rosalie." She grabbed her arm. "I didn't call him."

"And why the hell *didn't* you?" Alex tossed back.

"Because it's none of your business." Still gripping Rosalie, Bess swirled on him. "This is my home, and she's my guest."

"And you're a bigger idiot than I thought."

Sizing up the situation, Rosalie relaxed fractionally. "You two got a thing?"

"Yes," Alex shot back.

"No," Bess snapped, then sighed. "Something in between the two," she mumbled. She snatched her wallet out of her bag as she heard the elevator ding. "Excuse me. That's dinner."

While she herded the delivery boy inside to set up the meal, Alex and Rosalie stood eyeing each other with mutual dislike and suspicion.

"What's the game, Rosalie?"

"No game." She flashed a smile that was as feral as a shark's. "I'm a paid consultant. Your lady hired me."

"The hell with that." He paused a moment, studying her bruised eye. "Bobby do that?"

Rosalie angled her chin. "I walked into a door."

"Sure you did." He did care. Bess might have been surprised at how much he cared. Rosalie certainly would have been stunned. But he also knew there were things that couldn't be fixed. "You'll want to watch your step."

"I don't make the same mistake twice."

He turned away from her, his hands balled into fists in his pockets. "McNee, I want to talk to you."

"Oh, just shut up." She didn't bother to look up as she counted out bills. "Can't you see I'm trying to figure the tip? There you go."

"Thanks, lady." The delivery boy tucked the bills away. "Enjoy your dinner."

"There's enough for three," Bess stated, turning toward Alex. "But you're not going to stay if you're rude."

"Rude?" The single word bounced off her ceiling. He was beside her in two strides. "You think it's rude for me to ask you if you've lost your mind when I walk in and find you've invited a hooker to dinner?"

Her eyes narrowed. "Out."

"Damn it, Bess…"

"I said out." She gave him a hefty shove toward the door. "We went on one date," she reminded him. "*One.* Maybe I entertained the idea of something more, but that gives you no right to come into my house and tell me what to do and who to talk with."

He grabbed her hand before she could push him again. "One has nothing to do with the other."

"You're right. Absolutely right. What I should have said is that I run my life, Detective." She snatched her hand away so that she could poke a finger at his chest. "Me. Alone. Get the picture?"

"Yeah." He wondered how she'd like a nice clip on that pointy little chin of hers. "I've got a picture for you." He hauled her up and kissed her hard. No gentle touch, no finesse. All steam heat. It lasted only seconds, but he succeeded in shocking her speechless. "Things change, McNee." Dark, furious eyes pinned her to the spot. "Get used to it."

With that, he stormed out, slamming the door behind him.

"Well." Bess took one breath, then another. Her throat felt scalded. "Of all the incredible nerve. Who the hell does he think he is, marching in here that way?" Hands on her hips, she spun to face Rosalie. "Did you see that?"

"Hard to miss it." Grinning, Rosalie snatched a french fry from a plate.

"If he thinks he's getting away with that—that *attitude*—he's very much mistaken."

"Man's nuts about you."

"Excuse me?"

"Girl, that was one lovesick puppy."

Bess snatched up her wine and gulped. "Don't be ridiculous. He was just showing off."

"Uh-huh. If I had me a man who looked at me like that, I'd do one of two things."

"Which are?"

"I'd either sit back and enjoy, or I'd run for my life."

Frowning, Bess sat down and picked up her fork. "I don't like to be pushed."

"Seems to me it depends on who's doing the pushing." She sat, as well, and dug right into her steak. "He sure is one fine-looking man—for a cop."

Bess stabbed at her salad. "I don't want to talk about him."

"You're paying the tab," Rosalie said agreeably.

With a grunt of assent, Bess tried to eat. Damn cop, she thought. He'd ruined her appetite.

* * *

There was something to be said for beating the hell out of inanimate objects. Alex had always found the therapy of a pair of boxing gloves and a punching bag immeasurably rewarding. With those so easily accessible, he could never figure out why so many people felt the need for a psychiatrist's couch.

Until recently.

Twenty minutes of sweating and pounding hadn't relieved his basic frustration. He often used the gym—in the middle of a difficult case, when one went wrong, when a good arrest turned sour in court. The same ingredients had worked equally well for him whenever he'd fought with family, or friends, or had female problems.

Not this time.

Whatever hold Bess McNee had on him, Alex couldn't seem to punch himself out of it.

"So much energy, so early."

The familiar voice had Alex blinking away the sweat that had dripped through his headband into his eyes. His brother Mikhail, and Alex's ten-month-old nephew, Griff, were standing hand in hand, grinning identical grins.

"Got your papa out early, did you, tough guy?" Alex swung Griff up for a smacking kiss.

Griff babbled out happily. The only word Alex could decipher in the odd foreign language of a toddler was *Mama*.

"Sydney's tired," Mikhail explained. "She has some wheeling and dealing keeping her up at night. This one's an early riser." He ruffled his son's hair. "So I thought we'd come down and lift weights. Right?"

Griff grinned and cocked his elbows. "Papa."

"Your muscle's bigger," Alex assured him.

"Hey, it's the Griff-man!" Rocky, the former light-weight who ran the gym, gave a whistle and held out his wiry arms. "Come see me, champ."

With a squeal of pleasure, Griff wiggled out of Alex's arms to toddle off on his almost steady legs. "Better watch out, Rock," Mikhail called out. "He's slippery."

"I can handle him." With the confidence of a four-time grandfather, he hefted Griff. "We got things to do," he told Mikhail. "Why don't you talk to your brother there and find out why this is the third time this week he's come in to pound on my equipment?"

"Nosy," Alex muttered. "He's worse than an old woman."

Mikhail tilted a brow when Alex went back to pounding the bag. "Speaking of women…"

"We weren't."

"Why do men come to such places as this unless it's to talk of women?" The music of the Ukraine flavored Mikhail's voice. Alex wondered if his brother knew how much he sounded like their father.

"To hit things," he retorted. "To talk dirty and to sweat."

"That, too. So, it is a woman, yes?"

"It's always a damn woman," Alex said between gritted teeth.

"This one's named Bess."

Alex's punch stopped in midswing. Turning, he used his forearm to swipe his brow. "How do you know about Bess?"

"Rachel tells me." Pleased, Mikhail grinned. "She also tells me that this Bess is not beautiful so much as unique, and that she's smart. This isn't your usual type, Alexi."

"She's nobody's type." Alex turned back to the bag, feinted with his right, then jabbed with his left. "Unique," he said with a snort. "That's her, all right. Her face. It was like God was distracted that day and mixed up the features for five different women. Her eyes are too big, her chin's pointed, her nose is crooked." His gloved fist plowed into the bag. "And she has skin like an angel. I touch it and my mouth waters."

"Mmm... I'll have to get a look at this one."

"I've sworn off," Alex told him between grunts. "I don't need the aggravation. She doesn't have all her circuits working at the same time. Maybe Rachel thinks she's smart because she went to college."

"Radcliffe," Mikhail supplied. "She had lunch with Rachel, and Rachel asked."

"Radcliffe?" Letting out a breath, Alex leaned against the bag. "It figures."

"She also told Rachel that the two of you had a... misunderstanding."

"I understood perfectly. Look, maybe she went to some fancy college, but you couldn't fill up a teaspoon with her common sense. I don't need to get involved with someone that flaky."

Mikhail's bark of laughter echoed through the gym. "This from a man who once dated Miss Lug Wrench."

"It was Miss Carburetor."

"Ah, that's different."

A smile twitched, and Alex punched halfheartedly at the bag. Working up a sweat hadn't relaxed him, but five minutes with Mikhail was doing the job. "Anyway, we're finished before we got started. And both better off."

"Undoubtedly you're right."

"I know I'm right. We'd always be coming at things from different angles. Hers is cross-eyed. She doesn't see anything the way she should."

"A difficult woman."

"Difficult." Alex held out his hands so that Mikhail could unlace his gloves. "That doesn't begin to describe her. She acts so mild and relaxed, you wouldn't think you could rile her with a cattle prod. Then you point out an obvious mistake, for her own good, and she jumps on you with both feet. Kicks you out of the house."

Mikhail tucked his tongue in his cheek. "You're better off without her."

"You're telling me." Alex tossed his gloves aside and flexed his hands. "Who needs unreasonable women?"

"Men."

"Yeah." With a sigh, Alex sent his brother a miserable look. "I want her so much I can't breathe."

"I know the feeling." He punched his brother's sweaty shoulder. "So go get her."

"Go get her," Alex repeated.

"Put her in her place."

A dangerous light, one Mikhail recognized, flickered in Alex's eyes. "Her place. Right."

"Hey!" Mikhail called out when his brother strode off. "The showers are that way."

"I'll catch one at the station. See you later."

"Later," Mikhail agreed. He wandered off to find his son, wondering how soon he would meet this unique, unreasonable woman without common sense.

She sounded perfect for his baby brother.

* * *

Bess was never at her best in the morning, and she suspected anyone who was. Her alarm was buzzing when she heard the pounding on her door. She'd been ignoring the first for nearly ten minutes, but the incessant knocking had her dragging herself out of bed.

Bleary-eyed, pulling a skimpy silk robe over an equally skimpy nightshirt, she stumbled to the door. "What the hell?" she demanded. "Is it a fire or what?"

"Or what," Alex told her when she yanked open the door.

Struggling to focus, she dragged a hand through her hair. The robe drooped off one shoulder. "How'd you get up here?"

"Flashed my badge for the security guard." After closing the door behind him, he looked his fill. There was a great deal to be said for a sleepy woman in rumpled white silk. "Get you up, McNee?"

"What time is it?" She turned away, following the scent from her coffeemaker, which was set to brew at 7:20 each morning. "What day is it?"

"Thursday." He followed her weaving progress through the living area and into a big white-and-navy kitchen. There was a huge arrangement of fresh orchids on the center island. Orchids in the kitchen, he thought. Only Bess. "About 7:30."

"In the morning?" Blindly she groped for a mug. "What are you doing here at 7:30 on a Thursday morning?"

"This." He spun her around. The taste of her mouth, warm and soft from sleep, had him groaning. Before she could think—he didn't want either of them to think— he slipped his tongue between her lips to seduce hers.

Her body went stiff, then melted, softening against his like candle wax touched by a flame.

Through the roaring of his blood, he heard the crash as the china mug she'd held slipped from her fingers and smashed on the tiles.

Was she still dreaming? Bess wondered. Her dreams had always been very vivid, but this... It wouldn't be possible to feel so much, need so desperately, in a dream.

And she could taste him. Really taste him. A mingling of man and desire and salty sweat. Delicious. His mouth was so hot, so unyielding, just as his hands were through the thin silk she wore.

She could feel the cool tiles beneath her feet, a shivery contrast to the heat roaring around her. Under her palms, his cheeks were rough, arousingly rough. And she heard her own voice, a muffled, confused sound, as she tried to say his name.

"I have to wake up," she managed when his mouth left hers to cruise over her throat. "I really have to."

"You are awake." He had to touch her—just once. However unfair his advantage, he had to. So he cupped her breasts in his hands, molding their firmness through the silk, brushing his thumbs, feather-light, over straining nipples. "See?"

She'd never been the swooning type, but she was afraid this would be a first. "I have to—" She gasped, for as she'd started to step back, he'd swept her up into his arms. A skitter of panic, completely unfamiliar, raced down her spine. "Alexi, don't."

He covered her mouth again, felt her trembling surrender. And knew he could. And could not. "Your feet are bare," he said, and set her on the counter. "I made you drop your cup."

Shaken, she stared down at the shards of broken crockery. "Oh."

"You have a broom?"

"A broom." She was awake now, wide-awake. But her mind was still mush. "Somewhere. Why?"

He was making her stupid, he realized, and grinned. "So I can clean it up before you cut yourself. Stay there." He walked to a likely-looking closet and located a dustpan and broom. Because he was a man whose mother had trained him well in such matters, he went about the sweeping job quickly and competently. "So, have you missed me?"

"I haven't given you a thought." She blew the hair out of her eyes. "Hardly."

"Me either." He dumped the shards into the trash, replaced the broom and dustpan. "How about some coffee?"

"Sure." Maybe that would help her regain her normal composure. As he poured, she caught a whiff of him over the homey morning aroma. "You smell like a locker room."

"Sorry. I was at the gym." When he handed her the coffee, she sat where she was and sipped. Half a cup later, she was able to take her first clear-eyed look at him.

He looked fabulous. Rough and sweaty and ready for action. The thick tangle of hair was falling over a faded gray sweatband. His face was unshaven, his NYPD T-shirt was ripped and darkened in a vee down the chest, his sweatpants were loose and frayed at the cuffs. When she lifted her gaze back to his, he smiled.

"Good morning, McNee."

"Good morning."

He skimmed a finger over her thigh. She was sensitive there, he noted. He could tell by the way her eyes darkened and the pulse in her throat picked up the beat. "I'm not apologizing this time."

"You should be."

"No. I'm right about this." He put a finger over her lips before she could speak. "Trust me. I'm a cop."

He could have all but seduced her in her own kitchen before her eyes were even open, but she had a point to make. Closing a hand over his wrist, she drew his hand away. "My personal decisions, whether they have to do with my professional or my private life, are just that. Personal. I've been making those decisions, right or wrong, for a long time. I don't intend to stop now."

"I'm not going to see you hurt."

"That's very sweet, Alexi." Softening a bit, she brushed a hand through his hair. "I don't intend to be hurt."

"You don't know what you're dealing with. Oh, you think you do," he continued, recognizing the look in her eyes. "But all you know is the surface. There are things that go on in the streets, every day, every night, that you have no conception of. You never will."

She couldn't argue, not with what she saw in his face. "Maybe not. I don't see what you see, or know what you know. Maybe I don't want to. My friendship with Rosalie—"

"Friendship?"

"Yes." The expression on her face dared him to contradict her. "I feel something for her—about her." With a helpless gesture, Bess set her cup aside. "I can't possibly explain it to you, Alexi. You're not a woman. I can help her. Don't tell me it's a fairy tale to believe I can save her from the streets and what she's chosen to be. I've gotten that advice already."

"From someone with at least half a brain," he surmised. "I had no idea this had gotten so out of hand. You said you wanted to talk to her for background stuff for your story."

"That's true enough." But Bess remembered the bruise on Rosalie's face too well. "Is it so impossible that I might able to make a difference in her life? Has being a cop made you so hard you aren't willing to give someone a chance to change?"

He gripped her hands, hard. "This isn't about me."

"No," she said, and smiled. "It's not."

He swore and let go of her to pace to the coffee maker. "Okay, point taken. It's none of my business. But I'm going to ask for a promise."

"You can ask."

"Don't go out on the streets with her. Don't go anywhere near Bobby's territory."

She thought of the man with the silver hair and the vicious eyes. "That I can promise. Feel better?"

"I'm not through. Don't let her up here unless you're sure she's alone. Meet her down at your office, or in some public place."

"Really, Alexi…"

"Please."

She said nothing for a moment, and then, because she could see how much it had cost him to use that word, she relented. "All right." Bess scooted away from the counter, then opened the bread drawer. "Want a bagel?"

"Sure."

She popped two into the toaster oven before going to the refrigerator for cream cheese. "There's something I should tell you."

"I'm hoping there's a lot of things."

With a puzzled smile, she turned back. "I'm sorry?"

"I want to know about this personal life of yours, McNee. I want to know all about you, then I want to take you to bed and make love with you until we both forget our own names."

"Ah…" It didn't seem to take more than one of those long, level looks of his to make her forget a great deal more than her name. "Anyway…"

"Anyway?" he repeated helpfully as the toaster oven dinged.

"I was going to tell you about Angie Horowitz."

The lazy smile vanished. His eyes went cool and flat. "What do you know about her?"

"Boy, it really does click off," Bess murmured. "I feel like I just stepped into one of those rooms with the two-way mirror and the rubber hoses."

"Angie Horowitz," he repeated. "What do you know about her?"

"I don't know much of anything, but I thought I should tell you what Rosalie told me." She got out plates, then began to spread the bagels generously. "She said that Angie was really happy to have hooked up with this one guy. He'd hired her a couple of times and slipped her some extra money. Treated her well, promised her some presents. In fact, he gave her this little pendant. A gold heart with a crack down the center."

Alex's face remained impassive. There had been a broken neck chain wrapped in Angie's hand when they found her, just as there had been with the first victim.

That little detail had been kept out of the press. There hadn't been a heart, he thought now. But someone had broken the chain for a reason.

"She wore it all the time—according to Rosalie," Bess went on. "Rosalie also told me Mary Rodell had one just like it. She was the other victim, wasn't she?" she asked Alex. "She had it on the last time Rosalie saw her alive."

"Is that it?"

Bess was disappointed that he wasn't more pleased with the information. "There's a little more." Sulking a bit, she bit into her bagel. "Angie called the guy Jack, and she bragged to Rosalie that he was a real gentleman, and was built like…" She trailed off, cleared her throat, but her eyes were bright with humor, rather than embarrassment. "Women have colorful terms for certain things, just like men."

"I get the picture."

"He had a scar."

"What kind?"

"I don't know. A scar, on his hip. Angie told Rosalie he got upset when she asked him about it. That's all she told me, Alexi, but I figured the coincidence of the pendants, you might want to know about this guy."

"It never hurts." He gave her an easy smile, though his instincts were humming. "Probably nothing, but I'll look into it." He tugged on her hair. "Do yourself a favor, and don't tell Rosalie you passed this along to me."

"I'm softhearted, Detective. Not softheaded. She thinks you have a really nice butt—but you're still a cop."

He grimaced. "I don't think I like you discussing my anatomy with a—"

"Friend," she supplied, with a warning lift of her brow. "I also had lunch with your sister. We discussed your nasty temperament."

"I heard." He stole her bagel. "Radcliffe, huh?"

"So?"

"So nothing. Want to go dancing with me?"

She debated with herself for almost a full second. "Okay. Tonight?"

"Can't. Tomorrow?"

It meant canceling dinner at Le Cirque with L.D. Strater. That debate took nearly half a second. "That's fine. Sexy or sedate?"

"Sexy. Definitely."

"Good. Why don't you come by around—" She glanced at the clock, stared, then yelped. "Damn it! Now I'm going to be late. I'll owe Lori twenty dollars if I'm late one more time this month." She began pushing Alex out of the kitchen. "It's all your fault. Now beat it, so I can throw on some clothes and get out of here."

"Since you're already late…" He had some very good moves. Even as she shoved him toward the door, he was turning to catch her close. "I can arrange it so you're a lot later."

"Smooth talker," she said with a laugh. "Take a hike."

"You've already lost twenty. I'm just offering to make it worth your while."

"I don't know how I can resist that incredibly romantic gesture, but somehow I find I have the strength."

"You want romance?" There was a gleam in his eyes as he headed for the door. "Tomorrow night. We'll just see how strong you are."

Chapter 6

After spending most of the morning kicking his heels in court, waiting to testify in an assault case, Alex returned to the station to find his partner hip-deep in paperwork. "The boss wants to see you," Judd said through a mouthful of chocolate bar.

"Right." Alex shrugged out of his jacket and dragged off his court-appearance tie. With his free hand, he picked up his pile of messages.

"I think he meant now," Judd said helpfully.

"I got it." As he passed Judd's desk, Alex peeked over his shoulder at the report in the typewriter. "Two *p's* in apprehend, Einstein."

Judd backspaced and scowled. "You sure?"

"Trust me." He swung through the squad room and knocked on Captain Trilwalter's glass door.

"Come."

Trilwalter glanced up. If Alex often thought he was swamped in paperwork, it was nothing compared to what surrounded his captain. Trilwalter's desk was heaped with it. The overflowing files, stacks of reports and correspondence gave Trilwalter a bookish, accountantlike look. This was enhanced by the half glasses perched on his long, narrow nose, the slightly balding head and the ruthlessly knotted knit tie.

But Alex knew better. Trilwalter was a cop down to the bone, and he might still be on the street but for the bullet that had damaged his left lung.

"You wanted to see me, Captain?"

"Stanislaski." Trilwalter crooked his finger, then pointed it, gesturing to Alex to come in and shut the door. He leaned back in his chair, folded his hands over his flat belly and scowled.

"What the hell is all this about soap operas?"

"Sir?"

"Soap operas," Trilwalter repeated. "I just had a call from the mayor."

Testing his ground, Alex nodded slowly. "The mayor called you about soap operas?"

"You look confused, Detective." A rare, and not entirely humor-filled, smile curved Trilwalter's mouth. "That makes two of us. The name McNee mean anything to you? Bess McNee?"

Alex closed his eyes a moment. "Oh, boy."

"Rings a bell, does it?"

"Yes, sir." Alex gave himself a brief moment to contemplate murder. "Miss McNee and I have a personal relationship. Sort of."

"I'm not interested in your personal relationship, sort of or otherwise. Unless they come across my desk."

"When I arrested her—"

"Arrested her?" Trilwalter held up one hand while he took off his glasses. Slowly, methodically, he massaged the bridge of his nose. "I don't think I have to know about that. No, I'm sure I don't."

Despite himself, Alex began to see the humor in it. "If I could say so, Captain, Bess tends to bring that kind of reaction out in a man."

"She's a writer?"

"Yes, sir. For 'Secret Sins.'"

Trilwalter lifted tired eyes. "'Secret Sins.' Apparently the mayor is quite a fan. Not only a fan, Detective, but an old chum of your Bess McNee's. *Old chum* was just how he put it."

Finding discretion in silence, Alex said nothing as Trilwalter rose. The captain walked to the watercooler wedged between two file cabinets in the corner of his office. He poured out a paper cupful and drank it down.

"His honor, the mayor, requests that Miss McNee be permitted to observe a day in your life, Detective."

Alex made a comment normally reserved for locker rooms and pool halls. Trilwalter nodded sagely.

"My sentiments exactly. However, one of the less appealing aspects of working this particular desk is playing politics. You lose, Detective."

"Captain, we're closing in on that robbery on Lexington. I've got a new lead on the hooker murders and a message on my desk from a snitch who could know something about that stiff we found down on East Twenty-third. How am I supposed to work with some ditzy woman hanging over my shoulder?"

"This is the ditzy woman you have a personal relationship with?"

Alex opened his mouth, then closed it again. How to explain Bess? "Sort of," he said at length. "Look, Captain, I already agreed to talk to McNee about police work, in general, now and again. I never agreed to specifics. I sure as hell don't want her riding shotgun while I work."

"A day in your life, Stanislaski." With that same grim smile, Trilwalter crushed his cup and tossed it. "Monday next, to be exact."

"Captain—"

"Deal with it," Trilwalter said. "And see that she stays out of trouble."

Dismissed, Alex stalked back to his desk. He was still muttering to himself when Judd wandered over with two cups of coffee.

"Problem?"

"Women," Alex said.

"Tell me about it." Because he'd been waiting all morning for the chance, Judd sat on the edge of Alex's desk. "Speaking of women, did you know that Bess was engaged to L.D. Strater?"

Alex's head snapped up. "What?"

"Used to be," Judd explained. "One of the teachers at Holly's school's a real gossip-gatherer. Reads all the tabloids and stuff. She was telling Holly how Strater and Bess were a thing a few months ago."

"Is that so?" Alex remembered how they'd danced together at her party. Kissed. His mouth flattened into a grim line as he lifted the cup.

"A real whirlwind sort of thing—according to my sources. Before that, she was engaged to Charles Stutman."

"Who the hell is that?"

"You know, the writer. He's got that hot play on Broadway now. *Dust to Dust*. Holly really wants to see it. I thought maybe Bess could wangle some tickets."

The sound Alex made was neither agreement nor denial. It was more of a growl.

"Then there was George Collaway—you know, the son of that big publisher? That was about three years ago, but he married someone else."

"The lady gets around," Alex said softly.

"Yeah, and in top circles. And, hey, Holly was really blown away when she found out that Bess was Roger K. McNee's daughter. You know, the camera guy."

"Camera guy?" Alex repeated, feeling a hole spreading in the pit of his stomach. "As in McNee-Holden?"

"Yeah. First camera I ever bought was a Holden 500. Use their film all the time, too. Hell, so does the department. Well." He straightened. "If you get a chance, maybe you could ask Bess about those tickets. It sure would mean a lot to Holly."

McNee-Holden. Alex ran the names over in his head while the noise of the squad room buzzed around him. For God's sake, he had one of their cameras himself. He'd bought their little red packs of film hundreds of times over the years. The department used their developing paper. He was pretty sure NASA did too.

Wasn't Bess just full of secrets!

So she was rich. Filthy rich. He picked up his messages again, telling himself it wasn't such a big deal. Wouldn't have been, he corrected silently, if she'd told him about it herself.

Engaged, he thought with a frown. Three times engaged. Shrugging, he picked up the phone. None of his business, he reminded himself as he punched in numbers. If she'd been married three times, it would be none of his business. He was taking her dancing, not on a honeymoon.

But it was a long time before he was able to shuffle her into a back corner of his mind and get on with his job.

Sexy, the man had said, Bess remembered, turning in front of her cheval glass. It looked as though she were going to oblige him.

Snug teal silk hugged every curve and ended abruptly at midthigh. Over the strapless, unadorned bodice, she wore a short, body jacket of fuchsia. Long, wand-shaped crystals dangled at her ears. After stepping into her heels, she gave her hair a last fluff.

She felt like dancing.

When her buzzer sounded, she grinned at her reflection. Leave it to a cop to be right on time. Grabbing her purse—a small one that bulged with what she considered the essentials—she hurried to the intercom.

"I'll come down. Hold on."

She found him on the sidewalk, looking perfect in gray slacks and a navy shirt. His hands were tucked in the pockets of his bomber jacket.

"Hi." She kissed him lightly, then tucked an arm through his. "Where are we going?"

It gave him a jolt, the way their eyes and mouths lined up. As they would if they were in bed. "Downtown," he said shortly, and steered her left toward the corner to catch a cab.

He couldn't have pleased her more with his choice of the noisy, crowded club. The moment she stepped inside, Bess's blood started to hum. The music was loud, the dancing in full swing. They squeezed up to the bar to wait for a table.

"Vodka, rocks," Alex ordered, raising his voice over the din.

"Two," Bess decided, and smiled at him. "I think I was here before, a few months ago."

"I wouldn't be surprised." Not his business, Alex reminded himself. Her background, the men in her life. None of it.

The hell it wasn't.

"It doesn't look like the kind of place Strater would bring you."

"L.D.?" Her eyes laughed. "No, not his style." She angled herself around. "I love to watch people dance, don't you? It's one of the few legal forms of exhibitionism in this country." When he handed her her drink, she murmured a thank-you. "Take that guy there." She gestured with the glass at a man who was strutting on the floor, thumbs in his belt loops, hips wiggling. "That's definitely one of the standard urban white male mating dances."

"Did you do a lot of dancing with Stutman?" Alex heard himself ask.

"Charlie?" She sampled the vodka, pursed her lips. "Not really. He was more into sitting in some smoky club listening to esoteric music that he could obsess to." Still scanning the crowd, she caught the eye of a man in black leather. He cocked a brow and started toward her. One hard look from Alex, and he veered away.

Bess chuckled into her glass. "That put him in his place." Rattling her ice, she grinned up at him. "Were you born with that talent, or did you have to develop it?"

Alex plucked the glass out of her hand and set it aside. "Let's dance."

Always willing to dance, Bess let him pull her onto the floor. But instead of bopping to the beat, he wrapped his arms around her. While legs flashed and arms waved around them, and the music rocked, they glided.

"Nice." Smiling into his eyes, she linked her arms around his neck. "I see why you like to make your own moves, Detective."

"I believe I promised you romance." He skimmed his lips over her jaw to her ear.

"Yes." Her breath came out slow and warm as she closed her eyes. "You did."

"I'm not sure what a woman like you considers romantic."

Her skin shivered under his lips. "This is a good start."

"It's tough." He drew away so that their lips were an inch apart. "It's tough for a cop to compete with tycoons and playwrights."

Her eyes were half-closed and dreamy through her lashes. "What are you talking about?"

"A couple of your former fiancés."

The lashes lifted fractionally. "What about them?"

"I wondered when you were going to mention them. Or the fact that your father runs one of the biggest conglomerates known to man. Or the little detail about your chum the mayor calling my captain."

They continued to dance as he spoke, but Bess could see the anger building in his eyes. "Do you want to take them as separate issues, or all in one piece?"

She was a cool one, he thought. He was feeling anything but cool. "Why don't we start with the mayor? You had no right."

"I didn't ask him to call, Alexi." She spoke carefully, feeling the taut strength of his fingers at her waist. "We were having dinner, and—"

"You often have dinner with the mayor?"

"He's an old family friend," she said patiently. "I was telling him how helpful you'd been, and one thing led to another. I didn't know he'd called your captain until after it was done. I admit I liked the idea, and if it's caused you any trouble, I'm sorry."

"Great."

"My work's as important to me as yours is to you," she shot back, struggling with her own temper. "If you'd prefer, I can arrange to spend Monday observing another cop."

"You'll spend Monday where I can keep my eye on you."

"Fine. Excuse me." She broke away and worked her way through the crowd to the rest room. The music pulsed against the walls as she paced the small room, ignoring the chatter from the two women freshening their lipstick at the mirror. Losing her temper would be unproductive, she reminded herself. Better, much better, to handle this situation calmly, coolly.

When she was almost sure she could, she walked back out.

He was waiting for her. Taking her arm, he led her to a table in the rear, where they could talk without shouting.

"I think we should go. There's no use staying when you're so angry with me," she began, but he merely scraped back her chair.

"Sit."

She sat.

"When were you going to tell me about your family?"

"I don't see it as an issue." And that was true enough. "Why should it be? This is only the second time we've gone out."

The look he sent her had her jiggling a foot under the table. "You know damn well there's more going on between us than a couple of dates."

"All right, yes, I do." She picked up her drink, then set it down again, untouched. "But that's not the point. You're acting as though I deliberately hid something from you, or lied. That's just not true."

He picked up the fresh drink he'd ordered. "So tell me now."

"What? Didn't you run a make on me?" His narrowed eyes gave her some small sense of satisfaction. "Okay, Detective, I'll fill you in since you're so interested. My family owns McNee-Holden, which, since its inception in 1873, has expanded from still cameras and film to movies, television, satellites, and all manner of things. Shall I have them send you a prospectus?"

"Don't get smart."

"I'm just warming up." She hooked an arm over the back of her chair. "My father heads the company, and my mother entertains and does good works. I'm an only child, who was born rather late in life to them. My father's name is Roger, and he enjoys a racketing good game of polo. My mother's name is Susan—never Sue or Susie—and she prefers a challenging rubber of bridge. What else would you like to know?"

Despite his temper, he wanted to take her hand and soothe her. "Damn it, Bess, it isn't an interrogation."

"Isn't it? Let me make it easy for you, Alexi. I was born in New York, spent the early part of my childhood on our estate on Long Island, in the care of a very British nanny I was extremely fond of, before going off to boarding school. Which I detested. This, however, left my mother free to pursue her many charitable causes, and my father free to pursue his business. We are not close. From time to time we did travel together, but I was not a pretty child, nor a tractable one, and my parents usually left my care up to the servants."

"Bess—"

"I'm not finished." Her eyes were hard and bright. "This isn't a poor-little-rich-girl story, Alexi. I wasn't neglected or unhappy. Since I had no more in common with my parents than they had with me, I was content to go my own way. They don't interfere, and we get along very well. Because I prefer making my own way, I don't trumpet the fact that I'm Roger K. McNee's little girl. I don't hide it, either—otherwise, I would have changed my name. It's simply a fact. Satisfied?"

He took her hand before she could rise. His voice was calm again, and too gentle to resist. "I wanted to know who you are. I have feelings for you, so it matters."

Slowly her hand relaxed under his. The hard gleam faded from her eyes. "I understand that someone with your background would feel that their family, who and what they came from, are part of what they are. I don't feel that way about myself."

"Where you come from means something, Bess."

"Where you are means more. What does your father do?"

"He's a carpenter."

"Why aren't you a carpenter?"

"Because it wasn't what I wanted." He drummed his fingers on the table as he studied her. "Your point," he acknowledged. "Look, I'm sorry I pushed. It was just weird hearing all this from Judd."

"From Judd?"

"He got it from Holly, who got it from some other teacher who reads the tabloids." Even as he said it, it struck him as ridiculous. He grinned.

"See?" Relaxed again, she leaned forward. "Life really is a soap opera."

"Yours is. *Three* ex-fiancés?"

"That depends on how you count." She took Alex's hand, because she liked the feel of it in hers. "I wasn't engaged to L.D. He did give me a ring, and I didn't have the heart to tell him it was ostentatious. But marriage wasn't discussed."

"One of the ten richest men in the country gave you an ostentatious ring, but marriage wasn't discussed?"

"That's right. He's a very nice man—a little pompous, sometimes, but who wouldn't be, with so many people ready to grovel? Can we get some chips or something?"

"Sure." He signaled to a waitress. "So you didn't want to marry him."

"I never thought about it." Since he asked, she did so now. "No, I don't think I would have liked it very much. He wouldn't have either. L.D. finds me amusing and a little unconventional. Being a tycoon isn't all fun and games, you know."

"If you say so."

She chuckled. "But he'd prefer a different type for his

next wife." She dived in immediately when the waitress set baskets of chips and pretzels on the table. "I enjoyed being in love with him for a few weeks, but it wasn't the romance of the century."

"What about the other one, the writer?"

"Charlie." There was a trace of wistfulness now. "I was really stuck on Charlie. He has this kind of glow about him. He's so interested in people, in emotions, in motivations." She gestured with half a pretzel. "The thing about Charlie is, he's good. Deep-down good. Entirely too good for me." She finished off the pretzel. "See, I do things like join Greenpeace. Charlie flies to Alaska to help clean up oil spills. He's committed. That's why Gabrielle is perfect for him."

"Gabrielle?"

"His wife. They met at a whale rally. They've been married almost two years now."

Alex was determined to get it right. "You were engaged to a married man?"

"No." Insulted, she poked out her lip. "Of course not. He got married after we were engaged—that is, after we weren't engaged anymore. Charlie would never cheat on Gabrielle. He's too decent."

"Sorry. My mistake." He considered changing the subject, but this one was just too fascinating. "How about George? Was he between Charlie and Strater?"

"No, George was before Charlie and after Troy. Practically in another life."

"Troy? There was another one?"

"Oh, you didn't know about him." She propped her chin on her hand. "I guess your source didn't dig back far enough. Troy was while I was in college, and we weren't engaged for very long. Only a couple of weeks. Hardly counts."

Alex picked up his drink again. "Hardly."

"Anyway, George was a mistake—though I'd never admit it to Lori. She gloats."

"George was a mistake? The others weren't?"

She shook her head. "Learning experiences. But George, well… I was a little rash with him. I felt sorry for him, because he was always sure he was coming down with some terminal illness, and he'd been in therapy since kindergarten. We should never have gotten involved romantically. I was really relieved when he decided to marry Nancy instead."

"Is this like a hobby?" Alex asked after a moment.

"No, people plan hobbies. I never plan to fall in love. It just happens." Her smile was amused and tolerant. "It feels good, and when it's over, no one's hurt. It isn't a sexual thing, like with Vicki. She goes from man to man because of the sense of sexual power it gives her. I know most people think if you have a relationship with a man—particularly if you're engaged to him—you must be sleeping with him. But it's not always true."

"And if you're not engaged to him?"

Because the question demanded it, she met his eyes levelly. "Every situation has its own rules. I don't know what they are for this one yet."

"Things may get serious."

There was a slight pressure around her heart. "That's always a possibility."

"They're serious enough right now for me to ask if you're seeing anyone else."

She knew it was happening. Bess had never been

able to prevent that slow, painless slide into love. "Are you asking me if I am, or are you asking me not to?"

It wasn't painless for him. It was terrifying. With what strength of will he had left, Alex held himself on that thin, shaky edge. "I'm asking you not to. And I'm telling you that I don't want anyone else. I can't even think of anyone else."

Her eyes were warm as she leaned over to touch her lips to his. "There is no one else."

He laid a hand on her cheek to keep her mouth on his for another moment. Even as he kissed her, he wondered how many other men had heard her say those same words.

He told himself he was a jealous idiot. With an effort, he managed to smother the feeling. Rising, he took her hands and pulled her to her feet.

"We're supposed to be dancing."

"So I was told. Alexi." Snuggling into love as she would have into a cozy robe, she cupped his face in her hands.

"What?"

"I'm just looking. I want to make sure you're not mad at me anymore."

"I'm not mad at you." To prove it, he kissed the tip of her crooked nose.

No, not angry, she thought, searching his eyes. But there was something else shadowed there. She couldn't quite identify it. "My middle name's Louisa."

With a half smile on his lips, he tilted his head. "Okay."

"I'm trying to think if there's something else you might want to know that I haven't told you." Needing to be close, she rested her cheek against his. "I really don't have any secrets."

He turned his face into her hair. God, what was she doing to him to tie him up in knots like this? He pulled her against him, wrapping his arms tight around her. "I know all I need to know," he said quietly. "We're going to have to figure out those rules, Bess. We're going to have to figure them out fast."

"Okay." She wasn't sure what was holding her back. It would have been so easy to hurry out of the club with him, to go home and be with him. Her body was straining for him. And yet...

The first tremor of panic shocked her enough to have her pull back and smile, too brightly. She wasn't afraid, she assured herself. And she didn't need to overanalyze. When the time was right to move forward, she'd know it. That was all.

"Come on, Detective." Still smiling, she pulled him away from the table. "Let's see if you can keep up with me on the dance floor."

Chapter 7

Alex read over a particularly grisly autopsy report on half of a suspected murder-suicide, and tried to ignore the fact that Bess was sitting in a chair to his right, scribbling in her notebook. She was as good as her word, he was forced to admit. Though she did tend to mumble to herself now and again, she was quiet, unobtrusive, and once she'd realized he wouldn't answer her questions—much less acknowledge her presence—she'd directed them to Judd.

He couldn't say she was a problem. But, of course, she *was* a problem. She was there. And because she was there, he thought about her.

She'd even dressed quietly, in bone-colored slacks and a navy blazer. As if, he thought, the conservative clothes would help her fade into the background and make him forget she was bothering him. Fat chance, when he was aware of her in every cell.

He could smell her, couldn't he? he thought, seething with resentment. That fresh and seductive scent had been floating at the edges of his senses all morning. Sneaking into his brain the way a good second-story man sneaks through a window.

And he could sense her, too. He didn't need a cop's instincts to know she was behind him, to picture those big green eyes drawing a bead on his every move. To imagine those never-still hands making notes, or that soft, agile mouth curving when a fresh idea came to her.

She could have dressed in cardboard and made him needy.

He was so damn cute, Bess was thinking, smiling at the back of his head. She enjoyed watching him work— the way he scooped his hand through all that gorgeous black hair when he was trying to think. Or shifted the phone from one ear to the other so that he could take notes. The sound of his voice, clipped and no-nonsense or sly and persuasive, depending on what he wanted from the listener.

And she particularly enjoyed the way he moved his shoulders, restlessly, annoyance in every muscle, when he became too aware of her presence.

She had a terrific urge to press a kiss to the back of his neck—and to see what he was reading.

After a couple of scowls from him, she scooted her chair back and stopped peeking over his shoulder.

She was cooperating fully, Alex was forced to admit. Which only made it worse. He wanted her to go away. How could he explain that it was impossible for him to concentrate on his job when the woman he was falling in love with was watching him read an autopsy report?

"Here you go." Bess gave him a cup of coffee and a friendly smile. "You look like you could use it."

"Thanks." Cream, no sugar, he noted as he sipped. She'd remembered. Was that part of her appeal? he wondered. The fact that she absorbed those little details about people? "You must be getting bored."

Taking a chance, she sat on the edge of his desk. "Why?"

"Nothing much going on." He gestured to indicate the pile of paperwork. Maybe, just maybe, he could convince her she was wasting her time. "If you have your TV cop doing this, it isn't going to up your ratings."

"We'll want to show different aspects of his work." She broke a candy bar in half and offered Alex a share. "Like the fact that he'd have to concentrate and handle this sort of paperwork and detail in the middle of all this chaos."

He took a bite. "What chaos?"

She smiled again, jotting down notes. He didn't even see it any longer, she realized. Or hear it. All the noise, the movement, the rush. Dozens of little dramas had taken place that morning, fascinating her, unnoted by him.

"They brought a drug dealer in over there." She gestured with a nod as she continued to write. "Skinny guy in a white fedora and striped jacket, wearing a heavy dose of designer cologne."

"Pasquale," Alex said, noting the description. "So?"

"You saw him?"

"I smelled him." He shrugged. "Wasn't my collar."

Chuckling to herself, Bess crossed her legs and got

comfortable. "A Korean shopkeeper came rushing in shouting about vandalism at his store. He was so excited he lost most of his English. They sent out for an interpreter."

"Yeah, it happens." What was her point? he wondered.

She only smiled and finished her chocolate. "Right after that, they brought in a woman who'd been knocked around by her boyfriend. She was sitting over there—defending him, even while her face was swelling. The detective at the far end had a fight with his wife over the phone. He forgot their anniversary."

"Must have been Rogers. He's always fighting with his wife." Impatience rippled back. "What's that got to do with anything?"

"Atmosphere," she told him. "You've stopped noticing it and become a part of it. It's interesting to see. And you're very organized," she added, licking chocolate from her thumb. "Not like Judd over there, with all his neat little piles, but in the way you spread things out and know just where to find the right piece of paper at the right time."

"I hate having you stare at me when I work." He slapped her hand away from the autopsy report.

"I know." Unoffended, she grinned. She leaned a little closer. There was something in her eyes besides humor, he noted. He wasn't sure if he'd ever seen desire and amusement merged in the same expression before. And he certainly hadn't realized how the combination could make a man's blood hum. "You look very sexy plowing your way through all this, gun strapped to your side, your hair all messed up from raking your fingers through it. That keen, dangerous look in your eyes."

Mortified, he shifted in his chair. "Cut it out, McNee."

"I like the way your eyes get all dark and intense when you're taking down some important tidbit of information over the phone."

"For all you know, that was my dry cleaner."

"Uh-uh." She took his coffee to wash down the last bite of candy bar. "Tell me something, Alexi. Are you annoyed that I'm here, or are you nervous that I'm here?"

"Both." He rose. There must be something he had to do someplace else.

"That's what I thought." She hooked a finger around the strap of his holster. She wasn't afraid of the gun he wore. In fact, she was counting on talking him into letting her hold it one day. So that she could see how it felt. How he felt when he was forced to draw it. "You know, you haven't even kissed me."

"I'm not going to kiss you. Here."

She lifted her eyes, slowly. There was a definite dare in them. "Why not?"

"Because the next time I kiss you—" watching her, he slid a hand around her throat, his thumb caressing her collarbone, until her cocky smile faded away "—really kiss you, it's just going to be you and me. Alone. And I'm going to keep right on kissing you, and all sorts of other things, until there aren't any more rules. Any more reasons."

Was that what she wanted? She thought it was. Right now, when her skin was humming where his fingers lay, she thought it was exactly what she wanted. But there was something else, some complex mixture of yearning and fear, so unfamiliar it caused her to step back.

"What's wrong, McNee?" Delighted by her reaction, he let his hand slide down her shoulder and away. "Who's making who nervous now?"

"We're supposed to be working," she reminded him. "Not making each other nervous."

"Today, when I go off the clock, so do you."

"Stanislaski."

Alex's eyes stayed on hers another moment before flicking behind her. "Captain."

"Sorry to interrupt your social hour," he said sourly. "I need that report."

"Right here." Even as Alex was turning to reach for it, Bess was offering her hand to Trilwalter.

"Captain, it's so nice to meet you. I'm Bess McNee. I wanted to let you know how much I appreciate the department's cooperation today."

Trilwalter scowled at her a moment, then, remembering, stifled a sigh. "Right. You're the writer." A sneer twisted his mouth. "Soap operas."

"Yes, I am." Her smile made the fluorescents overhead dim. "I wonder…if I can have just a moment of your time? I know you're very busy, so I won't keep you."

He didn't want any part of her. He knew it, she knew it, and so did any of the cops hovering close enough to hear. But riding a desk had taught him that diplomacy was often his only weapon. Besides, once he made his feelings known, she'd be out of his hair and off finding another precinct to haunt.

"Why don't you come into my office, Ms. McNee?"

"Thank you." She shot a grin over her shoulder at Alex as she followed Trilwalter.

"You going to let her go in there alone?" Judd murmured.

"Yeah." Alex bit back a chuckle as he heard the glass

of Trilwalter's door rattle. "Oh, yeah. And I'm going to enjoy it."

Ten minutes later, Alex was surprised by a burst of laughter. Swiveling in his chair, he spotted Trilwalter leading Bess out of his office. The two of them were chuckling together like two old friends over a private joke.

"I'm going to remember that one, Bess."

"Just don't tell the mayor where you heard it."

"I know how to respect a source." Still smiling, he glanced over at a slack-jawed Alex. "Detective, you take care of Ms. McNee. Make sure she gets what she needs."

"Sir." He cut his eyes over to Bess. She merely batted her lashes, managing to look about as innocent as a smoking gun. "I have every intention of making certain Ms. McNee gets exactly what she needs."

Bess laid her hand in Trilwalter's. "Thank you again, Donald."

"My pleasure. Don't be a stranger."

"Donald?" Alex said, the moment the captain was out of earshot.

"Yes." Bess made a production out of brushing dust from her sleeve. "That is his name."

"We use several other names for him around here. What the hell did you do in there?"

"Why, we chatted. What else?"

Glancing over her shoulder, Alex noticed money changing hands. The odds had been even that Trilwalter would chew her up, then spit her out, within ten minutes. Since he'd lost twenty on the deal himself, Alex wasn't particularly pleased.

"Sit down and be quiet," he told her. "I've got work."

"Of course."

Before she could take her seat, his phone rang. "Stan-islaski. Yeah." He listened a moment, then pulled out his notepad to scribble. "I hear you. You know how it works, Boomer. It depends on what it's worth." Nodding to himself, he replaced the pad. "Yeah, we'll talk. I'll be there. In ten."

When Alex hung up the phone and grabbed for his jacket, Bess was right behind him. "What is it?"

"I've got someplace to go. Judd, let's hit it."

"I'm going with you."

Alex didn't even glance back as he started out. He was already working on tucking her in some far corner of his mind. "Forget it."

"I'm going with you," she repeated, and snagged his arm. "That's the deal."

It surprised him when he tried to shake her off and she wouldn't shake. The lady had a good grip, he noted. "I didn't make any deal."

She could be just as tough and cold-blooded as he, she thought. She planted her feet, angled her chin. "Your captain did. I ride with you, Detective, wherever you may be going. A day in the life, remember?"

"Fine." Frustration vibrated through him as he stared her down. "You ride—and you stay in the car. No way you're scaring off my snitch."

"Want me to drive?" Judd offered as they headed down the steps to the garage.

"No." Alex's answer was flat and left no room for argument. Judd sent Bess a good-natured shrug. Then, because Alex made no move to do so, he opened the back door of their nondescript unmarked car for her.

"Where are we going?" Bess asked, determined to be pleasant.

"To talk to the scum of the earth," Alex shot back as he pulled out of the garage.

"Sounds fascinating," Bess said, and meant it.

She didn't think she'd ever been in this part of town before. Many of the shop windows were boarded up. Those still in business were grubbier than usual. People still walked as though they were in a hurry, but it didn't look as if they had anyplace to go.

Funny, she thought, how Alex seemed to blend with the surroundings. It wasn't simply the jeans and battered jacket he wore, or the hair he'd deliberately mussed. It was a look in the eyes, a set of the body, a twist of the mouth. No one would look twice at him, she thought. Or if they bothered, they wouldn't see a cop, they'd see another street tough obviously on the edge of his luck.

Taking her cue from him, she pulled out her bag of cosmetics, darkening her mouth, adding just a little too much eyeliner and shadow. She tried a couple of bored looks in the mirror of her compact and decided to tease up her hair.

Alex glanced back at her and scowled. "What the hell are you doing to your face?"

"Getting into character," she said blithely. "Just like you. Are we going to bust somebody?"

He only turned away and muttered.

Just his luck, he thought. He wanted to slip into Boomer's joint unobtrusively, and he was stuck with a redhead who thought they were playing cops and robbers.

Unoffended, Bess put away her mirror and scanned the area. Parking wasn't a problem here. Bess decided that if anyone left his car unattended in this neighborhood for above ten minutes, he'd come back and be lucky to find a hubcap.

Alex swung over the curb and swore. He couldn't leave her in the car here, damn it. Any of the hustlers or junkies on the streets would take one look, then eat her alive.

"You listen to me." He turned, leaning over the seat to make his point. "Stay close to me, and keep your mouth shut. No questions, no comments."

"All right, but where—"

"No questions." He slammed out of his door, then waited for her. With his hand firm on her arm, he hauled her to the sidewalk. "If you step out of line, I swear, I'll slap the cuffs on you."

"Romantic, isn't he?" she said to Judd. "Just sends shivers down my spine."

"Keep a lid on it, McNee," Alex told her, refusing to be amused. He pulled her through a grimy door into an airless shop.

It took her a minute to get her bearings in the dim light. There were shelves and shelves crowded with dusty merchandise. Radios, picture frames, kitchenware. A tuba. A huge glass display counter with a diagonal crack across it dominated one wall. Security glass ran to the ceiling. Cutting through it was a window, like a bank teller's, studded with bars.

"A pawnshop," Bess said, with such obvious delight that Alex snarled at her.

"One word about atmosphere, I'll clobber you."

But she was already dragging out her notebook. "Go ahead, do what you have to do. You won't even know I'm here."

Sure, he thought. How would anyone know she was

there, simply because that sunshine scent of hers cut right through the grime and must? He stepped up to the counter just as a scrawny man in a loose white shirt came through the rear door.

"Stanislaski."

"Boomer. What have you got for me?"

Grinning, Boomer passed a hand over his heavily greased black hair. "Come on, I got some good stuff, and you know I make a point of cooperating with the law. But a man's got to make a living."

"You make one ripping off every poor slob who walks through the door."

"Aw, now you hurt my feelings." Boomer's pale blue eyes glittered. "Rookie?" he asked, nodding at Judd.

"He used to be."

After an appraising look, Boomer glanced over at Bess. She was busy poking through his merchandise. "Looks like I got me a customer. Hang on."

"She's with me." Alex shot him a knife-edged look that forestalled any questions. "Just forget she's here."

Boomer had already appraised the trio of rings on Bess's right hand, and the blue topaz drops at her ears. He sighed his disappointment. "You're the boss, Stanislaski. But listen, I like to be discreet."

Alex leaned on the counter, like a man ready to shoot the bull for hours. His voice was soft, and deadly. "Jerk my chain, Boomer, and I'm going to have to come down here and take a hard look at what you keep in that back room."

"Stock. Just stock." But he grinned. He didn't have any illusions about Alex. Boomer knew when he was detested, but he also knew they had an agreement of sorts. And, thus far, it had been advantageous to both of them. "I got something on those hookers that got sliced up."

Though his expression didn't change, though he didn't move a muscle, Alex went on alert. "What kind of something?"

Boomer merely smiled and rubbed his thumb and forefinger together. When Alex drew out a twenty, it disappeared quickly through the bars. "Twenty more, if you like what I have to say."

"If it's worth it, you'll get it."

"You know I trust you." Smelling of hair grease and sweat, Boomer leaned closer. "Word on the street is you're looking for some high roller. Guy's name's Jack."

"So far I'm not impressed."

"Just building up to it, pal. The first one that was wasted? She was one of Big Ed's wives. I recognized her from the newspaper picture. Now, she was fine-looking. Not that I ever used her services."

"Turn the page, Boomer."

"Okay, okay." He shot a grin at Judd. "He don't like conversation. I heard both those unfortunate ladies were in possession of a certain piece of jewelry."

"You've got good ears."

"Man in my position hears things. It so happens I had a young lady come in just yesterday. She had a certain piece of jewelry she wanted to exchange." Opening a drawer, Boomer pulled out a thin gold chain. Dangling from it was a heart, cracked down the center. When Alex held out a hand, Boomer shook his head. "I gave her twenty for it."

Saying nothing, Alex pulled another bill out of his wallet.

"Seems to me I'm entitled to a certain amount of profit."

Eyes steady, Alex pulled the twenty back an inch. "You're entitled to go in and answer a bunch of nasty questions down at the cop shop."

With a shrug, Boomer exchanged the bill for the heart. He'd only given ten for it, in any case. "She wasn't much more than a kid," Boomer added. "Eighteen, maybe twenty at a stretch. Still pretty. Bottle blonde, blue eyes. Little mole right here." He tapped beside his left eyebrow.

"Got an address?"

"Well, now..."

"Twenty for the address, Boomer." Alex's tone told the man to take it. "That's it."

Satisfied, Boomer named a hotel a few blocks away. "Signed her name Crystal," he added, wanting to keep the partnership intact. "Crystal LaRue. Figure she made it up."

"Let's check it out," he said to Judd, then tapped Bess on the shoulder. She was apparently absorbed in an ugly brass lamp in the shape of a rearing horse. "Let's go."

"In a minute." She turned a smile on Boomer. "How much?"

"Oh, for you—"

"Forget it." Alex was dragging her to the door.

"I want to buy—"

"It's ugly."

Annoyed at the loss, but pleased to have recorded the entire conversation, she sighed. "That's the point." But she climbed meekly into the car and began to scribble her impressions in her book.

Cramped shop. Very dirty. Mostly junk. Excellent place for props. Proprietor a complete sleaze. Alexi in complete control of exchange—a kind of game-playing. Quietly disgusted but willing to use the tools at hand.

By the time she'd finished scribbling, Alex was pulling to the curb again.

"Same rules," he said to Bess as they climbed out of the car.

"Absolutely." Lips pursed, she studied the crumbling hotel. She recognized it as a rent-by-the-hour special. "Is this where she lives?"

"Who?"

"The girl you were talking about." She lifted a brow. "I have ears, too, Alexi."

He should have known. "As long as you keep your mouth shut."

"There's no need to be rude," she told him as they started in. "Tell you what, just to show there's no hard feelings, I'll buy you both lunch."

"Great." Judd gallantly opened the door for her.

"You're so easy," Alex muttered to his partner as they entered the filthy lobby.

"Hey, we gotta eat sometime."

He hated to bring her in here, Alex realized. Into this dirty place that smelled of garbage and moldy dreams. How could she be so unaffected by it? he wondered, then struggled to put thoughts of her aside as he approached the desk clerk.

"You got a Crystal LaRue?"

The clerk peered over his newspaper. There was an unfiltered cigarette dangling from the corner of his mouth and total disinterest in his eyes. "Don't ask for names."

Alex merely pulled out his badge, flashed it. "Blonde, about eighteen. Good-looking. A beauty mark beside her eyebrow. Working girl."

"Don't ask what they do for a living, neither." With a shrug, the clerk went back to his paper. "Two-twelve."

"She in?"

"Haven't seen her go out."

With Bess trailing behind, they started up the steps. To entertain herself, she read the various tenants' suggestions and statements that were scrawled on the walls.

There was a screaming match in progress behind one of the doors on the first floor. Someone was banging on the wall from a neighboring room and demanding—in colorful terms—that the two opponents quiet down.

A bag of garbage had spilled on the stairs between the second and first floors. It had gone very ripe.

Alex rapped on the door of 212, waited. He rapped again and called out. "Crystal. Need to talk to you."

With a glance at Judd, Alex tried the door. The knob turned easily. "In a place like this, you'd think she'd lock it," Judd commented.

"And wire it with explosives," Alex added. He slipped out his gun, and Judd did the same. "Stay in the hall," he ordered Bess without looking at her. They went through the door, guns at the ready.

She did exactly what she was told. But that didn't stop her from seeing. Crystal hadn't gone out, and she wouldn't be walking the streets again. As the door hung open, Bess stared at what was sprawled across the sagging mattress inside. The stench of blood—and worse—streamed through the open doorway.

Death. Violent death. She had written about it, discussed it, watched gleefully as it was acted out for the cameras.

But she'd never seen it face-to-face. Had never known how completely a human being could be turned into a thing.

From far away, she heard Alex swear, over and over, but she could only stare, frozen, until his body blocked her view. He had his hands on her shoulders, squeezing. God, she was cold, Bess thought. She'd never been so cold.

"I want you to go downstairs."

She managed to lift her gaze from his chin to his eyes. The iced fury in them had her shivering. "What?"

He nearly swore again. She was white as a sheet, and her pupils had contracted until they were hardly bigger than the point of a pin. "Go downstairs, Bess." He tried to rub the chill out of her arms, knowing he couldn't. "Are you listening to me?" he said, his voice quiet, gentle.

"Yes." She moistened her lips, pressed them together. "I'm sorry, yes."

"Go down, stay in the lobby. Don't say anything, don't do anything, until Judd or I come down. Okay?" He gave her a little shake, and wondered what he would do if she folded on him. "Okay?"

She took one shaky breath, then nodded. "She's... so young." With an effort, she swallowed the sickness that kept threatening to rise in her throat. "I'm all right. Don't worry about me. I'm all right," she repeated, then turned away to go downstairs.

"She shouldn't have seen this," Judd said. His own stomach was quivering.

"Nobody should see this." Banking down on every emotion, Alex closed the door at his back.

* * *

She stuck it out, refusing to budge when Judd came down to drive her home. After finding an old chair, she settled into a corner while the business of death went on around her. From her vantage point, she watched them come and go—forensics, the police photographer, the morgue.

Detached, she studied the people who crowded in, asking questions, making comments, being shuffled out again by blank-faced cops.

There was grief in her for a girl she hadn't known, a fury at the waste of a life. But she remained. Not because of the job. Because of Alex.

He was angry with her. She understood it, and didn't question it. When they were finished at the scene, she rode in silence in the back of the car. Back at the station, she took the same chair she'd had that morning.

Hours went by, endlessly long. At one point she slipped out and bought Alex and Judd sandwiches from a deli. After a time, he went into another room. She followed, still silent, noted a board with pictures tacked to it. Horrible pictures.

She looked away from them, took a chair and listened while Alex and other detectives discussed the latest murder and the ongoing investigation.

Later, she rode with him back to the pawnshop. Waited patiently while he questioned Boomer again. Waited longer while he and Judd returned to the motel to reinterview the clerk, the tenants.

Like them, she learned little about Crystal LaRue. Her name had been Kathy Segal, and she'd once lived in Wisconsin. It had been hard, terribly hard, for Bess to listen when Alex tracked down and notified her parents.

Hard, too, to understand from Alex's end of the conversation that they didn't care. For them, their daughter had already been dead.

She'd been nobody's girl. She'd worked the streets on her own. Two months after she moved into the tiny little room with the sagging mattress, she had died there. No one had known her. No one had wanted to know her.

No one had cared.

Alex couldn't talk to Bess. It was impossible for him. Intolerable. He shared this part of his life with no one who mattered to him. It was true that his sister Rachel saw some of it as a public defender but as far as Alex was concerned that was too much. Perhaps that was why he kept all the pieces he could away from the rest of his family and loved ones.

He hated remembering the look on Bess's face as she'd stood in that doorway. There should have been a way to protect her from that, to shield her from her own stubbornness.

But he hadn't protected her, he hadn't shielded her, though that was precisely what he had sworn to do for people he'd never met from the first day he'd worn a badge. Yet for her, for the woman he was—God, yes, the woman he was in love with—he'd opened the door himself and let her in.

So he didn't talk to her, not even when it was time to turn it off and go home. And in the silence, his anger built and swelled and clawed at his guts. He found the words when he stepped into her apartment and closed the door.

"Did you get enough?"

Bess was in no mood to fight. Her emotions, always close to the surface, had been wrung dry by what she'd seen and heard that day. She would let him yell, if that was what he needed, but she was tired, she was aching, and her heart went out to him.

"Let me get you a drink," she said quietly, but he snagged her arm and whirled her back.

"Is it all in your notes?" That cold, terribly controlled fury swiped out at her. "Can you find a way to use it to entertain those millions of daytime viewers?"

"I'm sorry." It was all she could think of. "Alexi, I'm so sorry." She took a deep breath. "I want a brandy. I'll get us both one."

"Fine. A nice, civilized brandy is just what we need."

She walked away to choose a bottle from an old lacquered cabinet. "I don't know what you want me to say." Very carefully, very deliberately, she poured two snifters. "I'll apologize for choosing today to do this, if that helps. I'll apologize for making it more difficult for you by being there when this happened." She brought the snifter to him, but he didn't take it. "Right now, I'd be willing to say anything you'd like to hear."

He couldn't get beyond it, no matter what she said. He couldn't get beyond knowing he'd opened the door on the kind of horror she'd never be able to forget. "You had no business being there. You had no business seeing any of that."

With a sigh, she set both snifters aside. Maybe brandy wouldn't help after all. "You were there. You saw it."

His eyes flashed white heat. "It's my damn job."

"I know." She lifted a hand to his cheek, soothing. "I know."

Compelled, he grabbed her wrist, held tight a moment before he turned away. "I don't want you touched by it. I don't want you touched by it ever again."

"I can't promise that." Because it was her way, she wrapped her arms around his waist, rested her cheek against his back. He was rigid as steel, unyielding as granite. "Not if you want something between us."

"It's because I do want something between us."

"Alexi." So many emotions, she thought. Always before it had been easy to sort them out, to drift with them. But this time… It had been a long, hard day, she reminded herself. There would be time to think later. "If what you want is someone you can tuck in a comfortable corner, it isn't me. What you do is part of what you are." When he turned, she brushed her hands over his cheeks again, refusing to let him retreat. "You want me to say I was appalled by what I saw in that room? I was. I was appalled by the cruelty of it, sickened by the terrible, terrible waste."

That sliced at him, a long, thin blade through the heart. "I shouldn't have let you go with me. That part of my life isn't ever going to be part of yours."

"Stop." The sorrow that had paled her face hardened into determination. "Do you think that because I write fantasy I don't know anything about the real world? You're wrong. I know, it just doesn't overwhelm my life. And I know that what you faced today you may face tomorrow. Or worse. I know that every time you walk out the door you may not come back." The quick lick of fear reminded her to slow down and speak carefully. "What you are makes that a very real possibility. But I won't let that overwhelm me, either. Because there's nothing about you I'd change."

For a moment, he simply stared at her, a hundred

different feelings fighting for control inside him. Then, slowly, he lowered his brow to hers and shut his eyes. "I don't know what to say to you."

"You don't have to say anything. We don't have to talk at all."

He knew what she was offering, even before she tilted her head and touched her lips to his. He wanted it, and her. More than anything, he wanted to steep himself in her until the rest of the world went away.

He took his hands through her hair, letting his fingers toy with those loose, vivid curls. "We haven't come up with those rules."

Her lips curved, slanted over his. "We'll figure them out later."

He murmured his agreement, drawing her closer. "I want you. I need to be with you. I think I'd go crazy if I couldn't be with you tonight."

"I'm here. Right here."

"Bess." His mouth moved from hers to skim along those sharp cheekbones. "I'm in love with you."

She felt her heart stutter. That was the only way she could describe this sensation she'd never experienced before. "Alexi—"

"Don't." He closed his mouth over hers again. "Don't say it. It comes too easy to you. Just come to bed." He buried his face against her neck. "For God's sake, let me take you to bed."

Chapter 8

Hurt. Oh, she'd read the stories and the poetry, watched the movies. She'd even written the scenes. But she'd never believed that love and pain existed together, could twine into one clenched fist to batter the soul.

Yet his words had hurt her—immeasurably—even as her heart opened to give and accept.

This time it was different. How could she possibly explain that to him, when she was still groping for the answers herself? And what good were words now, when there was so much need?

A touch would be enough, she promised herself as they swayed toward the steps. Tonight would be enough, and tomorrow all the aches would only be memories.

His mouth came back to hers, restless, insistent, as they began the climb. The first helpless sigh caught in her throat as he pulled her close and aroused her unbearably with a long, sumptuous meeting of lips.

Her fingers trembled when she tugged at his jacket. Had they ever trembled for a man before? she wondered. No. And as the leather slid away, leaving her free to grip those magnificent shoulders, she knew that none of this had happened before. Not the trembling, not the raw scrape of nerves, not the sting of bright tears, not the sweet, slow throb of her blood.

This was the first time for so many things.

He didn't know how much longer he could perform the simple act of drawing breath in and out of his lungs. Not when her body was shivering against his. Not when he could hear those small, desperately needy sounds in her throat. The staircase seemed to stretch interminably. With a muffled oath, he swept her up into his arms.

Her eyes met his, and though her heart seemed ready to burst, she managed to smile. She knew he needed smiles tonight. "And I said you weren't romantic."

"I have my moments."

Shaky, she nuzzled her face into the curve of his neck. "I'm awfully glad I'm here for this one."

"Keep it up," he said in a strained voice as she ran nibbling kisses from throat to ear, "and I'll do something really romantic, like falling on my face and dropping you."

"Oh, I trust you, Detective." She caught the lobe of his ear in her teeth and felt the quick jerk of reaction. "Completely."

With his heart roaring in his head, he reached the top. She was teasing his jawline now, making little murmurs of approval as she sampled his flesh. He headed for the first door. "This better be the bedroom."

"Mmm-hmm…" While she worked her way to his mouth, her fingers were busy unbuttoning his shirt.

He recognized her scent first. Even as he passed through the doorway, it wrapped its alluring woman's fingers around him. That cheerful, sexy fragrance hung in the air, the result, no doubt, of spilled powder and an unstoppered bottle of perfume. Her clothes were a colorful mess of silk blouses, bright cotton pants, tangled hose. His quick scan passed over a life-size stuffed ostrich, a pair of thriving ficus trees flanking the wide window, and a collection of antique bottles, elegant in jewel colors, before he focused on the bed.

It was a long, wide ocean of cool blue sheets, topped by a lush mountain of vivid-toned pillows. All satins and silks.

Because his mouth was beginning to water, he took one long, slow breath. But the air, so fragrant, burned his lungs. "That looks big enough for six close friends."

"I like a lot of room." Even as his stomach quivered at the images that evoked, she was continuing. "I used to fall out of bed a lot when I was a kid."

"Is that how you broke your nose?"

"No. But I chipped a tooth once."

He set her down beside the bed, pleased that her arms stayed linked around his neck. "I think we can probably keep from falling out of this one. If we work on it."

She raised up on her toes, just a little, just enough to bring them eye-to-eye. "I'm willing to risk it."

Determined to steady himself, he kissed her brow, her cheeks. "Let me take my gun off."

He stripped off the holster, set it on the floor. With fingers that were suddenly numb and awkward, she reached for the buttons of her blazer.

"No." It was that one quick flash of nerves in her eyes that had settled his own. He closed his hands over hers. "Let me." He unfastened buttons, then took his hands slowly up her sides, his thumbs just brushing her breasts. "You're shaking."

"I know."

Watching her, he slid the jacket from her shoulders. "Are you afraid of me?"

"No." She couldn't swallow. "Of this, a little. It's silly."

He toyed with the first button of her blouse, then the second. Her skin quivered as his knuckle skimmed over it. "I like it."

"That's good." She tried to laugh, but only managed one trembling breath. "Because I can't seem to stop."

"There's plenty of time to relax." The blouse slipped away, and desire curled its powerful fist in his stomach. Midnight-blue silk shimmered in the dimming light, gleaming against ivory skin. "There's no hurry."

"I—" Her head fell back as he traced a finger over the silk. Gently, so gently, over the swell of her breasts, as though hers was the first body he'd touched. The only one he wanted to touch. "God, Alexi…"

"I've spent a lot of time imagining this. Step out of your shoes," he suggested while he unhooked her slacks. In a daze, she obeyed as the slacks slithered down her legs. "I'm going to spend a lot more time enjoying it. I want all of you." Lazily, testingly, he ran a finger under the lace cut high on her thigh. Ah, the skin there was like rose petals dewed with morning. Her eyes went wide and dark; her body quaked. "All of you," he repeated.

She couldn't move. Every muscle in her body had

turned to water. Hot, rushing water. She couldn't speak, not when so many emotions clogged her throat. As she stood swaying, helplessly seduced, he watched her. Touched her. Clever fingers brushing, stroking, exploring. He trailed them up her arms, slid them over her shoulders. Then back to silk, until her body burned like fever.

His eyes never left hers. Even when he kissed her, lightly, tormenting her hungry lips with the barest of tastes, his eyes stayed open and aware.

"You're making me crazy." Her voice hitched out through trembling lips.

"I know. I want to."

He caught her wrists when she reached for him, then ran their tangled fingers over her, so that she felt her own response to him, inside and out, as he touched his mouth to hers again. Patiently, erotically, he deepened the kiss, until her hands went limp and her pulse thundered. Then he brought her hands up, spread them over his chest. Together they spread his open shirt apart. With his mouth still clinging to hers, he tugged it off. His heart gave a quick, hard lurch as her hands, hot and eager, raced over him.

Yanking her close, he took off his shoes. His skin was already damp when he fumbled for the snap of his jeans.

"I want you under me." He tore his mouth from hers to savor her throat. "I want to feel you move under me."

They lowered to the bed, rolled once, then twice, over silk. He used every ounce of control, every degree of will, to keep himself from plunging into her and taking the quick, desperate release his body craved. His mind, his soul, wanted more than that.

She seemed smaller like this. Slighter. It helped him remember that passion could outstrip tenderness. So, while the blood pounded and burned in his veins, he loved her slowly.

She discovered that a woman could drown willingly in sweetness. She knew there was a gun on the floor beside them and that he had used it at least once to kill. But the hands that moved over her were those of a gentle man. One who cared. She rested a palm on his cheek as she floated away on the kiss. One who loved.

Who loved her.

Staggered by the knowledge, she poured everything she had into the kiss, needing to show him that whatever he felt was returned, equally. Then his mouth slid from hers to trail down her throat, over her shoulder. All thought, all reason, skittered away.

In a warm, slippery pool of silk and satin, he showed her what it was to ache for someone. To yearn for the sharp, thin point of pain the poets call ecstasy. Her hips arched under his, desperately offering. But he only continued that tormenting journey over her with teasing lips and gentle hands.

When his tongue flicked under the line of lace that clung tenuously to her breasts, she moaned, pressing an urgent hand to the back of his head. The taste there— honey, dampened by her arousal—nearly unraveled the taut knot of his control. So he pleased them both, closing a greedy mouth over that firm, scented swell.

Gasping out with pleasure, she bucked under him, straining for more, her nails digging heedlessly into his back as she whimpered and struggled for what was just out of reach. Maddened by her response, he brought his mouth to hers again, crushing her lips as he slithered a hand down to cup the heat between her thighs. Prayers and pleas trembled on her tongue, but before she could voice them, he slipped under the silk to stroke.

The unbearable pleasure shattered. Fractured lights, whirling colors, spun behind her eyes to blind her. She heard herself cry out; his name was nearly a sob. Then there was his groan, a sound of sweet satisfaction as her body went limp in release.

Never before. Her hands slid away from him, boneless. Sweet Lord, never like this. She felt weak, wrecked, weepy. As her breath sobbed out, as her eyes fluttered closed, they both knew that her mind, her body, were totally his for the taking.

He'd never felt stronger. Her wild response, her absolute surrender, filled him with a kind of intense power he'd never experienced before. Silk rustled against silk as he drew the teddy down, tossed it aside. Her skin, slick with passion, glowed in the shadows. He touched where he chose, watching, fascinated, as his own hands molded her. Gold against ivory. He tasted wherever he liked, feeling her muscles quiver involuntarily as he traced openmouthed kisses over her rib cage, down to her stomach. Heat to heat.

Then, wanting that instant of sheer pleasure again, he drove her up a second time, shuddering himself as her body convulsed and flowed with the crest of the wave.

At last, unable to wait a moment longer, he slipped inside that hot, moist sheath. Her groan of stunned delight echoed his own.

Slowly, as in a dream, her arms lifted to wrap around him. She rose to meet him, to take him deep. They moved gently at first, treasuring the intimacy, willing to prolong it. But need outpaced them, driving them faster, until, thrust for thrust, they sprinted toward the final crest.

His hand fisted in her hair as the last link of control snapped clean. Her name exploded from his lips like an oath as he emptied himself into her.

She wondered how she could ever have thought herself experienced. While it was true she hadn't been with as many men as some thought, she hadn't come to Alexi an innocent.

Yet things had happened tonight that had never happened before. And, because she was a woman who understood herself well, she knew that nothing she had experienced here would happen again—unless it was with him.

Relaxed now, she rubbed her cheek over his chest, content to remain as she'd been since he rolled over and dragged her across him. Tucked in the cocoon of his arms, she felt as cozy as a cat, and she arched lazily as he ran a hand down her spine.

"Will you tell me again?" she asked.

"What?"

She pressed her lips against him, feeling his heart beating strong and fast beneath them. "What every woman wants to hear."

"I love you." When she lifted her head, he laid a hand gently over her lips. He knew it would hurt to hear her say it, when she didn't mean it as he did.

Suddenly she was glad it was dark, and he couldn't see the smile fade away from her face. "Even after this," she said carefully, "you don't want me to love you back."

More than anything, he thought. More than life. "Let's just leave things as they are." He traced her face with a fingertip, enjoying those odd angles. "Tell me how you broke your nose."

She was silent a moment, gathering her composure. She couldn't offer what he didn't want to take. "Fist-fight."

He chuckled and drew her back to cuddle, instinctively soothing the tension out of her. "I should have figured."

She made an effort to relax against him. There was time to convince him. Hadn't he said they had plenty of time? "At boarding school," she added. "I was twelve and homely as a duck. Too skinny, funny hair, dumb face."

"I like your face. And your hair." His hand cupped her breast comfortably. "And your body."

"You didn't know me when I was twelve. When you're odd in any way, you're a target."

"I know."

Interested, she lifted her head again. "Do you?"

"I didn't learn English until I was five. Before my father's business got off the ground, times were rough." He turned his face into her hair to breathe in the scent. "I was this little Ukrainian kid, wearing my brother's hand-me-downs. And back then, Soviets weren't particularly popular with Americans."

"Well, you made such great villains." She kissed his cheek, comforting the small boy he'd been. "It must have been difficult for you."

"I had the family. We had each other. School was a little rugged at first. Name-calling, playground scuffles. Even some of the parents weren't too keen on having their kids play with the Russkie. No point in trying to explain we were Ukrainian." He shifted, tangled his legs with hers. "So, after a few black eyes and bloody noses, I earned a reputation for being tough. After a while, we kind of got absorbed into the neighborhood."

"What neighborhood?"

"Brooklyn. My parents still live there. Same house." With a shake of his head, he drew back. He could make her out now in the dark, could see the way her eyes were smiling at him. "How come we're talking about me, when I asked you about your nose?"

"I like hearing it."

"There was a fistfight," he said, prompting her.

Bess sighed. "One of those girl cliques," she began. "You know the type. The cool kids, all hair and teeth and attitude. I was the nerd they liked to pick on."

"You were never a nerd."

"I was a *champion* nerd. Gawky, top of the class academically, socially inept."

"You?"

There was such pure disbelief in the tone, she laughed. "Which of those descriptions don't you buy, Alexi?"

He considered a moment. "Any of them."

"I guess I'm two-thirds flattered and one-third insulted. I was tall for my age and skinny. A very late bloomer in the bosom and hips department."

"You might have bloomed slow," he began, proving his point with a sweep of his hand, "but you bloomed very well."

"Thank you. My mind, however, had developed quite nicely. Straight *A*'s."

"No kidding?" He grinned in the dark. "And you were the kid who always trashed the grading curve for the rest of us."

"That's the idea. Added to that, I was more comfortable with a book, or thinking, than I was tittering. Young girls do a lot of tittering. Because I was hard-headed, I automatically took a dislike to anything that was popular or fashionable at the time. As a result, I took a lot of flak. Bess the Mess, that sort of thing."

She paused long enough to shift some pillows. "Anyway, we had this history exam coming up. One of the cool kids—her name was Dawn Gallagher... Heart-shaped face, perfect features, long, flowing blond hair. You get the picture."

"Prom-queen type."

"Exactly. She was flunking big-time and wanted me to let her copy from my paper. She'd made my life adolescent hell, and she figured if she was nice to me for a couple of days, let me stand within five feet of her, maybe sit at the same lunch table, I'd be so grateful, I'd let her."

"But you hung tough."

"I don't cheat for anybody. The upshot was, she flunked the exam, and her parents were called to the school for a conference. Dawn retaliated by pinching me whenever I got too close, getting into my room and breaking my things, stealing my books. Small-time terrorism. One day on the basketball court—"

"You shot hoop?"

"Team captain. I was an athletic nerd," she explained. "Anyway, she tripped me. If that wasn't bad enough, she had a few friends on the other team. They elbowed the hell out of me during the game. I had bruises everywhere."

An immediate flood of resentment had him tightening his hold. "Little bitches."

Pleased with the support, she cuddled closer. "It was an epiphany for me. Suddenly I saw that pacifism, while morally sound, could get you trampled into dust. I waited for Dawn outside the science lab one day. We started out with words—I've always been good at them. We progressed to pushing and shoving and drew quite a crowd. She swung first. I didn't expect it, and she bopped me right on the nose. Let me tell you, Detective, pain can be a great motivator."

"Separates the nerds from the toughs."

"You got it. It took three of them to pull me off her, but before they did, I'd blackened her baby-blues, split her Cupid's-bow mouth and loosened several of her pearly-whites."

"Good for you, McNee."

"It was good," she said with a sigh. "In fact, it felt so good, I've had to be careful with my temper ever since. I didn't just want to hurt her, you see. I wanted to mangle her."

He took her hand, curled it into a fist and raised it to his lips. "I'll have to watch my step. Did you take much heat?"

"We both got suspended. My parents were appalled and embarrassed enough by my behavior to cancel my summer plans and switch me to another school."

"But—" He cut himself off. Not every family was as supportive as his.

"It was the best thing that could have happened to me," she told him. "I started off with a clean slate. I was still ugly, but I knew how to handle myself."

Even if she didn't realize she was carrying around some emotional scars, he did. He rolled over her, cupping her face in his hands. "Listen, McNee, you're beautiful."

Amused, she grinned. "Sure I am."

He didn't smile. In the dim light, his eyes were very

intense. "I said, you're beautiful. Why else haven't I been able to get you out of my mind since the first time I saw you?"

"Intriguing," she corrected. "Unusual."

"Gorgeous," he murmured, and watched her blink in surprise. "Ivory for skin, fire for hair, jade for eyes. And these." He traced a fingertip over a sprinkling of freckles. "Gold dust."

"You've already gotten me into bed, Alexi," she said lightly. She had to speak lightly, or she'd humiliate herself with tears. "But the flattery is appreciated." With a grin, she linked her arms around his neck. "But haven't you heard the one about actions speaking louder than words?"

He arched a brow. "If you insist."

"Oh, I do," she murmured, as his mouth came down to hers. "I absolutely do."

With her bag slapping hard against her hip, Bess raced into the office, ten minutes late. "I have a good excuse," she called to Lori.

Her perpetually prompt partner was standing by the coffeepot, her back to the door. "It's all right. I'm running behind myself."

"You?" Bess dropped her bag, stretched her shoulders. She might have skipped her workout that morning, but she was feeling as limber as a snake. "What is it, a national holiday?" She crossed to the pot herself, chattering as she poured a cup. "Well, I'd save my excuse for another time, but I can hardly stand not to tell you." She lifted shining eyes, then stopped after one look at Lori's face. "What is it, honey?"

"It's nothing." After giving herself a shake, Lori

sipped her coffee. "It's just that Steven caught me on my way in."

"Did he say something to upset you?"

"He said he loved me." She pressed her lips together. She'd be damned if she'd cry over him again. "The sonofabitch."

"Let's sit down." Bess curled a comforting arm around Lori's shoulder. "You might not want to hear this, but I think he means it."

"He doesn't even know what it means." Furious, Lori dashed one rogue tear away. "I'm not going to let him do this to me again. Get me believing, get me all churned up, just so he can back off when things get serious. Let him have the fantasy life. I've got reality."

Because she'd been waiting for an opening just like this, Bess crouched down in front of her. "Which is?"

"A job, paying your bills—"

"Boring," Bess finished, and Lori's brimming eyes flashed.

"Then I'm boring."

"No, you're not." Sighing, Bess set her coffee aside and took one of Lori's hands. "Maybe you're afraid to take risks, but that doesn't make you boring. And I know you want more out of life than a job and a good credit rating."

"What's wrong with those things?"

"Nothing, as long as that's not all you have. Lori, I know you're still in love with him."

"That's my problem."

"His, too. He's miserable without you."

Suddenly weary, Lori rubbed her fingers between her brows. "He's the one who broke things off. He said he didn't want complications, a long-term commitment."

"He was wrong. I'd bet the bank that he knows he's wrong. Why don't you just talk to him?"

"I don't know if I can." She squeezed her eyes tight. "It hurts."

An odd light flickered in Bess's eyes. "Is that how you know it's real? When it hurts?"

"It's one of the top symptoms." She opened her eyes again. This time, there was a trace of hope mixed with the tears. "Do you really think he's unhappy?"

"I know he is. Just talk, Lori. Hear each other out."

"Maybe." She gave Bess's hand a quick squeeze, then reached for her coffee again. "I wasn't going to dump this on you first thing."

"What are pals for?"

"Well, pal, we'd better get to work, or a lot of people will be out of a job."

"Great. I've been playing with the dialogue in that scene between Storm and Jade. We want to bump up the sexual tension."

Lori was already nodding and booting up the computer. "You're the dialogue champ," she began, then glanced up. "So why were you late?"

"It's not important. We've got them running into each other at the station house. The long look first, then—"

"Bess, you're only making me more curious. Get it out of the way, or I won't be able to work."

"Okay." She was all but bursting to tell, in any case. "I was with Alexi."

"I thought that was yesterday."

"It was." Bess's smile spread. "And last night. And this morning. Oh, Lori, it's incredible. I've never felt this way about anyone."

"Right." She started to pick up her reading glasses,

then looked up again. For a moment, she did nothing but study Bess's face. "Say that again."

"I've never felt this way about anyone."

"Good grief." On a quick huff of breath, Lori sat back. "I think you mean it."

"It's different." With a half laugh, Bess pressed a hand to her cheek. "It's scary, and it hurts, and sometimes I look at him and I can't even breathe. I'm so afraid he might take a good look at me and realize his mistake." She let her hand drop away. "It's supposed to be easy."

"No." Slowly Lori shook her head. "That was always *your* mistake. It's supposed to be hard, and scary and real."

"There's this clutching around my heart."

"Yeah."

"And…and…" Frustrated, Bess turned, scooting around a chair so that she could pace the length of the table. "And my stomach's all tied up in knots one minute. The next I feel so happy I can hardly bear it. When we were together last night…" No way to describe it, she thought. No possible way. "Lori, I swear, no one's ever made me feel like that. And this morning, when I woke up beside him, I didn't know whether to laugh or cry."

Lori rose, held out a hand. "Congratulations, McNee. You've finally made it."

"Looks that way." With a laugh, she threw her arms around Lori and squeezed. "Why didn't you ever tell me how it feels?"

"It's something you have to experience firsthand. How about him?"

"He loves me." She felt foolish and weepy. Digging through her bag she found a tattered tissue. "He told me. He looked at me, and he told me. But—"

"Oh-oh."

"He doesn't want me to tell him how I feel." Hissing a breath through her teeth, she pressed a hand to her stomach. "Oh, God, it hurts. It hurts everywhere when I realize he doesn't trust me enough. He thinks it's like all the other times. Why shouldn't he? But I want him to know it's not—and I don't know how."

"He only has to look at you."

"It's not enough." Calmer now, Bess blew her nose. "Everything's different this time. I guess I have to prove myself. I do love him, Lori."

"I can see that. I wasn't sure I ever would." Touched, she lifted a hand to Bess's hair. "You could take your own advice, and talk to him."

"We have talked. But he doesn't want to hear this, at least not yet. He wants things to stay as they are."

Lori lifted her brows. "What do you want?"

"For him to be happy." She chuckled and stuffed the mangled tissue back in her purse. "That makes me sound like a wimp. You know I'm not."

"Who knows you better? It only makes you sound like a woman in the first dizzy stages of love."

Bess gave her a watery smile. "Does it get worse or better?"

"Both."

"That's good news. Well, while it's getting worse and better, I'll have time to show him how I feel." She picked up her coffee, then set it aside again. "Lori, there's one more thing."

"What could be bigger?" Lori demanded.

"Alexi wants me to have dinner with his family on Sunday."

After a quick gurgle of laughter, Lori's eyes widened. "He's taking you home to Mother?"

"And Father," Bess put in. "And brothers and sisters and nieces and nephews. A couple times a month they have a big family dinner on Sunday."

"Obviously the man is crazy about you."

"He is. I know he is." Then she shut her eyes and dropped into a chair. "His family is enormously important to him. You can hear it every time he mentions one of them." She grabbed another tissue and began to tear it to shreds. "I want to meet them. Really. But what if they don't like me?"

"You have got it bad. Take it from me, you just be the Bess McNee we all know and love, and they'll be crazy about you, too."

"But what if—"

"What if you pull yourself together?" This time Lori picked up her glasses, perched them on her nose. "Put some of this angst into Storm and Jade's heartbreak. Millions of viewers will thank you."

After a deep breath, Bess nodded. "Okay, okay. That might work. And if we don't get the morning session out of the way, we won't be ready when Rosalie comes in at noon for a consulting session."

"Your deal, sister." Frowning, Lori gestured with a pencil. "That particular lady makes me nervous."

"Don't worry about Rosalie. I know what I'm doing."

"How many times have I heard that?"

But Bess only smiled and let her mind drift. "Okay. Storm and Jade." She closed her eyes, envisioned the scene. "So, they run into each other at the station..."

Chapter 9

"And then," Bess continued as she zipped through traffic, "Jade turns back, devastated, and says, 'But what you want isn't always what you need.' Music swells, fade out."

"It's not that I'm not fascinated by the twists and turns of those people in Holbrook…"

"Millbrook."

"Right." Alex winced as she cut off a sedan. "I just wish you'd watch the road. It would be really embarrassing if you got a ticket while I was in the car with you."

"I'm not speeding." Frowning, she glanced down at her speedometer. "Hardly."

She handled the five-speed like a seasoned veteran of the Indianapolis 500, Alex thought. And at the moment she was treating the other, innocent drivers on the road like competitors. "Maybe you could find a home in one lane and stay there."

"Killjoy." But she did as he asked. "I hardly ever get to drive. I love it."

He had to smile. The wind whipping in through the open sunroof was blowing her hair everywhere. "I'd never have guessed."

"The last time I had a chance was when L.D. and I went to some fancy do on Long Island." She checked her mirror and, unable to resist, shot into the next lane. "One trip with me and he insisted on taking his car and driver every damn place." She sent Alex a smile, then sobered instantly when she saw his expression. "I'm sorry."

"For what?"

"For bringing him up."

"I didn't say anything."

No, he hadn't said anything, she admitted. A man didn't have to say a word when his eyes could go that cold. Her hands tightened on the wheel. Now she stared straight ahead.

"He was a friend, Alexi. That's all he ever was. I didn't…" She took a long, careful breath. "I never slept with him."

"I didn't ask one way or the other," he said coolly.

"Maybe you should. One minute you want to know all there is about me, and the next you don't. I think—"

"I think you're driving too fast again." He reached over and brushed his knuckles down her cheek. "And you should relax. Okay?"

"Okay." But her fingers remained tight on the wheel. "I'd like—sometime—for us to talk about it."

"Sometime." Damn it, didn't she realize he didn't

want to talk about the other men who'd been part of her life? He didn't want to think about them. Especially now, now that he was in love, and he knew what it was like to be with her.

He knew the sound of that little sigh she made when she turned toward him in the night. The way her eyes stayed unfocused and heavy, long after she awakened in the morning. He knew she liked her showers too hot and too long. And that she smelled so good because she rubbed some fragrant cream all over before she'd even dried off.

She was always losing things. An earring, a scribbled note, money. She never counted her change, and she always overtipped.

He knew those things, was coming to treasure them. Why should he talk about other men who had come to know them?

"Turn here."

"Hmm?"

"I said turn..." He trailed off with a huff of breath as she breezed by the exit. "Okay, take the next one, and we'll double back."

"The next what?"

"Turn, McNee." He reached over and gave her hair a quick tug. "Take the next turn, which means you have to get over in the right lane."

"Oh." She did, punching the gas and handily cutting off another car. At the rude blast of its horn, she only lifted a hand and waved.

"He wasn't being friendly," Alex pointed out—after he took his hands from in front of his eyes.

"I know. But that's no reason for me to be rude, too."

"Some people consider cutting off another driver rude."

"No. That's an adventure."

Somehow they made it without mishap. But the moment she'd squeezed into a parking place two doors down from his parents' row house, he held out his hand. "Keys."

Sulking, she jingled them in her hand. "I didn't get a ticket."

"Probably because there wasn't a traffic cop brave enough to pull you over. Let's have them, McNee. I've had enough adventure for one day."

"You just want to drive." Her eyes narrowed suspiciously. "It's a man thing."

"It's a survival thing." He plucked them from her hand. "I just want to live." Not that he was going to object to handling the natty little Mercedes. But he decided against bringing that up as they climbed out of opposite doors.

"Pretty neighborhood," she commented, taking in the trees and freshly painted house trim and flowering plants, the scatter of kids riding over the uneven sidewalk on bikes and skateboards.

A few of them called out to Alex. Bess found herself being given the once-over by a group of teenage boys before they sent hoots and whistles and thumbs-up signs in Alex's direction.

"Ah, the first stamp of approval." But she rubbed her damp palm surreptitiously against her skirt before taking his hand. "Did you used to ride bikes along the sidewalk?"

"Sure."

Battling nerves, she strolled with him toward the

house. "And sit on the curb in the summer and lie about girls?"

"I didn't have to lie," he told her with a wicked grin. He glanced up the steps as the door opened and Mikhail came out, Griff on his hip.

"You're late again." He started down, jiggling Griff.

"She missed the turn."

"He's always late." Mikhail smiled. "You're Bess."

"Yes. Hello." She held out a hand and found that his was hard as rock. Griff had already leaned over to give Alex a kiss, and now, still puckered, he leaned toward Bess. Laughing, she pressed her mouth to his. "And hello to you, too, handsome."

"Griff likes the ladies," Mikhail told her. "Takes after his uncle."

"Don't start," Alex muttered.

Mikhail ignored him and continued to study Bess until she was fighting the need to squirm. "Do I have dirt on my face, or what?"

"No, sorry." He shifted his gaze to his brother. "You're improving, Alexi," he said in Ukrainian. "This one is well worth a few sweaty mornings in the gym."

"Tak." He skimmed a hand down to the nape of Bess's neck. "If you tell her about that, I'll strangle you in your sleep."

Mikhail's grin flashed. The resemblance was startling, Bess thought. Those wild, dark looks, that simmering sexuality. And the child had the looks, as well, she realized. Lord help the women of the twenty-first century.

"Guy talk?" she asked.

"Bad manners," Mikhail said apologetically, deciding he liked not only her unusual looks, but the intelligence in her eyes, as well. Yes, indeed, he thought, Alex was definitely improving. "I was complimenting my brother on his taste. Take her in, Alex. Griff wants to watch the kids ride awhile."

"Sydney?" he asked as he mounted the steps.

"She's here, but she's tired."

"She works too hard."

"There is that." The grin spread again. "And she's pregnant."

Alex stopped, turned. "Yeah?" He went down the steps again to catch Mikhail and Griff in a bear hug. "It's good?"

"It's great. We want our children close, our family big."

"You're off to the right start." He grabbed Bess's hand as Mikhail lifted Griff onto his shoulders and crossed the street. Griff was clapping his hands and shouting toddler gibberish to the other kids. "I'm still trying to get used to him being a papa, and now he's going to have another."

She'd forgotten her nerves. Perhaps the child's sweet, unaffected kiss had done it. She slipped an arm around Alex's waist. "Come on, Uncle Alex. I want to meet the rest of them."

"They're loud," he warned as they started back up the door.

"I like loud."

"They can be nosy."

"So can I."

At the door, he took both of her hands. He'd brought women into his home before, but it had never been important. This was vital. "I love you, Bess." Before she could speak, he kissed her, then pushed open the door.

* * *

They certainly were loud, Bess discovered. No one seemed to mind if everyone talked at once, or if the big, droopy-eared dog barked and raced around the living room to hide behind chairs. And they were nosy, though they were charming with it. She'd hardly had a chance to get her bearings before she was sitting next to Alex's father, Yuri, and being cagily interrogated.

"So you write stories for TV." He nodded his big, shaggy head approvingly. "You have brains."

"A few." She smiled up at Zack when he offered her a glass of wine.

"Rachel says more than a few." He sent his wife a wink as she sat with her hands folded over her enormous belly. "She's been watching your show."

"Oh, yeah?"

"I admit I was curious." Rachel wanted to shift to get comfortable, but she knew it was useless. "After we met, I taped it a couple of times. Then, when I gave in to Zack's hounding me about taking maternity leave, I realized how easy it is to get hooked. I'm not sure I've got all the characters straight yet, but it's amazingly entertaining. Nick's caught it with me." She glanced at her brother-in-law.

To his credit, Nick didn't blush, but he did squirm. "I was just keeping you company." He might have come a long way from trying to prove his manhood with gangs like the Cobras, but even at nearly twenty-one, he wasn't quite secure enough to admit he'd gotten caught up in the "Secret Sins" of Millbrook. He shrugged, shook back his shaggy blond hair, then caught the quick grins of his family. "It wasn't like I was really watching." His green eyes glinted with humor. "Except for the babes."

"That's what they all say." Bess smiled back, enjoying him. Too bad he wasn't an actor, she thought. Those brooding good looks—tough, with just a hint of vulnerability beneath—would shine on-screen. "So, who's your type, Nick? LuAnne, our sensitive ingenue with the big, weepy eyes, who suffers in silence, or the scheming Brooke, who uses her sexuality to destroy any man who crosses her?"

Considering, he ran his tongue around his teeth. "Actually, I go for Jade. I've got this thing for older women."

Zack caught him in a headlock.

"Hey." Nick laughed, not bothering to try to free himself. "We're having a conversation here. I'm trying to make time with Alex's lady."

"Kill him in the other room, will you?" Alex said easily. "We have to eat in here."

"I watch your show many times," Nadia said as she popped in from the kitchen. Alex's mother's handsome face was flushed pink from oven heat. "I like it."

"Well, that Vicki's not hard to watch." Zack stood behind his wife now, rubbing her shoulders.

"Men always go for the cheap floozies," Rachel put in. "How about you, Alex? Caught any 'Secret Sins'?"

"No." Not that he'd admit. "McNee keeps me up on what's happening in Millbrook."

"It must be hard." Sydney, looking pale but blissfully relaxed in her corner of the couch, sipped her ginger ale. "The pace."

"It's murder." Bess grinned. "I love it."

"So, how is it you meet Alexi?" Yuri asked.

"He arrested me."

There was a moment of silence, while Alex aimed a

killing look at Bess. Then a burst of laughter that sent
the dog careening around the room again.

"Did I miss a joke?" Mikhail demanded as he swung
through the door with Griff.

"No." Rachel chuckled again while her brother sat
on the arm of the couch, beside his wife. "But I have
a feeling it's going to be a good one. Come on, Bess,
this I have to hear."

She told them, while Alex interrupted a half-dozen
times to disagree or correct or put in his own perspec-
tive. Even as they sat at the big old table to enjoy Nadia's
pot roast, they were shouting with laughter or calling
out questions.

"He put you in a cell, but you still go out with him."
This from Mikhail.

"Well." Bess ran her tongue over her teeth. "He is
kind of cute."

With a hearty laugh, Yuri slapped his son on the
back. "The ladies, they always say so."

Alex scooped up potatoes. "Thanks, Papa."

"Is good to be attractive to women." He wiggled his
brows at his wife. "Then, when you pick one, she is
helpless to resist."

"I picked you," Nadia told him, passing biscuits to
Nick. "You were very slow. Like a bear with, ah…" She
struggled for the right word. "Soft brains." She ignored
Yuri's snort of objection. "He did not come to court me.
So I courted him."

"Every time I turn, there she is. In my way." When
he looked at his wife, Bess saw memories and more in
his eyes. "There was no prettier girl in the village than
Nadia. Then she was mine."

"I liked your big hands and shy eyes," she told him.

Her smile was quick and lovely. "Soon you were not so shy. But my boys," she added, turning the smile on Bess, "they were never shy with the girls."

"Why waste time?" On impulse, Alex put a hand on Bess's cheek and turned her face to his. Her smile was puzzled. Then surprise shot into her eyes as he covered her mouth with his. Not a quick, friendly kiss, this, but a searing one that made her head buzz.

She had no way of knowing that he'd never kissed a woman not of his family at his mother's table. Nor that by doing so, he was telling those he loved that this was *the* woman.

As the table erupted with applause, Bess cleared her throat. "No," she managed. "Not a bit shy."

Nadia blinked back tears and raised her glass. She understood what her son had told her and felt the bittersweet pleasure that came from knowing the last of her children had given his heart. "Welcome," she said to Bess.

A little confused, Bess reached for her glass as all the others were lifted. "Thank you." She sipped, relieved when the chattering started again.

How easy to fall in love with them, she realized. All of them were so warm, so open, so comfortable with each other. Her parents would never have had such a sweetly intimate conversation at the table. Nor had they ever embraced her with the verve and passion both Yuri and Nadia showed their children.

Was this what she'd been missing all of those years? Bess wondered. Had lacking something like this caused her to be so socially clumsy as a child, and, making up for it, so socially active as an adult?

Still, what she had had, and what she hadn't, had

forged her into what she was, so she couldn't regret it. Well, perhaps a little, she mused, falling unknowingly into the family tradition by sneaking the dog bits of food under the table. It was hard not to regret it a little when you saw how lovely it could be to be part of such a solid whole.

Absorbing everything, she glanced around the table. And found Mikhail's eyes on her. This time she smiled. "You're doing it again," she told him.

"Yes. I want to carve you."

"I beg your pardon?"

"Your face." He reached out to take it in his hand. The conversation continued around them, as if he handled women at the dinner table regularly. "Very fascinating. Mahogany would be best."

Amused, she sat patiently while he turned her face this way and that. "Is this a joke?"

"Mikhail never jokes about his work," Sydney commented, coaxing one more green bean into her son. "I'm just surprised it's taken him so long to demand you sit for him."

"Sit?" She shook her head, and then her eyes widened as it all came together. "Oh, of course. Stanislaski. The artist. I've seen your work. Lusted after it, actually."

"You will sit for me, and I'll give you a piece. You'll choose it."

"I could hardly turn down an offer like that."

"Good." Satisfied, he went back to his meal. "She's very beautiful," he said to Alex, in such an offhand way that Bess laughed.

"I'd say that Stanislaski taste runs to the odd, but your wife proves me wrong."

Mikhail brushed a hand over Sydney's halo of auburn hair, stroked a finger down her classically lovely face. "There are different kinds of beauty. You'll come to the studio next week."

"Don't bother to argue." Sydney caught Mikhail's hand, squeezed it. "It won't do you a bit of good."

At the other end of the table, Rachel winced. Nadia leaned closer, spoke gently. "How far apart?"

Rachel gave a little sigh. "Eight, ten minutes. They're very mild yet."

"What's mild?" Zack glanced at her, and then his mouth all but dropped to his knees. "Oh, God, now? *Now?*"

"Not this very minute." She would be calm, Rachel told herself and took a deep, cleansing breath to prove it. "I think you have time for some of Mama's cream cake."

"She's in labor." He gaped across the table at his equally panicked brother.

"We're not ready here." Nick stumbled to his feet. "We're ready back at home. I'm supposed to call the doctor, but I don't have the number."

"Mama does," Rachel assured her husband's younger brother. Then she lifted a hand to her husband's. "Take it easy, Muldoon. There's plenty of time."

"Time, hell. We're going now. Shouldn't we go now?" Zack demanded of Nadia.

She smiled and nodded. "It would be best for you, Zack."

"But, Mama—"

Rachel's protest was cut off by Nadia's gentle flow of Ukrainian, the gist of which had a great deal to do with placating frightened husbands.

"She should put her feet up," Mikhail announced. "This helped you, yes?"

"Yes," Sydney agreed. "But I think we should wait until she gets to the hospital."

"Nine-one-one." Alex shoved away from the table and sprang to his feet. "I'll call."

"Oh, sit down." Rachel waved an annoyed hand at him. "I don't need a cop."

"An ambulance," he insisted.

"I'm not sick, I'm in labor."

"I take her in the truck." Yuri was already up, prepared to lift his baby girl into his big arms. "We get there very fast."

While the men began to argue in a mixture of languages, Nadia rose quietly and went into the kitchen to call Rachel's obstetrician.

"I've already been through this," Mikhail was saying to Alex. "I know how to handle it."

"Ha." Their father pushed them both aside and pounded a fist on his broad chest. "Me, four times. You know nothing."

"We don't have the tape recorder or the music." Nick ran a hand through his flow of sandy hair. He was desperately afraid he'd be sick. Though no one was listening to him, he continued to babble. "The video camera. We've got to get the video camera."

"Honey, you want some water? You want some juice?" When she yelped, Zack turned dead white. "Another one? It hasn't been ten minutes, has it?"

"You're breaking my hand." Rachel shook it free and sent a pleading look to Sydney.

"Okay, guys, back off." The steel under velvet that made Sydney a successful businesswoman snapped into

her voice. "Alex, go upstairs and get your sister a pil-
low for the ride. Yuri, go start the truck. That's a very
good idea. Nick, you, Mikhail and Griff go back to your
apartment and get what Rachel needs. We'll meet you
at the hospital."

"How do you get there?" Mikhail demanded.

"I have a car." Bess was watching the family drama
with fascinated eyes. "We can fit three in a pinch."

"Wonderful." Dispersing the troops with all the flair
of a general, Sydney gave her husband a kiss and a
shove. "Get going. Zack and Nadia will ride with Yuri
and Rachel. I'll go with Alex and Bess."

As the next contraction hit, Rachel began to breathe
slowly, steadily. "Sorry," she said to Bess in between
breaths, "to put you out."

"No problem." She had to bite her tongue to prevent
herself asking what it felt like to go into labor at a family dinner. There'd be time for that later.

"I called the doctor, and Natasha." Nadia came back
into the room, pleased that Sydney had organized the
troops. "Natasha and her family are coming."

"We should go." Zack helped Rachel to her feet and
swallowed hard. "Shouldn't we go?"

By the time they arrived at the hospital, Sydney and
Bess were the best of friends. It was difficult to be otherwise, when they'd been crammed together in one seat
while Alex drove like a madman back to Manhattan.

They talked about clothes, a few mutual friends they'd
discovered, and the Stanislaski men. Sydney agreed that
it was very forbearing of Bess not to mention the quality of Alex's driving, after he'd been so critical of hers.

By the time they found their way to the maternity

level, Rachel was already settled in a birthing room, Zack had gotten over the first stages of panic, and Yuri was patting a pocket full of cigars.

"She's in the early stages," Nadia explained to them in the corridor. "Company is good for her."

Alex strode straight through the door, but Bess hung back. "I don't want to intrude," she said to Nadia.

"This is not intrusion. This is family." Nadia cocked her head. "Are you uneasy with childbirth?"

"Oh, no. I couldn't be, after I've written so many."

Alex poked his head back out. "How'd you research that, McNee?"

"I did rounds with an obstetrician." Her dimple winked out. "And found a few mothers-to-be who didn't object to having me hang around during labor and delivery. Have you ever seen one?"

"No." His eyes changed. Just like a man. "They, ah, show us films, just in case, but I've never been at ground zero."

"It's pretty great." She laughed, perfectly able to read his thoughts. "Don't worry. I'll hold your hand."

They passed the time in the big, airy birthing room telling stories, giving advice, joking with Zack once Mikhail and Nick arrived with Rachel's things. Griff was happily settled in with Zack's cook, Rio, so there was little to do but wait.

When Rachel felt like walking, they took turns leading her around the corridors, rubbing her back, making small talk to take her mind off the discomfort between contractions.

"I can see your mind working," Alex murmured to Bess. "'How can I use this?'"

"It's ingrained." She murmured her thanks when

he passed her his cold drink. "Your family," she said, glancing around the room. "I've never known anyone like them. My parents—they'd be appalled to be expected to take part in something like this."

"It's our baby, too."

She smiled and lifted a hand to his cheek. "That's what I mean. You're all very special."

"I'm glad you're here." As he leaned over to kiss her, Yuri slapped him on the back.

"Now all my children make babies but you." He wiggled his brows at Bess. "You start soon, yes?"

"Papa…" Not sure how to take Bess's chuckle, Alex rose and spoke, firmly and quietly, in his mother tongue. "When I decide to make babies, I'll let you know."

"What decide?" Yuri gestured toward Bess. "She's the one you want, isn't she?"

"Yes."

Now Yuri gestured expansively with both hands. "Then?"

"I have my reasons for waiting. They're my reasons."

Though the shake of Yuri's head was a gesture of sadness, there was a twinkle in his eye. "How is it all my children are so stubborn?"

"How is it my papa is so nosy?"

With a laugh, Yuri embraced Alex and kissed both his cheeks. "Go take this pretty girl for a walk, steal some kisses. Your sister will be some time yet."

"That's advice I'll take." He reached for Bess's hand and pulled her to her feet. "Come on, let's get some air."

"Alexi." Bess had to quicken her pace to keep up with him. "Don't be angry with him. He didn't mean to embarrass you."

"Yes, he did, but I'm not angry with him."

"What were you two rattling on about?"

He punched the button for the elevator. "You know, I don't think I'll teach you any Ukrainian. It comes in too handy."

"But it's—"

"Rude," he finished for her, grinning. "I know."

By the time they came back again, Alex had taken his father's advice to heart. Bess's head was still spinning when they walked past the waiting room. It was Alex who spotted Nick, pacing and smoking in the smoking lounge like the cliché expectant daddy.

"How's it going, kid?"

"It's been an awfully long time." Nick's hand shook a bit as he lifted the cigarette to his lips. "I mean, Sydney was only in a couple of hours for Griff. It's getting really intense, and Rachel kicked me and the camera out. How come they don't do something?"

"I don't know a lot about it," Alex mused. "But I think babies come when they're ready."

"It's only been a little more than six hours." Bess moved in to soothe, touched that Nick should have such deep concern for his sister-in-law.

"Feels like six days," Zack commented as he staggered in. He plucked the cigarette from Nick's hand and took a deep drag. "She's swearing at me. I know what some of those names are now, even if they aren't in English."

"That's a good sign," Bess assured him. "It means things are moving along."

"She swore at the doctor, too." With a sigh, he passed the cigarette back to Nick. "But she didn't take a swing at *him*."

"If she missed," Alex commented, "she must be in really bad shape."

Wincing, Zack rubbed his shoulder. "She didn't. I'd better get back."

"Let's go give him some support," Alex began, but then he spotted a woman rushing off the elevator. "Tash!"

"Oh, Alex!"

Bess watched the woman fly into the waiting room, Gypsy hair flowing. There was concern in her eyes and laughter on her lips as she swung into Alex's arms.

"Alexi, how is Rachel?"

"Swearing at her doctor and punching Zack."

"Ah." She relaxed instantly. "That's good. Nick." She held out a hand for his. "Don't look so worried. Your niece or nephew will be along soon. Spence is parking the car. We were going to leave the children, but they were so disappointed, we brought them. Freddie's looking forward to seeing you."

Nick brightened a bit. "How's she doing?"

"She's taller than me now, and so pretty. Alex, where's Rachel?"

"I'll take you. Oh, this is Bess."

"Bess?" Natasha turned, one hand still on her brother's arm. Of course, she'd heard about Bess. West Virginia might be a fair distance from New York, but family business traveled fast on phone wires. "I'm sorry. I didn't realize."

"That's all right. You've got a lot on your mind." And then Bess said the first thing that came to hers. "What fabulous genes you all have."

Natasha's brows lifted. Then, below them, her eyes lit with laughter. "Rachel said I would like you. I hope we have time to talk before we leave town. I'm sorry to rush off."

"Don't worry about it. I think Nick and I'll go to the cafeteria, rustle up some food for this group."

Three hours later, Bess had delivered sandwiches and coffee, bounced Natasha's youngest daughter, Katie, on her knee and introduced herself to Spence Kimball and helped him entertain his very cranky son. She'd met Freddie and noted that the pretty, pixielike teenager was deep in puppy love with Nick.

As time dragged on, she added her support when Mikhail pressured his very tired wife to rest in the waiting room, took a few minutes to interrogate some nurses to help her beef up some hospital scenes and soothed Alex's nerves as his sister's labor reached the final stages.

"It won't be much longer."

"That's what they said an hour ago."

They were standing in the waiting room. Alex refused to sit. After a yawn and a good stretch, Bess wrapped her arms around him.

"She's fully dilated, and the baby was crowning. The last glance I had of the fetal monitor showed a really strong heartbeat. A fast one. I think it's a girl."

"How do you know so much?"

"Research." She settled her head on his shoulder. "I was figuring earlier that I've delivered twelve babies, including one set of twins. In a matter of speaking."

When her voice slurred, he tipped up her chin. "You're asleep on your feet, McNee. I should have sent you home."

"You couldn't have pried me away."

No, that was true, he realized. It was just one more aspect to her beauty. "I owe you."

"Then pay up." She lifted her mouth, sighing into the kiss.

"Mama." Though he'd enjoyed watching his brother, Mikhail shot to his feet when he spotted his parents in the doorway.

"We have a new member of the family." There were tears in Nadia's eyes and in Yuri's as he stood with his arm tight around his wife.

"What is it?" Nick and Alex demanded together.

"You will come see. They bring the baby to the glass in a moment."

"Rachel is resting." Yuri dashed away a tear. "You will kiss her good-night soon."

They trooped out together, to wait by the nursery window for the first glimpse.

"I'm an uncle," Nick said to Freddie. The girl's cheeks turned pink as he gave her a hard hug. "Hey, there's Zack." He kept his arm around her as his brother walked forward, holding a tiny bundle. The bundle was squalling, and Zack was grinning from ear to ear.

He held the baby up. Atop the curling black hair was a bright pink bow.

"It's a girl," Alex murmured, and held Bess hard against him. "She's beautiful."

"Man" was the best Nick could do. "Oh, man." Overcome for a moment, he glanced down and found himself looking at Freddie, who was still tucked under his arm. He drew back, brushed a fingertip along her cheek and caught a tear on the tip. "What's this?"

"It's just so sweet." Freddie's eyelashes were spiky and her eyes swam as she looked up at him. He thought for a moment—an uncomfortable moment—that it would be easy to drown in those eyes.

"Yeah, it's great." He let out a careful breath. She was his cousin, he reminded himself. Well, a kind of cousin. And she was hardly more than a kid. "I, ah, don't have a handkerchief or anything."

"It's all right." Freddie felt a drop roll down her cheek, but she didn't mind. After all, these were the very best kind of tears. "Do *you* ever think about having babies?" she asked with disarming candor.

"Having—" Nick would have stepped back then, way back, but the family was crowding him in. "No," he said firmly, and made himself look away from her damp, glowing face. "No way."

"I do." She sighed and let her head rest against his arm.

Mikhail was whispering something to Sydney that had her nodding and wiping away tears. Behind Freddie, Natasha shifted Katie in her arms and turned to her husband. He had one hand on Freddie's shoulder, and his sleeping son lay curved on his own.

"Every one is a miracle."

He bent his head to kiss her damp cheeks. "Just say the word anytime you decide you'd like another miracle of our own."

"I am a man blessed." Yuri grabbed the closest body. It happened to be Bess's, and she found herself whirled in a circle. "Two grandsons. Now three granddaughters." He tossed Bess up. She came down laughing, gripping his shoulders.

"Congratulations." She pleased him enormously by kissing him firmly on the mouth. "Grandpapa."

"It's a good day." He reached in his pocket. "Have a cigar."

Chapter 10

Rosalie considered herself an excellent judge of people, and she had already decided Bess was one strange lady. But she kept coming back.

Sure, the money was good, Rosalie thought as she sat drinking a diet soda in Bess's basement office. And for a woman with a retirement plan, that had to be number one. Yet it was more than making an extra buck that kept her taking the trip up and across town several days each week. More, too, that kept her hanging around after they finished what Bess liked to call 'consulting sessions.'

Rosalie was human enough to get a charge out of being connected, however remotely, to the entertainment world. She couldn't deny that she'd been excited, awed and impressed when she watched a couple of tapings.

But there was another factor, a much more basic one. Rosalie enjoyed Bess's company.

Besides being a strange lady, Bess had class. Rosalie didn't figure a person had to possess class to recognize it in another. Class wasn't just a matter of pedigree—though she'd discovered Bess had one. It was more than having an old lady in the DAR, or an old man in *Who's Who*. It was hazier than that. Though Rosalie couldn't quite come up with the terms she wanted, she had recognized in Bess those rare and often nebulous qualities, grace and compassion.

She was procrastinating over taking the trip back downtown by dawdling over her drink. Bess didn't seem to mind if Rosalie hung around while she worked. In the few weeks since they'd hooked up, Rosalie had noted that Bess worked hard and long. Harder, in Rosalie's opinion, than she herself, or any of the other ladies in her profession. Certainly Bess's hours were longer.

It amused Rosalie to compare the two. In fact, she and Bess had gotten into a very interesting discussion on the similarities and differences between Bess's selling her mind and Rosalie her body.

What a kick that had been, Rosalie thought now, while Bess typed and mumbled. Philosophical discussions weren't the norm in Rosalie's world.

The simple term she had not quite grasped for their relationship was *friendship*. They had become friends.

"How late you gonna work?" Rosalie asked, and Bess glanced up absently from the computer screen.

"Oh...not much longer." Her eyes were still slightly unfocused when she blew her hair away from them. Brock was on the verge of seducing Jessica. "I just had this idea for a little twist on a scene for tomorrow." She smiled then. It was quick, and a little wicked. "Of course, several members of the cast are going to want to murder me when I toss this at them in the morning. But that's show biz."

Rosalie took a drag on her cigarette. "What time did you get in here this morning?"

"Today? About nine-thirty. I was…" She thought of Alex. "Running a little late."

Lips pursed, Rosalie looked at the fake designer watch on her wrist. "And it's after seven now." Her grin flashed. "Girlfriend, you'd only put in half that many hours in my line of work."

"Yeah, but I get to sit down." Bess rubbed at the dull ache in the back of her neck. She really was going to have to work on her posture. "Hungry?" she asked. "Want to order something in?"

With a little tug of regret, Rosalie stabbed out the cigarette. "No. I gotta get to work, too."

"You could take the night off." Casually Bess ran a finger lightly over the keyboard. "Maybe we could catch a movie."

Chuckling, Rosalie dug in her purse for a mirror to check her makeup. "You said you weren't going to try to reform me."

"I lied." Bess sat back in her chair while Rosalie painted her mouth bloodred. She'd tried very hard not to pontificate, not to pressure, not to preach. And thought she had succeeded. But she hadn't tried not to care. That would have been useless. "I really worry about you. Especially since the last murder."

The odd twisting in Rosalie's stomach had her shifting her eyes from her compact mirror to Bess. She couldn't remember if anyone had ever worried about her before. Certainly not in years. "Didn't I tell you I could take care of myself?"

"Yes, but—"

"No buts about it, honey." With a second dip into her purse, Rosalie pulled out a stiletto. One flick of the wrist, and the long, razor-sharp blade zipped out. "What I can't handle, this can."

Bess managed to close her mouth, but her eyes stayed riveted to the knife. In the overhead lights, it gleamed silver, bright as sudden death. She couldn't say it was elegant. But it was fascinating, deathly fascinating. "Can I?"

With a shrug of her shoulders, Rosalie passed the weapon to her. "Don't mess with the blade," she warned. "It's as sharp as it looks."

Bess took a good grip on the handle, twisting her wrist this way and that, like a fencer. She wondered if Jade/Josie might carry one. She was already imagining a scene where the tormented Jade found the knife— maybe with the blade smeared with blood—in one of her practical handbags. No, her briefcase. Better.

"Have you ever—"

"Not yet." Rosalie held out a hand to take it back. "But there's always a first time." She pressed the button, and the blade whisked away again. "So don't lose any sleep over me." After dropping the weapon back into her bag, she took out an atomizer and sprayed scent generously on her skin. The air bloomed with roses. "Couple more months, I'll have enough put away. I'm going to be spending the winter in the Florida sunshine while you slog through dirty snow." She rose, tugging her tight off-the-shoulder top provocatively down, so that the rise of her breasts swelled invitingly over it. "See you around."

"Wait." Bess scrambled through her own purse and

came up with her mini recorder. "If it won't bother your ethics, I thought you might use this." At Rosalie's wry glance, Bess's cheeks heated. "I don't mean to record that part. Just the streets, conversations with the other women, maybe a couple of, ah…transactions."

"You're the boss." Taking the recorder, Rosalie slipped it away.

"Be careful," Bess added, though she knew Rosalie would laugh.

She did, sending a last cocky look over her bare shoulder. "Girlfriend, I'm always careful."

Still chuckling, Rosalie headed down the narrow corridor toward the freight elevator. She was already picturing the way Bess's eyes would pop out when she listened to the tape and discovered that her "consultant" had recorded *everything.* The prospect of pulling such a fine joke had her grinning as the doors slid open. Her amusement died a quick death when Alex walked off.

While they eyed each other with mutual suspicion, Alex pressed two fingers to the Door Open button. "How's the moonlighting going, Rosalie?"

"It passes the time."

When she started past him, he raised an arm to block the elevator opening. "What do you know about Crystal LaRue?"

"I know she's dead." Rosalie fisted a hand on her hip, cocked it. "Something else you want?"

Alex let her see that her snide invitation only amused him. "What do you know about her before she was dead?"

"Nothing." She would have given him the same answer if she'd been Crystal's most intimate friend, but as it was, she was telling the simple truth. "I never met her. Heard she was new, didn't have a man yet."

"Now, I heard that, too," Alex said conversationally. "And I heard that Bobby wanted to make her one of his wives."

"Maybe. Bobby likes to start them young."

Alex struggled with his disgust. She'd been seventeen, he thought. A runaway who hadn't known the rules and would never have a chance to learn them. "Did Bobby roust her, put on the pressure?"

"Can't say."

"Can't say? Or won't?"

Rosalie opened the hand on her hip and began to drum her fingers there. "Listen, I don't know what Bobby did. I've been keeping out of his way lately."

Saying nothing, Alex studied her face. The bruising had faded. "Seems to me Bess is paying you enough that you could stay out of his way altogether."

"That's my business."

"And hers," Alex said evenly. "I don't want him finding out about this sideline of yours and going after her." His eyes were cold and passionless. "Then I'd have to kill him."

"You think I'd turn Bobby on to her?" Arrogance was sidelined as fury snapped into Rosalie's voice. "I *owe* her."

"What?"

"Respect," she said, with an innate and graceful dignity that had Alex softening. "She had me eat at her table. She even said I could stay in her extra bedroom. Like a guest." Her lips thinned at Alex's expression. "Don't sweat it, honey. I didn't take her up on it. Sure, she's paying me, and maybe you don't think that's any different than me taking money from some slob off the street. But she treats me like somebody. Not some *thing,* some*body.*" Embarrassed by her own vehemence, she shrugged. "She doesn't have the sense not to."

"She's got sense, all right. Not all good." Alex's lips twitched, even as Rosalie's did. "Maybe she hasn't gone so wrong here. I just don't want her hurt."

"Neither do I." Rosalie tapped a scarlet nail on his chest. "You got a bad case, cop. Stars in your eyes." The little wisp of envy came and went, almost unnoticed. "Make sure you keep them in hers, or you'll answer to me."

His grin flashed before he could prevent it. The charm of it nearly had Rosalie changing her mind about cops. "Yes, ma'am." Like Bess, he wanted to say something that would stop her from going back on the streets. Unlike Bess, he accepted that there was nothing that would do it.

"Maybe I see why she's so stuck on you." When he moved his blocking arm, she stepped into the elevator, turned. "You be good to her, Stanislaski. She deserves good."

The elevator doors clunked shut. Alex stood studying them a moment before he turned and wandered down the corridor to find Bess.

She was bent over the keys, rapping out a machine-gun fire of words onto the monitor. Her fingers moved like lightning, but her eyes were far away. In Millbrook, he thought, smiling to himself.

She had her legs crossed under her, up on the chair. The way her shoulders were hunched, he imagined her muscles would complain loudly the moment she came back to earth.

She was wearing a skirt again, a little leather number in bold blue that was hiked high up on her thighs. The hot-pink blouse she'd tucked into it should have clashed with her hair, but it didn't. The blouse looked like silk and was carelessly shoved up to her elbows. A half-dozen gold bracelets clanged at her wrist as she worked. Rings flashed on her fingers, and the big Gypsy hoops she wore at her ears peeked out of her tousled hair.

His heart ached with love for her. And his loins… Alex let out a little breath. He wanted, quite simply, to devour her. Inch by delicious inch.

What the hell was he going to do, he wondered, when she tried to slither out of his life? He was sure she would, as she'd done with others before. He could lock her up, carry her off. He could beg or threaten. He already knew he would do whatever he had to in order to keep her in his life.

What had ever made him think he would one day find some nice, pretty woman with simple tastes and a quiet style? Someone who would be content to sit home while he worked his crazy hours? Who would have and help him raise the houseful of children he so badly wanted?

With Bess, nothing was simple, nothing was quiet. She would never be content to sit home but would badger him incessantly, picking at him until he gave in and talked about the darker aspects of his work, those pieces of his life that he wanted to keep locked away from everyone who mattered. As for children… He didn't know how the devil to get and keep a ring on her finger, much less ask her to help make a family.

Being in love with her left him helpless, made him

stupid, brought him a kind of fear he'd never faced as a cop. Not fear for his life. Fear for his heart.

He could only take his own advice and leave things as they were. Handle each day until she was so used to him she'd want to stay.

As he watched, she stopped typing, lifted a hand to her neck for a quick, impatient rub. Her skirt hiked higher as she shifted. It took all his control not to lick his lips. She punched a few buttons, had the machine clicking. A moment later, the printer beside her began to hum.

With a smile on his face and lust in his heart, Alex closed the door quietly at his back. Locked it.

She jumped like a rabbit when his hands came down on her shoulders. "Didn't anyone ever teach you to sit in a chair?"

"Alexi." She pressed a hand to her galloping heart. "You scared— Oh…" Her sigh was long and heartfelt as he massaged away the aches. "That's wonderful."

"You're going to do permanent damage if you keep sitting like that all day."

"I was planning on soaking in a hot tub for two or three days." She leaned into his hands.

"Where's Lori?"

"She wasn't feeling too terrific." As the printer continued to rattle, Bess closed her eyes. "I told her I was leaving, too. Then I snuck back. I wanted to make a few changes for tomorrow." She brought her hand up to one of his, skimming her fingers over it to the wrist. "You said you might have to work late."

"Lead fizzled. We'll work on tracing the heart necklace down, but that's better during business hours."

"Trace it down?"

"Hit the jewelers," he explained, "see if we can track down to when it was bought. Long shot, but..."

"Do you think the heart has a personal meaning for him?"

"Like some woman broke his heart, so he gives them a symbol of it before he whacks them?" He gave a little grunt as he continued to knead her muscles. "It's a little too obvious to dismiss. Psychiatric profile figures him as sexually inadequate on a normal level, so he pays for women to perform. He wants them and detests himself for that, as much as he detests them for being available. The fact that he goes through a short courtship routine shows that—" He broke off as she reached for a pad. "Hold on, McNee." He gave her shoulders a hard squeeze. "I don't know how you do it. One minute I'm thinking about getting you out of these clothes and the next you've got me talking about a case." He pressed a kiss to the top of her head. "No notes."

Her fingers retreated from the pad, but with obvious reluctance. "I like hearing you talk about your work. I want you to be able to talk to me about anything."

"Apparently I can. Even the stuff I don't want you to hear. I've got a problem with you, Bess. You won't let me tuck you into that nice safe corner where I want you to be."

"You only think that's where you want me to be." Smiling, she tugged his hand around so that she could kiss it. "You like me right where I am." Turning his hand over, she pressed her lips to his palm. "I'm going to stay there."

She felt his fingers tense, then relax slowly as he spread them over her cheek. "I was watching you while you worked."

A rippling thrill raced through her at the words and at the shimmer of desire she heard in them. "Were you?"

"And thinking." His hands slid down over her breasts, sampled their weight, molded them. "Fantasizing."

Her head fell back against the chair. Her breathing quickened. "About?"

"The things I'd like to do with you." Through layers of silk, he caught her nipples, tugging gently. "To you."

When she tried to shift in the chair to face him, he increased the pressure, held her still. Her dazzled eyes focused on the monitor. She could still see the ghost of herself there, and his hands moving. Sliding. Stroking.

Impossibly erotic to see, and to feel. Dry-mouthed, she watched his fingers undo her buttons and saw the dark shadow of his hair as he pressed a hot mouth to her throat. She lifted a hand, hooked it around his neck as she tilted her head to offer more.

"I can shut down in thirty seconds."

He bit her lightly, just above the collarbone. "I'm not going to give you a chance to shut down."

She laughed shakily, even as she lifted her other arm to capture him in a reverse embrace. "I meant the computer."

He would have laughed himself, but he'd stopped breathing. "I know what you meant."

"But I—" He slipped a hand under her skirt, and it was so sudden, so searing. Before she could gasp out in shock, he had driven her ruthlessly to the peak.

"I watched you." Each word burned his throat as she poured into his hand. "I wanted you." Half demented, he whipped her up again, pressing his face into her neck as her body shuddered. "Do you remember the first time I found you here?"

"What?" She couldn't remember her own name. There was only this need he was ruthlessly building inside her again. "Alexi, please. Come home with me. I need—" This time she cried out as the third high, hard wave swamped her.

"I wanted you then." In one violent move, he spun her chair around and dragged her to her feet, and her already weakened system went limp at what she read in his face. "Let me show you exactly what I wanted."

This wasn't the smooth and patient lover of the night before. This man with the fierce eyes and bruising hands wouldn't cuddle her and whisper exotic endearments. This was the warrior she'd only glimpsed. He would plunder. Whether or not she was ready, he was showing her that dark, reckless side of him that he kept so tightly controlled.

In the moment when he stared at her, the look in his eyes hot and concentrated, she understood that excitement took a twist into the primitive when it carried a touch of fear.

He fisted a hand in her hair and yanked her against him. His body was like rock, vibrating from deep within, as if from an erupting volcano. For that moment, there was only the strength and the fury of the inevitable.

His mouth burned over hers, his tongue diving deep, while his free hand tugged the snap of her skirt free. He wanted her flesh, craved it. That heated silk, those alluring curves and taut muscles. Time and place had lost all impact. There was only here. Only now. Only her.

Shivery fingers of fear ran up her spine. She hadn't known what it was to be wanted this way. It was so huge, so violent, so glorious. Before, he had given her more than she had ever dreamed of. Now, he seemed compelled to give her more than she had ever *dared* dream.

Beside them, the printer stopped its practical clatter and dropped into a hum. The low, waiting sound was drowned out by the thundering of her heart. The bright working lights overhead seemed to dim as he took her hips and pressed her hard against him.

"You make a war inside me," he muttered as his teeth scraped roughly down her throat. "There's no end to it. No peace from it. Say my name. I want to hear you say my name."

"Alexi." When his lips crushed down on hers again, he felt her breathe it, warm, into his mouth. "Take me. Now."

The wild need slammed into her so that her mouth was as turbulent, her hands as frantic. Dozens of tiny explosions burst inside her body, merging into one huge tumult of sensation that battered, bruised and bewitched. She was all but sobbing with it as she tugged and pulled at his clothes.

She was quivering for him. Couldn't stop. The power and pressure growing inside her was all but unbearable. And the heat, the furnace blast of heat, had her skin slicked and her head spinning. Glorying in it, she brought her mouth to his bare shoulder, savoring the taste of flesh. His busy, bruising hands had her bearing down with teeth and nails. His breath hissed in her ear as she reached down to curl impatient fingers around him.

Confused and tangled phrases whirled in his mind. He heard them burst from his lips to hang on the thick air as he fought to catch his breath. On an oath, he gripped her shoulders and hauled her back.

Her face was flushed, her eyes were glowing. He'd

marked that ivory skin. He could see where his fingers had pressed, where his roughened cheeks had scraped. But the part of him that would have been shocked by his lack of care was far overshadowed by a dark and desperate desire to conquer, to consume. To mate.

He saw them now as brands, signs that made her his. Only his.

With a jerk of his head, he tossed his hair back. The way it swayed and settled had new emotion burning her throat. Naked, muscles bunched as if to fight, he looked so magnificent he dazzled her eyes.

Then he looked at her, and the smile that had nearly formed on her face froze into wonder.

"No one makes you feel like this but me."

His accent had thickened, and the sound of it sent chills along her heated skin. She could only shake her head.

"No one touches you like me." He took his hands from her shoulders and gripped the bodice of her chemise. "No one has you, ever again, but me."

"Alexi—"

But he shook his head. He could feel her heart pounding under his hands, and his own chest was heaving. "Understand me. You're mine now." Her eyes widened with shock as he jerked his hands and ripped the chemise in half. "All of you."

He pushed her back against the table, watching the play of stunned excitement over her face. Yes, he wanted to excite her. And shock her. Stagger her.

His fingers dug into her hips as he lifted her. He was braced, straining like a stallion at the bit. "Hold on to me," he demanded, but her fluttering hands slid off his sweat-slick arms. His breath heaved out, his fingers dug into her smooth, taut flesh. "Hold!"

She met his eyes then, and felt that wild whip of power. Drunk on it, she gripped his hair and wrapped her legs around him. When he plunged inside her, her body arched back, absorbing that first rocketing flash of heat. It was like being consumed from the inside out.

She felt the cool surface of the table against her back first, then his weight on her. Greedy for more, she tightened around him, matching his fast, frantic rhythm, dragging his mouth back to hers so that they could echo the intimacy with their tongues.

He lost himself. There was only her now, and the need to possess her. The desperate craving to be possessed by her. Images reeled through his brain, all dark and sharp-edged, until he thought he would go mad.

And went mad.

In a frenzy of movement, he dragged her farther onto the table, crushing papers, knocking aside empty cups, scattering pencils. He couldn't take his eyes from her face, the way her eyes clouded, like fog over moss, the way her lips trembled with each gasping breath. There was a bloom on her skin now, a rose under glass. He was hammering himself into her, empowered by a rabid fury of emotion that had its razor-tipped fingers around his throat.

Too much, she thought frantically. Never enough. The harsh overhead lights fractured into rainbows that blinded her eyes. They seemed to arch around his head, but she didn't think of angels. His eyes were so dark, so fiercely focused. Even as her own grew leaden, she refused to close them.

Oh, to watch him wanting her. Taking her.

She couldn't understand the words he murmured, over and over again. But she understood what was in those eyes. They were tearing each other apart, and they couldn't stop. The animal had taken over, and it had diamond-sharp claws and jagged teeth.

There was nothing left but the sound of their mixed labored breathing, the solid slap of flesh against flesh, and the heady scent of hot, desperate sex.

She felt his body go rigid, felt the rippling muscles in the arms she gripped turn to stone. He groaned out her name as his eyes sharpened like daggers. When he poured himself into her, she cried out in triumph, then again in wonder as he drove her over that crumbling edge with him.

The strength that had screamed through him switched off like a light, and he collapsed, panting, his full weight on her. Fighting for breath, he wallowed in her hair, drawing in the scent of it and the fragrance they'd made together. He couldn't find his center, the focus that was so vital for survival. He no longer had one without her.

God, he could feel her vibrating beneath him, shuddering from the aftershocks. And there were tears mixed with the dew of sweat on her face.

With breath still burning his lungs, he levered himself on his elbows and shook his head to try to clear it. At the movement, she made a small, whimpering sound in her throat that both aroused and dismayed. Trying to find the gentleness that had always been so easy for him, he shifted their positions and began to stroke her hair, her shoulders, her back.

Murmuring apologies, he cradled her like a child. "*Milaya,* I'm sorry. I hurt you. I must have hurt you. Don't cry."

"I'm not crying." But, of course, she was. He could feel the tears fall even as she ran kisses over his face and throat. "Just tell me you love me. Please tell me you love me."

"I love you. Shh." He covered her mouth tenderly with his. "You know I love you."

"I love you." She pressed those wet, shaky kisses to his cheeks, to his jaw. "You have to believe that I love you."

A hot fist clenched in his gut, but he kept his hands gentle. "Just let me hold you."

Tearing up again, she pressed her face to his shoulder. "Even now you don't believe me. Alexi, what more can I do?"

"I believe you." But they both knew he said it only to comfort. "You belong to me. I believe that."

"You're everything I want." She relaxed against him, satisfied that he would take that much.

"No more tears?"

"No."

He tilted her chin up to search her face. "How badly did I hurt you?"

"I don't think the results will be in for days." She smiled a little. "How badly did I hurt you?"

His eyes narrowed, and her smile widened. "You're not...upset?"

"About what?"

"I was an animal." With a hand that had yet to steady, he brushed her tumbled hair out of her face. "I took you on a table like a lunatic."

"I know." After one long, satisfied sigh, she slid her body lazily over his. "It was wonderful."

"Yes?" Guilt began to turn to pride. "You liked it?"

After being so thoroughly ravished, it wasn't difficult to stroke his ego. "It was like being dragged off by some barbarian. I couldn't even understand what you were saying. It was exciting." She kissed his cheek. "Frightening." And the other. "It was also the most erotic experience of my life."

"You were crying."

"Alexi." She touched a hand to his face. "You didn't just overpower me. You overwhelmed me. No one's ever made me feel more wanted. More irresistible."

"I can't resist you, but I'm sorry I put bruises on you."

"I don't mind—under the circumstances." After another luxurious sigh, she glanced around the room. "I don't know how I'll ever work in here again, though."

Now he grinned, wickedly. "Maybe it'll inspire you."

"There is that." She shifted to straddle him and watched his sleepy eyes skim down to her breasts and back. Possibilities, she thought. There were definite possibilities in that look. "Being a cop, I imagine you've been through arduous physical training."

The possibilities had occurred to him, as well. "Absolutely."

"And you'd probably have amazing recuperative powers."

His brow lifted. "Under the right conditions."

"Good." To be certain she created them, she ran her hands over his still-gleaming chest.

With a half laugh, he caught her wrists. "McNee, wouldn't you rather pick this up in bed?"

For an answer, she leaned over, letting her lips hover a breath away from his. The tip of her tongue darted out to trace the shape of his mouth, to dip teasingly inside, then retreat. Slowly, she tilted her head. Softly, she tasted his lips. Achingly, achingly, she deepened the kiss.

"Does that give you a clue, Detective?"

Chapter 11

"I can't believe you want to spend the best part of a Saturday morning in a sweaty gym." Alex was stalling, even as he walked with Bess up the iron steps that led to Rocky's.

"It's your sweaty gym," Bess said, and kissed him.

The past few days had been almost like a honeymoon, she thought. If she took out the hours they'd both been at work. But they'd made the most of what time they'd had together, snuggling on the couch in her place, cooking a meal in his, wrestling in bed in both.

She was starting to hope that he believed she loved him. And, once he did, she wanted nothing more than for them to take that next step. The step that would lead to an authentic honeymoon, with all the trimmings.

"You picked me up at my gym yesterday," she pointed out.

"That wasn't a gym." There was the faintest trace of a masculine sneer in his voice. "That was an exercise palace. Fancy lighting, piped-in music. All those mirrors."

"At least I'll be able to see when my butt starts to drop."

He gave it a friendly pat. "I'll let you know."

"Do, and die," she said smartly, and pushed through the frosted glass doors.

She immediately thought of every bad boxing film she'd ever seen. The huge room echoed with grunts and slaps and thumps. It smelled of mildew and sweat and… She took a testing sniff and decided she didn't want to know what else. There were exposed pipes along the ceilings and walls, and there was a hardwood floor that looked as though it had been gouged by spikes. The boxing ring that was set up in one corner was already occupied by two compact, dancing men in tiny shorts who were trying to pop each other in the eye.

A trio of punching bags hung at strategic points. A half-naked man with a body like a cement truck was currently trying to whip the tar out of one of them.

Weights were being employed as well. She watched tendons bulge and muscles bunch.

They didn't worry about mirrors and lighting here. Nor did she spot any of the high-tech equipment she was accustomed to. This was down-and-dirty—squat, sweat and punch. She sincerely doubted there would be a juice bar in the vicinity, either.

"Had enough?" Alex asked. He was obviously amused at the thought of her stripping down to her leotard and having a go with the boys.

Bess closed her mouth, then answered his grin with a cool stare. "I haven't even started yet."

It was his turn to drop his jaw when she peeled off her sweatshirt. Beneath she wore a snug, low-cut crop top in zigzagging stripes of green and purple. As she shimmied out of her baggy street shorts, he shoved the discarded shirt in front of her.

"Come on, Bess, put your clothes on. Sweet Lord." The bottom half was worse. Over formfitting tights she had on a teeny strip of spandex that covered little more than a G-string. "You can't wear that in here."

"Is it illegal?" She bent over to stuff her sweats into her gym bag and heard the heavy thump of weights as they were dropped. Maintaining position, she turned her head and smiled at the pop-eyed man staring at her.

The catcalls and whistles started immediately, the sound swelling and bouncing off the cinder-block walls. Alex was very much afraid there would be a riot—one he was likely to incite himself. "Damn it, put something on before I have to kill somebody."

"They look harmless." She straightened again and lifted her arms to tie the short curls at the nape of her neck into a stubby ponytail. "Anyway, I came to work out." With a challenging grin, she flexed a muscle. "How much can you bench-press?"

"McNee, don't you dare—" He broke off with an oath as she blithely strolled across the room to chat with the weightlifter. The two hundred pounds of muscle began to babble like a teenager. Alex had no choice but to send out a warning snarl, much as a guard dog might to a pack of encroaching wolves, before he went after her.

She pulled it off, of course. He should have known

she would. The men started out drooling, kicked over into laughing and finally wound up competing with each other to show her the proper way to perform squat lifts, chin-ups and leg curls.

Before an hour was over, she'd been shown pictures of wives and children, listened to sob stories over sweethearts and stopped being ogled—unless it was at a discreet distance.

"You sure you want to do this?" Alex asked again, tapping his gloved hands together.

"Absolutely." She smiled at Rocky as he himself laced up her gloves. "I couldn't leave without one sparring match."

"You watch out for his left—it's a good one," Rocky advised her. "Kid could've been a contender if he hadn't wanted to be a cop."

She winked at Rocky. "I've got fast feet. He won't lay a glove on me."

Two of her new admirers held open the ropes for her so that she could step into the ring. Enjoying the sensation, she adjusted her padded helmet. "Aren't we supposed to wear those funny retainers?"

"The what— Oh, mouth guards?" He couldn't resist, and he leaned over and kissed her to an accompaniment of hoots. "Baby, I'm not going to hit you." In a friendly gesture, he tapped his gloves to hers. "Okay, put your hands up." When she did, lifting them toward the ceiling, he rolled his eyes. "It's not an arrest, McNee." Patiently he adjusted her hands until they were in a defensive position.

"Now, you want to guard, see? Keep your left up, keep it up. If I come in like this—" he did a slow-motion jab at her jaw "—you block, jab back. That's it."

"And I fake with my left," she said, and did so.

"If you want." Lord, she was sweet. "Now try for here." He tapped his own chin. "Go ahead, you don't have to pull it." When she punched halfheartedly, he shook his head. "No, you punch like a girl. Put your body behind it. Pretend I'm Dawn Gallagher."

Her eyes lit, and she swung full-out, only to come up solidly against his block. "Hey, that's good." Impressed, she swung again. "But I've got to move around, right? Fake you out with my grace and fancy footwork."

She did a quick boogie that had the onlookers clapping and Alex grinning at her. "You got style. Let's work on it."

He was enjoying himself, showing her the moves. And it certainly didn't hurt for a woman living in the city to learn how to defend herself with something more than an ammonia-filled water pistol.

"It's fun." She ducked her head as he'd shown her and tried two quick jabs with her left.

"Always room for another flyweight," Rocky called out to her. "Come on, Bess, body blow."

Chuckling, she aimed for Alex's midsection and dodged his light tap toward her chin. "You look so cute in gym shorts," she murmured.

"Don't try to distract me."

"Well, you do." She danced around him again, and, laughing, he turned toward her.

"Okay, that ought to—" He ended on a grunt when she connected hard with his jaw and set him down on his butt.

"Oh, God." She crouched instantly, battering his face with her gloves as she tried to stroke it. "Oh, Alexi, I'm sorry. Did I hurt you?"

He wiggled his jaw, sending her a dark look. "Right cross," he muttered as men climbed through the ropes to cheer and hold Bess's arms in the air.

"I'm really sorry," Bess said again as they started down the iron steps. But she was fingering the little bit of tarnished metal Rocky had pinned—with some ceremony—to her sweatshirt. "You said not to pull my punches."

"I know what I said." He'd be lucky if he didn't have a bruise, Alex thought. And how the hell would he explain that? "You only got through because I was finished."

She ran her tongue over her teeth and stepped outside. "Uh-huh."

"Don't get smart with me, McNee." He snatched her up and swung her around. "Or I'll demand a rematch."

Wildly in love, she tossed her arms around his neck. "Anytime."

"Oh, yeah? How about..." He trailed off with a grimace as his beeper sounded. "Sorry."

"It's all right." She only sighed a little as he tracked down a phone and called in. As she stood beside him, watching his face, listening to his terse comments, she realized that their plans for a picnic in the park and some casual shopping were about to go bust.

"You have your cop's face on," she said when he hung up. "Do you have to go in?"

"Yeah." But he didn't tell her they'd found another victim. It was bad enough that he was spoiling their plans for the day. "It's probably going to take a while. I'm really sorry, Bess."

"Look." She framed his face with her hands. "I understand. This is part of it."

He brought those hands to his lips. "I…" But he didn't tell her he loved her, because she would echo the words, and it made him nervous to hear them. "I appreciate it," he said instead. "And I'll make it up to you."

"Tell you what—why don't I finish up what I have to do, then stop by the market? I'll make dinner. Something that won't spoil if it has to be warmed up a couple of times."

Though his mind was already drifting away from her, he managed a pained smile. "You're going to cook."

"I'm not that bad. I'm not," she insisted with a bit of a huff when he grinned. "I only burned the potatoes the other night because you kept distracting me."

"I guess it's the least I can do." He kissed her lightly once, then again, longer. "I'll try to call."

"If you can." She waved him off, then stood watching while he jogged down into the subway. With a quick laugh, she spun around, hugging herself.

She felt just like a cop's wife.

"I hope you don't mind me dropping by."

"Of course not." Rachel took a look at the bulging shopping bags in Bess's hands. "Been busy?"

"Whenever I get started with that little plastic card, I can't seem to stop." She dumped her purchases inside the apartment door. "You look wonderful. How can you look wonderful less than a week after going through childbirth?"

"Strong genes." Pleased in general, and with Bess in particular, Rachel kissed her on both cheeks. "Come sit down."

"Thanks. I— Oops." She dipped into the bag and pulled out a gold-foiled candy box. "For Mom."

"Oh." Rachel's eyes took on the glow a woman's get when she looks at a lover—or a five-pound box of exclusive chocolates. "I think you just became my best friend."

Chuckling, Bess dug into the bags again. "Well, I know that people tend to drop by with baby gifts." She held out a box wrapped in snowy white with bright red lollipops scattered over it. "And, though I couldn't resist the tradition, I figured you deserved something really sinful for yourself."

"I do." Rachel tucked the baby box under her other arm. "It's really sweet of you, Bess, and unnecessary. You and Alex already brought Brenna that wonderful stuffed dragon."

"That was from us. This is from me. It's a girl thing. I saw this tiny little white organdy dress with all these flounces and little pink bows and I couldn't resist."

Rachel's new-mother's heart melted. "Really?"

"I figure in another year she might want to wear motorcycle boots, so this may be your only chance to play dress-up."

"I swore that whatever I had, I wouldn't make sexist decisions in dress or attitude." She sighed over the box. "White organdy?"

"Six flounces. I counted."

"I can't wait to put her in it."

"Ah, company." Mikhail strode out of the bedroom with Brenna tucked in his arm. "Hello, Aunt Bess." He kissed both of her cheeks, then her mouth.

"You said you wouldn't wake her up." This from Rachel, who was already leaning over to coo.

"I didn't. Exactly. What's this?" Recognizing the gold foil box, he flipped it open and dived in.

"Mine," Rachel said in a huff. "If you eat more than one, I'll break your fingers."

"She was always greedy," he said over the first piece. "Where's Alexi?"

"He got called in."

"Good. Now you have time to sit down. I'll sketch you."

"Now?" Womanlike, Bess lifted a hand to her hair. "I'm not exactly dressed for it."

"I want your face." Obviously well used to making himself at home, he opened the drawer on an end table and rummaged for a pad. "Perhaps I'll do your body later. It's a good one."

Her laugh was quick. "Thanks."

"You might as well cooperate," Rachel told her, and crossed over to take the baby. "Once the artist in him takes over, you haven't got a chance."

"I'm flattered, really."

"There's no reason to be," he said absently as he unearthed a suitable pencil. "You have the face you were born with."

"Thank God that's not always true."

That caught his interest. "You had it fixed?"

"No. I just sort of grew into it."

"Not there," he told her before Bess could sit. "Over there, closer to the window, in the light. Rachel, when do I get the drink you promised me?"

"On its way." She stopped nuzzling Brenna long enough to look up. "What can I get you, Bess?"

"Anything cold—and a shot at holding the baby."

"I can accommodate you on both counts." Rachel

laid her daughter gently in Bess's arms. "She hardly ever cries. And I think her eyes may stay blue. Like Zack's."

"She's a beauty." Bess leaned down to brush her lips over the curling dark hair and to draw in the indescribably sweet scent of baby. "Like all of you."

"Move," Mikhail ordered his sister. "You're in my way."

Shooting off a mild Ukrainian insult, she headed for the kitchen.

"Talk if you like." Mikhail gestured with his pencil, and began to sketch.

"It's one of my best things." She'd already forgotten to be self-conscious. "Where's Sydney and Griff?"

"Griff has the sniffles." The pencil was moving with quick, deft strokes over the pad. "Sydney fusses over him, but she says *I'm* fussing over him and sends me out on errands."

"Which he does by coming by and plaguing me," Rachel called out.

"She's happy to see me," Mikhail said. "Because she's lonely, with Zack and Nick over checking on the progress of the new apartment."

"Oh, that's right, you're moving." Comfortable, Bess tucked up her legs. "Alexi mentioned it."

"We need a bigger place. Of course, it was supposed to be ready a month ago, but things never run on time. I'll miss this one," she said, coming back in with a tray of cold drinks. "And having Nick underfoot. But I imagine he'll like having this place to himself."

Bess reached for her drink with her free hand, gently jiggling the baby with the other. "I guess he had as big a crush on you as Freddie has on him."

For a moment, Rachel only stared. Then she let out her breath in a quiet laugh. "Alex said you saw things."

"Just part of the job."

Rachel didn't consider herself a slouch in the reading-people department. "So, how big a crush do you have on Alexi?"

"The biggest." Bess smiled and rubbed her cheek over Brenna's. "He thinks I'm flighty. Fickle. But I'm not. Not with him."

"Why would he think that?"

"I have a varied track record. But it's different with him." When Bess lowered her head to murmur to the baby, Rachel glanced at her brother. They exchanged a great deal without uttering a word. "It makes me envy people like your sister, Natasha," Bess went on. "Those three beautiful children, a husband who after years together still looks at her as if he can't believe she belongs to him. Work she loves. I envy all that."

"You'd like a family?"

"I never had one."

Rachel knew it was the lawyer in her, but she couldn't help moving along the line of questioning. "Does it bother you that he's a cop?"

"Bother me?" Bess's brows lifted in surprise. "No. Do you mean, will I worry? I suppose I will. But it's not something I could change, or that I want to change. I love who he is."

"He's making you sad," Mikhail said quietly.

"No." Bess's denial was quick enough to startle the dozing baby. She soothed her automatically as she shook her head. "No, of course he isn't."

"I see what's in your eyes."

He would, she realized, and felt the warmth creep

into her cheeks. "It's only that I know he doesn't trust me—my feelings. Or, I suppose, the endurance of my feelings. It's not his fault."

"He was always one to pick things apart." There was brotherly disgust in Mikhail's voice. "Never one to take anything on faith. I'll speak to him."

"Oh, no." This time, she laughed. "He'd be furious with both of us. All that Slavic pride and male ego."

Instantly Mikhail's eyes narrowed. "What's wrong with that?"

"Nothing." She grinned at Rachel. "Not a thing. I'll just wear him down in my own way. In fact, I'm going to start tonight. I'm cooking dinner. I thought maybe I could call your mother, find out if he has a favorite dish."

"I can tell you that," Rachel offered. "Anything."

"Well, that certainly widens my choices. Do you think she'd mind if I called her, asked for some pointers? My kitchen skills are moderate at best."

"She'd love it." Rachel smiled to herself, knowing her mother would hang up the phone and immediately start planning the wedding.

It was after midnight when Alex let himself into Bess's apartment with the key she'd given him. He was punchy with fatigue, and his head was buzzing from too much coffee. Those were usual things, as much a part of his work as filing reports or following a lead. But the sick weight in his stomach was something new.

He would have to tell her.

She'd left the television on. In an old black-and-white movie a woman screamed in abject terror and fled down a moonlit beach. As he shrugged out of his jacket, Alex moved across the room to switch it off. Before he reached the set, he saw her, curled on the couch.

She'd waited for him. The sweetness of that speared through him as he crouched beside her. For so many years now, he'd come home alone, to no one. Gently he brushed the dark red curls from her cheek and replaced them with his lips. She stirred, murmuring. Her eyes fluttered open.

"I'm just going to carry you into bed," he whispered. "Go back to sleep."

"Alexi." She lifted a hand to rub over the cheek he hadn't shaved that morning. Her voice was thick with sleep, her eyes glazed with it. "What time is it?"

"It's late. You should have gone to bed."

She made a vague sound of disagreement and pushed up on one elbow. "I was waiting up, but the movie was so bad." Her laugh was groggy, and she rubbed her eyes like a child. "It zapped me." She circled her shoulders before leaning forward to kiss him. "You had a long day, Detective."

"Yeah." And maybe, because she was half-asleep, he could put off the rest. "So have you. I'll cart you in."

"No, I'm okay." She sat up, yawning. "Did you eat something?"

"I caught a sandwich. I'm really sorry, I tried to call."

"And got the machine," she said with a rueful nod. "Because I'd forgotten the paprika and had to run back out to the market."

"You cooked?" The idea both touched him and accented his guilt.

"I amazed myself." It felt good to settle against him when he joined her on the couch and slipped an arm around her. Cozy, right, and wonderfully simple. "Your mother's recipe for chicken and dumplings—Hungarian-style."

"Csirke paprikas?" Normally it would have made his mouth water. "That's a lot of work."

"It was a culinary adventure—and the cleaning lady will probably quit on Monday, after one look at the kitchen." She laughed up at him, then scrubbed her knuckles over his cheek when she caught the look in his eyes. "Don't worry. It'll heat up just fine for tomorrow's lunch. Then again…" She snuggled closer. "If you're feeling really guilty, I'll take you up on that ride to the bedroom—and whatever else you can think of."

But instead of chuckling and scooping her up, he pushed away to pace to the television and snap it off. "We have to talk."

His tone had nerves skittering in her stomach, but she nodded. "All right."

He thought it might be best—for both of them—if they had some of the brandy she had offered him during an earlier crisis. Trying out the words in his head, he walked to the lacquered cabinet.

"It's bad," she murmured, and pressed her lips together, hard. Her first thought was that he had changed his mind about her. That he had finally taken that good look she'd been afraid of and realized his mistake.

"It's bad," he concurred, then brought the snifters to the couch. "Here. Drink a little."

"It's all right. I don't make scenes."

He tilted the brandy toward her lips himself. "Just a little, *milaya.*"

She closed her eyes and did as he asked. He couldn't say that sweet word to her in that loving tone if he'd changed his mind. "Okay." A deep breath, and she opened her eyes again.

"There was another murder last night."

"Oh, Alexi." Instantly the image of Crystal LaRue's mangled body flashed behind her eyes. "Oh, God." She caught his hand in hers and squeezed. "Last night?"

"The desk clerk found her this morning. They had an arrangement. She only used that room for work, and he was ticked that she hadn't checked out and slipped him his usual tip." He was taking it slow, deliberately, so that the general horror would pass before he hit her with the specifics. Again he tipped the brandy up to her lips. "She'd rented the room three times last night. He caught a glimpse of the third john when they went up, so we've had him looking over mug shots most of the day."

"You'll catch him."

"Oh, yeah. There's no doubt about it this time. He didn't find the guy in the books, but he gave the police artist a fair description. We'll be broadcasting it. This time we should have his blood type, too. DNA. Couple of other things."

"You'll have him soon."

"Not soon enough. Bess, the woman…" His fingers tightened on hers, but he told her the worst as gently as he knew how. "It was Rosalie."

She only stared, and he watched, helpless, as the color simply slid out of her face. "No." She was tugging her hand from his, but he only held tighter. "You're wrong. You made a mistake. I just saw her. I just talked to her a couple of days ago."

"There's no mistake." His voice toughened, for her sake. "I ID'd her myself. Rechecked that with prints, and the desk clerk's ID. Bess, it was Rosalie."

The moan came out brokenly as she wrapped her arms around herself and began to rock. "Don't," she said when he tried to gather her close. "Don't, don't, don't."

She sprang up, needing the distance, desperate to find something to do with the helpless rage that was building inside her. "She didn't have to die. It isn't right. It isn't right for her to die like that."

"It's never right."

It was his tone, the cool detachment of it, that had her whirling on him. "But she was just a hooker. Don't get involved, right? Don't feel anything. Isn't that what you told me?"

He went very still, as if she'd pulled a gun and taken aim. "I guess I did."

"I wanted to help her, but you told me I couldn't. You told me it was a waste of my time and energy. And you were right, weren't you, Alexi? How fine it must be to always be so right."

He took the blow. What else could he do? "Why don't you sit down, Bess? You'll make yourself sick."

She wanted to break something, to smash it—but nothing was precious enough. "I *cared,* damn you. I cared about her. She wasn't just a story line to me. She was a person. All she wanted was to go south, buy a trailer." When her breath began to hitch, she covered her mouth with her hands. "She shouldn't have died like that."

"I wish I could change it." The bitter sense of failure turned his voice to ice. "I wish to God I could." Before he realized the glass was leaving his hand, he was heaving the snifter against the wall. "How do you know what I felt when I walked into that filthy room and found her like that? How the hell do you know what it's like to face it and know you couldn't stop it? She was a person to me, too."

"I'm sorry." The tears that spilled over now spilled for all of them. "Alexi, I'm sorry."

"For what?" He tossed back. "It was the truth."

"Facts. Not truth." He'd tried to soften the blow, to cushion her when his own emotions were raw. He'd needed to comfort. His eyes had been dazed with fatigue and pain and the kind of grief she might never understand, but he'd needed to shield her. And she hadn't allowed it. "Hold me, please. I need you to hold me."

For a moment she was afraid he wouldn't move. Then he crossed to her. Though his arms were rigid with tension, they came around her.

"I didn't mean to hurt you," she murmured, but he only shook his head and stroked her hair. Grieving, she turned her face into his throat. "I wanted to make it a lie somehow. To make you wrong so it could all be wrong." She squeezed her eyes closed and held tight. "She was somebody."

He stared blankly over her shoulder as he remembered one of the last things Rosalie had said to him. *She treats me like somebody.* "I know."

"You'll catch him," she said fiercely.

"We'll catch him. We'll put him away. He won't hurt anybody else." Though her words still scraped against him, he rocked her. He would tell her the rest and hoped it helped. "She had a knife."

"I saw it. She showed me."

"She used it. I don't know how bad she hurt him, but she put up a hell of a fight. It's recorded."

"Recorded?" Eyes dull with shock, she leaned back. "My God. The tape. I gave her my mini recorder."

"I figured as much. For whatever consolation it is, the fact that you did give it to her, and she decided to use it, is going to make a difference. A big one."

"You heard them," she said through dry lips. "You heard—"

"We got everything, from the deal on the street until…the end. Don't ask me, Bess." He lifted a hand to cup her face. "Even if I could tell you what was on the tape, I wouldn't."

"I wasn't going to ask. I don't think I could bear to know what happened in that room."

Calmer now, he searched her face. "I've only got a few hours. I have to go in first thing in the morning. Do you want me to stay with you tonight, or would you rather I go?"

She'd hurt him more than she'd realized. Perhaps the only way she could heal the wound was to admit, and to show him, that she needed comfort. Needed it from him. Drawing him close, she laid her head on his shoulder.

"I want you with me, Alexi. Always. And tonight— I don't think I'd make it through tonight without you."

She began to cry then. Alex picked her up and carried her to the couch, where they could lie down and grieve together.

Chapter 12

Judd flexed his hand on the steering wheel as he turned on West Seventy-sixth. He wasn't nervous this time. He was eager. The idea of bringing Wilson J. Tremayne III—a U.S. senator's grandson—in for questioning in the murders of four women had him chafing at the bit.

They had him, Judd thought. He knew they had the creep. The artist's sketch, the blood type, the voiceprint. It had been quick work on that, he mused. Flavored with luck. Bess's tape had been one of those twisted aspects of police work that never failed to fascinate him.

It was Trilwalter who'd identified Tremayne from the sketch. Judd remembered that the boss had taken a long, hard look at the artist's rendering and then ordered Alex to the newspaper morgue. The desk clerk had picked the reprint of Tremayne's newspaper picture from a choice of five.

From there, Alex had used a connection at one of the local television stations and had finessed a videotape of Tremayne campaigning for his grandfather. The lab boys had jumped right on it, and had matched the voice to the one on Bess's tape.

It still made him queasy to think about what had been on that tape, but that was something he didn't want to show to Alex. Just as he knew better than to let Alex spot his eagerness now.

"So," he said casually, "you think the Yankees have got a shot this year?"

Alex didn't even glance over. He could all but taste his partner's excitement. "When a cop starts licking his lips, he forgets things. Miranda rights, probable cause, makes all kinds of little procedural mistakes that help slime ooze out of courtrooms and back onto the street."

Judd clenched his jaw. "I'm not licking my lips."

"Malloy, you'll be drooling any minute." Alex looked over at the beautiful old building while Judd hunted up a parking space. The Gothic touches appealed to him, as did the tall, narrow windows and the scattering of terrace gardens. Tremayne lived on the top floor, in a plush two-level condo with a view of the park and a uniformed doorman downstairs.

He came and went as he pleased, wearing his Italian suits and his Swiss watch.

And four women were dead.

"Don't take it personally," Alex said when they got out of the car. "Stanislaski's rule number five."

But Judd was getting good, very good, at reading his partner. "You want him as bad as I do."

Alex looked over, his eyes meeting, then locking on

Judd's. There wasn't eagerness in them or excitement or even satisfaction. They were all cold fury. "So let's go get the bastard."

They flashed their badges for the doorman, then rode partway up in the elevator with a plump middle-aged woman and her yipping schnauzer. Alex glanced up and spotted the security camera in the corner. It might come in handy, he thought. The DA would have to subpoena the tapes for the nights of the murders. If they were dated and timed, so much the better. But, if not, they would still show Tremayne going and coming.

The schnauzer got off at four. They continued on to eight. Side by side, they approached 8B.

Though the door was thick, Alex could hear the strains of an aria from *Aida* coming from the apartment. He'd never cared much for opera, but he'd liked this particular one. He wondered if it would be spoiled for him now. He rang the buzzer.

He had to ring it a second time before Tremayne answered. Alex recognized him. It was almost as though they were old friends now that Alex had pored over the newspaper shots and stories, the videotape. And, of course, he knew his voice. Knew it when it was calm, when it was amused and when it was darkly, sickly, thrilled.

Dressed in a thick velour robe that matched his china-blue eyes, Tremayne stood dripping, rubbing a thick monogrammed towel over his fair hair.

"Wilson J. Tremayne?"

"That's right." Tremayne glanced pleasantly from face to face. He didn't have the street sense to smell cop. "I'm afraid you've caught me at a bad time."

"Yes, sir." Never taking his eyes off Tremayne's,

Alex took out his badge. "Detectives Stanislaski and Malloy."

"Detectives?" Tremayne's voice was bland, only mildly curious, but Alex saw the flicker. "Don't tell me my secretary forgot to pay my parking tickets again."

"You'll have to get dressed, Mr. Tremayne." Still watching, Alex replaced his shield. "We'd like you to come with us."

"With you?" Tremayne eased backward a step. Judd noted that his hand eased down toward the doorknob, closed over it. Knuckles whitened. "I'm afraid that would be very inconvenient. I have a dinner engagement."

"You'll want to cancel that," Alex said. "This may take a while."

"Detective—?"

"Stanislaski."

"Ah, Stanislaski. Do you know who I am?"

Because it suited him, because he wanted it, Alex let Tremayne see the knowledge. "I know exactly who you are, Jack." Alex allowed himself one quick flash of pleasure at the fear that leaped into Tremayne's eyes. "We're going downtown, Mr. Tremayne. Your presence is requested for questioning on the murders of four women. Mary Rodell." His voice grew quieter, more dangerous, on each name. "Angie Horowitz, Crystal LaRue and Rosalie Hood. You're free to call your attorney."

"This is absurd."

Alex slapped a hand on the door before Tremayne could slam it shut. "We can take you in as you are—and give your neighbors a thrill. Or you can get dressed."

Alex saw the quick panic and was braced even as Tremayne turned to run. He knew better—sure he

did—but it felt so damn good to body-slam the man up
against that silk-papered wall. A small, delicate statue
tipped from its niche and bounced on the carpet. When
he hauled Tremayne up by the lapels, he saw the gold
chain, the dangling heart with a crack running through
it that was the twin of the one they had in evidence. And
he saw the fresh white bandage that neatly covered the
wounds Rosalie had inflicted as she fought for her life.

"Give me a reason." Alex leaned in close. "I'd love
it."

"I'll have your badges." Tears began to leak out of
Tremayne's eyes as he slid to the floor. "My grandfather will have your badges."

In disgust, Alex stood over him. "Go find him some
pants," he said to Judd. "I'll read him his rights."

With a nod, Judd started for the bedroom. "Don't
take it personally, Stanislaski."

Alex glanced over with something that was almost
a smile. "Kiss off, Malloy."

They had him cold, Alex thought as he turned into
Bess's building. They could call out every fancy lawyer on the East Coast, and it wouldn't mean a damn
thing. The physical evidence was overwhelming—particularly since they'd found the murder weapon in the
nightstand drawer.

Opportunity was unlikely to be a problem, and as for
motive—he'd leave that up to the shrinks. Undoubtedly
they'd cop an insanity plea. Maybe they'd even pull it
off. One way or the other, he was off the streets.

It went a long way toward easing the bitterness he'd
felt over Rosalie's death. He hoped it helped Bess with
her grief.

He'd nearly called her from the station, but he'd wanted to tell her face-to-face. As he waited for the elevator, he shifted the bunch of lilacs he held. Maybe it was a weird time to bring her flowers, but he thought she needed them.

Stepping into the car, he tucked a hand in his pocket and felt the jeweler's box. It was even a weirder time to propose marriage. But he knew he needed it.

It scared him just how much he'd come to depend on having her with him. To talk to him, to listen to him, to make him laugh. To make love with him. He knew he was rushing things, but he justified it by assuring himself that if he got her to marry him quickly enough, she wouldn't have time to change her mind.

She believed she was in love with him. After they were committed, emotionally and legally, he would take as much time as necessary to make certain it was true.

The elevator opened, and Alex dug for his keys. They'd order in tonight, he decided. Put on some music, light some candles. He grimaced as he fit the key into the lock. No, she'd probably had that routine before, and he'd be damned if he'd follow someone else's pattern. He'd have to think of something else.

He opened the door with his arms full of nodding lilacs, his mind racing to think of some clever, innovative way to ask Bess to be his wife. The color went out of his face and turned his eyes to midnight. He felt something slam into his chest. It was like being shot.

She was standing in the center of the room, her laughter just fading away. In another man's arms, her mouth just retreating from another man's lips.

"Charlie, I—" She heard the sound of the door and

turned. The bright, beaming smile on her face froze, then faded away like the laughter. "Alexi."

"I guess I should have knocked." His voice was dead calm. Viciously calm.

"No, of course not." There were butterflies in her stomach, and their wings were razor-sharp. "Charlie, this is Alexi. I've told you about him."

"Sure. Think I met you at Bess's last party." Lanky, long-haired and obviously oblivious to the tension throbbing in the air, he gave Bess's shoulders a squeeze. "She gives the best."

Alex set the flowers aside. One fragile bloom fell from the table and was ignored. "So I've heard."

"Well, I've got to be going." Charlie bent to give Bess another kiss. Alex's hands clenched. "You won't let me down?"

"Of course not." She worked up a smile, grateful that Charlie was too preoccupied to sense the falseness of it. "You know how happy I am for you, Charlie. I'll be in touch."

He went out cheerfully, calling out a last farewell before he shut the door. In the silence, Alex noticed the music for the first time. Violins and flutes whispered out of her stereo. Very romantic, he thought, and his teeth clenched like his fists.

"Well." Her eyes were burning dry, though her heart was weeping. "I can see I should explain." She walked over to the wine she'd poured for Charlie and topped off her glass. "I can also see that you've already made up your mind, so explanations would be pointless."

"You move fast, Bess."

She was glad she had her back to him for a moment.

Very glad, because her hand trembled as she lifted the wine. "Do you think so, Alexi?"

"Or maybe you've been seeing him all along."

"You can say that?" Now she turned, and the first flashes of anger burst through her. "You can stand there and say that to me?"

"What the hell do you expect me to say?" he shot back. He didn't go near her. Didn't dare. "I walk in here and find you with him. A little music, a nice bottle of wine." He wished he had been shot. It couldn't possibly hurt more than this bite of betrayal. "Do you think I'm an idiot?"

"No. No, I don't." She needed to sit, but she locked her knees straight. "But I must be to have been so careless as to have an assignation here when you were bound to find me out." Her eyes were like glass as she toasted him. "Caught me."

He took a step forward, stopped himself. "Are you going to tell me you didn't sleep with him?"

In the thrum of silence, the flutes sang. "No, I'm not going to tell you that. I'm not ashamed that I once cared enough for a very good man to be intimate with him. I'd tell you that I haven't been with Charlie or anyone else since I met you, but the evidence is against me, isn't it, Detective?"

She was so tired, Bess thought, so terribly tired, and the scent of the lilacs made her want to weep. Rosalie's funeral had been that morning, and she'd quietly made the arrangements herself. She'd gone alone, without mentioning it to Alex. But she'd needed him.

"You let him kiss you."

"Yes, I let him kiss me. I've let lots of men kiss me. Isn't that the problem?" She set down the wine before she could do something rash, like tossing it to the floor. "You didn't come to me a virgin, Alexi, nor did I expect you to. That's one of the big differences between us."

"There's a bigger difference between a virgin and a—"

He broke off, appalled with himself. He wouldn't have meant it. Stumbling, horrified apologies whirled through his head. But he could see by the way her head jerked up, the way her color drained, that there would be no taking back even the unsaid.

"I think," she said in an odd voice, "you'd better go."

"We haven't finished."

"I don't want you here. Even a whore can choose."

His face was as pale as hers. "Bess, I didn't mean that. I could never mean that. I want to understand—"

"No, you don't." She cut him off, her voice so thick with tears that she had to fight for every word. "You never wanted to understand, Alexi. You never wanted to hear the one thing I needed you to believe. Now the only thing you need to understand is that I don't want to see you again."

He felt something rip apart in his gut. "You can't have that."

"If you don't leave now, I'll call Security. I'll call your captain, I'll call the mayor." Desperation was rising like a flood. "Whatever it takes to keep you away from me."

His eyes narrowed, sharpened. "You can call God Almighty. It won't stop me."

"Maybe this will." She gripped her hands tightly together and looked just over his shoulder. "I don't love you, I don't want you, I don't need you. It was fun while it lasted, but the game's over. You can let yourself out."

She turned away and walked quickly up the stairs. There had been hurt in his eyes. If there had been anger, she knew, he would have come after her, but there had been hurt, and she made it to the bedroom alone. With her hands over her face, she waited, biting back sobs, until she heard the door close downstairs. With a sound of mourning, she lowered herself to the floor and tasted her own tears. They were bitter.

Impatient and unsympathetic, Mikhail paced the floor of Alex's sparsely furnished apartment. "You don't answer your phone," he was saying. "You don't return messages." He kicked a discarded shirt aside. The apartment was a shambles. "Lucky for you I came instead of Mama. She'd box your ears for living like a pig."

"I gave the staff the month off." With the concentrated care of the nearly drunk, Alex poured another glass of vodka from the half-empty bottle on the table.

"And drinking alone in the middle of the day."

"So, join me." Alex gestured carelessly toward the kitchen, where dishes were piled high. "Bound to be a clean glass somewhere."

Mikhail washed one out before coming back to the table. He sat, poured. "What is this, Alexi?"

"Celebration. My day off." Alex took a swallow and waited for the vodka to join the rest swimming through his system. "I caught the bad guy." With a half laugh, he toasted himself. "And lost the girl."

Mikhail drummed his fingers on the table as he drank. It was no less than he'd expected. "You fought with Bess?"

"Fought?" Lips pursed, Alex studied the clear, potent liquid in his glass. "I don't know that's the term, exactly. Found her with another man."

Mikhail's glass froze halfway to his lips. "You're wrong."

"Nope." Alex reached for the bottle with an almost steady hand. "Walked in and found her lip-locked to this guy she used to be engaged to. Bess has this hobby of getting engaged."

Mikhail merely shook his head. Something was not quite right with this picture. "Did you kill him?"

"Thought about it." Before he drank again, Alex ran his tongue over his teeth. Good, he thought. They were nearly numb. The rest would follow. "Too damn bad I'm a cop."

"What was her explanation?"

"Didn't give me one. Got pissed, is all." He set the glass down so that he could use both hands to rub his face.

"Because you accused without trusting."

"I didn't accuse," Alex shot back, then pressed his fingers to his burning eyes. "I didn't have to. What I didn't say was unforgivable. She tossed me out on my ear, but not before she told me she didn't love me anyway."

"She lies." Before Alex could lift his glass again, Mikhail grabbed his wrist. "I tell you, she lies. A few days ago she visited Rachel and the baby. I made her sit for me and sketched her while she talked of you. There's no mistaking what I saw in her eyes, Alexi. You're blind if you haven't seen it yourself."

He had seen it, and the pain of remembering what he'd seen clawed through him so that he stumbled to his feet as if to escape it. "She falls in love easily."

"So? There is love, and love. How many times have you taken the fall?"

"This is the first."

"For this kind, yes. There were others."

"They were different."

"Ah." Patient and amused, Mikhail held up a finger. "So it's okay for you to play with love until you find the truth, but it's not okay for Bess."

"It's—" Put that way, it was tough to argue with. Especially when his head was reeling. "Damn it, I was jealous. I have a right to be jealous."

"You have a right to make an ass of yourself, too." Pleased, now that he knew it could be fixed, Mikhail kicked back and crossed his booted feet. "Did you?"

"Big-time." Alex swayed, then sat down heavily. "I was going to ask her to marry me, Mik. I had the ring in my pocket and these stupid lilacs. I was scared to death she'd say yes. More scared that she'd say no." He propped his spinning head in his hands. "What the hell was she doing kissing that son of a bitch?"

"Maybe if you had asked nicely, she would have told you."

With a lopsided grin, Alex turned his bleary eyes on his brother. "Would you have asked nicely?"

"No, I would have broken his arms, maybe his legs, too. Then I would have asked." With a sigh, Mikhail patted Alex's shoulder. "But that is me. You were always more impulsive."

"We could go find him." Alex considered and, warming to the idea, leaned over to give Mikhail a sloppy hug. "We'll go beat him up together. Like old times."

"We'll try something different." Rising, Mikhail hauled Alex to his feet.

"Where we going?"

"I'm going to put you in a cold shower until your head's clear."

Alex staggered and linked an arm around his brother's neck. "What for?"

"So you can go find your woman and grovel."

Unsure of his footing, Alex stared at the tilting floor. "I don't wanna grovel."

"Yes, you do. It's best to get used to it before you marry her. I have more experience in this."

"Oh, yeah?" Enjoying the idea of his big brother crawling at Sydney's feet, he grinned as Mikhail thrust him, fully clothed, into the shower. "Can I watch next time?"

"No." With immense satisfaction, Mikhail turned the cold water on full and listened to his brother's pained shout bounce viciously on the tiles. "This is a very good start," he decided.

"You son of a bitch." They were both laughing when Alex grabbed Mikhail in a headlock and dragged him under the spray.

He was nearly sober by the time he walked into Bess's office, but he wasn't laughing. It was hard to laugh when your throat was thick with nerves.

He was going to be reasonable, he promised himself. They would discuss the entire matter like civilized adults. And if she didn't give him the right answers, he'd strangle her. He could always arrest himself afterward.

But he saw only Lori sitting at the keyboard, frantically typing. "I'll have the damn changes by six," she called out. Her brow was furrowed in concentration as she glanced up. Her eyes frosted over.

"What the hell do you want?"

"I need to see Bess."

"You're out of luck." Nobody hurt her friend and got away with it. Nobody. "She's not here."

"Where?"

She offered an anatomically impossible suggestion, offered it so coolly he nearly smiled. But it wasn't enough. She leapt up and slammed the door shut. Locked it. "Sit down, buster, I've got an earful for you."

"Tell me where she is."

"When hell freezes over. Do you know what you did to her?" She took the flat of her hand to push him back. "Why didn't you just cut out her heart and slice it into little pieces while you were at it?"

"What *I* did?" He jammed his hands into his pockets so he wouldn't shove her back. "I'm the one who walked in and found her snuggled up to that pretty-faced playwright."

"You don't know what you found."

"Then why don't you tell me?"

She'd die first. "You don't know her at all, do you? You didn't have a clue how lucky you were. She's the most loving, most generous, most unselfish person I've ever known. She'd have crawled through broken glass for you." Afraid she'd do something violent if she didn't move, Lori began to pace. "I was so happy when she told me about you. I could see how much in love she was. Really in love. She wasn't just taking you under her wing until she could find someone for you."

"Find someone for me?"

"What do you think she did with all those other men who were dazzled by her?" Lori tossed back. "Oh, she'd try to talk herself into being in love, and thinking they loved her back, and the whole time she'd listen to their problems like some den mother. Then she'd steer them in the direction of some woman she'd decided was perfect for them. She was usually right."

"She was going to marry—"

"She was never going to marry anyone. Whenever she said yes, it was because she couldn't bear to hurt anyone's feelings. And, okay, because she always wanted to have someone she could count on. But however loyal, however sensitive, she is to other people's feelings, she's not stupid. She'd tell herself she was going to get married, then she'd go into overdrive finding the guy a substitute."

"Substitute? Why—?" But Lori wasn't ready to let him get a word in.

"Not that she ever calculated it that way. But after you watched it happen a couple of times, you saw the pattern. But you…" She whirled back to him. "You broke the pattern. She needed you. You made her cry." Angry tears glazed Lori's own eyes. "Not once did I ever see her cry over any man. She'd just slip seamlessly into the my-pal-Bess category, and everyone was happy. But she's cried buckets over you."

He felt sick, and small, and he was beginning to understand a great deal about groveling. "Tell me where she is. Please."

"Why the hell should I?"

"I love her."

She wanted to snarl at him for daring to say so, but she recognized the same misery in his eyes she'd seen in her friend's. "Charlie was—"

"No." He shook his head quickly. "It doesn't matter."

What did matter was trust, and it was time he gave it. "I don't need to know. I just need her."

With a sigh, Lori fingered the square-cut diamond on her left hand. Bess had pushed her into taking the right step with Steven. She could only hope she was doing the same in return. "If you hurt her again, Alex—"

"I won't." Then he sighed. "I don't want to hurt her again, but I probably will."

She weakened, because it was exactly the thing a man in love would say. "I sent her home. She wasn't in any shape to work."

"Dyakuyu."

"What?"

"Thanks."

She hated feeling this way. The only way Bess could get from one day to the next was by telling herself it would get better. It had to get better.

But she didn't believe it.

She hadn't had the heart to throw out the lilacs. She'd tried to. She'd even stood holding them over the trash can, weeping like a fool. But the thought of parting with them had been too much. Now she tormented herself with the fragile scent whenever she came downstairs.

She thought about taking a trip—anywhere. She certainly had the vacation time coming, but it didn't seem fair to leave Lori in the lurch, especially since Lori had added wedding plans to her work load.

A lot of good she was doing Lori, or the show, this way, she thought. But the problems of the people in Millbrook seemed terribly petty when compared to hers. Too bad she couldn't write herself out of this one, she thought, as she stood in the kitchen, trying to talk herself into fixing something to eat.

Well, she'd certainly made the grade, Bess told herself, and pressed her fingers against her swollen eyes. She'd fallen in love and had her heart broken. Great research for the next troubled relationship she invented for the television audience.

The hell with food. She was going to go up to bed and will herself to sleep. Tomorrow she would find some way to put her life back together.

When she stepped out of the kitchen, what was left of her life shattered at her feet.

He was standing by the table, one hand brushing over the lilacs. All he did was look at her, turn his head and look, and she nearly crumpled to her knees.

"What are you doing here?" The pain made her voice razor-sharp.

"I still have my key." He lowered his hand slowly. Her eyes were still puffy from her last bout of tears, and there were smudges of fatigue under them. Nothing that had been said to him, nothing he'd said to himself, had lashed more sharply.

"You didn't have to bring it by." If composure was all she had left, she would cling to it. "You could have dropped it in the mail. But thanks." Her smile was so cold it hurt her jaw. "If that's all, I'm in a hurry. I was just on my way up to change before I go out."

"You can't look at me when you lie." He said it half to himself, remembering how her eyes had drifted away from his face when she said she didn't love him.

She forced her gaze back to his, held it steady. "What do you want, Alexi?"

"A great many things. Maybe too many things. But first, for you to forgive me."

Her face crumpled at that. She put a hand up to cover it, knowing it was too late. "Leave me alone."

"*Milaya,* let me—"

"Don't." She cringed away, crossing her arms over herself in self-defense, and his hands stopped an inch away. There was an odd catch in his breath as he drew them back and let them fall to his sides.

"I won't touch you." His voice was quiet and strained. "Please, let me say what I've come to say."

"What else could there be?" She turned away. "I know what you think of me. You made that clear."

"What I did was hurt you and make a fool of myself."

"Oh, yes, you hurt me." She was still trembling from it. "But not just that last time. You hurt me every time you pulled back when I needed to tell you how much I loved you. I thought, I won't let it matter, because he'll have to see it. God, he'll have to see it, because it's right there every time I look at him. Every time I think about him. And he loves me. He wants me. In my whole life, no one wanted me. Not really."

"Bess."

She jerked away from his hands. "My parents," she began, turning back. "How many times I heard them say to each other, 'Where did she come from?' As if I was some stray pet that had wandered in by mistake."

When she began to roam the room, her shoulders still hunched protectively, he said nothing. How could he tell her he was sorry he'd opened up old wounds, and sorry, as well, that it had taken that to have her reveal those smothered feelings to him?

"I handled it." Those stiff shoulders jerked as she

tried to shrug it off. "What else could I do? It wasn't their fault, really. They've always been so perfect, in their way, and I could never be. Not for them. Not even for you."

"Do you think that's what I want?"

She glanced back then. The tears had dried up. There was no point in them. "I don't know what you want, Alexi. I only know it keeps circling around. I went from my parents into school. Those awful teenage years, when all the girls were so bright and pretty, and falling in and out of love. No one wanted me. Oh, I had friends. Somewhere along the line I'd learned that if you didn't try so hard, if you just relaxed and acted naturally, that there were a lot of people who'd like you for what you were. But there was never anyone to love. There has never been anybody to love until you."

"There's never going to be anyone else." He waited until she turned back. "I love you, Bess. Please, give me another chance."

"It won't work." She rubbed at her drying tears with the heel of her hand. "I thought it would, I wanted it to. I was so sure love would be enough. But it's not. Not without hope. Certainly not without faith."

The calm way she said it had panic streaking through him. "Do you want me to crawl?" He ignored her defensive retreat and gripped her arms. "Then I will. You're not going to push me out of your life because I was stupid, because I was afraid. I won't let you."

Was this how a man crawled? she wondered. With his eyes flashing fire and his voice booming? "And the next time you see me kissing an old friend?"

"I won't care." With a sound of disgust, he released

her to stalk the room. "I will care. I'll kill the next one who touches you."

"Then New York would be littered with bodies." It should be funny, she thought. Why wasn't it funny? "I can't change what I am for you, Alexi. I wouldn't ask you to change for me."

"No, you wouldn't." He scrubbed his hands over his face and struggled to find some balance. "I know a kiss between friends is harmless, Bess. I'm not quite that big a fool. But the other night, when I walked in—"

"You assumed I was betraying you."

"I don't know what I assumed." It was as honest as he could get. "When I saw you, I felt… It was all feeling," he said carefully. "So I didn't think. In my heart, in my head, I know better than to assume anything. One of my own rules that I broke. There were reasons." Calmer now, he walked back and took her hands. "We'd just finished the bust, and I was wired from it. I knew I'd tell you about it, all about it. I'd gone beyond trying to separate that part of my life—any part of it—from you. It was going to upset you to think about it, because of Rosalie. I knew that, too. Damn it, I knew you'd gone to that funeral alone, and I felt like the lowest kind of creep for letting you."

He was prying her heart open again, inch by inch. "I didn't think you knew."

"I knew." His voice was flat. All he could think was how desperately he wanted to hold her. "You leave notes everywhere. All these pieces of paper scattered around, with scribbling on them about dry-cleaning and dialogue and appointments. I saw the one about the flowers you'd ordered for her, and the directions to the cemetery." He looked down at their hands. "If things hadn't been moving so fast in the investigation, I would have taken the time. I would have tried to."

That she didn't doubt. "It was more important to me that you catch the man who killed her than that you go stand over her grave."

"I wasn't with you," he said, more slowly. "And I wanted to be. And when I got here, I wanted to…" This was hardly the time to bring up the ring in his pocket. "I was churned up about a lot of things, Bess. My response was way out of line, and I'll apologize for it as often as you like. But I'd like you to hear me out."

"It's all right." She gave his hands a squeeze, hoping he'd release hers. He didn't. "Alexi, Charlie was here because—"

"I don't need to know." Now he let her hands go to bring his own to her face. He wanted her to see what was in his eyes. "You don't have to explain yourself to me. You don't have to change yourself for me."

She felt something move inside her heart and was afraid to believe it was healing. "I'd rather clear the air. I was too angry to do it before. He came by to tell me that Gabrielle was expecting. He was like a little boy at Christmas, and he wanted to share his good news with a friend. And to ask me if I'd be godmother—even though it's seven and a half months down the road."

He lowered his brow to hers. "You should have slugged me, McNee." When he moved his mouth toward hers, he felt her retreat. Patiently he stroked his thumbs over her temples. "Just once," he murmured and tasted her lips.

He didn't mean to deepen the kiss, didn't mean to crush her against him and hold her so tightly neither of them could breathe. But he couldn't stop himself until he felt her body shake with a fresh bout of tears.

"Don't. Please don't." He pressed his face into her hair and rocked her. "I'll break apart."

Turning her face into his shoulder, she fought back the worst of the tears. "I didn't want you to come back. I didn't want to feel this again."

He deserved that, he thought as he squeezed his eyes tight. "You were right to send me away. I want a chance to prove to you that you're right to let me back in." He brushed a hand through her hair. "You're so good at listening, Bess. I have to ask you to listen to me now."

"You don't need to apologize again." She could do nothing but love him, she realized, and, drawing back, she managed a smile. "And I can't let you back in, because you were always here."

Her words brought a pressure to his chest. He pressed their joined hands against it to try to ease it away. "Just that easy?"

"It's not easy." She supposed it would never be easy. "It's just the way it is."

"Mikhail said I would grovel," he murmured. "Bess, you humble me."

"Let's put it behind us." She drew a deep breath, then kissed both his cheeks as a sign of peace. "I'm good at fresh starts."

"No." Taking her hand, he pulled her to the couch. "I like our other start. We don't need a new one, only to play this one out. Sit." He pulled her down with him, keeping her hand close to his heart. "You explained, now I will. I was afraid to believe in you. No woman has ever meant what you mean, and I let myself imagine that you'd be with me forever. Just as I let myself imagine that you'd turn away. And because I was more afraid of the second, it seemed more real."

"It's hard to be afraid." She turned her cheek to his hand. "I know."

"You don't know all." He glanced away, toward the flowers subtly scenting the room. "You kept the lilacs."

"I tried not to." She smiled again. "But they were so beautiful."

"I brought you something besides lilacs that day." He reached into his pocket and drew out the box. Her hand went limp in his. He watched her lips tremble apart. "I don't think it's ostentatious." When she only continued to stare, he shifted. "That was a joke."

"Okay." The two syllables came out in a whisper. "Are you—are you going to let me see it?"

For an answer, he opened the box himself. Inside was a gold band set with a rainbow of gems. He knew what they were only because he'd asked the jeweler to identify each of them. The amethyst, the peridot, the blue topaz, the citrine.

"I know it's not traditional," he said when she remained silent. "But it reminded me of you, and I wanted—hell, I wanted something no one else would have thought to give you."

"No one has," she managed, barely breathing. "No one would."

"If you don't like it, we can look for something else."

She was afraid she would cry again and knew it would do neither of them any good. "It's lovely. Beautiful." She managed to tear her gaze from it. "You bought me this before? You had it with you the other night? You were going to give it to me, then you walked in and saw me with Charlie." Laughing, she lifted a hand to her cheek. "I'm surprised you didn't gun us both down. I couldn't have written it better myself."

"Then you forgive me?"

She already had, but since he was looking so nervous, she nodded. "Anyone with such good taste deserves a second chance."

"I bought this days ago, but it took me a while to work up the nerve. Facing a junkie with an Uzi seemed easier." But he was into it now, and he was going to finish. "My idea was to pressure you to accept it, then push for a quick wedding so you wouldn't change your mind. But that was wrong." He closed the box, and was encouraged by Bess's quick gasp of dismay. "It was stupid, and it showed a lack of faith in both of us. I'm sorry."

"I— You—" She let out a frustrated breath. "I don't mind."

"Of course you do," he said. "It was calculating, even devious, when a proposal of marriage should be romantic. So, when we're both ready, I'll ask you properly."

Her face fell. "When we're both ready?"

"I don't want to push you when you might be feeling a little vulnerable. Especially since a long engagement is out. So I'll give you time."

"Time," she echoed, ready to scream.

"It's fair." He waited a beat. "Okay, I'm ready."

Before she could laugh, he was down on one knee. "What are you doing?"

"A proper proposal of marriage." He nearly launched into his humble little speech. Instead, his eyes darkened when she continued to laugh. "You don't want one."

"Damn right I want one. But I want you up here." She took his hand to tug him back to the couch so that they were at eye level with each other. "I want you to look me right in the eye."

"Okay, then I get something I want, too."

"Name it."

"I want to hear you say it." He caught her hand, brought it to his cheek. "I want very much to hear you say it. I need to hear the words from you."

"I love you, Alexi." For the first time, she said the words smiling, knowing they would be taken as they were meant. "I'm going to love you forever."

He turned his face so that his lips pressed into her palm. Taking the ring out of the box, he slipped it onto her finger. It shot out a rainbow of color. As he linked his fingers with hers, he lifted his head. "Be my family." He shook his head before she could speak and felt himself stumble. "I meant to be romantic. Let me—"

"No." Overwhelmed, she laid a hand over his lips. "That was perfect. Don't change it. Don't change anything."

"Then say yes."

"Yes." She threw her arms around him and laughed. "Oh, yes...."

* * * * *